The Sweetness at the Bottom of the Pie

ALAN BRADLEY

Delacorte Press

THE SWEETNESS AT THE BOTTOM OF THE PIE
A Delacorte Press Book / May 2009

Published by Bantam Dell
A Division of Random House, Inc.
New York, New York

Book design by Catherine Leonardo
Cover design by Joe Montgomery

Delacorte Press is a registered trademark of Random House, Inc.,
and the colophon is a trademark of Random House, Inc.

Library of Congress Cataloging-in-Publication Data
Bradley, C. Alan, 1938–
The sweetness at the bottom of the pie / Alan Bradley.
p. cm.
ISBN 978-0-385-34230-8 (hardcover)
978-0-440-33846-8 (e-book)
1. Detectives—England—Fiction. 2. Motherless families—Fiction.
3. Sisters—Fiction. 4. England—Fiction. I. Title.
PR9199.4.B7324S94 2009
813'.6—dc22
2008041787

Printed in the United States of America

www.bantamdell.com

10 9 8 7 6 5 4 3 2 1
BVG

For Shirley

UNLESS SOME SWEETNESS AT THE BOTTOM LIE,
WHO CARES FOR ALL THE CRINKLING OF THE PIE?
William King, *The Art of Cookery* (1708)

The Sweetness at the Bottom of the Pie

one

IT WAS AS BLACK IN THE CLOSET AS OLD BLOOD. THEY had shoved me in and locked the door. I breathed heavily through my nose, fighting desperately to remain calm. I tried counting to ten on every intake of breath, and to eight as I released each one slowly into the darkness. Luckily for me, they had pulled the gag so tightly into my open mouth that my nostrils were left unobstructed, and I was able to draw in one slow lungful after another of the stale, musty air.

I tried hooking my fingernails under the silk scarf that bound my hands behind me, but since I always bit them to the quick, there was nothing to catch. Jolly good luck then that I'd remembered to put my fingertips together, using them as ten firm little bases to press my palms apart as they had pulled the knots tight.

Now I rotated my wrists, squeezing them together until I felt a bit of slack, using my thumbs to work the silk down until the knots were between my palms—then between my fingers. If they had been bright enough to think of tying my thumbs together, I should never have escaped. What utter morons they were.

With my hands free at last, I made short work of the gag.

Now for the door. But first, to be sure they were not lying in wait for me, I squatted and peered out through the keyhole at the attic. Thank heavens they had taken the key away with them. There was no one in sight; save for its perpetual tangle of shadows, junk, and sad bric-a-brac, the long attic was empty. The coast was clear.

Reaching above my head at the back of the closet, I unscrewed one of the wire coat hooks from its mounting board. By sticking its curved wing into the keyhole and levering the other end, I was able to form an L-shaped hook which I poked into the depths of the ancient lock. A bit of judicious fishing and fiddling yielded a gratifying click. It was almost too easy. The door swung open and I was free.

I SKIPPED DOWN THE BROAD stone staircase into the hall, pausing at the door of the dining room just long enough to toss my pigtails back over my shoulders and into their regulation position.

Father still insisted on dinner being served as the clock struck the hour and eaten at the massive oak refectory table, just as it had been when Mother was alive.

"Ophelia and Daphne not down yet, Flavia?" he asked peevishly, looking up from the latest issue of *The British Philatelist*, which lay open beside his meat and potatoes.

"I haven't seen them in ages," I said.

It was true. I hadn't seen them—not since they had gagged and blindfolded me, then lugged me hog-tied up the attic stairs and locked me in the closet.

Father glared at me over his spectacles for the statutory four seconds before he went back to mumbling over his sticky treasures.

I shot him a broad smile, a smile wide enough to present him with a good view of the wire braces that caged my teeth. Although they gave me the look of a dirigible with the skin off, Father always liked being reminded that he was getting his money's worth. But this time he was too preoccupied to notice.

I hoisted the lid off the Spode vegetable dish and, from the depths of its hand-painted butterflies and raspberries, spooned out a generous helping of peas. Using my knife as a ruler and my fork as a prod, I marshaled the peas so that they formed meticulous rows and columns across my plate: rank upon rank of little green spheres, spaced with a precision that would have delighted the heart of the most exacting Swiss watchmaker. Then, beginning at the bottom left, I speared the first pea with my fork and ate it.

It was all Ophelia's fault. She was, after all, seventeen, and therefore expected to possess at least a modicum of the maturity she should come into as an adult. That she should gang up with Daphne, who was thirteen, simply wasn't fair. Their combined ages totalled thirty years. Thirty years!—against my eleven. It was not only unsporting, it was downright rotten. And it simply screamed out for revenge.

NEXT MORNING I WAS BUSY among the flasks and flagons of my chemical laboratory on the top floor of the east wing when Ophelia barged in without so much as a la-di-dah.

"Where's my pearl necklace?"

I shrugged. "I'm not the keeper of your trinkets."

"I know you took it. The Mint Imperials that were in my lingerie drawer are gone too, and I've observed that missing mints in this household seem always to wind up in the same grubby little mouth."

I adjusted the flame on a spirit lamp that was heating a beaker of red liquid. "If you're insinuating that my personal hygiene is not up to the same high standard as yours you can go suck my galoshes."

"Flavia!"

"Well, you can. I'm sick and tired of being blamed for everything, Feely."

But my righteous indignation was cut short as Ophelia peered shortsightedly into the ruby flask, which was just coming to the boil.

"What's that sticky mass in the bottom?" Her long manicured fingernail tapped at the glass.

"It's an experiment. Careful, Feely, it's acid!"

Ophelia's face went white. "Those are my pearls! They belonged to Mummy!"

Ophelia was the only one of Harriet's daughters who referred to her as "Mummy": the only one of us old enough to have any real memories of the flesh-and-blood woman who had carried us in her body, a fact of which Ophelia never tired of reminding us. Harriet had been killed in a mountaineering accident when I was just a year old, and she was not often spoken of at Buckshaw.

Was I jealous of Ophelia's memories? Did I resent them? I don't believe I did; it ran far deeper than that. In rather an odd way, I despised Ophelia's memories of our mother.

I looked up slowly from my work so that the round lenses of my spectacles would flash blank white semaphores of light at her. I knew that whenever I did this, Ophelia had the horrid impression that she was in the presence of some mad black-and-white German scientist in a film at the Gaumont.

"Beast!"

"Hag!" I retorted. But not until Ophelia had spun round on her heel—quite neatly, I thought—and stormed out the door.

Retribution was not long in coming, but then with Ophelia, it never was. Ophelia was not, as I was, a long-range planner who believed in letting the soup of revenge simmer to perfection.

Quite suddenly after dinner, with Father safely retired to his study to gloat over his collection of paper heads, Ophelia had too quietly put down the silver butter knife in which, like a budgerigar, she had been regarding her own reflection for the last quarter of an hour. Without preamble she said, "I'm not really your sister, you know . . . nor is Daphne. That's why we're so unlike you. I don't suppose it's ever even occurred to you that you're adopted."

I dropped my spoon with a clatter. "That's not true. I'm the spitting image of Harriet. Everybody says so."

"She picked you out at the Home for Unwed Mothers because of the striking resemblance," Ophelia said, making a distasteful face. ·

"How could there be a resemblance when she was an adult and I was a baby?" I was nothing if not quick on the uptake.

"Because you reminded her of her own baby pictures. Good Lord, she even dragged them along and held them up beside you for comparison."

I appealed to Daphne, whose nose was firmly stuck in a leather-bound copy of *The Castle of Otranto*. "That's not true, is it, Daffy?"

"'Fraid so," Daphne said, idly turning an onionskin page. "Father always said it would come as a bit of a shock to you. He made both of us swear never to tell. Or at least until you were eleven. He made us take an oath."

"A green Gladstone bag," Ophelia said. "I saw it with my own eyes. I watched Mummy stuffing her own baby pictures into a green Gladstone bag to drag off to the home. Although I was only six at the time—almost seven—I'll never forget her white hands...her fingers on the brass clasp."

I leapt up from the table and fled the room in tears. I didn't actually think of the poison until next morning at breakfast.

As with all great schemes, it was a simple one.

BUCKSHAW HAD BEEN THE HOME of our family, the de Luces, since time out of mind. The present Georgian house had been built to replace an Elizabethan original burnt to the ground by villagers who suspected the de Luces of Orange sympathies. That we had been ardent Catholics for four hundred years, and remained so, meant nothing to the inflamed citizenry of Bishop's Lacey. "Old House," as it was called, had gone up in flames, and the new house which had replaced it was now well into its third century.

Two later de Luce ancestors, Antony and William de

Luce, who had disagreed about the Crimean War, had spoiled the lines of the original structure. Each of them had subsequently added a wing, William the east wing and Antony the west.

Each became a recluse in his own dominion, and each had forbidden the other ever to set foot across the black line which they caused to be painted dead center from the vestibule in the front, across the foyer, and straight through to the butler's W.C. behind the back stairs. Their two yellow brick annexes, pustulantly Victorian, folded back like the pinioned wings of a boneyard angel which, to my eyes, gave the tall windows and shutters of Buckshaw's Georgian front the prim and surprised look of an old maid whose bun is too tight.

A later de Luce, Tarquin—or Tar, as he was called—in the wake of a sensational mental breakdown, made a shambles of what had promised to be a brilliant career in chemistry, and was sent down from Oxford in the summer of Queen Victoria's Silver Jubilee.

Tar's indulgent father, solicitous of the lad's uncertain health, had spared no expense in outfitting a laboratory on the top floor of Buckshaw's east wing: a laboratory replete with German glassware, German microscopes, a German spectroscope, brass chemical balances from Lucerne, and a complexly shaped mouth-blown German Geisler tube to which Tar could attach electrical coils to study the way in which various gases fluoresce.

On a desk by the windows was a Leitz microscope, whose brass still shone with the same warm luxury as it had the day it was brought by pony cart from the train at Buckshaw Halt. Its reflecting mirror could be angled to catch the first pale rays of the morning sun, while for cloudy days or for use after dark, it was equipped with a paraffin microscope lamp by Davidson & Co. of London.

There was even an articulated human skeleton on a wheeled stand, given to Tar when he was only twelve by the great naturalist Frank Buckland, whose father had eaten the mummified heart of King Louis XIV.

Three walls of this room were lined from floor to ceiling with glass-fronted cabinets, two of them filled row upon row with chemicals in glass apothecary jars, each labeled in the meticulous copperplate handwriting of Tar de Luce, who in the end had thwarted Fate and outlived them all. He died in 1928 at the age of sixty in the midst of his chemical kingdom, where he was found one morning by his housekeeper, one of his dead eyes still peering sightlessly through his beloved Leitz. It was rumored that he had been studying the first-order decomposition of nitrogen pentoxide. If that was true, it was the first recorded research into a reaction which was to lead eventually to the development of the A-bomb.

Uncle Tar's laboratory had been locked up and preserved in airless silence, down through the dusty years until what Father called my "strange talents" had begun to manifest themselves, and I had been able to claim it for my own.

I still shivered with joy whenever I thought of the rainy autumn day that Chemistry had fallen into my life.

I had been scaling the bookcases in the library, pretending I was a noted Alpinist, when my foot slipped and a heavy book was knocked to the floor. As I picked it up to straighten its creased pages, I saw that it was filled not just with words, but with dozens of drawings as well. In some of them, disembodied hands poured liquids into curiously made glass containers that looked as if they might have been musical instruments from another world.

The book's title was *An Elementary Study of Chemistry,* and within moments it had taught me that the word *iodine* comes from a word meaning "violet," and that the name *bromine* was derived from a Greek word meaning "a stench." These were the sorts of things I needed to know! I slipped the fat red volume under my sweater and took it upstairs, and it wasn't until later that I noticed the name *H. de Luce* written on the flyleaf. The book had belonged to Harriet.

Soon, I found myself poring over its pages in every spare moment. There were evenings when I could hardly wait for bedtime. Harriet's book had become my secret friend.

In it were detailed all the alkali metals: metals with fabulous names like lithium and rubidium; the alkaline earths such as strontium, barium, and radium. I cheered aloud when I read that a woman, Madame Curie, had discovered radium.

And then there were the poisonous gases: phosphine, arsine (a single bubble of which has been known to prove fatal), nitrogen peroxide, hydrogen sulfide...the lists went on and on. When I found that precise instructions were given for formulating these compounds, I was in seventh heaven.

Once I had taught myself to make sense of the chemical equations such as $K_4FeC_6N_6 + 2K = 6KCN + Fe$ (which describes what happens when the yellow prussiate of potash is heated with potassium to produce potassium cyanide), the universe was laid open before me: It was like having stumbled upon a recipe book that had once belonged to the witch in the wood.

What intrigued me more than anything was finding out the way in which everything, all of creation—all of it!—was held together by invisible chemical bonds, and I found a strange, inexplicable comfort in knowing that somewhere, even though we couldn't see it in our own world, there was real stability.

I didn't make the obvious connection at first, between the book and the abandoned laboratory I had discovered as a child. But when I did, my life came to life—if that makes any sense.

Here in Uncle Tar's lab, row on row, were the chemistry books he had so lovingly assembled, and I soon discovered that with a little effort most of them were not too far beyond my understanding.

Simple experiments came next, and I tried to remember to follow instructions to the letter. Not to say that there weren't a few stinks and explosions, but the less said about those the better.

As time went on, my notebooks grew fatter. My work was becoming ever more sophisticated as the mysteries of Organic Chemistry revealed themselves to me, and I rejoiced in my newfound knowledge of what could be extracted so easily from nature.

My particular passion was poison.

I SLASHED AWAY at the foliage with a bamboo walking stick pinched from an elephant-foot umbrella stand in the front hall. Back here in the kitchen garden, the high red-brick walls had not yet let in the warming sun; everything was still sodden from the rain that had fallen in the night.

Making my way through the debris of last year's uncut grass, I poked along the bottom of the wall until I found what I was looking for: a patch of bright leaves whose scarlet gloss made their three-leaved clusters easy to spot among the other vines. Pulling on a pair of cotton gardening gloves that had been tucked into my belt, and launching into a loudly whistled rendition of "Bibbidi-Bobbidi-Boo," I went to work.

Later, in the safety of my sanctum sanctorum, my Holy of Holies—I had come across that delightful phrase in a biography of Thomas Jefferson and adopted it as my own—I stuffed the colorful leaves into a glass retort, taking care not to remove my gloves until their shiny foliage was safely tamped down. Now came the part I loved.

Stoppering the retort, I connected it on one side to a flask in which water was already boiling, and on the other to a coiled glass condensing tube whose open end hung suspended over an empty beaker. With the water bubbling furiously, I watched as the steam found its way through the tubing and escaped into the flask among the leaves. Already they were beginning to curl and soften as the hot vapor opened the tiny pockets between their cells, releasing the oils that were the essence of the living plant.

This was the way the ancient alchemists had practiced their art: fire and steam, steam and fire. Distillation.

How I loved this work.

Distillation. I said it aloud. "Dis-till-ation!"

I looked on in awe as the steam cooled and condensed in the coil, and wrung my hands in ecstasy as the first limpid drop of liquid hung suspended, then dropped with an audible *plop!* into the waiting receptacle.

When the water had boiled away and the operation was complete, I turned off the flame and cupped my chin in my palms to watch with fascination as the fluid in the beaker settled out into two distinct layers: the clear distilled water on the bottom, a liquid of a light yellow hue floating on top. This was the essential oil of the leaves. It was called urushiol and had been used, among other things, in the manufacture of lacquer.

Digging into the pocket of my sweater, I pulled out a shiny gold tube. I removed its cap, and couldn't help smiling as a red tip was revealed. Ophelia's lipstick, purloined from the drawer of her dressing table, along with the pearls and the Mint Imperials. And Feely—Miss Snotrag—hadn't even noticed it was gone.

Remembering the mints, I popped one into my mouth, crushing the sweet noisily between my molars.

The core of lipstick came out easily enough, and I relit the spirit lamp. Only a gentle heat was required to reduce the waxy stuff to a sticky mass. If Feely only knew that lipstick was made of fish scales, I thought, she might be a little less eager to slather the stuff all over her mouth. I must remember to tell her. I grinned. Later.

With a pipette I drew off a few millimeters of the distilled oil that floated in the beaker and then, drop by drop, dripped it gently into the ooze of the melted lipstick, giving the mixture a vigorous stir with a wooden tongue depressor.

Too thin, I thought. I fetched down a jar and added a dollop of beeswax to restore it to its former consistency.

Time for the gloves again—and for the iron bullet

mold I had pinched from Buckshaw's really quite decent firearm museum.

Odd, isn't it, that a charge of lipstick is precisely the size of a .45 caliber slug. A useful bit of information, really. I'd have to remember to think of its wider ramifications tonight when I was tucked safely into my bed. Right now, I was far too busy.

Teased from its mold and cooled under running water, the reformulated red core fitted neatly back inside its golden dispenser.

I screwed it up and down several times to make sure that it was working. Then I replaced the cap. Feely was a late sleeper and would still be dawdling over breakfast.

"WHERE'S MY LIPSTICK, you little swine? What have you done with it?"

"It's in your drawer," I said. "I noticed it when I purloined your pearls."

In my short life, bracketed by two sisters, I had of necessity become master of the forked tongue.

"It's not in my drawer. I've just looked, and it isn't there."

"Did you put on your specs?" I asked with a smirk.

Although Father had had all of us fitted with spectacles, Feely refused to wear hers and mine contained little more than window glass. I wore them only in the laboratory to protect my eyes, or to solicit sympathy.

Feely slammed down the heels of her hands on the table and stormed from the room.

I went back to plumbing the depths of my second bowl of Weetabix.

Later, I wrote in my notebook:

Friday, 2nd of June 1950, 9:42 A.M. Subject's appearance normal but grumpy.
(Isn't she always?) Onset may vary from 12 to 72 hours.

I could wait.

MRS. MULLET, WHO WAS short and gray and round as a
millstone and who, I'm quite sure, thought of herself as a
character in a poem by A. A. Milne, was in the kitchen
formulating one of her pus-like custard pies. As usual, she
was struggling with the large Aga cooker that dominated
the small, cramped kitchen.

"Oh, Miss Flavia! Here, help me with the oven, dear."

But before I could think of a suitable response, Father
was behind me.

"Flavia, a word." His voice was as heavy as the lead
weights on a deep-sea diver's boots.

I glanced at Mrs. Mullet to see how she was taking it.
She always fled at the slightest whiff of unpleasantness,
and once when Father raised his voice, she had rolled herself up in a carpet and refused to come out until her husband was sent for.

She eased the oven door shut as if it were made of
Waterford crystal.

"I must be off," she said. "Lunch is in the warming
oven."

"Thank you, Mrs. Mullet," Father said. "We'll manage." We were always managing.

She opened the kitchen door—and let out a sudden
shriek like a cornered badger. "Oh, good Lord! Beggin'
your pardon, Colonel de Luce, but, oh, good Lord!"

Father and I had to push a bit to see round her.

It was a bird, a jack snipe—and it was dead. It lay on its back on the doorstep, its stiff wings extended like a little pterodactyl, its eyes rather unpleasantly filmed over, the long black needle of its bill pointing straight up into the air. Something impaled upon it shifted in the morning breeze—a tiny scrap of paper.

No, not a scrap of paper, a postage stamp.

Father bent down for a closer look, then gave a little gasp. And suddenly he was clutching at his throat, his hands shaking like aspen leaves in autumn, his face the color of sodden ashes.

two

MY SPINE, AS THEY SAY, TURNED TO ICE. FOR A MO-
ment I thought he was having a heart attack, as sedentary
fathers often do. One minute they are crowing at you to
chew every mouthful twenty-nine times and the next you
are reading about them in *The Daily Telegraph*:

> Calderwood, Jabez, of The Parsonage, Frinton. Suddenly at his
> residence on Saturday, the 14th inst. In his fifty-second year.
> Eldest son of et cetera...et cetera...et cetera...survived by
> daughters, Anna, Diana, and Trianna...

CALDERWOOD, JABEZ, AND HIS ILK had the habit of
popping off to heaven like jacks-in-the-box, leaving behind, to fend for themselves, an assortment of dismal-
sounding daughters.

Hadn't I already lost one parent? Surely Father wouldn't
pull such a rotten trick.

Or would he?

No. He was now sucking air noisily up through his nose like a cart horse as he reached out towards the thing on the doorstep. His fingers, like long, unsteady white tweezers, deskewered the stamp delicately from the dead bird's bill, and then shoved the punctured scrap hastily into one of his waistcoat pockets. He pointed a trembling forefinger at the little carcass.

"Dispose of that thing, Mrs. Mullet," he said in a strangled voice that sounded like someone else's: the voice of a stranger.

"Oh my, Colonel de Luce," Mrs. Mullet said. "Oh my, Colonel, I don't . . . I think . . . I mean to say . . ."

But he was already gone, to his study, stumping off, huffing and puffing like a freight engine.

As Mrs. M went, hand over mouth, for the dustpan, I escaped to my bedroom.

THE BEDROOMS AT BUCKSHAW WERE VAST, dim Zeppelin hangars, and mine, in the south—or Tar—wing, as we called it, was the largest of the lot. Its early-Victorian wallpaper (mustard yellow, with a spattering of things that looked like bloodred clots of string) made it seem even larger: a cold, boundless, drafty waste. Even in summer the trek across the room to the distant washstand near the window was an experience that might have daunted Scott of the Antarctic; just one of the reasons I skipped it and climbed straight up into my four-poster bed where, wrapped in a woolen blanket, I could sit cross-legged until the cows came home, pondering my life.

I thought, for instance, of the time I used a butter knife to scrape off samples of my jaundiced wall covering. I remembered Daffy's wide-eyed recounting of one of A. J. Cronin's books in which some poor sod sickened and died after sleeping in a room in which one of the wallpaper's prime coloring ingredients was arsenic. Filled with hope, I carried my scrapings up to the laboratory for analysis.

No stodgy old Marsh's test for me, thank you very much! I favored the method by which the arsenic was first converted to its trioxidic, then heated with sodium acetate to produce cacodyl oxide: not only one of the most poisonous substances ever known to exist on this planet Earth, but one with the added advantage of giving off a most unbelievably offensive odor: like the stink of rotten garlic, but a million times worse. Its discoverer, Bunsen (of burner fame), noted that just one whiff of the stuff would not only make your hands and feet tingle, but also your tongue would develop a vile black coating. Oh, Lord, how manifold are thy works!

You can imagine my disappointment when I saw that my sample contained no arsenic: It had been colored by a simple organic tincture, most likely one made from the common goat-willow (*Salix caprea*) or some other harmless and supremely boring vegetable dye.

Somehow that caused my thoughts to go flying back to Father.

What had frightened him so at the kitchen door? And *was* it really fear I had seen in his face?

Yes, there seemed little doubt of that. There was nothing else it could have been. I was already far too familiar with his anger, his impatience, his fatigue, his sudden bleak moods: all of them states which drifted now and then across his face like the shadows of the clouds that moved across our English hills.

He was not afraid of dead birds, that much I knew. I had seen him tuck into many a fat Christmas goose, brandishing his knife and fork like an Oriental assassin. Surely it couldn't be the presence of feathers? Or the bird's dead eye?

And it couldn't have been the stamp. Father loved stamps more dearly than he loved his offspring. The only thing he had ever loved more than his pretty bits of paper was Harriet. And she, as I have said, was dead.

Like that snipe.

Could that be the reason for his reaction?

"No! No! Get away!" The harsh voice came in at my open window, derailing and wrecking my train of thought.

I threw off the blanket, leaped from my bed, ran across the room, and looked down into the kitchen garden.

It was Dogger. He was flattened against the garden wall, his dark, weathered fingers splayed out across the faded red bricks.

"Don't come near me! Get away!"

Dogger was Father's man: his factotum. And he was alone in the garden.

It was whispered—by Mrs. Mullet, I might as well admit—that Dogger had survived two years in a Japanese prisoner-of-war camp, followed by thirteen more months of torture, starvation, malnutrition, and forced labor on the Death Railway between Thailand and Burma where, it was thought, he had been forced to eat rats.

"Go gently, dear," she told me. "His nerves are something shocking."

I looked down at him there in the cucumber patch, his thatch of prematurely white hair standing on end; his eyes upturned, seemingly sightless, to the sun.

"It's all right, Dogger!" I shouted. "I've got them covered from up here."

For a moment, I thought he hadn't heard me, but then his face turned slowly, like a sunflower, towards the sound of my voice. I held my breath. You never know what someone might do in such a state.

"Steady on, Dogger," I called out. "It's all right. They've gone."

Suddenly he went limp, like a man who has been holding a live electrical wire in which the current has just been switched off.

"Miss Flavia?" His voice quavered. "Is that you, Miss Flavia?"

"I'm coming down," I said. "I'll be there in a jiff."

Down the back stairs I ran, pell-mell, and into the kitchen. Mrs. Mullet had gone home, but her custard pie sat cooling at the open window.

No, I thought: What Dogger needed was something to drink. Father kept his Scotch locked tightly in a bookcase in his study, and I could not intrude.

Luckily, I found a pitcher of cool milk in the pantry. I poured out a tall glass of it, and dashed into the garden.

"Here, drink this," I said, holding it out to him.

Dogger took the drink in both hands, stared at it for a long moment as if he didn't know what to do with it, and then raised it unsteadily to his mouth. He drank deeply until the milk was gone. He handed me the empty glass.

For a moment, he looked vaguely beatific, like an angel by Raphael, but that impression quickly passed.

"You have a white mustache," I told him. I bent down to the cucumbers and, tearing off a large, dark green leaf from the vine, used it to wipe his upper lip.

The light was coming back into his empty eyes.

"Milk and cucumbers..." he said. "Cucumbers and milk..."

"Poison!" I shouted, jumping up and down and flapping my arms like a chicken, to show him that everything was under control. "Deadly poison!" And we both laughed a little.

He blinked.

"My!" he said, looking round the garden as if he were a princess coming awake from the deepest dream, "isn't it turning out to be a lovely day!"

FATHER DID NOT APPEAR AT LUNCH. To reassure myself, I put an ear to his study door and listened for a few minutes to the flipping of philatelic pages and an occasional clearing of the paternal throat. Nerves, I decided.

At the table, Daphne sat with her nose in Walpole (Horace), her cucumber sandwich beside her, soggy and forgotten on a plate. Ophelia, sighing endlessly, crossing, uncrossing, and recrossing her legs, stared blankly off into space, and I could only assume she was trifling in her mind with Ned Cropper, the jack-of-all-trades at the Thirteen Drakes. She was too absorbed in her haughty reverie to notice when I leaned in for a closer look at her lips as she reached absently for a cube of cane sugar, popped it into her mouth, and began sucking.

"Ah," I remarked, to no one in particular, "the pimples will be blooming in the morning."

She made a lunge for me, but my legs were faster than her flippers.

Back upstairs in my laboratory, I wrote:

Friday, 2nd of June 1950, 1:07 p.m. No visible reaction as yet. "Patience is a necessary ingredient of genius."
—(Disraeli)

TEN O'CLOCK HAD COME and gone, and still I couldn't sleep. Mostly, when the light's out I'm a lump of lead, but tonight was different. I lay on my back, hands clasped behind my head, reviewing the day.

First there had been Father. Well, no, that's not quite true. First there had been the dead bird on the doorstep—and then there had been Father. What I thought I had seen on his face was fear, but still there was some little corner of my brain that didn't seem to believe it.

To me—to all of us—Father was fearless. He had seen things during the War: horrid things that must never be put into words. He had somehow survived the years of Harriet's vanishing and presumed death. And through it all he had been stalwart, staunch, dogged, and unshakeable. Unbelievably British. Unbearably stiff upper lip. But now...

And then there was Dogger: Arthur Wellesley Dogger, to give him his "full patronymic" (as he called it on his better days). Dogger had come to us first as Father's valet, but then, as "the full vicissitudes of that position" (his words, not mine) bore down upon his shoulders, he found it "more copacetic" to become butler, then chauffeur, then Buckshaw's general handyman, then chauffeur again for a while. In recent months, he had rocked gently down, like a falling autumn leaf, before coming to rest in his present post of gardener, and Father had donated our Hillman estate wagon to St. Tancred's as a raffle prize.

Poor Dogger! That's what I thought, even though

Daphne told me I should never say that about anyone: "It's not only condescending, it fails to take into account the future," she said.

Still, who could forget the sight of Dogger in the garden? A great simple hulk of a helpless man just standing there, hair and tools in disarray, wheelbarrow overturned, and a look on his face as if...as if...

A rustle of sound caught my ear. I turned my head and listened.

Nothing.

It is a simple fact of Nature that I happen to possess acute hearing: the kind of hearing, Father once told me, that allows its owner to hear spiderwebs clanging like horseshoes against the walls. Harriet had possessed it too, and sometimes I like to imagine I am, in a way, a rather odd remnant of her: a pair of disembodied ears drifting round the haunted halls of Buckshaw, hearing things that are sometimes better left unheard.

But, listen! There it was again! A voice reflected; hard and hollow, like a whisper in an empty biscuit tin.

I slipped out of bed and went on tiptoes to the window. Taking care not to jiggle the curtains, I peeked out into the kitchen garden just as the moon obligingly came out from behind a cloud to illuminate the scene, much as it would in a first-rate production of A *Midsummer Night's Dream*.

But there was nothing more to see than its silvery light dancing among the cucumbers and the roses.

And then I heard a voice: an angry voice, like the buzzing of a bee in late summer trying to fly through a closed windowpane.

I threw on one of Harriet's Japanese silk housecoats

(one of the two I had rescued from the Great Purge), shoved my feet into the beaded Indian moccasins that served as slippers, and crept to the head of the stairs. The voice was coming from somewhere inside the house.

Buckshaw possessed two Grand Staircases, each one winding down in a sinuous mirror image of the other, from the first floor, coming to earth just short of the black painted line that divided the checker-tiled foyer. My staircase, from the "Tar," or east wing, terminated in that great echoing painted hall beyond which, over against the west wing, was the firearm museum, and behind it, Father's study. It was from this direction that the voice was emanating. I crept towards it.

I put an ear to the door.

"Besides, Jacko," a caddish voice was saying on the other side of the paneled wood, "how could you live in the light of discovery? How could you ever go on?"

For a queasy instant I thought George Sanders had come to Buckshaw, and was lecturing Father behind closed doors.

"Get out," Father said, his voice not angry, but in that level, controlled tone that told me he was furious. In my mind I could see his furrowed brow, his clenched fists, and his jaw muscles taut as bowstrings.

"Oh, come off it, old boy," said the oily voice. "We're in this together—always have been, always will be. You know it as well as I."

"Twining was right," Father said. "You're a loathsome, despicable excuse for a human being."

"Twining? Old Cuppa? Cuppa's been dead these thirty years, Jacko—like Jacob Marley. But, like said Marley, his ghost lingers on. As perhaps you've noticed."

"And we killed him," Father said, in a flat, dead voice.

Had I heard what I'd heard? How could he—

By taking my ear from the door and bending to peer through the keyhole I missed Father's next words. He was standing beside his desk, facing the door. The stranger's back was to me. He was excessively tall, six foot four, I guessed. With his red hair and rusty gray suit, he reminded me of the Sandhill Crane that stood stuffed in a dim corner of the firearm museum.

I reapplied my ear to the paneled door.

"...no statute of limitations on shame," the voice was saying. "What's a couple of thousand to you, Jacko? You must have come into a fair bit when Harriet died. Why, the insurance alone—"

"Shut your filthy mouth!" Father shouted. "Get out before I—"

Suddenly I was seized from behind and a rough hand was clapped across my mouth. My heart almost leaped out of my chest.

I was being held so tightly I couldn't manage a struggle.

"Go back to bed, Miss Flavia," a voice hissed into my ear.

It was Dogger.

"This is none of your business," he whispered. "Go back to bed."

He loosened his grip on me and I struggled free. I shot him a poisonous look.

In the near-darkness, I saw his eyes soften a little.

"Buzz off," he whispered.

I buzzed off.

Back in my room I paced up and down for a while, as I often do when I'm thwarted.

I thought about what I'd overheard. Father a murderer? That was impossible. There was probably some quite simple explanation. If only I'd heard the rest of the conversation between Father and the stranger...if only Dogger hadn't ambushed me in the dark. Who did he think he was?

I'll show him, I thought.

"With no further ado!" I said aloud.

I slipped José Iturbi from his green paper sleeve, gave my portable gramophone a good winding-up, and slapped the second side of Chopin's Polonaise in A flat Major onto the turntable. I threw myself across the bed and sang along:

"DAH-dah-dah-dah, DAH-dah-dah-dah, DAH-dah-dah-dah, DAH-dah-dah-dah..."

The music sounded as if it had been composed for a film in which someone was cranking an old Bentley that kept sputtering out: hardly a selection to float you off to dreamland...

WHEN I OPENED MY EYES, an oyster-colored dawn was peeping in at the windows. The hands of my brass alarm clock stood at 3:44. On Summer Time, daylight came early, and in less than a quarter of an hour, the sun should be up.

I stretched, yawned, and climbed out of bed. The gramophone had run down, frozen in mid-Polonaise, its needle lying dead in the grooves. For a fleeting moment I thought of winding it up again to give the household a Polish reveille. And then I remembered what had happened just a few hours before.

I went to the window and looked down into the garden. There was the potting shed, its glass panes clouded with the dew, and over there, an angular darkness that was Dogger's overturned wheelbarrow, forgotten in the events of yesterday.

Determined to put it right, to make up to him somehow, for something of which I was not even certain, I dressed and went quietly down the back stairs and into the kitchen.

As I passed the window, I noticed that a slice had been cut from Mrs. Mullet's custard pie. How odd, I thought; it was certainly none of the de Luces who had taken it. If there was one thing upon which we all agreed—one thing that united us as a family—it was our collective loathing of Mrs. Mullet's custard pies. Whenever she strayed from our favorite rhubarb or gooseberry to the dreaded custard, we generally begged off, feigning group illness, and sent her packing off home with the pie, and solicitous instructions to serve it up, with our compliments, to her good husband, Alf.

As I stepped outside, I saw that the silver light of dawn had transformed the garden into a magic glade, its shadows darkened by the thin band of day beyond the walls. Sparkling dew lay upon everything, and I should not have been at all surprised if a unicorn had stepped from behind a rosebush and tried to put its head in my lap.

I was walking towards the wheelbarrow when I tripped suddenly and fell forward onto my hands and knees.

"Bugger!" I said, already looking round to make sure that no one had heard me. I was now plastered with wet black loam.

"Bugger," I said again, a little less loudly.

Twisting round to see what had tripped me up, I spotted

it at once: something white protruding from the cucumbers. For a teetering moment there was a part of me that fought desperately to believe it was a little rake, a cunning little cultivator with white curled tines.

But reason returned, and my mind admitted that it was a hand. A hand attached to an arm: an arm that snaked off into the cucumber patch.

And there, at the end of it, tinted an awful dewy cucumber green by the dark foliage, was a face. A face that looked for all the world like the Green Man of forest legend.

Driven by a will stronger than my own, I found myself dropping further to my hands and knees beside this apparition, partly in reverence and partly for a closer look.

When I was almost nose to nose with the thing its eyes began to open.

I was too shocked to move a muscle.

The body in the cucumbers sucked in a shuddering breath . . . and then, bubbling at the nose, exhaled it in a single word, slowly and a little sadly, directly into my face.

"*Vale*," it said.

My nostrils pinched reflexively as I got a whiff of a peculiar odor—an odor whose name was, for an instant, on the very tip of my tongue.

The eyes, as blue as the birds in the Willow pattern, looked up into mine as if staring out from some dim and smoky past, as if there were some recognition in their depths.

And then they died.

I wish I could say my heart was stricken, but it wasn't. I wish I could say my instinct was to run away, but that would not be true. Instead, I watched in awe, savoring every detail: the fluttering fingers, the almost imperceptible bronze metallic cloudiness that appeared on the skin, as if, before my very eyes, it were being breathed upon by death.

And then the utter stillness.

I wish I could say I was afraid, but I wasn't. Quite the contrary. This was by far the most interesting thing that had ever happened to me in my entire life.

three

I RACED UP THE WEST STAIRCASE. MY FIRST THOUGHT was to waken Father, but something—some great invisible magnet—stopped me in my tracks. Daffy and Feely were useless in emergencies; it would be no good calling them. As quickly and as quietly as possible, I ran to the back of the house, to the little room at the top of the kitchen stairs, and tapped lightly on the door.

"Dogger!" I whispered. "It's me, Flavia."

There wasn't a sound within, and I repeated my rapping.

After about two and a half eternities, I heard Dogger's slippers shuffling across the floor. The lock gave a heavy *click* as the bolt shot back and his door opened a couple of wary inches. I could see that his face was haggard in the dawn, as if he hadn't slept.

"There's a dead body in the garden," I said. "I think you'd better come."

As I shifted from foot to foot and bit my fingernails,

Dogger gave me a look that can only be described as re-proachful, then vanished into the darkness of his room to dress. Five minutes later we were standing together on the garden path.

It was obvious that Dogger was no stranger to dead bodies. As if he'd been doing it all his life, he knelt and felt with his first two fingers for a pulse at the back angle of the jawbone. By his deadpan, distant look I could tell that there wasn't one.

Getting slowly to his feet, he dusted off his hands, as if they had somehow been contaminated.

"I'll inform the Colonel," he said.

"Shouldn't we call the police?" I asked.

Dogger ran his long fingers over his unshaven chin, as if he were mulling a question of earth-shattering conse-quence. There were severe restrictions on using the tele-phone at Buckshaw.

"Yes," he said at last. "I suppose we should."

We walked together, too slowly, into the house.

Dogger picked up the telephone and put the receiver to his ear, but I saw that he was keeping his finger firmly on the cradle switch. His mouth opened and closed several times and then his face went pale. His arm began shaking and I thought for a moment he was going to drop the thing. He looked at me helplessly.

"Here," I said, taking the instrument from his hands. "I'll do it."

"Bishop's Lacey two two one," I said into the tele-phone, thinking as I waited that Sherlock might well have smiled at the coincidence.

"Police," said an official voice at the other end of the line.

"Constable Linnet?" I said. "This is Flavia de Luce speaking from Buckshaw."

I had never done this before, and had to rely on what I'd heard on the wireless and seen in the cinema.

"I'd like to report a death," I said. "Perhaps you could send out an inspector?"

"Is it an ambulance you require, Miss Flavia?" he said. "We don't usually call out an inspector unless the circumstances are suspicious. Wait till I find a pencil..."

There was a maddening pause while I listened to him rummaging through stationery supplies before he continued:

"Now then, give me the name of the deceased, slowly, last name first."

"I don't know his name," I said. "He's a stranger."

That was the truth: I didn't know his name. But I did know, and knew it all too well, that the body in the garden—the body with the red hair, the body in the gray suit—was that of the man I'd spied through the study keyhole. The man Father had—

But I could hardly tell them that.

"I don't know his name," I repeated. "I've never seen him before in my life."

I had stepped over the line.

MRS. MULLET AND THE POLICE ARRIVED at the same moment, she on foot from the village and they in a blue Vauxhall sedan. As it crunched to a stop on the gravel, its front door squeaked open and a man stepped out onto the driveway.

"Miss de Luce," he said, as if pronouncing my name aloud put me in his power. "May I call you Flavia?"

I nodded assent.

"I'm Inspector Hewitt. Is your father at home?"

The Inspector was a pleasant-enough-looking man, with wavy hair, gray eyes, and a bit of a bulldog stance that reminded me of Douglas Bader, the Spitfire ace, whose photos I had seen in the back issues of *The War Illustrated* that lay in white drifts in the drawing room.

"He is," I said, "but he's rather indisposed." It was a word I had borrowed from Ophelia. "I'll show you to the corpse myself."

Mrs. Mullet's mouth fell open and her eyes goggled. "Oh, good Lord! Beggin' your pardon, Miss Flavia, but, oh, good Lord!"

If she had been wearing an apron, she'd have thrown it over her head and fled, but she didn't. Instead, she reeled in through the open door.

Two men in blue suits, who, as if awaiting instructions, had remained packed into the backseat of the car, now began to unfold themselves.

"Detective Sergeant Woolmer and Detective Sergeant Graves," Inspector Hewitt said. Sergeant Woolmer was hulking and square, with the squashed nose of a prize-fighter; Sergeant Graves a chipper little blond sparrow with dimples who grinned at me as he shook my hand.

"And now if you'll be so kind," Inspector Hewitt said.

The detective sergeants unloaded their kits from the boot of the Vauxhall, and I led them in solemn procession through the house and into the garden.

Having pointed out the body, I watched in fascination as Sergeant Woolmer unpacked and mounted his camera on a wooden tripod, his fingers, fat as sausages, making surprisingly gentle microscopic adjustments to the little silver controls. As he took several covering exposures of the garden, lavishing particular attention on the cucumber patch, Sergeant Graves was opening a worn leather case in which were bottles ranged neatly row on row, and in which I glimpsed a packet of glassine envelopes.

I stepped forward eagerly, almost salivating, for a closer look.

"I wonder, Flavia," Inspector Hewitt said, stepping gingerly into the cucumbers, "if you might ask someone to organize some tea?"

He must have seen the look on my face.

"We've had rather an early start this morning. Do you think you could manage to rustle something up?"

So that was it. As at a birth, so at a death. Without so much as a kiss-me-quick-and-mind-the-marmalade, the only female in sight is enlisted to trot off and see that the water is boiled. Rustle something up, indeed! What did he take me for, some kind of cowboy?

"I'll see what can be arranged, Inspector," I said. Coldly, I hoped.

"Thank you," Inspector Hewitt said. Then, as I stamped off towards the kitchen door, he called out, "Oh, and Flavia . . ."

I turned, expectantly.

"We'll come in for it. No need for you to come out here again."

The nerve! The bloody nerve!

OPHELIA AND DAPHNE WERE already at the breakfast table. Mrs. Mullet had leaked the grim news, and there had been ample time for them to arrange themselves in poses of pretended indifference.

Ophelia's lips had still not reacted to my little prepara-
tion, and I made a mental note to record the time of my
observation and the results later.

"I found a dead body in the cucumber patch," I told
them.

"How very like you," Ophelia said, and went on preen-
ing her eyebrows.

Daphne had finished *The Castle of Otranto* and was
now well into *Nicholas Nickleby*. But I noticed that she was
biting her lower lip as she read: a sure sign of distraction.

There was an operatic silence.

"Was there a great deal of blood?" Ophelia asked at
last.

"None," I said. "Not a drop."

"Whose body was it?"

"I don't know," I said, relieved at an opportunity to
duck behind the truth.

"The Death of a Perfect Stranger," Daphne proclaimed
in her best BBC Radio announcer's voice, dragging herself
out of Dickens, but leaving a finger in to mark her place.

"How do you know it's a stranger?" I asked.

"Elementary," Daffy said. "It isn't you, it isn't me, and it
isn't Feely. Mrs. Mullet is in the kitchen, Dogger is in the
garden with the coppers, and Father was upstairs just a few
minutes ago splashing in his bath."

I was about to tell her that it was me she had heard in
the tub, but I decided not to; any mention of the bath led
inevitably to gibes about my general cleanliness. But after
the morning's events in the garden, I had felt the sudden
need for a quick soak and a wash-up.

"He was probably poisoned," I said. "The stranger, I
mean."

"It's always poison, isn't it?" Feely said with a toss of her hair. "At least in those lurid yellow detective novels. In this case, he probably made the fatal mistake of eating Mrs. Mullet's cooking."

As she pushed away the gooey remains of a coddled egg, something flashed into my mind like a cinder popping out of the grate and onto the hearth, but before I could examine it, my chain of thought was broken.

"Listen to this," Daphne said, reading aloud. "Fanny Squeers is writing a letter:

" '. . . my pa is one mask of brooses both blue and green likewise two forms are steepled in his Goar. We were kimpelled to have him carried down into the kitchen where he now lays . . .

" '. . . When your nevew that you recommended for a teacher had done this to my pa and jumped upon his body with his feet and also langwedge which I will not pollewt my pen with describing, he assaulted my ma with dreadful violence, dashed her to the earth, and drove her back comb several inches into her head. A very little more and it must have entered her skull. We have a medical certifiket that if it had, the tortershell would have affected the brain.'

"Now listen to this next bit:

" 'Me and my brother were then the victims of his feury since which we have suffered very much which leads us to the arrowing belief that we have received some injury in our insides, especially as no marks of violence are visible externally. I am screaming out loud all the time I write—' "

It sounded to me like a classic case of cyanide poisoning, but I didn't much feel like sharing my insight with these two boors.

" 'Screaming out loud all the time I write,' " Daffy repeated. "Imagine!"

"I know the feeling," I said, pushing my plate away, and, leaving my breakfast untouched, I made my way slowly up the east staircase to my laboratory.

WHENEVER I WAS UPSET, I made for my sanctum sanctorum. Here, among the bottles and beakers, I would allow myself to be enveloped by what I thought of as the Spirit of Chemistry. Here, sometimes, I would reenact, step by step, the discoveries of the great chemists. Or I would lift down lovingly from the bookcase a volume from Tar de Luce's treasured library, such as the English translation of Antoine Lavoisier's *Elements of Chemistry*, printed in 1790 but whose leaves, even after a hundred and sixty years, were still as crisp as butcher's paper. How I gloried in the antiquated names just waiting to be plucked from its pages: Butter of Antimony . . . Flowers of Arsenic.

"Rank poisons," Lavoisier called them, but I reveled in the recitation of their names like a hog at a spa.

"King's yellow!" I said aloud, rolling the words round in my mouth—savoring them in spite of their poisonous nature.

"Crystals of Venus! Fuming Liquor of Boyle! Oil of Ants!"

But it wasn't working this time; my mind kept flying back to Father, thinking over and over about what I had seen and heard. Who was this Twining—"Old Cuppa"—the man Father claimed they had killed? And why had Father not appeared at breakfast? That had me truly worried. Father always insisted that breakfast was "the body's banquet," and to the best of my knowledge, there was nothing on earth that would compel him to miss it.

Then, too, I thought of the passage from Dickens that

Daphne had read to us: the bruises blue and green. Had Father fought with the stranger and suffered wounds that could not be hidden at the table? Or had he suffered those injuries to the insides described by Fanny Squeers: injuries that left no external marks of violence. Perhaps that was what had happened to the man with the red hair. Which should explain why I had seen no blood. Could Father be a murderer? Again?

My head was spinning. I could think of nothing better to calm it down than the Oxford English Dictionary. I fetched down the volume with the Vs. What was that word the stranger had breathed in my face? "*Vale*"! That was it.

I flipped the pages: vagabondical . . . vagrant . . . vain . . . here it was: *vale*: Farewell; good-bye; adieu. It was pronounced *val-eh*, and was the second person singular imperative of the Latin verb *valere*, to be well.

What a peculiar thing for a dying man to say to someone he didn't know.

A sudden racket from the hall interrupted my thoughts. Someone was giving the dinner gong a great old bonging. This huge disk, which looked like a leftover from the opening of a film by J. Arthur Rank, had not been sounded for ages, which could explain why I was so startled by its shattering noise.

I ran out of the laboratory and down the stairs to find an oversized man standing at the gong with the striker still in his hand.

"Coroner," he said, and I took it he was referring to himself. Although he did not trouble to give his name, I recognized him at once as Dr. Darby, one of the two partners in Bishop's Lacey's only medical practice.

Dr. Darby was the spitting image of John Bull: red face, multiple chins, and a stomach that bellied out like a sail full of wind. He was wearing a brown suit with a checked yellow waistcoat, and he carried the traditional doctor's black bag. If he remembered me as the girl whose hand he had stitched up the year before after the incident with a wayward bit of laboratory glassware, he gave no outward sign but stood there expectantly, like a hound on the scent.

Father was still nowhere in sight, nor was Dogger. I knew that Feely and Daffy would never condescend to respond to a bell ("So utterly Pavlovian," Feely said), and Mrs. Mullet always kept to her kitchen.

"The police are in the garden," I told him. "I'll show you the way."

As we stepped out into the sunshine, Inspector Hewitt looked up from examining the laces of a black shoe that protruded rather unpleasantly from the cucumbers.

"Morning, Fred," he said. "Thought you'd best come have a look."

"Um," Dr. Darby said. He opened his bag and rummaged inside for a moment before pulling out a white paper bag. He reached into it with two fingers and extracted a single crystal mint, which he popped into his mouth and sucked with noisy relish.

A moment later he had waded into the greenery and was kneeling beside the corpse.

"Anyone we know?" he asked, mumbling a bit round the mint.

"Shouldn't seem so," Inspector Hewitt said. "Empty pockets...no identification...reason to believe, though, that he's recently come from Norway."

Recently come from Norway? Surely this was a deduction worthy of the great Holmes himself—and I had heard it with my own ears! I was almost ready to forgive the Inspector his earlier rudeness. Almost . . . but not quite.

"We've launched inquiries, ports of call and so forth."

"Bloody Norwegians!" said Dr. Darby, rising and closing his bag. "Flock over here like birds to a lighthouse, where they expire and leave us to mop up. It isn't fair, is it?"

"What shall I put down as the time of death?" Inspector Hewitt asked.

"Hard to say. Always is. Well, not always, but often."

"Give or take?"

"Can't tell with cyanosis: takes a while to tell if it's coming or going, you know. Eight to twelve hours, I should say. I'll be able to tell you more after we've had our friend up on the table."

"And that would make it . . . ?"

Dr. Darby pushed back his cuff and looked at his watch.

"Well, let me see . . . it's eight twenty-two now, so that makes it no sooner than about that same hour last evening and no later than, say, midnight."

Midnight! I must have audibly sucked in air, since both Inspector Hewitt and Dr. Darby turned to look at me. How could I tell them that, just a few hours ago, the stranger from Norway had breathed his last breath into my face?

The solution was an easy one. I took to my heels. I found Dogger trimming the roses in the flower bed under the library window. The air was heavy with their scent: the delicious odor of tea chests from the Orient.

"Father not down yet, Dogger?" I asked.

"Lady Hillingdons are especially fine this year, Miss Flavia," he said, as if ice wouldn't melt in his mouth; as if our furtive encounter in the night had never taken place. Very well, I thought, I'll play his game.

"Especially fine," I said. "And Father?"

"I don't think he slept well. I expect he's having a bit of a lie-in."

A lie-in? How could he be back in bed when the place was alive with the law?

"How did he take it when you told him about the—you know—in the garden?"

Dogger turned and looked me directly in the eye. "I didn't tell him, miss."

He reached out and with a sudden snip of his secateurs, pruned a less-than-perfect bloom. It fell with a plop to the ground, where it lay with its puckered yellow face gazing up at us from the shadows.

We were both of us staring at the beheaded rose, thinking of our next move, when Inspector Hewitt came round the corner of the house.

"Flavia," he said, "I'd like a word with you."

"Inside," he added.

four

"AND THE PERSON OUTSIDE TO WHOM YOU WERE speaking?" Inspector Hewitt asked.

"Dogger," I said.

"First name?"

"Flavia," I said. I couldn't help myself.

We were sitting on one of the Regency sofas in the Rose Room. The Inspector slapped down his Biro and turned at the waist to face me.

"If you are not already aware of it, Miss de Luce—and I suspect you are—this is a murder investigation. I shall brook no frivolity. A man is dead and it is my duty to discover the why, the when, the how, and the who. And when I have done that, it is my further duty to explain it to the Crown. That means King George the Sixth, and King George the Sixth is not a frivolous man. Do I make myself clear?"

"Yes, sir," I said. "His given name is Arthur: Arthur Dogger."

"And he's the gardener here at Buckshaw?"

"He is now, yes."

The Inspector had opened a black notebook and was taking notes in a microscopic hand.

"Was he not always?"

"He's a jack-of-all-trades," I said. "He was our chauffeur until his nerve gave out . . ."

Even though I looked away, I could still feel the intensity of his detective eye.

"The war," I said. "He was a prisoner of war. Father felt that . . . he tried to—"

"I understand," Inspector Hewitt said, his voice gone suddenly soft. "Dogger's happiest in the garden."

"He's happiest in the garden."

"You're a remarkable girl, you know," he said. "In most cases I should wait to talk to you until a parent was present, but with your father indisposed . . ."

Indisposed? Oh, of course! I'd nearly forgotten my little lie.

In spite of my momentary look of puzzlement, the Inspector went on: "You mentioned Dogger's stint as chauffeur. Does your father still keep a motorcar?"

He did, in fact: an old Rolls-Royce Phantom II, which now resided in the coach house. It had actually been Harriet's, and it had not been driven since the day the news of her death had come to Buckshaw. Furthermore, although Father was not a driver himself, he would permit no one else to touch it.

Consequently, the coachwork of this magnificent old

thoroughbred, with its long black bonnet and tall nickel-plated Palladian radiator with intertwined *R*s, had long ago been breached by field mice that had found their way up through the wooden floorboards and nested in its mahogany glove box. Even in its decrepitude, it was sometimes still spoken of as "The Royce," as people of quality often call these vehicles.

"Only a ploughman would call it a Rolls," Feely had said once when I'd momentarily forgotten myself in her presence.

Whenever I wanted to be alone in a place where I could count on being undisturbed, I would clamber up into the dim light of Harriet's dust-covered Roller, where I would sit for hours in the incubator-like heat, surrounded by drooping plush upholstery and cracked, nibbled leather.

At the Inspector's unexpected question, my mind flew back to a dark, stormy day the previous autumn, a day of pelting rain and a mad torrent of wind. Because the risk of falling branches had made it too dangerous to hazard a walk in the woods above Buckshaw, I had slipped away from the house and fought my way through the gale to the coach house to have a good think. Inside, the Phantom stood glinting dully in the shadows as the storm howled and screamed and beat at the windows like a tribe of hungry banshees. My hand was already on the door handle of the car before I realized there was someone inside it. I nearly leaped out of my skin. But then I realized that it was Father. He was just sitting there with tears running down his face, oblivious to the storm.

For several minutes I had stood perfectly still, afraid to move, scarce daring to breathe. But when Father reached slowly for the door handle, I had to drop silently to my hands like a gymnast and roll underneath the car. From the corner of my eye I saw one of his perfectly polished half-Wellingtons step down from the running board, and as he walked slowly away, I heard something like a shuddering sob escape him. For a long while I lay there staring up at the floorboards of Harriet's Rolls-Royce.

"Yes," I said. "There's an old Phantom in the coach house."

"And your father doesn't drive."

"No."

"I see."

The Inspector laid down his Biro and notebook as carefully as if they were made of Venetian glass.

"Flavia," he said (and I couldn't help noticing that I was no longer "Miss de Luce"), "I'm going to ask you a very important question. The way in which you answer it is crucial, do you understand?"

I nodded.

"I know that you were the one who reported this . . . incident. But who was it that first discovered the body?"

My mind went into a tailspin. Would telling the truth incriminate Father? Did the police already know that I had summoned Dogger to the cucumber patch? Obviously not; the Inspector had only just learned Dogger's identity, so it seemed reasonable to assume they had not yet questioned him. But when they did, how much would he tell them? Which of us should he protect: Father or me? Was there some new test by which they would know that the victim was still alive when I discovered him?

"I did," I blurted out. "I found the body." I felt like Cock Robin.

"Just as I thought," Inspector Hewitt said.

And here was one of those awkward silences. It was broken by the arrival of Sergeant Woolmer, who used his massive body to herd Father into the room.

"We found him in the coach house, sir," he said. "Holed up in an old motorcar."

"Who are *you*, sir?" Father demanded. He was furious, and for an instant I caught a glimpse of the man he must once have been. "Who are you, and what are you doing in my house?"

"I'm Inspector Hewitt, sir," the Inspector said, getting to his feet. "Thank you, Sergeant Woolmer."

The sergeant took two steps back until he was clear of the door frame, and then he was gone.

"Well?" Father said. "Is there a problem, Inspector?"

"I'm afraid there is, sir. A body has been found in your garden."

"What do you mean, a body? A dead body?"

Inspector Hewitt nodded. "Yes, sir," he said.

"Whose is it? The body, I mean."

It was at that moment I realized Father had no bruises, no scratches, no cuts, no abrasions...at least none that were visible. I also noticed that he had begun to turn white round the edges, except for his ears, which had begun to go the color of pink plasticine.

And I noticed that the Inspector had spotted it too. He did not answer Father's question at once, but left it hanging in the air.

Father turned and walked in a long arc to the liquor cabinet, touching with the tips of his fingers the horizontal surface of every piece of furniture he passed. He mixed himself a Votrix-and-gin and downed it, all with a swift, fluid efficiency that suggested more practice than I had imagined possible.

"We haven't identified the person as yet, Colonel de Luce. Actually, we were hoping you could offer us assistance."

At this, Father's face went whiter, if possible, than it had been before, and his ears burned redder.

"I'm sorry, Inspector," he said, in a voice that was nearly inaudible. "Please don't ask me to...I'm not very good with death, you see..."

Not very good with death? Father was a military man, and military men lived with death; lived *for* death; lived *on* death. To a professional soldier, oddly enough, death was life. Even I knew that.

I knew instantly, too, that Father had just told a lie, and suddenly, without warning, somewhere inside me, a little thread broke. It felt as if I had just aged a little and something old had snapped.

"I understand, sir," Inspector Hewitt said, "but unless other avenues present themselves..."

Father pulled a handkerchief from his pocket and mopped his forehead, then his neck.

"Bit of a shock, you know," he said, "all this..."

He waved an unsteady hand at his surroundings, and as he did so, Inspector Hewitt took up his notebook, flipped back the cover, and began to write. Father walked slowly to the window where he pretended to be taking in the prospect, one which I could see perfectly in my mind's eye: the artificial lake; the island with its crumbling Folly; the fountains, now dry, that had been shut off since the outbreak of war; the hills beyond.

"Have you been at home all morning?" the Inspector asked with no preliminaries.

"What?" Father spun round.

"Have you been out of the house since last evening?"

It was a long time before Father spoke.

"Yes," he said at last. "I was out this morning. In the coach house."

I had to suppress a smile. Sherlock Holmes once remarked of his brother, Mycroft, that you were as unlikely to find him outside of the Diogenes Club as you were to meet a tramcar coming down a country lane. Like Mycroft, Father had his rails, and he ran on them. Except for church and the occasional short-tempered dash to the train to attend a stamp show, Father seldom, if ever, stuck his nose out-of-doors.

"What time would that have been, Colonel?"

"Four, perhaps. Perhaps a bit earlier."

"You were in the coach house for—" Inspector Hewitt glanced at his wristwatch. "—five and a half hours? From four this morning until just now?"

"Yes, until just now," Father said. He was not accustomed to being questioned, and even though the Inspector did not notice it, I could sense the rising irritation in his voice.

"I see. Do you often go out at that time of day?"

The Inspector's question sounded casual, almost chatty, but I knew that it wasn't.

"No, not really, no, I don't," Father said. "What are you driving at?"

Inspector Hewitt tapped the tip of his nose with his Biro, as if framing his next question for a parliamentary committee. "Did you see anyone else about?"

"No," Father said. "Of course I didn't. Not a living soul."

Inspector Hewitt stopped tapping long enough to make a note. "No one?"

"No."

As if he'd known it all along, the Inspector gave a sad and gentle nod. He seemed disappointed, and sighed as he tucked his notebook into an inner pocket.

"Oh, one last question, Colonel, if you don't mind," he said suddenly, as if he had just thought of it. "What were you doing in the coach house?"

Father's gaze drifted off out the window and his jaw muscles tightened. And then he turned and looked the Inspector straight in the eye.

"I'm not prepared to tell you that, Inspector," he said.

"Very well, then," Inspector Hewitt said. "I think—"

It was at this very moment that Mrs. Mullet pushed open the door with her ample bottom, and waddled into the room with a loaded tray.

"I've brought you some nice seed biscuits," she said. "Seed biscuits and tea and a nice glass of milk for Miss Flavia."

Seed biscuits and milk! I hated Mrs. Mullet's seed biscuits the way Saint Paul hated sin. Perhaps even more so. I wanted to clamber up onto the table, and with a sausage on the end of a fork as my scepter, shout in my best Laurence Olivier voice, "Will no one rid us of this turbulent pastry cook?"

But I didn't. I kept my peace.

With a little curtsy, Mrs. Mullet set down her burden in front of Inspector Hewitt, then suddenly spotted Father, who was still standing at the window.

"Oh! Colonel de Luce. I was hoping you'd turn up. I

wanted to tell you I got rid of that dead bird what we found on yesterday's doorstep."

Mrs. Mullet had somewhere picked up the idea that such reversals of phrase were not only quaint, but poetic.

Before Father could deflect the course of the conversation, Inspector Hewitt had taken up the reins.

"A dead bird on the doorstep? Tell me about it, Mrs. Mullet."

"Well, sir, me and the Colonel and Miss Flavia here was in the kitchen. I'd just took a nice custard pie out of the oven and set it to cool in the window. It was that time of day when my mind usually starts thinkin' about gettin' home to Alf. Alf is my husband, sir, and he doesn't like for me to be out gallivantin' when it's time for his tea. Says it makes him go all over fizzy-like if his digestion's thrown off its time. Once his digestion goes off, it's a sight to behold. All buckets and mops, and that."

"The time, Mrs. Mullet?"

"It was about eleven, or a quarter past. I come for four hours in the morning, from eight to twelve, and three in the afternoon, from one to four, though," she said, with a surprisingly black scowl at Father, who was too pointedly looking out the window to notice it, "I'm usually kept behind my time, what with this and that."

"And the bird?"

"The bird was on the doorstep, dead as Dorothy's donkey. A snipe, it was: one of them jack snipes. God knows I've cooked enough on 'em in my day to be certain of that. Gave me a fright, it did, lyin' there on its back with its feathers twitchin' in the wind, like, as if its skin was still alive when its heart was already dead. That's what I said to

Alf. 'Alf,' I said, 'that bird was lyin' there as if its skin was still alive—' "

"You have a very keen eye, Mrs. Mullet," Inspector Hewitt said, and she puffed up like a pouter pigeon in a glow of iridescent pink. "Was there anything else?"

"Well, yes, sir, there was a stamp stuck on its little bill, almost like it was carryin' it in its mouth, like a stork carries a baby in a nappy, if you know what I mean, but in another way, not like that at all."

"A stamp, Mrs. Mullet? What sort of stamp?"

"A postage stamp, sir—but not like the ones you sees nowadays. Oh no—not like them at all. This here stamp had the Queen's head on it. Not Her Present Majesty, God bless her, but the old Queen...the Queen what was... Queen Victoria. Leastways she should have been on it if that bird's bill hadn't been stickin' through where her face ought to have been."

"You're quite sure about the stamp?"

"Cross my heart and hope to die, sir. Alf had a stamp collection when he was a lad, and he still keeps what's left of it in an old Huntley and Palmers biscuit tin under the bed in the upstairs hall. He doesn't take them out as much as he did when both of us were younger—makes him sad, he says. Still and all, I knows a Penny Black when I sees one, dead bird's bill shoved through it or no."

"Thank you, Mrs. Mullet," said Inspector Hewitt, helping himself to a seed biscuit, "you've been most helpful."

Mrs. Mullet dropped him another curtsy and went to the door.

" 'It's funny,' I said to Alf, I said, 'You don't generally see jack snipes in England till September.' Many's the jack snipe I've turned on the spit and served up roasted on a nice bit of toast. Miss Harriet, God bless her soul, used to fancy nothing better than a nice—"

There was a groan behind me, and I turned just in time to see Father fold in the middle like a camp chair and slither to the floor.

I MUST SAY THAT Inspector Hewitt was very good about it. In a flash he was at Father's side, clapping an ear to his chest, loosening his tie, checking with a long finger for airway obstruction. I could see that he had not slept through his St. John Ambulance classes. A moment later he flung open the window, put first and fourth fingers to his lower lip, and let out a whistle I should have given a guinea to learn.

"Dr. Darby!" he shouted. "Up here, if you please. Quickly! Bring your bag."

As for me, I was still standing with my hand to my mouth when Dr. Darby strode into the room and knelt beside Father. After a quick one-two-three examination, he pulled a small blue vial from his bag.

"Syncope," he said to Inspector Hewitt; to Mrs. Mullet and me, "That means he's fainted. Nothing to worry about."

Phew!

He unstoppered the glass, and in the few moments before he applied it to Father's nostrils, I detected a familiar scent: It was my old friend *Ammon. Carb.*, Ammonium Carbonate, or, as I called it when we were alone together in the laboratory, *Sal Volatile*, or sometimes just plain Sal. I knew that the "ammon" part of its name came from ammonia, which was named on account of its being first discovered not far from the shrine of the god Ammon in ancient Egypt, where it was found in camel's urine. And I knew that later, in London, a man after my own heart had patented a means by which smelling salts could be extracted from Patagonian guano.

Chemistry! Chemistry! How I love it!

As Dr. Darby held the vial to his nostrils, Father gave out a snort like a bull in a field, and his eyelids flew up like roller blinds. But he uttered not a word.

"Ha! Back among the living, I see," the doctor said, as Father, in confusion, tried to prop himself up on his elbow and look round the room. In spite of his jovial tone, Dr. Darby was cradling Father like a newborn baby. "Wait a bit till you get your bearings. Just stay down on the old Axminster a minute."

Inspector Hewitt stood gravely by until it was time to help Father to his feet.

Leaning heavily on Dogger's arm—Dogger had been summoned—Father made his way carefully up the staircase to his room. Daphne and Feely put in a brief appearance: no more, really, than a couple of blanched faces behind the banisters.

Mrs. Mullet, scurrying by on her way to the kitchen, stopped to put a solicitous hand on my arm.

"Was the pie good, luv?" she asked.

I'd forgotten the pie until that moment. I took a leaf from Dr. Darby's notebook.

"Um," I said.

Inspector Hewitt and Dr. Darby had returned to the garden when I climbed slowly up the stairs to my laboratory. I watched from the window with a little sadness and almost a touch of loss as two ambulance attendants came round the side of the house and began to shift the stranger's remains onto a canvas stretcher. In the distance, Dogger was working his way round the Balaclava fountain on the east lawn, busily decapitating more of the Lady Hillingdons.

Everyone was occupied; with any luck, I could do what I needed to do and be back before anyone even realized I was gone.

I slipped downstairs and out the front door, pulled Gladys, my ancient BSA, from where she was leaning against a stone urn, and minutes later was pedaling furiously into Bishop's Lacey.

What was the name Father had mentioned?

Twining. That was it. "Old Cuppa." And I knew precisely where to find him.

five

BISHOP LACEY'S FREE LIBRARY WAS LOCATED IN COW Lane, a narrow, shady, tree-lined track that sloped from the High Street down to the river. The original building was a modest Georgian house of black brick, whose photograph had once appeared in color on the cover of *Country Life*. It had been given to the people of Bishop's Lacey by Lord Margate, a local boy who had made good (as plain old Adrian Chipping) and had gone on to fame and fortune as the sole purveyor of BeefChips, a tinned bully beef of his own invention, to Her Majesty's Government during the Boer War.

The library had existed as an oasis of silence until 1939. Then, while closed for renovations, it had taken fire when a pile of painter's rags spontaneously combusted just as Mr. Chamberlain was delivering to the British people his famous "As long as war has not begun, there is always hope that it may be prevented" speech. Since the entire adult population of Bishop's Lacey had been huddled round one another's wireless sets, no one, including the six members of the volunteer fire department, had spotted the blaze until it was far too late. By the time they arrived with their hand-operated pumping engine, nothing remained of the place but a pile of hot ashes. Fortunately, all of the books had escaped, having been stored for protection in temporary quarters.

But with the outbreak of war then, and the general fatigue since the Armistice, the original building had never been replaced. Its site was now nothing more than a weed-infested patch in Cater Street, just round the corner from the Thirteen Drakes. The property, having been given in perpetuity to the villagers of Bishop's Lacey, could not be sold, and the once-temporary premises that housed its holdings had now become the Free Library's permanent home in Cow Lane.

As I turned off the High Street, I could see the library, a low box of glass-brick and tile, which had been erected in the 1920s to house a motorcar showroom. Several of the original enamel signs bearing the names of extinct motor-cars, such as the Wolseley and the Sheffield-Simplex, were still attached to one of its walls below the roofline, too high up to have attracted the attention of thieves or vandals.

Now, a quarter century after the last Lagonda had rolled out of its doors, the building had fallen, like old crockery in the servant's quarters, into a kind of chipped and broken decrepitude.

Behind and beyond the library, a warren of decaying outbuildings, like tombstones clustered round a country church, subsided into the long grass between the old show-room and the abandoned towpath that followed the river. Several of these dirt-floored hovels housed the overflow of books from the library's long gone and much larger Georgian predecessor. Makeshift structures that had once been a cluster of motor repair shops now found their dim interiors home to row upon row of unwanted books, their subjects labeled above them: History, Geography, Philosophy, Science. Still reeking of antique motor oil, rust, and primitive water closets, these wooden garages were called the stacks—and I could see why! I often came here to read and, next to my chemical laboratory at Buckshaw, it was my favorite place on earth.

I was thinking this as I arrived at the front door and turned the knob.

"Oh, scissors!" I said. It was locked.

As I stepped to one side to peer in the window, I noticed a handmade sign crudely drawn with black crayon and stuck to the glass: CLOSED.

Closed? Today was Saturday. The library hours were ten o'clock to two-thirty, Thursday through Saturday; they were clearly posted in the black-framed notice beside the door. Had something happened to Miss Pickery?

I gave the door a shake, and then a good pounding. I cupped my hands to the glass and peered inside, but except for a beam of sunlight falling through motes of dust before coming to rest upon shelves of novels there was nothing to be seen.

"Miss Pickery!" I called, but there was no answer.

"Oh, scissors!" I said again. I should have to put off my researches until another time. As I stood outside in Cow

Lane, it occurred to me that Heaven must be a place where the library is open twenty-four hours a day, seven days a week.

No ... eight days a week.

I knew that Miss Pickery lived in Shoe Street. If I left my bicycle here and took a shortcut through the outbuildings at the back of the library, I'd pass behind the Thirteen Drakes, and come out beside her cottage.

I picked my way through the long wet grass, watching carefully to avoid tripping on any of the rotting bits of rusty machinery that jutted out here and there like dinosaur bones in the Gobi Desert. Daphne had described to me the effects of tetanus: One scratch from an old auto wheel and I'd be foaming at the mouth, barking like a dog, and falling to the ground in convulsions at the sight of water. I had just managed to work up a gob of spit in my mouth for practice when I heard voices.

"But how could you let him, Mary?" It was a young man's voice, coming from the inn yard.

I flattened myself behind a tree, then peeked round it. The speaker was Ned Cropper, the odd-jobs boy at the Thirteen Drakes.

Ned! The very thought of him had the same effect upon Ophelia as an injection of novocaine. She had taken it into her head that he was the spitting image of Dirk Bogarde, but the only similarity I could see was that both had arms and legs and stacks of brilliantined hair.

Ned was sitting on a beer barrel outside the back door of the inn, and a girl I recognized as Mary Stoker was sitting on another. They did not look at one another. As Ned dug an elaborate maze in the ground with the heel of his boot, Mary kept her hands clasped tightly in her lap as she gazed at nothing in midair.

Although he had spoken in an urgent undertone, I could hear every word perfectly. The plaster wall of the Thirteen Drakes functioned as a perfect sound reflector.

"I told you, Ned Cropper, I couldn't help myself, could I? He come up behind me while I was changing his sheets."

"Whyn't you let out a yell? I know you can wake the dead . . . when you feel like it."

"You don't much know my pa, do you? If he knew what that bloke had done he'd have my hide for gumboots!"

She spat into the dust.

"Mary!" The voice came from somewhere inside the inn, but still it rolled out into the yard like thunder. It was Mary's father, Tully Stoker, the innkeeper, whose abnormally loud voice played a prominent part in some of the village's most scandalous old wives' tales.

"Mary!"

Mary leaped to her feet at the sound of his voice.

"Coming!" she shouted. "I'm coming!"

She hovered: torn, as if making a decision. Suddenly she darted like an asp across to Ned and planted a sharp kiss on his mouth, then, with a flick of her apron—like a conjurer flourishing his cape—she vanished into the dark recess of the open doorway.

Ned sat for a moment longer, then wiped his mouth with the back of his hand before rolling the barrel to join the other empties along the far side of the inn yard.

"Hullo, Ned!" I shouted, and he turned, half embarrassed. I knew he'd be wondering if I'd overheard him with Mary, or witnessed the kiss. I decided to be ambiguous.

"Nice day," I said with a sappy grin.

Ned inquired after my health, and then, in order of careful precedence, about the health of Father, and of Daphne.

"They're fine," I told him.

"And Miss Ophelia?" he asked, getting round to her at last.

"Miss Ophelia? Well, to tell you the truth, Ned, we're all rather worried about her."

Ned recoiled as if a wasp had gone up his nose.

"Oh? What's the trouble? Nothing serious, I hope."

"She's gone all green," I said. "I think it's chlorosis. Dr. Darby thinks so too."

In his *1811 Dictionary of the Vulgar Tongue*, Francis Grose called chlorosis "Love's Fever," and "The Virgin's Disease." I knew that Ned did not have the same ready access to Captain Grose's book as I did. I hugged myself inwardly.

"Ned!"

It was Tully Stoker again. Ned took a step towards the door.

"Tell her I was asking after her," he said.

I gave him a Winston Churchill V with my fingers. It was the least I could do.

SHOE STREET, like Cow Lane, ran from the High Street to the river. Miss Pickery's Tudor cottage, halfway along, looked like something you'd see on the lid of a jigsaw puzzle box. With its thatched roof and whitewashed walls, its diamond-pane leaded-glass windows, and its red-painted Dutch door, it was an artist's delight, its half-timbered walls floating like a quaint old ship upon a sea of old-fashioned flowers such as anemones, hollyhocks, gillyflowers, Canterbury bells, and others whose names I didn't know.

Roger, Miss Pickery's ginger tomcat, rolled on the front doorstep, exposing his belly for a scratching. I obliged.

"Good boy, Roger," I said. "Where's Miss Pickery?"

Roger strolled slowly off in search of something interesting to stare at, and I knocked at the door. There was no answer.

I went round into the back garden. No one home.

Back in the High Street, after stopping for a look at the same old flyblown apothecary jars in the chemist's window, I was just crossing Cow Lane when I happened to glance to my left and saw someone stepping into the library. Arms outstretched, I dipped my wings and banked ninety degrees. But by the time I reached the door, whoever it was had already let themselves in. I turned the doorknob, and this time, it swung open.

The woman was putting her purse in the drawer and settling down behind the desk, and I realized I had never seen her before in my life. Her face was as wrinkled as one of those forgotten apples you sometimes find in the pocket of last year's winter jacket.

"Yes?" she said, peering over her spectacles. They teach them to do that at the Royal Academy of Library Science. The spectacles, I noted, had a slightly grayish tint, as if they had been steeped overnight in vinegar.

"I was expecting to see Miss Pickery," I said.

"Miss Pickery has been called away on a private family matter."

"Oh," I said.

"Yes, very sad. Her sister, Hetty, who lives over in

Nether-Wolsey, had a tragic accident with a sewing machine. It appeared for the first few days that all might be
well, but then she took a sudden turn and it seems now as
if there's a real possibility she might lose the finger. Such a
shame—and she with the twins. Miss Pickery, of course..."

"Of course," I said.

"I'm Miss Mountjoy, and I'd be happy to assist you in
her stead, as it were."

Miss Mountjoy! The retired Miss Mountjoy! I had
heard tales about "Miss Mountjoy and the Reign of
Terror." She had been Librarian-in-Chief of the Bishop's
Lacey Free Library when Noah was a sailor. All sweetness
on the outside, but on the inside, "The Palace of Malice."
Or so I'd been told. (Mrs. Mullet again, who reads detective novels.) The villagers still held novenas to pray she
wouldn't come out of retirement.

"And how may I help you, dearie?"

If there is a thing I truly despise, it is being addressed as
"dearie." When I write my magnum opus, A Treatise Upon
All Poisons, and come to "Cyanide," I am going to put under "Uses" the phrase "Particularly efficacious in the cure
of those who call one 'Dearie.'"

Still, one of my Rules of Life is this: When you want
something, bite your tongue.

I smiled weakly and said, "I'd like to consult your newspaper files."

"Newspaper files!" she gurgled. "My, you do know a lot,
don't you, dearie?"

"Yes," I said, trying to look modest, "I do."

"The newspapers are in chronological order on the
shelves in the Drummond Room: That's the west rear, to

the left, at the top of the stairs," she said with a wave of her hand.

"Thank you," I said, edging towards the staircase.

"Unless, of course, you want something earlier than last year. In that case, they'll be in one of the outbuildings. What year are you looking for, in particular?"

"I don't really know," I said. But, wait a minute—I *did* know! What was it the stranger had said in Father's study?

"Twining—Old Cuppa's been dead these—" What?

I could hear the stranger's oily voice in my head: "Old Cuppa's been dead these . . . thirty years!"

"The year 1920," I said, as cool as a trout. "I'd like to peruse your newspaper archive for 1920."

"Those are likely still in the Pit Shed—that is, if the rats haven't been at them." She said this with a bit of a leer over her spectacles as if, at the mention of rats, I might throw my hands in the air and run off screaming.

"I'll find them," I said. "Is there a key?"

Miss Mountjoy rummaged in the desk drawer and dredged up a ring of iron keys that looked as if they might once have belonged to the jailers of Edmond Dantès in *The Count of Monte Cristo*. I gave them a cheery jingle and walked out the door.

The Pit Shed was the outbuilding farthest from the library's main building. Tottering precipitously on the river's bank, it was a conglomeration of weathered boards and rusty corrugated tin, all overgrown with moss and climbing vines. In the heyday of the motor showroom, it had been the garage where autos had their oil and tires changed, their axles lubricated, and other intimate underside adjustments seen to.

Since then, neglect and erosion had reduced the place to something resembling a hermit's hovel in the woods.

I gave the key a twist and the door sprang open with a rusty groan. I stepped into the gloom, being careful to edge round the sheer sides of the deep mechanic's pit which, though it was boarded over with heavy planks, still occupied much of the room.

The place had a sharp and musky smell with more than a hint of ammonia, as if there were little animals living beneath its floorboards.

Half of the wall closest to Cow Lane was taken up with a folding door, now barred, which had once rolled back to allow motorcars to enter and park astride the pit. The glass of its four windows had been painted over, for some unfathomable reason, with a ghastly red through which the sunlight leaked, giving the room a bloody and unsettling tint.

Round the remaining three walls, rising like the frames of bunk beds, were ranged wooden shelves, each one piled high with yellowed newspapers: *The Hinley Chronicle*, *The West Counties Advertiser*, *The Morning Post-Horn*, all arranged by year and identified with faded handwritten labels.

I had no trouble finding 1920. I lifted down the top pile, choking with the cloud of dust that flew up into my face like an explosion in a flour mill as tiny shards of nibbled newsprint fell to the floor like paper snow.

Tub and loofah tonight, I thought, like it or not.

A small deal table stood near a grimy window: just enough light and enough room to spread the papers open, one at a time.

The Morning Post-Horn caught my eye: a tabloid whose front page, like the *Times of London*, was chock-full of adverts, snippets of news, and agony columns:

> Lost: brown paper parcel tied with butcher's twine.
> Of sentimental value to distressed owner. Generous reward offered.
> Apply "Smith," c/o The White Hart, Wolverston

Or this:

> Dear One: He was watching. Same time Thursday next. Bring soapstone. Bruno.

AND THEN SUDDENLY I REMEMBERED! Father had attended Greyminster...and wasn't Greyminster near Hinley? I tossed *The Morning Post-Horn* back onto its bier, and pulled down the first of four stacks of *The Hinley Chronicle*.

This paper had been published weekly, on Fridays. The first Friday of that year was New Year's Day, so that the year's first issue was dated the following Friday: the eighth of January, 1920.

Page followed page of holiday news—Christmas visitors from the Continent, a deferred meeting of the Ladies' Altar Guild, a "good-sized pig" for sale, Boxing Day revels at The Grange, a lost tire from a brewer's dray.

The Assizes in March were a grim catalogue of thefts, poaching, and assaults.

On and on I went, my hands blackening with ink that had dried twenty years before I was born. The summer brought more visitors from the Continent, market days, laborers wanted, Boy Scout camps, two fêtes, and several proposed road works.

After an hour I was beginning to despair. The people who read these things must have possessed superhuman eyesight, the type was so wretchedly small. Much more of this and I knew I'd have a throbbing headache.

And then I found it:

Popular Schoolmaster Plummets to Death

In a tragic accident on Monday morning, Grenville Twining, M.A. (Oxon.), 72, Latin scholar and respected housemaster at Greyminster School, near Hinley, fell to his death from the clock tower of Greyminster's Anson House. Those familiar with the facts have described the accident as "simply inexplicable."

"He climbed up onto the parapet, gathered his robes about him, and gave us the palm-down Roman Salute. *'Vale!'* he shouted down to the boys in the quad," said Timothy Greene of the sixth form at Greyminster, ". . . and down he came!"

"Vale"? My heart gave a leap. It was the same word the dying man had breathed into my face! "Farewell." It could hardly be coincidence, could it? It was just too bizarre. There *had* to be some connection—but what could it be?

Damn! My mind was racing away like mad and my wits were standing still. The Pit Shed was hardly the place for speculation; I'd think about it later.

I read on:

"The way his gown fluttered, he seemed just like a falling angel," said Toby Lonsdale, a rosy-cheeked lad who was near tears as he was shepherded away by his comrades before giving way and breaking down altogether nearby.

Mr. Twining had recently been questioned by police in the matter of a missing postage stamp: a unique and extremely valuable variation of the Penny Black.

"There is no connection," said Dr. Isaac Kissing, who has been Headmaster at Greyminster since 1915. "No connection whatsoever. Mr. Twining was revered and, if I may say so, loved by all who knew him."

The Hinley Chronicle has learned that police inquiries into both incidents are continuing.

The newspaper's date was the 24th of September, 1920.

I reshelved the paper, stepped outside, and locked the door. Miss Mountjoy was still sitting idle at her desk when I returned the key.

"Did you find what you were looking for, dearie?" she asked.

"Yes," I said, making a great show of dusting off my hands.

"May I inquire further?" she asked coyly. "I might be able to direct you to related materials."

Translation: She was perishing with nosiness.

"No, thank you, Miss Mountjoy," I said.

For some reason I suddenly felt as if my heart had been ripped out and swapped with a counterfeit made of lead.

"Are you all right, dearie?" Miss Mountjoy asked. "You seem a little peaked."

Peaked? I felt as if I were about to puke.

Perhaps it was nervousness, or perhaps it was an unconscious attempt to stave off nausea, but to my horror I found myself blurting out, "Did you ever hear of a Mr. Twining, of Greyminster School?"

She gasped. Her face went red, then gray, as if it had caught fire before my eyes and collapsed in an avalanche of ashes. She pulled a lace handkerchief from her sleeve, knotted it, and jammed it into her mouth, and for a few moments, she sat there, rocking in her chair, gripping the lace between her teeth like an eighteenth-century seaman having his leg amputated below the knee.

At last, she looked up at me with brimming eyes and said in a shaky voice, "Mr. Twining was my mother's brother."

six

WE WERE HAVING TEA. MISS MOUNTJOY HAD EXCA-vated a battered tin kettle from somewhere, and after a dig in her carry-bag, come up with a scruffy packet of Peek Freans.

I sat on a library ladder and helped myself to another biscuit.

"It was tragic," she said. "My uncle had been house-master of Anson House forever—or so it seemed. He took great pride in his house and in his boys. He spared no pains in urging them always to do their best; to prepare them-selves for life.

"He liked to joke that he spoke better Latin than Julius Caesar himself, and his Latin grammar, *Twining's Lingua Latina*—published when he was just twenty-four, by the way—was a standard text in schools round the world. I still keep a copy beside my bed, and even though I can't read much of it, I sometimes like to hold it for the comfort it brings me: *qui, quae, quod*, and all that. The words have such a comforting sound about them.

"Uncle Grenville was forever organizing things: He encouraged his boys to form a debating society, a skating club, a cycling club, a cribbage circle. He was a keen amateur conjurer, although not a very good one—you could always see the ace of diamonds peeping out of his cuffs with the bit of elastic dangling down from it. He was an enthusiastic stamp collector, and taught the boys to learn the history and the geography of the issuing countries, as well as to keep neat, orderly albums. And that was his downfall."

I stopped chewing and sat expectantly. Miss Mountjoy had slipped into a kind of reverie and seemed unlikely to go on without encouragement.

Little by little, I had come under her spell. She had talked to me woman-to-woman, and I had succumbed. I felt sorry for her . . . really I did.

"His downfall?" I asked.

"He made the great mistake of putting his trust in several wretched excuses for boyhood who had wormed themselves into his favor. They pretended great interest in his little stamp collection, and feigned an even greater interest in the collection of Dr. Kissing, the headmaster. In those days, Dr. Kissing was the world's greatest authority on the Penny Black—the world's first postage stamp—in all of its many variations. The Kissing collection was the envy—and I say that advisedly—of all the world. These vile creatures convinced Uncle Grenville to intercede and arrange a private viewing of the Head's stamps.

"While examining the crown jewel of this collection, a

Penny Black of a certain peculiarity—I've forgotten the details—the stamp was destroyed."

"Destroyed?" I asked.

"Burned. One of the boys set it alight. He meant it to be a joke."

Miss Mountjoy took up her tea and drifted like a wisp of smoke to the window, where she stood looking out for what seemed like a very long time. I was beginning to think she'd forgotten about me, but then she spoke again:

"Of course, my uncle was blamed for the disaster..."

She turned and looked me in the eye. "And the rest of the story you've learned this morning in the Pit Shed."

"He killed himself," I said.

"He did *not* kill himself!" she shrieked. The cup and saucer fell from her hand and shattered on the tile floor. "He was murdered!"

"By whom?" I asked, getting a grip on myself, even managing to get the grammar right. Miss Mountjoy was beginning to grate on my nerves again.

"By those monsters!" she spat out. "Those obscene monsters!"

"Monsters?"

"Those boys! They killed him as surely as if they had taken a dagger into their own hands and stuck him in the heart."

"Who were they, these boys... these monsters, I mean? Do you remember their names?"

"Why do you want to know? What right have you coming here to stir up these ghosts?"

"I'm interested in history," I said.

She passed a hand across her eyes as if commanding

herself to come out of a trance, and spoke in the slow voice of a woman drugged.

"It's so long ago," she said. "So very long ago. I really don't care to remember...Uncle Grenville mentioned their names, before he was—"

"Murdered?" I suggested.

"Yes, that's right, before he was murdered. Strange, isn't it? For all these years one of their names has stuck most in my mind because it reminded me of a monkey...a monkey on a chain, you know, with an organ grinder and a little round red hat and a tin cup."

She gave a tight, nervous little laugh.

"Jacko," I said.

Miss Mountjoy sat down heavily as if she'd been pole-axed. She stared at me with goggle eyes as if I'd just materialized from another dimension.

"Who are you, little girl?" she whispered. "Why have you come here? What's your name?"

"Flavia," I said as I paused for a moment at the door. "Flavia Sabina Dolores de Luce." The "Sabina" was real enough; "Dolores" I invented on the spot.

UNTIL I RESCUED HER from rusty oblivion, my trusty old three-speed BSA Keep Fit had languished for years in a toolshed among broken flowerpots and wooden wheelbarrows. Like so many other things at Buckshaw, she had once belonged to Harriet, who had named her l'Hirondelle: "the swallow." I had rechristened her Gladys.

Gladys's tires had been flat, her gears bone dry and crying out for oil, but with her own onboard tire pump and black leather tool bag behind her seat, she was entirely self-sufficient. With Dogger's help, I soon had her in tiptop running order. In the tool kit, I had found a booklet called *Cycling for Women of All Ages*, by Prunella Stack, the leader of the Women's League of Health and Beauty. On its cover was written with black ink, in beautiful, flowing script: *Harriet de Luce, Buckshaw*.

There were times when Harriet was not gone; she was everywhere.

As I raced home, past the leaning moss-covered head-stones in the heaped-up churchyard of St. Tancred's, through the narrow leafy lanes, across the chalky High Road, and into the open country, I let Gladys have her head, swooping down the slopes past the rushing hedges, imagining all the while I was the pilot of one of the Spitfires which, just five years ago, had skimmed these very hedgerows like swallows as they came in to land at Leathcote.

I had learned from the booklet that if I bicycled with a poker back like Miss Gulch in *The Wizard of Oz* at the cin-ema, chose varied terrain, and breathed deeply, I would glow with health like the Eddystone Light, and never suf-fer from pimples: a useful bit of information which I wasted no time in passing along to Ophelia.

Was there ever a companion booklet, *Cycling for Men of All Ages?* I wondered. And if so, had it been written by the leader of the Men's League of Health and Handsomeness?

I pretended I was the boy Father must always have wanted: a son he could take to Scotland for salmon fishing and grouse shooting on the moors; a son he could send out to Canada to take up ice hockey. Not that Father did any of these things, but if he'd had a son, I liked to think he might have done.

My middle name should have been Laurence, like his, and when we were alone together he'd have called me

Larry. How keenly disappointed he must have been when all of us had come out girls.

Had I been too cruel to that horror, Miss Mountjoy? Too vindictive? Wasn't she, after all, just a harmless and lonely old spinster? Would a Larry de Luce have been more understanding?

"Hell, no!" I shouted into the wind, and I chanted as we flew along:

> Oomba-chukka! Oomba-chukka
> Oomba-chukka-Boom!

But I felt no more like one of Lord Baden-Powell's blasted Boy Scouts than I did Prince Knick-Knack of Ali-Kazaam.

I was me. I was Flavia. And I loved myself, even if no one else did.

"All hail Flavia! Flavia forever!" I shouted, as Gladys and I sped through the Mulford Gates, at top speed, into the avenue of chestnuts that lined the drive at Buckshaw.

These magnificent gates, with their griffins rampant and filigreed black wrought iron, had once graced the neighboring estate of Batchley, the ancestral home of "The Dirty Mulfords." The gates were acquired for Buckshaw in the 1760s by one Brandwyn de Luce, who—after one of the Mulfords absconded with his wife—dismantled them and took them home.

The exchange of a wife for a pair of gates ("The finest this side Paradise," Brandwyn had written in his diary) seemed to have settled the matter, since the Mulfords and the de Luces remained best of friends and neighbors until the last Mulford, Tobias, sold off the estate at the time of the American Civil War and went abroad to assist his Confederate cousins.

"A WORD, FLAVIA," Inspector Hewitt said, stepping out of the front door.

Had he been waiting for me?

"Of course," I said graciously.

"Where have you been just now?"

"Am I under arrest, Inspector?" It was a joke—I hoped he'd catch on.

"I was merely curious."

He pulled a pipe from his jacket pocket, filled it, and struck a match. I watched as it burned steadily down towards his square fingertips.

"I went to the library," I said.

He lit his pipe, then pointed its stem at Gladys.

"I don't see any books."

"It was closed."

"Ah," he said.

There was a maddening calmness about the man. Even in the midst of murder he was as placid as if he were strolling in the park.

"I've spoken to Dogger," he said, and I noticed that he kept his eyes on me to gauge my reaction.

"Oh, yes?" I said, but my mind was sounding the kind of "Oogah!" warning they have on a submarine preparing to dive.

Careful! I thought. Watch your step. How much did Dogger tell him? About the strange man in the study? About the quarrel with Father? The threats?

That was the trouble with someone like Dogger: He was likely to break down for no reason whatsoever. Had he blabbed to the Inspector about the stranger in the study? Damn the man! Damn him!

"He says that you awakened him at about four A.M. and told him that there was a dead body in the garden. Is that correct?"

I held back a sigh of relief, almost choking in the process. Thank you, Dogger! May the Lord bless you and keep you and make his face to shine upon you, always! Good old faithful Dogger. I knew I could count on you.

"Yes," I said. "That's correct."

"What happened then?"

"We went downstairs and out the kitchen door into the garden. I showed him the body. He knelt down beside it and felt for a pulse."

"And how did he do that?"

"He put his hand on the neck—under the ear."

"Hmm," the Inspector said. "And was there? Any pulse, I mean?"

"No."

"How did you know that? Did he tell you?"

"No," I said.

"Hmm," he said again. "Did you kneel down beside it too?"

"I suppose I could have. I don't think so . . . I don't remember."

The Inspector made a note. Even without seeing it, I knew what it said: Query: Did D. (1) tell F. no pulse? (2) See F. kneel BB (Beside Body)?

"That's quite understandable," he said. "It must have been rather a shock."

I brought to mind the image of the stranger lying there in the first light of dawn: the slight growth of whiskers on his chin, strands of his red hair shifting gently on the faint stirrings of the morning breeze, the pallor, the extended leg, the quivering fingers, that last, sucking breath. And that word, blown into my face . . . "*Vale*."

The thrill of it all!

"Yes," I said, "it was devastating."

I HAD EVIDENTLY PASSED the test. Inspector Hewitt had gone into the kitchen where Sergeants Woolmer and Graves were busily setting up operations under a barrage of gossip and lettuce sandwiches from Mrs. Mullet.

As Ophelia and Daphne came down to lunch, I noticed with disappointment Ophelia's unusual clarity of complexion. Had my concoction backfired? Had I, through some freak accident of chemistry, produced a miracle facial cream?

Mrs. Mullet bustled in, grumbling as she set our soup and sandwiches on the table.

"It's not right," she said. "Me already behind my time, what with all this pother, and Alf expectin' me home, and all. The nerve of them, axin' me to dig that dead snipe out of the refuse bin," she said with a shudder, ". . . so's they could prop it up and take its likeness. It's not right. I showed them the bin and told them if they wanted the carcass so bad they could jolly well dig it out themselves; I had lunch to make. Eat your sandwiches, dear. There's nothing like cold meats in June—they're as good as a picnic."

"Dead snipe?" Daphne asked, curling her lip.

"The one as Miss Flavia and the Colonel found on my

yesterday's back doorstep. It still gives me the goose-pimples, the way that thing was layin' there with its eye all frosted and its bill stickin' straight up in the air with a bit of paper stuck on it."

"Ned!" Ophelia said, slapping the table. "You were right, Daffy. It's a love token!"

Daphne had been reading *The Golden Bough* at Easter, and told Ophelia that primitive courting customs from the South Seas sometimes survived in our own enlightened times. It was simply a matter of being patient, she said.

I looked from one to the other, blankly. There were whole aeons when I didn't understand my sisters at all.

"A dead bird, stiff as a board, with its bill sticking straight up in the air? What kind of token is that?" I asked.

Daphne hid behind her book and Ophelia flushed a little. I slipped away from the table and left them tittering into their soup.

"MRS. MULLET," I said, "didn't you tell Inspector Hewitt we never see jack snipe in England until September?"

"Snipes, snipes, snipes! That's all I hear about nowadays is snipes. Step to one side, if you please—you're standin' where it wants scrubbin'."

"Why is that? Why do we never see snipe before September?"

Mrs. Mullet straightened up, dropped her brush in the bucket, and dried her soapy hands on her apron.

"Because they're somewhere else," she said triumphantly.

"Where?"

"Oh, you know ... they're like all them birds what emigrate. They're up north somewhere. For all I know, they could be takin' tea with Father Christmas."

"By up north, how far do you mean? Scotland?"

"Scotland!" she said contemptuously. "Oh dear, no. Even my Alf's second sister, Margaret, gets as far as Scotland on her holidays, and she's no snipe.

"Although her husband is," she added.

There was a roaring in my ears, and something went "click."

"What about Norway?" I asked. "Could jack snipe summer in Norway?"

"I suppose they could, dear. You'd have to look it up."

Yes! Hadn't Inspector Hewitt told Dr. Darby that they had reason to believe the man in the garden had come from Norway? How could they possibly know that? Would the Inspector tell me if I asked?

Probably not. In that case I should have to puzzle it out for myself.

"Run along now," Mrs. Mullet said. "I can't go home till I finish this floor, and it's already one o'clock. Poor Alf's digestion is most likely in a shockin' state by now."

I stepped out the back door. The police and the coroner had gone, and taken the body with them, and the garden now seemed strangely empty. Dogger was nowhere in sight, and I sat down on a low section of the wall to have a bit of a think.

Had Ned left the dead snipe on the doorstep as a token of his love for Ophelia? She certainly seemed convinced of it. If it *had* been Ned, where did he get the thing?

Two and a half seconds later, I grabbed Gladys, threw my leg over her saddle, and, for the second time that day, was flying like the wind into the village.

Speed was of the essence. No one in Bishop's Lacey would yet know of the stranger's death. The police would not have told a soul—and nor had I.

Not until Mrs. Mullet finished her scrubbing and walked to the village would the gossip begin. But once she reached home, news of the murder at Buckshaw would spread like the Black Death. I had until then to find out what I needed to know.

seven

AS I SKIDDED TO A STOP AND LEANED GLADYS AGAINST
a pile of weathered timbers, Ned was still at work in the inn
yard. He had finished with the beer barrels and was now
showily unloading cheeses the size of millstones from the
back of a parked lorry.

"Hoy, Flavia," he said as he saw me, jumping at the opportunity to stop work. "Fancy some cheese?"

Before I could answer he had pulled a nasty-looking
jackknife from his pocket and sliced off a slab of Stilton
with frightening ease. He cut one for himself and tucked
into it on the spot with what Daphne would call "noisy
gusto." Daphne is going to be a novelist, and copies out
into an old account book phrases that strike her in her
day-to-day reading. I remembered "noisy gusto" from the
last time I snooped through its pages.

"Been home?" Ned asked, looking at me with a shy
sideways glance. I saw what was coming. I nodded.

"And how's Miss Ophelia? Has the doctor been round?"

"Yes," I said. "I believe he saw her this morning."

Ned swallowed my deception whole.

"Still green then, is she?"

"More of a yellow than before," I said. "A shade more sulphuric than cupric."

I had learned that a lie wrapped in detail, like a horse pill in an apple, went down with greater ease. But this time, as soon as I said it, I knew that I had overstepped.

"Haw, Flavia!" Ned said. "You're making sport of me."

I let him have my best slow-dawning country-bumpkin smile.

"You've caught me out, Ned," I said. "Guilty, as charged."

He gave me back a weird mirror image of my grin. For a fraction of a second I thought he was mocking me, and I felt my temper begin to rise. But then I realized he was honestly pleased to have puzzled me out. This was my opportunity.

"Ned," I said, "if I asked you a terrifically personal question, would you answer it?"

I waited as this sunk in. Communicating with Ned was like exchanging cabled messages with a slow reader in Mongolia.

"Of course I'd answer it," he said, and the roguish twinkle in his eye tipped me off to what was coming next. "'Course, I might not say the truth."

When we'd both had a good laugh, I got down to business. I'd start with the heavy artillery.

"You're frightfully keen on Ophelia, aren't you?"

Ned sucked his teeth and ran a finger round the inside of his collar. "She's a right nice girl, I'll give her that."

"But wouldn't you like to settle down with her one day in a thatched cottage and raise a litter of brats?"

By now, Ned's neck was a rising column of red, like a thick alcohol thermometer. In seconds he looked like one of those birds that inflate its gullet for mating purposes. I decided to help him out.

"Just suppose she wanted to see you but her father wouldn't allow it. Suppose one of her younger sisters could help."

Already his ruddy crop was subsiding. I thought he was going to cry.

"Do you mean it, Flavia?"

"Honest Injun," I said.

Ned stuck out his calloused fingers and gave my hand a surprisingly gentle shake. It was like shaking hands with a pineapple.

"Fingers of Friendship," he said, whatever that meant.

Fingers of Friendship? Had I just been given the secret handshake of some rustic brotherhood that met in moonlit churchyards and hidden copses? Was I now inducted, and would I be expected to take part in unspeakably bloody midnight rituals in the hedgerows? It seemed like an interesting possibility.

Ned was grinning at me like the skull on a Jolly Roger. I took the upper hand.

"Listen," I told him. "Lesson Number One: Don't leave dead birds on the loved one's doorstep. It's something that only a courting cat would do."

Ned looked blank.

"I've left flowers once or twice, hopin' she'd notice," he said. This was news to me; Ophelia must have whisked the bouquets off to her boudoir for mooning purposes before anyone else in the household spotted them.

"But dead birds? Never. You know me, Flavia. I wouldn't do a thing like that."

When I stopped to think about it for a moment, I knew that he was right; I did and he wouldn't. My next question, though, turned out to be sheer luck.

"Does Mary Stoker know you're sweet on Ophelia?" It was a phrase I had picked up at the cinema from some American film—*Meet Me in St. Louis* or *Little Women*— and this was the first opportunity I'd ever had to make use of it. Like Daphne, I remembered words, but without an account book to jot them down.

"What's Mary have to do with it? She's Tully's daughter, and there's an end of it."

"Come off it, Ned," I said. "I saw that kiss this morning as I was . . . passing by."

"She needed a little comfort. 'Twas no more than that."

"Because of whoever it was that crept up behind her?"

Ned leapt to his feet. "Damn you!" he said. "She don't want that getting out."

"As she was changing the sheets?"

"You're a devil, Flavia de Luce!" Ned roared. "Get away from me! Go home!"

"Tell her, Ned," said a quiet voice, and I turned to see Mary at the door.

She stood with one hand flat on the doorpost, the other clutching her blouse at the neck like Tess of the d'Urbervilles. Close up, I could see that she had raw red hands and a decided squint.

"Tell her," she repeated. "It can't make any difference to you now, can it?"

I detected instantly that she didn't like me. It's a fact of life that a girl can tell in a flash if another girl likes her. Feely says that there is a broken telephone connection between men and women, and we can never know which of us rang off. With a boy you never know whether he's smitten or gagging, but with a girl you can tell in the first three seconds. Between girls there is a silent and unending flow of invisible signals, like the high-frequency wireless messages between the shore and the ships at sea, and this secret flow of dots and dashes was signaling that Mary detested me.

"Go on, tell her!" Mary shouted.

Ned swallowed hard and opened his mouth, but nothing came out.

"You're Flavia de Luce, aren't you?" she said. "One of that lot from up at Buckshaw." She flung it at me like a pie in the face.

I nodded dumbly, as if I were some inbred ingrate from the squire's estate who needed coddling. Better to play along, I thought.

"Come with me," Mary said, beckoning. "Be quick about it—and keep quiet."

I followed her into a dark stone larder, and then into an enclosed wooden staircase that spiraled precipitously up to the floor above. At the top, we stepped out into what must once have been a linen press: a tall square cupboard now filled with shelves of cleaning chemicals, soaps, and waxes. In the corner, mops and brooms leaned in disarray amid an overwhelming smell of carbolic disinfectant.

"Shhh!" she said, giving my arm a vicious squeeze. Heavy footsteps were approaching, coming up the same staircase we had just ascended. We pressed back into a corner, taking care not to knock over the mops.

"That'll be the bloody day, sir, when a Cotswold horse takes the bloody purse! If I was you I'd take a flutter on Seastar, and be damned to any tips you get from some bloody skite in London what don't know his ark from his halo!"

It was Tully, exchanging confidential turf tips with someone at a volume loud enough to be heard at Epsom Downs. Another voice muttered something that ended in "Haw-haw!" as the sound of their footsteps faded away in the warren of paneled passages.

"No, this way," Mary hissed, tugging at my arm. We slipped round the corner and into a narrow corridor. She pulled a set of keys from her pocket and quietly unlocked the last door on the left. We stepped inside.

We were in a room which had not likely changed since Queen Elizabeth visited Bishop's Lacey in 1592 on one of her summer progresses. My first impressions were of a timbered ceiling, plastered panels, a tiny window with leaded panes standing ajar for air, and broad floorboards that rose and fell like the ocean swell.

Against one wall was a chipped wooden table with an *ABC Railway Guide* (October 1946) shoved under one leg to keep it from teetering. On the tabletop were an unmatched Staffordshire pitcher and ewer in pink and cream, a comb, a brush, and a small black leather case. In a corner near the open window stood a single piece of luggage: a cheap-looking steamer trunk of vulcanized fiber, plastered over with colored stickers. Beside it was a straight chair with a missing spindle. Across the room stood a wooden wardrobe of jumble-sale quality. And the bed.

"This is it," Mary said. As she locked us in, I turned to

look at her closely for the first time. In the gray dishwater light from the sooty windowpanes, she looked older, harder, and more brittle than the raw-handed girl I had just seen in the bright sunlight of the inn yard.

"I expect you've never been in a room this small, have you?" she said scornfully. "You lot at Buckshaw fancy the odd visit to Bedlam, don't you? See the loonies—see how we live in our cages. Throw us a biscuit."

"I don't know what you're talking about," I said.

Mary turned her face towards me so that I was receiving the full intensity of her glare. "That sister of yours—that Ophelia—sent you with a message for Ned, and don't tell me she didn't. She fancies I'm some kind of slattern, and I'm not."

And in that instant I decided that I liked Mary, even if she didn't like me. Anyone who knew the word *slattern* was worth cultivating as a friend.

"Listen," I said, "there's no message. What I said to Ned was strictly for cover. You have to help me, Mary. I know you will. There's been a murder at Buckshaw..."

There! I'd said it!

"...and nobody knows it yet but you and me—except the murderer, of course."

She looked at me for no more than three seconds and then she asked, "Who is it that's dead, then?"

"I don't know. That's why I'm here. But it makes sense to me that if someone turns up dead in the cucumbers, and even the police don't know who he is, the most likely place he'd be staying in the neighborhood—*if* he was staying in the neighborhood—is right here at the Thirteen Drakes. Can you bring me the register?"

"Don't need to bring it to you," Mary said. "There's only one guest right now, and that's Mr. Sanders."

The more I talked to Mary the more I liked her.

"And this here's his room," she added helpfully.

"Where is he from?" I asked.

Her face clouded. "I don't know, rightly."

"Has he ever stopped here before?"

"Not so far as I know."

"Then I need to have a look at the register. Please, Mary! Please! It's important! The police will soon be here, and then it will be too late."

"I'll try . . ." she said, and, unlocking the door, slipped from the room.

As soon as she was gone, I pulled open the door of the wardrobe. Except for a pair of wooden coat hangers it was empty, and I turned my attention to the steamer trunk, which was covered over with stickers like barnacles clinging to the hull of a ship. These colorful crustaceans, however, had names: Paris, Rome, Stockholm, Amsterdam, Copenhagen, Stavanger—and more.

I tried the hasp, and to my surprise, it popped open. It was unlocked! The two halves, hinged in the middle, swung easily apart, and I found myself face-to-face with Mr. Sanders's wardrobe: a blue serge suit, two shirts, a pair of brown Oxfords (with blue serge? Even I knew better than that!), and a floppy, theatrical hat that reminded me of photographs I'd seen of G. K. Chesterton in the *Radio Times*.

I pulled out the drawers of the trunk, taking care not to disturb their contents: a pair of hairbrushes (imitation tortoiseshell), a razor (Valet AutoStrop), a tube of shaving cream (Morning Pride Brushless), a toothbrush, toothpaste (thymol: "specially recommended to arrest the germs of dental decay"), nail clippers, a straight comb (xylonite), and a pair of square cuff links (Whitby jet, with a pair of initials inset in silver: *HB*).

HB? Wasn't this Mr. Sanders's room? What could *HB* stand for?

The door flew open and a voice hissed, "What are you doing?"

I nearly flew out of my skin. It was Mary.

"I couldn't get the register. Dad was— Flavia! You can't go through a guest's luggage like that! You'll get both of us in a pickle. Stop it."

"Right-ho," I said as I finished rifling the pockets of the suit. They were empty anyway. "When was the last time you saw Mr. Sanders?"

"Yesterday. Here. At noon."

"Here? In this room?"

She gulped, and nodded, looking away. "I was changing his sheets when he come up behind me and grabbed me. Put a hand over my mouth so's I shouldn't scream. Good job Dad called from the yard just then. Rattled him a bit, it did. Don't think I didn't get in a good kick or two. Him and his filthy paws! I'd have scratched his eyes out if I'd had half the chance."

She looked at me as if she'd said too much; as if a great social gulf had suddenly opened up between us.

"I'd have scratched his eyes out and sucked the holes," I said.

Her eyes widened in horror.

"John Marston," I told her. "*The Dutch Courtesan*, 1604."

There was a pause of approximately two hundred years. Then Mary began to giggle.

"Ooh, you are a one!" she said.

The gap had been bridged.

"Act Two," I added.

Seconds later the two of us were doubled over, hands covering our mouths, hopping about the room, snorting in unison like a pair of trained seals.

"Feely once read it to us under the blankets with a torch," I said, and for some reason, this struck both of us as being even more hilarious, and off we went again until we were nearly paralyzed from laughter.

Mary threw her arms round me and gave me a crushing hug. "You're a corker, Flavia," she said. "Really you are. Come here—take a gander at this."

She went to the table, picked up the black leather case, unfastened the strap, and lifted the lid. Nestled inside were two rows of six little glass vials, twelve in all. Eleven were filled with a liquid of a yellowish tinge; the twelfth was a quarter full. Between the rows of vials was a half-round indentation, as if some tubular object were missing.

"What do you make of it?" she whispered, as Tully's voice thundered vaguely in the distance. "Poisons, you think? A regular Dr. Crippen, our Mr. Sanders?"

I uncorked the partially filled bottle and held it to my nose. It smelled as if someone had dropped vinegar on the back of a sticking plaster: an acrid protein smell, like an alcoholic's hair burning in the next room.

"Insulin," I said. "He's a diabetic."

Mary gave me a blank look, and I suddenly knew how Archimedes felt when he said "Eureka!" in his bathtub. I grabbed Mary's arm.

"Does Mr. Sanders have red hair?" I demanded.

"Red as rhubarb. How did you know?"

She stared at me as if I were Madame Zolanda at the church fête, with a turban, a shawl, and a crystal ball.

"A wizard guess," I said.

eight

"CRIKEY!" MARY SAID, FISHING UNDER THE TABLE and pulling out a round metal wastepaper basket. "I almost forgot this. Dad'd have my hide for a hammock if he found out I didn't empty this thing. He's always on about germs, Dad is, even though you wouldn't think it to look at him. Good job I remembered before—oh, gawd! Just look at this mess, will you."

She pulled a wry face and held out the basket at arm's length. I peeked—tentatively—inside. You never know what you're getting into when you stick your nose in other people's rubbish.

The bottom of the wastebasket was covered with chunks and flakes of pastry: no container, just bits flung in, as if whoever had been eating it had had enough. It appeared to be the remains of a pie. As I reached in and extracted a piece of it, Mary made a gacking noise and turned her head away.

"Look at this," I said. "It's a piece of the crust, see? It's golden brown here, from the oven, with little crinkles of pastry, like decorations on one side. These other bits are from the bottom crust: They're whiter and thinner. Not very flaky, is it?

"Still," I added, "I'm famished. When you haven't eaten all day, anything looks good."

I raised the pie and opened my mouth, pretending I was about to gobble it down.

"Flavia!"

I paused with the crumbling cargo halfway to my gaping mouth.

"Huh?"

"Oh, you!" Mary said. "Give it over. I'll chuck it."

Something told me this was a Bad Idea. Something else told me that the gutted pie was evidence that should be left untouched for Inspector Hewitt and the two sergeants to discover. I actually considered this for a moment.

"Got any paper?" I asked.

Mary shook her head. I opened the wardrobe and, standing on tiptoe, felt along the top shelf with my hand. As I suspected, a sheet of newspaper had been put in place to serve as a makeshift shelf liner. God bless you, Tully Stoker!

Taking care not to break them, I tipped the larger remnants of the pie slowly out onto the *Daily Mail* and folded it up into a small neat package, which I shoved into my pocket. Mary stood watching me nervously, not saying a word.

"Lab test," I said, darkly. To tell the truth, I didn't have any idea yet what I was going to do with this revolting stuff. I'd think of something later, but right now I wanted to show Mary who was in charge.

As I set the wastepaper basket down on the floor, I was startled at a sudden slight movement in its depths, and I don't mind admitting that my stomach turned a primal handspring. What was in there? Worms? A rat? Impossible: I couldn't have missed something that big.

I peered cautiously into the container and sure enough, something *was* moving at the bottom of the basket. A feather! And it was moving gently, almost imperceptibly, back and forth with the room's air currents; stirring like a dead leaf on a tree—in the same way the dead stranger's red hair had stirred in the morning breeze.

Could it have been only this morning that he died? It seemed an eternity since the unpleasantness in the garden. Unpleasantness? You liar, Flavia!

Mary looked on aghast as I reached into the basket and extracted the feather and the bit of pastry impaled upon its quill end.

"See this?" I said, holding it out towards her. She shrank back in the way Dracula is supposed to do when you threaten him with a cross. "If the feather had fallen on the pastry in the wastepaper basket, it wouldn't be attached.

"Four-and-twenty blackbirds, baked in a pie," I recited. "See?"

"You think?" Mary asked, her eyes like saucers.

"Bang on, Sherlock," I said. "This pie's filling was bird, and I think I can guess the species."

I held it out to her again. "What a pretty dish to set before the King," I said, and this time she grinned at me.

I'd do the same with Inspector Hewitt, I thought, as I

pocketed the thing. Yes! I'd solve this case and present it to him wrapped up in gaily colored ribbons.

"No need for you to come out here again," he'd said to me in the garden, that saucepot. What bloody cheek!

Well, I'd show him a trick or two!

Something told me that Norway was the key. Ned hadn't been in Norway, and besides, he had sworn he didn't leave the snipe on our doorstep and I believed him, so he was out of the question—at least for now.

The stranger had come from Norway, and I had heard that straight from the horse's mouth, so to speak! Ergo (that means "therefore") the stranger could have brought the snipe with him.

In a pie.

Yes! That made sense! What better way to get a dead bird past an inquisitive H. M. Customs inspector?

Just one more step and we're home free: If the Inspector can't be asked how he knew about Norway, and nor can the stranger (obviously, since he is dead), who, then, does that leave?

And I suddenly saw it all, saw it spread out before me at my feet the way one must see from the top of a mountain. The way Harriet must have—

The way an eagle sees his prey.

I hugged myself with pleasure. If the stranger had come from Norway, dropped a dead bird on our doorstep before breakfast, and then appeared in Father's study after midnight, he must have been staying somewhere not far away. Somewhere within walking distance of Buckshaw. Somewhere such as right here in this very room at the Thirteen Drakes.

Now I knew it for certain: The corpse in the cucumbers *was* Mr. Sanders. There could be no doubt about it.

"Mary!"

It was Tully again, bellowing like a bull calf, and this time, it seemed, he was right outside the door.

"Coming, Dad!" she shouted, grabbing the wastebasket.

"Get out of here," she whispered. "Wait five minutes and then go down the back stairs—same way as we came up."

She was gone, and a moment later I heard her explaining to Tully in the hallway that she just wanted to give the wastebasket an extra clean-out, since someone left a mess in it.

"We wouldn't want somebody to die of germs they picked up at the Thirteen Drakes, would we, Dad?"

She was learning.

While I waited, I took a second look at the steamer trunk. I ran my fingers over the colored labels, trying to imagine where it had been in its travels, and what Mr. Sanders had been doing in each city: Paris, Rome, Stockholm, Amsterdam, Copenhagen, Stavanger. Paris was red, white, and blue, and so was Stavanger.

Was Stavanger in France? I wondered. It didn't sound French—unless, of course, it was pronounced "stah-vonj-yay" as in Laurence Olivier. I touched the label and it wrinkled beneath my finger, piled up like water ahead of the prow of a ship.

I repeated the test on the other stickers. Each one was pasted down tightly: as smooth as the label on a bottle of cyanide.

Back to Stavanger. It felt a little lumpier than the others, as if there were something underneath it.

The blood was humming in my veins like water in a millrace.

Again I pried the trunk open and took the safety razor from the drawer. As I extracted the blade, I thought how lucky it was that women—other than the occasional person like Miss Pickery at the library—don't need to shave. It was tough enough being a woman without having to lug all that tackle everywhere you went.

Holding the blade carefully between my thumb and forefinger (after the glassware incident I had been loudly lectured about sharp objects) I made a slit along the bottom of the label, taking great care to cut along the precise edge of a blue and red decorative line that ran nearly the full width of the paper.

As I lifted the incision slightly with the dull edge of the blade, something slid out and, with a whisper of paper, fell to the floor. It was a glassine envelope, similar to the ones I had noticed in Sergeant Graves's kit. Through its semi-transparency, I could see that there was something inside, something square and opaque. I opened the envelope and gave it a tap with my finger. Something fell out into the palm of my hand: two somethings, in fact.

Two postage stamps. Two bright orange postage stamps, each in its own tiny translucent jacket. Aside from their color, they were identical to the Penny Black that had been impaled upon the jack snipe's bill. Queen Victoria's face again. What a disappointment!

I didn't doubt that Father would have gone into positive raptures about the pristine perfection of the things, the enchantment of engraving, the pleasures of perforations, and the glories of glue, but to me they were no more

than the sort of thing you'd slap on a letter to dreadful
Aunt Felicity in Hampshire, thanking her for her thoughtful Christmas gift of a Neddy the Squirrel Annual.

Still, why bother putting them back? If Mr. Sanders
and the body in our garden were, as I knew they were,
one and the same, he was well past the need for postage
stamps.

No, I thought, I'll keep the things. They might come in
handy someday when I need to barter my way out of a
scrape with Father, who is incapable of thinking stamps
and discipline at the same time.

I shoved the envelope into my pocket, licked my forefinger, and moistened the inside edge of the slit in the label on the trunk. Then, with my thumb, I ironed it shut.
No one, not even Inspector Fabian of the Yard, could ever
guess it had been sliced open.

My time was up. I took one last look round the room,
slipped out into the dim hallway and, as Mary had in-
structed me, moved carefully towards the back staircase.

"You're about as useless as tights on a bull, Mary! How
the bloody hell can I stay on top of things when you're letting everything go to hell in a handbasket?"

Tully was coming up the back way; one more turning of
the stairs and we'd be face-to-face!

I flew on tiptoe in the other direction, through the
twisting, turning labyrinth of corridors: up two steps here,
down three there. A moment later, panting, I found myself
at the top of the L-shaped staircase that led down to the
front entrance. As far as I could see, there was no one
below.

I tiptoed down, one slow step at a time.

A long hallway, hung profusely with dark, water-stained sporting prints, served as a lobby, in which centuries of sacrificed kippers had left the smell of their smoky souls clinging to the wallpaper. Only the patch of sunshine visible through the open front door relieved the gloom.

To my left was a small desk with a telephone, a telephone directory, a small glass vase of red and mauve pansies, and a ledger. The register!

Obviously, the Thirteen Drakes was not a busy beehive: Its open pages bore the names of travelers who had signed in for the past week and more. I didn't even have to touch the thing.

There it was:

2nd June 10:25 A.M. F. X. Sanders London

NO OTHER GUESTS HAD REGISTERED the day before, and none since.

But London? Inspector Hewitt had said that the dead man had come from Norway and I knew that, like King George, Inspector Hewitt was not a frivolous man.

Well, he hadn't said exactly that: He'd said that the deceased had *recently* come from Norway, which was a horse of an entirely different hue.

Before I could think this through, there was a banging from above. It was Tully again; the ubiquitous Tully. I could tell by his tone that Mary was still getting the worst of it.

"Don't look at me like that, my girl, or I'll give you reason to regret it."

And now he was clomping heavily down the main staircase! In another few seconds he'd see me. Just as I was about to make a bolt for the front door, a battered black taxicab stopped directly in front of it, the roof piled high with luggage and the wooden legs of a photographer's tripod protruding from one of its windows.

Tully was distracted for a moment.

"Here's Mr. Pemberton," he said in a stage whisper. "He's early. Now then, girl, I told you this would happen, didn't I? Get a move on and dump those dirty sheets while I find Ned."

I ran for it! Straight back past the sporting prints, into the back vestibule, and out into the inn yard.

"Ned! Come and get Mr. Pemberton's luggage."

Tully was right behind me, following me towards the back of the inn. Although momentarily dazzled by the bright sunlight, I could see that Ned was nowhere about. He must have finished unloading the lorry and gone on to other duties.

Without even thinking about it, I sprang up and into the back of the lorry, lay down, and flattened myself behind a pile of cheeses.

Peering out from between the stacked rounds I saw Tully stride out into the inn yard, look round, and mop his red face with his apron. He was dressed for pumping pints. The bar must be open, I thought.

"Ned!" he bellowed.

I knew that, standing in the bright sunlight as he was, he could not see me in the lorry's dim interior. All I had to do was lie low and keep quiet.

I was thinking that when a couple more voices were added to Tully's bellowing.

"Wot cheer, Tully," one said. "Thanks for the pint."

"S'long, mate," said the other. "See you next Saturday."

"Tell George he can hang his shirt on Seastar. Just don't tell 'im which shirt!"

It was one of those stupid things men say simply to get in the last word. There was nothing remotely funny about it. Still, they all laughed, and were probably slapping their legs, at the witticism, and a moment later I felt the lorry dip on its springs as the two climbed heavily into the cab. Then the engine grated into life and we began to move— backwards.

Tully was folding and unfolding his fingers, beckoning the lorry as it reversed, indicating with his hands the clearance between its tailgate and the inn yard wall. I couldn't jump out now without leaping straight into his arms. I'd have to wait until we drove out through the archway and turned onto the open road.

My last glimpse of the yard was of Tully walking back towards the door and Gladys leaning where I had left her against a pile of scrap lumber.

As the lorry veered sharply and then accelerated, I was beaned by a wheel of toppling Wensleydale and followed it, sliding, across the rough wooden floor. By the time I'd braced myself, the high road behind us was flashing by in a blur of green hedges, and Bishop's Lacey was receding in the distance.

Now you've done it, Flave, I thought, you might never see your family again.

As attractive as this idea seemed at first, I realized quickly that I *would* miss Father—at least a little. Ophelia and Daphne I would soon learn to live without.

Inspector Hewitt would, of course, have already jumped to the conclusion that I had committed the murder, fled the scene, and was making my way by tramp steamer to British Guiana. He would have alerted all ports to keep an eye out for an eleven-year-old murderess in pigtails and sweater.

Once they put two and two together, the police would soon set the hounds to tracking a fugitive who smelt like an Olde Worlde Cheese Shoppe. I would need to find a place to take a bath, then: a meadow stream, perhaps, where I could wash my clothes and dry them on a bramble bush. They would, naturally, interview Tully, grill Ned and Mary, and find out my means of escape from the Thirteen Drakes.

The Thirteen Drakes.

Why is it, I wondered, that the men who choose the names of our inns and public houses are so desperately unimaginative? The Thirteen Drakes, Mrs. Mullet had once told me, was given its name in the eighteenth century by a landlord who simply counted up twelve other licensed Drakes in nearby villages and added another.

Why not something of practical value, like the Thirteen Carbon Atoms, for instance? Something that could be used as a memory aid? There were thirteen carbon atoms in tridecyl, whose hydride was marsh gas. What a jolly useful name for a pub!

The Thirteen Drakes, indeed. Leave it to a man to name a place for a bird!

I was still thinking about tridecyl when, at the open tailgate of the lorry, a rounded, whitewashed stone flashed by. It had a familiar look, and I realized almost at once that it was the turnoff marker for Doddingsley. In another half mile the driver would be forced to stop—even if only for a moment—before turning either right to St. Elfrieda's or left to Nether Lacey.

I slithered to the lip of the open box just as the brakes squealed and the vehicle began to slow. A moment later, like a commando being sucked out the drop-hole of a Whitley bomber, I slipped off the tailgate and hit the dirt on all fours.

Without a backwards glance, the driver turned to the left, and as the heavy lorry and its load of cheeses lumbered away in a cloud of dust, I set off for home.

It was going to be a fair old trudge across the fields to Buckshaw.

nine

I EXPECT THAT LONG AFTER MY SISTER OPHELIA IS dead and gone, whenever I think of her, the first memory that will come to mind will be her gentle touch at the piano. Seated at the keyboard of our old Broadwood grand in the drawing room, Feely becomes a different person.

Years of practice—come hell or high water—have given her the left hand of a Joe Louis and the right hand of a Beau Brummell (or so Daffy says).

Because she plays so beautifully, I have always felt it my bounden duty to be particularly rotten to her. For instance, when she is playing one of those early things by Beethoven that sounds as if it's been cribbed from Mozart, I will stop at the drop of a hat, whatever I may be doing, to stroll casually through the drawing room.

"First-rate flipper work," I'll say loudly enough to be heard above the music. "Arf! Arf! Arf!"

Ophelia has milky blue eyes: the sort of eyes I like to

imagine blind Homer might have had. Although she has most of her repertoire off by heart, she occasionally shifts herself on the piano bench, folds a bit forward at the waist like an automaton, and has a good squint at the sheet music.

Once, when I remarked that she looked like a disoriented bandicoot, she leapt up from the piano bench and beat me within an inch of my life with a rolled-up piano sonata by Schubert. Ophelia has no sense of humor.

As I climbed over the last stile and Buckshaw came into view across the field, it almost took my breath away. It was from this angle and at this time of day that I loved it most. As I approached from the west, the mellow old stone glowed like saffron in the late afternoon sun, well settled into the landscape like a complacent mother hen squatting on her eggs, with the Union Jack stretching itself contentedly overhead.

The house seemed unaware of my approach, as if I were an intruder creeping up on it.

Even from a quarter of a mile away I could hear the notes of the Toccata by Pietro Domenico Paradisi—the one from his Sonata in A Major—come tripping out to meet me.

The Toccata was my favorite composition; to my mind it was the greatest musical accomplishment in the entire history of the world, but I knew that if Ophelia found that out, she would never play the piece again.

Whenever I hear this music it makes me think of flying down the steep east side of Goodger Hill; running so fast that my legs can barely keep up with themselves as I swoop from side to side, mewing into the wind, like a rapturous seagull.

When I was closer to the house, I stopped in the field and listened to the perfect flow of notes, not too *presto*—just the way I liked it. I thought of the time I heard Eileen Joyce play the Toccata on the BBC Home Service. Father had it switched on, not really listening, as he fiddled with his stamp collection. The notes had found their way through the corridors and galleries of Buckshaw, floated up the spiral staircase and into my bedroom. By the time I realized what was being played, raced down the stairs, and burst into Father's study, the music had ended.

We had stood there looking at one another, Father and I, not knowing what to say, until at last, without a word, I had backed out of the room and gone slowly back upstairs.

That's the only problem with the Toccata: It's too short.

I came round the fence and onto the terrace. Father was sitting at his desk in the window of his study, intent on whatever it was he was working at.

The Rosicrucians claim in their adverts that you can make a total stranger turn round in a crowded cinema by fixing your gaze intently on the back of his neck, and I stared at him for all I was worth.

He glanced up, but he did not see me. His mind was somewhere else.

I didn't move a muscle.

And then, as if his head were made of lead, he looked down and went on with his work, and in the drawing room, Feely moved on to something by Schumann.

WHENEVER SHE WAS THINKING ABOUT NED, Feely played Schumann. I suppose that's why they call it romantic music. Once when she was playing a Schumann sonata with an excessively dreamy look on her face, I had re-marked loudly to Daffy that I simply adored bandstand music, and Feely flew into a passion—a passion that wasn't helped by my stalking out of the room and returning a few minutes later with a Bakelite ear-trumpet I had found in a closet, a tin cup, and a hand-lettered sign tied round my neck with a string: "Deafened in tragic piano accident. Please take pity."

Feely had probably forgotten that incident by now, but I hadn't. As I pretended to push past her to look out the window, I had a fleeting close-up of her face. Drat! Nothing for my notebook again.

"You're probably in trouble," she said, slamming down the lid on the keyboard. "Where have you been all day?"

"None of your horse-nails," I told her. "I'm not in your employ."

"Everyone's been looking for you. Daffy and I told them you'd run away from home, but no such bloody luck by the look of it."

"It's bloody poor form to say 'bloody,' Feely; you're not supposed to. And don't puff out your cheeks like that: It makes you look like a petulant pear. Where's Father?"

As if I didn't know.

"He hasn't stuck his nose out all day," Daffy said. "Do you suppose he's upset about what happened this morning?"

"The corpse on the premises? No, I shouldn't say so—nothing to do with him, is it?"

"That's what I thought," Feely said, and lifted the piano lid.

With a toss of her hair, she was off into the first of Bach's *Goldberg Variations*.

It was slow, but lovely nonetheless, although even on his best days Bach, to my way of thinking, couldn't hold a candle to Pietro Domenico Paradisi.

And then I remembered Gladys! I had left her at the Thirteen Drakes, where she could be spotted by anyone. If the police hadn't been there already, they soon would be.

I wondered if by now Mary or Ned had been made to tell them of my visit. But if they had, I reasoned, wouldn't Inspector Hewitt be at Buckshaw this very moment reading me the riot act?

Five minutes later, for the third time that day, I was on my way to Bishop's Lacey—this time on foot.

BY KEEPING TO THE HEDGEROWS and skulking behind trees whenever I heard the sound of an approaching vehicle, I was able to make my way, by a devious route, to the far end of the High Street which, this late in the day, was deep in its usual empty sleep.

A shortcut through Miss Bewdley's ornamental garden (water lilies, stone storks, goldfish, and a red lacquered footbridge) brought me to the brick wall that skirted the inn yard of the Thirteen Drakes, where I crouched and listened. Gladys, if no one had moved her, was directly on the other side.

Except for the hum of a far-off tractor, there wasn't a sound. Just as I was about to venture a peek over the top of the wall I heard voices. Or, to be more precise, one voice, and it was Tully's. I could have heard it even if I'd stayed home at Buckshaw with earplugs.

"Never laid eyes on the bloke in my life, Inspector. His first visit to Bishop's Lacey, I daresay. Would have remembered if he'd stopped here before: Sanders was my late wife's maiden name, God bless 'er, and I'd have marked it if someone by that name ever signed the register. You can put a fiver on that. No, he wasn't never out here in the yard; he come in the front door and went up to his room. If there's any clues, that's where you'll find 'em—there or in the saloon bar. He was in the saloon bar later for a bit. Drank a pint of half-and-half, chug-a-lug, no tip."

So the police knew! I could feel the excitement fizzing inside me like ginger beer, not because they had identified the victim, but because I had beaten them to it with one hand tied behind my back.

I allowed a smug look to flit across my face.

When the voices had faded, I used a bit of creeper for a screen and peeked over the top of the bricks. The inn yard was empty.

I vaulted over the wall, grabbed Gladys, and wheeled her furtively out into the empty High Street. Darting down Cow Lane, I retraced my tracks from earlier in the day by circling back behind the library, between the Thirteen Drakes, and along the rutted towpath beside the river, into Shoe Street, past the churchyard, and into the fields.

Bumpety-bump across the fields we went, Gladys and I. It was good to be in her company.

> "Oh the moon shone bright on Mrs. Porter
> And on her daughter
> They wash their feet in soda water."

It was a song Daffy had taught me, but only after exacting the promise that I would never sing it at Buckshaw. It seemed like a song for the great outdoors, and this was a perfect opportunity.

Dogger met me at the door.

"I need to talk to you, Miss Flavia," he said. I could see the tension in his eyes.

"All right," I said. "Where?"

"Greenhouse," he said, with a jerk of his thumb.

I followed him round the east side of the house and through the green door that was set into the wall of the kitchen garden. Once in the greenhouse, you might as well be in Africa; no one but Dogger ever set foot in the place.

Inside, open ventilation panes in the roof caught the afternoon sun, reflecting it down to where we stood among the potting benches and the gutta-percha hoses.

"What's up, Dogger?" I asked lightly, trying to make it sound a little bit—but not too much—like Bugs Bunny.

"The police," he said. "I have to know how much you told them about . . ."

"I've been thinking the same thing," I said. "You first."

"Well, that Inspector . . . Hewitt. He asked me some questions about this morning."

"Me too," I said. "What did you tell him?"

"I'm sorry, Miss Flavia. I had to tell him that you came and woke me when you found the body, and that I went to the garden with you."

"He already knew that."

Dogger's eyebrows flew up like a pair of seagulls.

"He did?"

"Of course he did. I told him."

Dogger let out a long slow whistle.

"Then you didn't tell him about . . . that row . . . in the study?"

"Certainly not, Dogger! What do you take me for?"

"You must never breathe a word of that, Miss Flavia. Never!"

Now here was a pretty kettle of flounders. Dogger was asking me to conspire with him in withholding information from the police. Who was he protecting? Himself? Father? Or could it be me?

These were questions I could not ask him outright. I thought I'd try a different tack.

"Of course I'll keep quiet," I said. "But why?"

Dogger picked up a trowel and began shoveling black soil into a pot. He did not look at me, but his jaw was set at an angle that signaled clearly that he had made up his mind about something.

"There are things," he said at last, "which need to be known. And there are other things which need not to be known."

"Such as?" I ventured.

The lines of his face softened and he almost smiled.

"Buzz off," he said.

IN MY LABORATORY, I pulled the paper-wrapped packet from my pocket and carefully opened out the folds.

I gave a groan of disappointment: My cycling and wall climbing had reduced the evidence to little more than particles of pastry.

"Oh, crumbs," I said, not without a little pleasure in the aptness of my words. "Now what am I going to do?"

I put the feather carefully into an envelope, and slipped it into a drawer among letters belonging to Tar de Luce that had been written and replied to when Harriet was my age. No one would ever think of looking there, and besides, as Daffy once said, the best place to hide a glum countenance is onstage at the opera.

Even in its mutilated form, the broken pastry reminded me that I had not eaten all day. Supper at Buckshaw was, by some archaic statute, always prepared earlier by Mrs. Mullet and warmed over for our consumption at nine o'clock.

I was starved, hungry enough to eat a ... well, to eat a slice of Mrs. Mullet's icky custard pie. Odd, wasn't it? She had asked me earlier, just after Father fainted, if I had enjoyed the pie ... and I hadn't eaten any.

When I had gone through the kitchen at four in the morning—just before I stumbled upon that body in the cucumber vines—the pie had still been on the windowsill where Mrs. Mullet had left it to cool. And there had been a piece missing.

A piece missing indeed!

Who could have taken it? I remembered wondering about that at the time. It hadn't been Father or Daffy or Feely; they would rather eat creamed worms on toast than Mrs. Mullet's cussed custard.

Nor would Dogger have eaten it; he wasn't the sort of man who helped himself to dessert. And if Mrs. Mullet had given him the slice, she wouldn't have thought I ate it, would she?

I walked downstairs and into the kitchen. The pie was gone.

The window sash was still in its raised position, just as Mrs. Mullet had left it. Had she taken the remains of the pie home to her husband, Alf?

I could telephone and ask her, I thought, but then I remembered Father's telephonic restrictions.

Father was of a generation that despised "the instrument," as he called it. Always ill at ease with the thing, he could be coaxed to talk into it only in the most dire circumstances.

Ophelia once told me that even when news had come of Harriet's death, it had to be sent by telegram because Father refused to believe anything he hadn't seen in print. The telephone at Buckshaw was subscribed to for use only in the event of fire or medical emergency. Any other use of "the instrument" required Father's personal permission, a rule which had been drummed into us from the day we climbed out of our cribs.

No, I would have to wait until tomorrow to ask Mrs. Mullet about the pie.

I took a loaf of bread from the pantry and cut a thick slice. I buttered it, then slathered on a blanket of brown sugar. I folded the bread twice in half, each time pressing it down flat with the palm of my hand. I stuck it in the warming oven and left it there for as long as it took me to sing three verses of "If I Knew You Were Comin' I'd've Baked a Cake."

It was not a true Chelsea bun, but it would have to do.

ten

EVEN THOUGH WE DE LUCES HAD BEEN ROMAN Catholics since chariot races were all the rage, that did not keep us from attending St. Tancred's, Bishop's Lacey's only church and a fortress of the Church of England if ever there was one.

There were several reasons for our patronage. The first was its handy location, and another the fact that Father and the Vicar had both (although at different times) been to school at Greyminster. Besides, Father had once pointed out to us, consecration was permanent, like a tattoo. St. Tancred's, he said, had been a Roman Catholic Church before the Reformation and, in his eyes, remained one.

Consequently, every Sunday morning without exception we straggled across the fields like ducks, Father slashing intermittently at the vegetation with his Malacca walking stick, Feely, Daffy, and me in that order, and Dogger, in his Sunday best, bringing up the rear.

No one at St. Tancred's paid us the slightest attention. Some years before, there had been a minor outbreak of grumbling from the Anglicans, but all had been settled without blood or bruises by a well-timed contribution to the Organ Restoration Fund.

"Tell them we may not be praying *with* them," Father told the Vicar, "but we are at least not actively praying *against* them."

Once, when Feely lost her head and bolted for the Communion rail, Father refused to speak to her until the following Sunday. Ever since that day, whenever she so much as shifted her feet in church, Father would mutter, "Steady on, old girl." He did not need to catch her eye; his profile, which was that of the standard-bearer in some particularly ascetic Roman legion, was enough to keep us in our places. At least in public.

Now, glancing over at Feely as she knelt with her eyes closed, her fingertips touching and pointed to Heaven, and her lips shaping soft words of devotion, I had to pinch myself to keep in mind that I was sitting next to the Devil's Hairball.

The congregation at St. Tancred's had soon become accustomed to our ducking and bobbing, and we basked in Christian charity—except for the time that Daffy told the organist, Mr. Denning, that Harriet had instilled in all of us her firm belief that the story of the Flood in Genesis was derived from the racial memory of the cat family, with particular reference to the drowning of kittens.

That had caused a bit of a stir, but Father had put things right by making a handsome donation to the Roof Repair Fund, a sum he deducted from Daffy's allowance.

"Since I don't have an allowance anyway," Daffy said, "no one's the loser. It's a jolly good punishment, actually."

I listened, unmoved, as the congregation joined in the General Confession:

"We have left undone those things which we ought to have done; And we have done those things which we ought not to have done."

Dogger's words flashed into my mind:

"There are things which need to be known. And there are other things which need not to be known."

I turned round and looked at him. His eyes were closed and his lips were moving. And so, I noticed, were Father's.

Because it was Trinity Sunday we were treated to a rare old romp from Revelation all about the sardine stone, the rainbow round about the throne, the sea of glass like unto crystal, and the four beasts full of eyes before and uncomfortably behind.

I had my own opinion about the true meaning of this obviously alchemical reference, but, since I was saving it for my Ph.D. thesis, I kept it to myself. And even though we de Luces were players on the opposing team, as it were, I couldn't help envying those Anglicans the glories of their Book of Common Prayer.

The glass, too, was glorious. Above the altar, morning sunlight washed in through three windows whose stained glass had been poured in the Middle Ages by half-civilized semivagrant glassmakers who lived and caroused on the verge of Ovenhouse Wood, the thin remains of which still bordered Buckshaw to the west.

On the left panel, Jonah sprang from the mouth of the great fish, looking back over his shoulder at the thing with a look of wide-eyed indignation. From the booklet that used to be given away in the church porch, I remembered that the creature's white scales had been achieved by firing the glass with tin, while Jonah's skin had been made brown with salts of ferric iron (which, interestingly enough—to me at least—is also the antidote for arsenical poisoning).

The panel on the right portrayed Jesus emerging from his tomb, as Mary Magdalene, in a red dress (also iron, or perhaps grated particles of gold), holds out to him a purple garment (manganese dioxide) and a loaf of yellow bread (silver chloride).

I knew that these salts had been mixed with sand and the ashes of a salt marsh reed called glasswort, fired in a furnace hot enough to have given even Shadrach, Meshach, and Abednego second thoughts, and then cooled until the desired color was obtained.

The central panel was dominated by our own Saint Tancred, whose body lay at this very moment somewhere beneath our feet in the crypt. In this view, he is standing at the open door of the church in which we sit (as it looked before the Victorians improved it), welcoming with outstretched arms a multitude of parishioners. Saint Tancred has a pleasant face: He's the sort of person you would like to invite over on a Sunday afternoon to browse through back issues of the *Illustrated London News*, or maybe even *Country Life*, and, since we share his faith, I like to imagine that while he snores away eternity down below, he has a particular soft spot for all of us at Buckshaw.

As my mind swam back to the present, I realized that the Vicar was praying for the man I had found dead in the garden.

"He was a stranger among us," he said. "It is not necessary that his name be known unto us . . ."

This would be news to Inspector Hewitt, I thought.

"...in order for us to ask God to have mercy on his soul, and to grant him peace."

So the word was out! Mrs. Mullet, I guessed, had wasted no time in scurrying across the lane yesterday to break the news to the Vicar. I could hardly believe he had heard it from the police.

There was a sudden hollow bang as a kneeling bench slammed up, and I looked round just in time to see Miss Mountjoy edging her way crab-wise out of the pews and fleeing along the side aisle to the transept door.

"I feel nauseous," I whispered to Ophelia, who let me slide past her without batting an eye. Feely had a particular aversion to having her shoes vomited on, a useful quirk of which I took advantage from time to time.

Outside, a wind had sprung up, whipping the branches of the churchyard yews, and sending ripples running through the unmowed grass. I caught a glimpse of Miss Mountjoy disappearing among the moss-covered tombstones, heading towards the crumbling, overgrown lych-gate.

What had upset her so? For a moment I considered running after her, but then I thought better of it: The river looped round St. Tancred's in such a way that the church was virtually on an island and, through the centuries, the meandering water had cut through the ancient lane beyond the lych-gate. The only possible way for Miss Mountjoy to make her way home without retracing her steps would be to take off her shoes and wade across the now-submerged stepping-stones that had once bridged the river.

It was obvious that she wanted to be alone.

I rejoined Father as he was shaking hands with Canon Richardson. What with the murder, we de Luces were all the rage as the villagers in their Sunday finery lined up to speak with us or, sometimes, simply to touch us as if we were talismans. Everyone wanted to have a word, but nobody wanted to say anything that mattered.

"Dreadful business that, up at Buckshaw," they'd say to Father, or Feely or me.

"Nasty," we'd reply, and shake hands, and then wait for the next petitioner to shuffle forward. Only when we'd serviced the entire congregation were we free to make our way home for lunch.

AS WE CROSSED THE PARK, the door of a familiar blue car opened and Inspector Hewitt came across the gravel to meet us. Having already decided that police investigations were likely shelved on Sundays, I was a little surprised to see him. He gave Father a brisk nod and touched the brim of his hat to Feely, to Daffy, and to me.

"Colonel de Luce, a few words... in private if you please."

I watched Father closely, fearing he might faint again, but aside from a slight tightening of his knuckles on the handle of his walking stick, he seemed not at all surprised. He might even, I thought, have been preparing himself for this moment.

Dogger, meanwhile, had quietly sloped off into the house, perhaps to change his stiff old-fashioned collar and cuffs for the comfort of his gardening overalls.

Father looked round at us as if we were a gaggle of intrusive geese.

"Come into my study," he said to the Inspector, then turned and walked away.

Daffy and Feely stood gazing off into the middle distance

as they are inclined to do when they don't know what to say. For a moment I thought of breaking the silence, but, on second thought, decided against it and walked away in a careless manner, whistling the "Harry Lime" theme from *The Third Man*.

Since it was Sunday, I thought it would be appropriate to go into the garden and have a look at the place where the body had lain. It would be, in a way, like those Victorian paintings of veiled widows crouching to place a handful of pathetic pansies—usually in a glass tumbler—upon the grave of their dead husband or mother. But somehow the thought made me sad, and I decided to skip the theatrics.

Without the dead man, the cucumber patch was oddly uninteresting, no more than a patch of greenery with here and there a broken stalk and something that looked suspiciously like the drag mark of a heel. In the grass, I could see the perforations where the sharp legs of Sergeant Woolmer's heavy tripod had pierced the turf.

I knew from listening to Philip Odell, the private eye on the wireless, that whenever there's a sudden and unexpected death, there's bound to be a postmortem, and I couldn't help wondering if Dr. Darby had yet had the body—as I had heard him remark to Inspector Hewitt—"up on the table." But again, that was something I dared not ask, at least not just yet.

I looked up at my bedroom window. Reflected in it, so close I could almost touch them, images of plump white clouds floated by in a sea of blue sky.

So close! Of course! The cucumber patch was directly below my window!

Why, then, had I heard nothing? Everyone knows that

the killing of a human being requires the exertion of a certain amount of mechanical energy. I forget the exact formula, although I know there is one. Force applied in a short span of time (for instance a bullet), makes a great deal of noise, whereas force applied more slowly may well make no noise at all.

What did this tell me? That if the stranger had been violently attacked, it had happened somewhere else, somewhere out of earshot. If he had been attacked where I found him, the killer had used a silent method: silent and slow since, when I found him, the man had been still, although barely, alive.

"*Vale*," the dying man had said. But why would he say farewell to me? It was the word Mr. Twining had shouted before jumping to his death, but what was the connection? Was the man in the cucumbers trying to link his own death with that of Mr. Twining? Had he been there when the old man jumped? Had he been part of it?

I needed to think—and to think without distractions. The coach house was out of the question since I was now aware that, in times of trouble, I might well encounter Father sitting there in Harriet's Phantom. That left the Folly.

On the south side of Buckshaw, on an artificial island in an artificial lake, was an artificial ruin, in the shadow of which was a little Greek temple of lichen-stained marble. Now sunk deep in neglect and overgrown with nettles, there had been a time when it was one of the glories of England: a little cupola on four exquisitely slender legs that might have been a bandstand on Parnassus. Countless eighteenth-century de Luces had poled their guests out to the Folly on festive flower-strewn barges, where they had picnicked upon cold game and pastry as they watched the swans glide across the glassy water, and looked through quizzing-glasses at the hired hermit as he gaped and yawned at the doorway of his ivy-clad cave.

The island, the lake, and the Folly had been designed by Capability Brown (although this attribution had been brought into question more than once in the pages of *Notes and Queries*, which Father read avidly, but only in case matters of philatelic interest should crop up), and there was still in the library at Buckshaw a large red leather portfolio containing a signed set of the landscaper's original drawings. These inspired a little witticism on Father's part: "Let those other wise men live in their own folly," he said.

There was a family tradition that it had been on a picnic at Buckshaw Folly that John Montague, the fourth Earl of Sandwich, invented the snack which was given his name when he first slapped cold grouse between two slices of bread while playing at cribbage with Cornelius de Luce.

"History be damned," Father had said.

Now, having waded out to the island through water no more than a foot deep, I sat on the steps of the little temple with my legs drawn up and my chin on my knees.

First of all, there was Mrs. Mullet's custard pie. Where had it gone?

I let my mind drift back to the early hours of Saturday morning: envisioned myself coming down the stairs, going through the hallway to the kitchen, and—yes, the pie had certainly been on the windowsill. And there had been a single piece cut out of it.

Later, Mrs. Mullet had asked if I enjoyed the pie. Why me? I wondered. Why didn't she ask Feely or Daffy?

And then it struck me like a thunderclap! The dead man had eaten it. Yes. Everything was making sense!

Here was a diabetic who had come on a long journey from Norway, bringing with him a jack snipe concealed in a pie. I had found the remains of that pie—complete with telltale feather—at the Thirteen Drakes, and the dead bird had been dumped on our doorstep. Not having eaten—even though, according to Tully Stoker, he had been served a drink in the saloon bar—the stranger had made his way to Buckshaw on Friday night, quarreled with Father, and on his way out passed through the kitchen and helped himself to a slice of Mrs. Mullet's custard pie. And he hadn't made it through the cucumbers before it brought him down!

What kind of poison could work that quickly? I ran through the most likely possibilities. Cyanide worked in minutes: after turning blue in the face, the victim was asphyxiated almost immediately. It left behind a smell of bitter almonds. But no, the case against cyanide was that, had it been used, the victim would have been dead before I found him. (Although I have to admit that I have a soft spot for cyanide—when it comes to speed, it is right up there with the best of them. If poisons were ponies, I'd put my money on cyanide.)

But was it bitter almonds I had smelt on his last breath? I couldn't think.

Then there was curare. It, too, had an almost instant effect and again, the victim died within minutes by asphyxiation. But curare could not kill by ingestion; to be fatal, it had to be injected. Besides that, who in the English countryside—besides me, of course—would be likely to carry curare in his kit?

What about tobacco? I recalled that a handful of

tobacco leaves left to soak in a jar of water in the sun for several days could easily be evaporated to a thick black molasses-like resin which brought death in seconds. But *Nicoteana* was grown in America, its fresh leaves unlikely to be found in England, or, for that matter, in Norway.

Query: would crumbled cigarette ends, cigars, or pipe tobacco produce an equally toxic poison?

Since nobody smoked at Buckshaw, I would have to gather my own samples.

Query: When (and where) are the ashtrays emptied at the Thirteen Drakes?

THE REAL QUESTION WAS THIS: Who put the poison in the pie? And, even more to the point, if the dead man had eaten the thing by accident, whom had it originally been intended for?

I shivered as a shadow passed across the island, and I looked up just as a darkening cloud blotted out the sun. It was going to rain—and soon.

But before I could scramble to my feet it came pouring down in buckets, one of those sudden brief but ferocious storms of early June that smashes flowers and plays havoc with drains. I tried to find a dry, sheltered spot in the precise center of the open cupola where I would be most sheltered from the pelting rain—not that it made much difference, what with the cold wind that had suddenly sprung up out of nowhere. I wrapped my arms round myself for warmth. I'd have to wait it out, I thought.

"Hullo! Are you all right?"

A man was standing at the far edge of the lake, looking across at me on the island. Through the sheets of falling rain, I could see no more than dabs of damp color, which gave him the appearance of someone in an Impressionist painting. But before I could reply, he had rolled up his trouser legs and removed his shoes, and was swiftly wading barefoot towards me. As he steadied himself with his long walking staff, he reminded me of Saint Christopher carrying the Christ Child piggyback across the river, although as he drew closer, I could see that the object on his shoulders was actually a canvas knapsack.

He was dressed in a baggy walking suit and wore a hat with a wide, floppy brim: a bit like Leslie Howard, the film star, I thought. He was fiftyish, I guessed, about Father's age but dapper in spite of it.

With a waterproof artist's sketchbook in one hand, he was the very image of the strolling artist-illustrator: Olde England, and all that.

"Are you all right?" he repeated, and I realized I hadn't answered him the first time.

"Perfectly well, thank you," I said, babbling a bit too much to make up for my possible rudeness. "I was caught in the rain, you see."

"I do see," he said. "You're saturated."

"Not so much saturated as drenched," I corrected him. When it came to chemistry, I was a stickler.

He opened his knapsack and pulled out a waterproof walking cape, the sort of thing worn by hikers in the Hebrides. He wrapped it round my shoulders and I was immediately warm.

"You needn't . . . but thank you," I said.

We stood there together in the falling rain, not

speaking, each of us gazing off across the lake, listening to the clatter of the downpour.

After a time he said, "Since we're to be marooned on an island together, I suppose there could be no harm in us exchanging names."

I tried to place his accent: Oxford with a touch of something else. Scandinavian, perhaps?

"I'm Flavia," I said. "Flavia de Luce."

"My name's Pemberton, Frank Pemberton. Pleased to meet you, Flavia."

Pemberton? Wasn't this the man who had arrived at the Thirteen Drakes just as I was making my escape from Tully Stoker? I wanted that visit kept quiet, so I said nothing.

We exchanged a soggy handshake, and then drew apart as strangers often do after they've touched.

The rain went on. After a bit he said, "Actually, I knew who you were."

"Did you?"

"Mmm. To anyone who takes a serious interest in English country houses, de Luce is quite a well-known name. Your family is, after all, listed in *Who's Who*."

"Do *you* take a serious interest in English country houses, Mr. Pemberton?"

He laughed. "A professional interest, I'm afraid. In fact I'm writing a book on the subject. I thought I would call it *Pemberton's Stately Homes: A Stroll Through Time*. Has rather an impressive ring, don't you think?"

"I expect it depends upon whom you're trying to impress," I said, "but it does, yes . . . rather, I mean."

"My home base is in London, of course, but I've been tramping through this part of the country for quite some time, scribbling in my notebooks. I'd rather hoped to have a look round the estate and interview your father. In fact, that's why I'm here."

"I don't think that will be possible, Mr. Pemberton," I said. "You see, there's been a sudden death at Buckshaw, and Father is . . . assisting the police with their inquiries."

Without thinking, I had pulled the phrase from remembered serials on the wireless, and, until I said it, not realized its import.

"Good Lord!" he said. "A sudden death? Not one of the family, I hope."

"No," I said. "A complete stranger. But since he was found in the garden at Buckshaw, you see, Father is bound to—"

At that moment it stopped raining as suddenly as it had begun. The sun came out to play in rainbows on the grass, and somewhere on the island, a cuckoo sang, precisely as it does at the end of the storm in Beethoven's Pastoral Symphony. I swear it did.

"I understand perfectly," he said. "I wouldn't dream of intruding. Should Colonel de Luce wish to be in contact at a later date, I'm at the Thirteen Drakes, in Bishop's Lacey. I'm sure Mr. Stoker would be happy to convey a message."

I removed the cape and handed it to him.

"Thank you," I said. "I'd best be getting back."

We waded back across the lake together like a couple of bathers holidaying at the seaside.

"It was a pleasure meeting you, Flavia," he said. "In time, I trust we shall become fast friends."

I watched as he strolled across the lawn towards the avenue of chestnuts and out of sight.

eleven

I FOUND DAFFY IN THE LIBRARY, PERCHED AT THE very top of a wheeled ladder.

"Where's Father?" I asked.

She turned a page and went on reading as if I had never been born.

"Daffy?"

I felt my inner cauldron beginning to boil: that bubbling pot of occult brew that could so quickly transform Flavia the Invisible into Flavia the Holy Terror.

I seized one of its rungs and gave the ladder a good shake, and then a shove to start it rolling. Once in motion, it was easy enough to sustain, with Daffy clinging to the top like a paralyzed limpet as I pushed the thing down the long room.

"Stop it, Flavia! Stop it!"

As the doorway approached at an alarming rate, I braked, then ran round behind the ladder and raced off again in the opposite direction, and all the while, Daffy teetering away up top like the lookout on a whaler in a North Atlantic blow.

"Where's Father?" I shouted.

"He's still in his study with the Inspector. Stop this! Stop it!"

As she looked a little green about the gills, I stopped.

Daffy came shakily down the ladder and stepped gingerly off onto the floor. I thought for a moment she would lunge at me, but she seemed to be taking an unusually long while regaining her land legs.

"Sometimes you scare me," she said.

I was about to retort that there were times I scared myself, but then I remembered that silence can sometimes do more damage than words. I bit my tongue.

The whites of her eyes were still showing, like those of a bolted cart-horse, and I decided to take advantage of the moment.

"Where does Miss Mountjoy live?"

Daffy looked blank.

"Miss Library Mountjoy," I added.

"I have no idea," Daffy said. "I haven't used the library in the village since I was a child."

Still wide-eyed, she peered at me over her glasses.

"I was thinking of asking her advice on becoming a librarian."

It was the perfect lie. Daffy's look became almost one of respect.

"I don't know where she lives," she said. "Ask Miss Cool, at the confectionery. She knows what's under every bed in Bishop's Lacey."

"Thanks, Daff," I said as she dropped down into an upholstered wingback chair. "You're a brick."

ONE OF THE CHIEF CONVENIENCES of living near a village is that, if required, you can soon be in it. I flew along on Gladys, thinking that it might be a good idea to keep a logbook, as aeroplane pilots are made to do. By now, Gladys and I must have logged some hundreds of flying hours together, most of them in going to and from Bishop's Lacey. Now and then, with a picnic hamper strapped to her black back-skirts, we would venture even farther afield.

Once, we had ridden all morning to look at an inn where Richard Mead was said to have stayed a single night in 1747. Richard (or Dick, as I sometimes referred to him) was the author of *A Mechanical Account of Poisons in Several Essays*. Published in 1702, it was the first book on the subject in the English language, a first edition of which was the pride of my chemical library. In my bedroom portrait gallery, I kept his likeness stuck to the looking-glass alongside those of Henry Cavendish, Robert Bunsen, and Carl Wilhelm Scheele, whereas Daffy and Feely had pin-ups of Charles Dickens and Mario Lanza respectively.

The confectioner's shop in the Bishop's Lacey High Street stood tightly wedged between the undertaker's premises on one side and a fish shop on the other. I leaned Gladys up against the plate-glass window and seized the doorknob.

I swore curses under my breath. The place was locked as tight as Old Stink.

Why did the universe conspire against me like this? First the closet, then the library, and now the confectioner's. My life was becoming a long corridor of locked doors.

I cupped my hands at the window and peered into the interior gloom.

Miss Cool must have stepped out or perhaps, like everyone else in Bishop's Lacey, was having a family emergency. I took the knob in both hands and rattled the door, knowing as I did so that it was useless.

I remembered that Miss Cool lived in a couple of rooms behind the shop. Perhaps she had forgotten to unlock the door. Older people often do things like that: they become senile and—

But what if she's died in her sleep? I thought. Or worse . . .

I looked both ways but the High Street was empty. But wait! I had forgotten about Bolt Alley, a dark, dank tunnel of cobblestones and brick that led to the yards behind the shops. Of course! I made for it at once.

Bolt Alley smelled of the past, which was said to have once included a notorious gin mill. I gave an involuntary shiver as the sound of my footsteps echoed from its mossy walls and dripping roof. I tried not to touch the reeking green-stained bricks on either side, or to inhale its sour air, until I had edged my way out into the sunlight at the far end of the passage.

Miss Cool's tiny backyard was hemmed in with a low wall of crumbling brick. Its wooden gate was latched on the inside.

I scrambled over the wall, marched straight to the door, and gave it a good banging with the flat of my hand.

I put my ear to the panel, but nothing seemed to be moving inside.

I stepped off the walk, waded into the unkempt grass, and pressed my nose to the bottom of the sooty window-pane. The back of a dresser was blocking my view.

In one corner of the yard was a decaying doghouse—all

that was left of Miss Cool's collie, Geordie, who had been run over by a speeding motorcar in the High Street.

I tugged at the sagging frame until it pulled free of the mounded earth and dragged it across the yard until it was directly under the window. Then I climbed on top of it.

From the top of the doghouse it was only one more step up until I was able to get my toes on the windowsill, where I balanced precariously on the chipped paint, my arms and legs spread out like Leonardo da Vinci's Vitruvian Man, one hand hanging on tightly to a shutter and the other trying to polish a viewing port in the grimy glass.

It was dark inside the little bedroom, but there was light enough to see the form lying on the bed; to see the white face staring back at me, its mouth gaping open in a horrid "O."

"Flavia!" Miss Cool said, scrambling to her feet, her words muffled by the window glass. "What on *earth*—?"

She snatched her false teeth from a tumbler and rammed them into her mouth, then vanished for a moment, and as I leaped to the ground I heard the sound of the bolt being shot back. The door opened inwards to reveal her standing there—like a trapped badger—in a housedress, her hand clutching and opening in nervous spasms at her throat.

"What on earth . . . ?" she repeated. "What's the matter?"

"The front door's locked," I said. "I couldn't get in."

"Of course it's locked," she said. "It's always locked on Sundays. I was having a nap."

She rubbed at her little black eyes, which were still squinting at the light.

Slowly it dawned on me that she was right. It *was*

Sunday. Although it seemed aeons ago, it was only this morning that I had been sitting in St. Tancred's with my family.

I must have looked crushed.

"What is it, dear?" Miss Cool said. "That horrid business up at Buckshaw?"

So she knew about it.

"I hope you've had the good sense to keep away from the actual scene of the—"

"Yes, of course, Miss Cool," I said with a regretful smile. "But I've been asked not to talk about that. I'm sure you'll understand."

This was a lie, but a first-rate one.

"What a good child you are," she said, with a glance up at the curtained windows of an adjoining row of houses that overlooked her yard. "This is no place to talk. You'd better come inside."

She led me through a narrow hallway, on one side of it her tiny bedroom, and on the other, a miniature sitting room. And suddenly we were in the shop, behind the counter that served as the village post office. Besides being Bishop's Lacey's only confectioner, Miss Cool was also its postmistress and, as such, knew everything worth knowing—except chemistry, of course.

She watched me carefully as I looked round with interest at the tiers of shelves, each one lined with glass jars of horehound sticks, bull's-eyes, and hundreds-and-thousands.

"I'm sorry. I can't do business on a Sunday. They'd have me up before the magistrates. It's the law, you know."

I shook my head sadly.

"I'm sorry," I said. "I forgot what day it was. I didn't mean to frighten you."

"Well, no real harm done," she said, suddenly recovering her usual garrulous powers as she bustled about the shop, aimlessly touching this and that.

"Tell your father there's a new set of stamps coming out soon, but nothing to go into raptures about, at least to my way of thinking, anyways. Same old picture of King George's head, God bless 'im, but tarted up in new colors."

"Thank you, Miss Cool," I said. "I'll be sure to let him know."

"I'm sure that lot at the General Post Office up in London could come up with something better than that," she went on, "but I've heard as how they're saving up their brains for next year to celebrate the Festival of Britain."

"I wonder if you could tell me where Miss Mountjoy lives," I blurted.

"Tilda Mountjoy?" Her eyes narrowed. "Whatever could you want with her?"

"She was most helpful to me at the library, and I thought it might be nice to take her some sweets."

I gave a sweet smile to match the sentiment.

This was a shameless lie. I hadn't given the matter a moment's thought until now, when I saw that I could kill two birds with one stone.

"Ah, yes," Miss Cool said. "Margaret Pickery off to tend the sister in Nether-Wolsey: the Singer, the needle, the finger, the twins, the wayward husband, the bottle, the bills . . . a moment of unexpected and rewarding usefulness for Tilda Mountjoy . . .

"Acid drops," she said suddenly. "Sunday or no, acid drops would be the perfect choice."

"I'll have sixpence worth," I said.

"... and a shilling's worth of the horehound sticks," I added. Horehound was my secret passion.

Miss Cool tiptoed to the front of the shop and pulled down the blinds.

"Just between you and me and the gatepost," she said in a conspiratorial voice.

She scooped the acid drops into a purple paper bag of such a funereal color that it simply cried out to be filled with a scoop or two of arsenic or *nux vomica*.

"That will be one-and-six," she said, wrapping the horehound sticks in paper. I handed her two shillings and while she was still digging in her pockets I said, "That's all right, Miss Cool, I don't require change."

"What a sweet child you are." She beamed, slipping an extra horehound stick into the wrappings. "If I had children of my own, I couldn't hope to see them half so thoughtful or so generous."

I gave her a partial smile and kept the rest of it for myself as she directed me to Miss Mountjoy's house.

"Willow Villa," she said. "You can't miss it. It's orange."

WILLOW VILLA WAS, as Miss Cool had said, orange; the kind of orange you see when the scarlet cap of a Death's Head mushroom has just begun to go off. The house was hidden in the shadows beneath the flowing green skirts of a monstrous weeping willow whose branches shifted uneasily in the breeze, sweeping bare the dirt beneath it like a score of witches' brooms. Their movement made me think of a piece of seventeenth-century music that Feely sometimes played and sang—very sweetly, I must admit— when she was thinking of Ned:

The willow-tree will twist, and the willow-tree will
     twine,
O I wish I was in the dear youth's arms that once had
     the heart of mine.

The song was called "The Seeds of Love," although
love was not the first thing that came to mind whenever I
saw a willow; on the contrary, they always reminded me of
Ophelia (Shakespeare's, not mine) who drowned herself
near one.

Except for a handkerchief-sized scrap of grass at one side,
Miss Mountjoy's willow filled the fenced-in yard. Even on
the doorstep I could feel the dampness of the place: the
tree's languid branches formed a green bell jar through
which little light seemed to penetrate, giving me the odd
sensation of being under water. Vivid green mosses made a
stone sponge of the doorstep, and water stains stretched
their sad black fingers across the face of the orange plaster.

On the door was an oxidized brass knocker with the
grinning face of the Lincoln Imp. I lifted it and gave a couple of gentle taps. As I waited, I gazed absently up into the
air in case anyone should be peeking out from behind the
curtains.

But the dusty lace didn't stir. It was as if there was no
breath of air inside the place.

To the left, a walk cobbled with old, worn bricks led
round the side of the house, and after waiting at the door
for a minute or two, I followed it.

The back door was almost completely hidden by long
tendrils of willow leaves, all of them undulating with a
slightly expectant swishing, like a garish green theater curtain about to rise.

I cupped my hands to the glass at one of the tiny windows. If I stood on tiptoe—

"What are you doing here?"

I spun round.

Miss Mountjoy was standing outside the circle of willow branches, looking in. Through the foliage, I could see only vertical stripes of her face, but what I saw made me edgy.

"It's me, Miss Mountjoy . . . Flavia," I said. "I wanted to thank you for helping me at the library."

The willow branches rustled as Miss Mountjoy stepped inside the cloak of greenery. She was holding a pair of garden shears in one hand and she said nothing. Her eyes, like two mad raisins in her wrinkled face, never left mine.

I shrank back as she stepped onto the walk, blocking my escape.

"I know well enough who you are," she said. "You're Flavia Sabina Dolores de Luce—Jacko's youngest daughter."

"You know he's my father?!" I gasped.

"Of course I know, girl. A person of my age knows a great deal."

Somehow, before I could stop it, the truth popped out of me like a cork from a bottle.

"The 'Dolores' was a lie," I said. "I sometimes fabricate things."

She took a step towards me.

"Why are you here?" she asked, her voice a harsh whisper.

I quickly plunged my hand into my pocket and fished out the bag of sweets.

"I brought you some acid drops," I said, "to apologize for my rudeness. I hope you'll accept them."

A shrill wheezing sound, which I took to depict a laugh, came out of her.

"Miss Cool's recommendation, no doubt?"

Like the village idiot in a pantomime, I gave half a dozen quick, bobbing nods.

"I was sorry to hear about the way your uncle—Mr. Twining—died," I said, and I meant it. "Honestly I was. It doesn't seem fair."

"Fair? It certainly was not fair," she said. "And yet it was not unjust. It was not even wicked. Do you know what it was?"

Of course I knew. I had heard this before, but I was not here to debate her.

"No," I whispered.

"It was murder," she said. "It was murder, pure and simple."

"And who was the murderer?" I asked. Sometimes my own tongue took me by surprise.

A rather vague look floated across Miss Mountjoy's face like a cloud across the moon, as if she had spent a lifetime preparing for the part and then, center stage in the spotlight, had forgotten her lines.

"Those boys," she said at last. "Those loathsome, detestable boys. I shall never forget them; not for all their apple cheeks and schoolboy innocence."

"One of those boys is my father," I said quietly.

Her eyes were somewhere else in time. Only slowly did they return to the present to focus upon me.

"Yes," she said. "Laurence de Luce. Jacko. Your father was called Jacko. A schoolboy sobriquet, and yet even the coroner called him that. Jacko. He said it ever so softly at the inquest, almost caressingly—as if all the court were in thrall with the name."

"My father gave evidence at the inquest?"

"Of course he testified—as did the other boys. It was the sort of thing that was done in those days. He denied everything, of course, all responsibility. A valuable postage stamp had been stolen from the headmaster's collection, and it was all, 'Oh no, sir, it wasn't me, sir!' As if the stamp had magically sprouted grubby little fingers and filched it-self!"

I was about to tell her "My father is not a thief, nor is he a liar," when suddenly I knew that nothing I could say would ever change this ancient mind. I decided to take the offensive.

"Why did you walk out of church this morning?" I asked.

Miss Mountjoy recoiled as if I had thrown a glass of wa-ter in her face. "You don't mince words, do you?"

"No," I said. "It had something to do with the Vicar's praying for the stranger in our midst, didn't it? The man whose body I found in the garden at Buckshaw."

She hissed through her teeth like a teakettle. "*You* found the body? *You?*"

"Yes," I said.

"Then tell me this—did it have red hair?" She closed her eyes, and kept them closed awaiting my reply.

"Yes," I said. "It had red hair."

"For what we have received may the Lord make us truly thankful," she breathed, before opening her eyes again. It seemed to me not only a peculiar response, but somehow an unchristian one.

"I don't understand," I said. And I didn't.

"I recognized him at once," she said. "Even after all these years, I knew who he was as soon as I saw that shock of red hair walking out of the Thirteen Drakes. If that hadn't been enough, his swagger, that overweening cockiness, those cold blue eyes—any one of those things—would have told me that Horace Bonepenny had come back to Bishop's Lacey."

I had the feeling that we were slipping into deeper waters than I knew.

"Perhaps now you can see why I could not take part in any prayer for the repose of that boy's—that man's—rancid soul."

She reached out and took the bag of acid drops from my hand, popping one into her mouth and pocketing the rest.

"On the contrary," she continued, "I pray that he is, at this very moment, being basted in hell."

And with that, she walked into her dank Willow Villa and slammed the door.

Who on earth was Horace Bonepenny? And what had brought him back to Bishop's Lacey?

I could think of only one person who might be made to tell me.

AS I RODE UP THE AVENUE of chestnuts to Buckshaw, I could see that the blue Vauxhall was no longer at the door. Inspector Hewitt and his men had gone.

I was wheeling Gladys round to the back of the house when I heard a metallic tapping coming from the greenhouse. I moved towards the door and looked inside. It was Dogger.

He was sitting on an overturned pail, striking the thing with a trowel.

Clang...clang...clang...clang. In the way the bell of St. Tancred's tolls for the funeral of some ancient in Bishop's Lacey, it went on and on, as if measuring the strokes of a life. Clang...clang...clang...clang...

His back was to the door, and it was obvious that he did not see me.

I crept away towards the kitchen door where I made a great and noisy ado by dropping Gladys with a loud clatter on the stone doorstep. ("Sorry, Gladys," I whispered.)

"Damn and blast!" I said, loudly enough to be heard in the greenhouse. I pretended to spot him there behind the glass.

"Oh, hullo, Dogger," I said cheerily. "Just the person I was looking for."

He did not turn immediately, and I pretended to be scraping a bit of clay from the sole of my shoe until he recovered himself.

"Miss Flavia," he said slowly. "Everyone has been looking for you."

"Well, here I am," I said. Best to take over the conversation until Dogger was fully back on the rails.

"I was talking to someone in the village who told me about somebody I thought you might be able to tell me about."

Dogger managed the ghost of a smile.

"I know I'm not putting that in the best way, but—"

"I know what you mean," he said.

"Horace Bonepenny," I blurted out. "Who is Horace Bonepenny?"

At my words, Dogger began to twitch like an experimental frog whose spinal cord has been hooked up to a galvanic battery. He licked his lips and wiped madly at his mouth with a pocket handkerchief. I could see that his eyes were beginning to dim, winking out much as the stars do just before sunrise. At the same time, he was making a great effort to pull himself together, though with little success.

"Never mind, Dogger," I said. "It doesn't matter. Forget it."

He tried to get to his feet, but was unable to lift himself from the overturned pail.

"Miss Flavia," he said, "there are questions which need to be asked, and there are questions which need not to be asked."

So there it was again: so like a law, these words that fell from Dogger's lips as naturally, and with as much finality, as if Isaiah himself had spoken them.

But those few words seemed utterly to have exhausted him, and with a loud sigh he covered his face with his hands. I wanted nothing more at that moment than to throw my arms round him and hug him, but I knew that he wasn't up to it. Instead, I settled for putting my hand on his shoulder, realizing even as I did so that the gesture was of greater comfort to me than it was to him.

"I'll go and get Father," I said. "We'll help you to your room."

Dogger turned his face slowly round towards me, a chalky white mask of tragedy. The words came out of him like stone grating upon stone.

"They've taken him away, Miss Flavia. The police have taken him away."

twelve

FEELY AND DAFFY WERE SITTING ON A FLOWERED DI-
van in the drawing room, wrapped in one another's arms
and wailing like air-raid sirens. I had taken a few steps into
the room to join in with them before Ophelia spotted me.

"Where have you been, you little beast?" she hissed,
springing up and coming at me like a wildcat, her eyes
swollen and as red as cycle reflectors. "Everyone's been
searching for you. We thought you'd drowned. Oh! How I
prayed you had!"

Welcome home, Flave, I thought.

"Father's been arrested," Daffy said matter-of-factly.
"They've taken him away."

"Where?" I asked.

"How should we know?" Ophelia spat contemptuously.
"Wherever they take people who have been arrested, I expect. Where have you been?"

"Bishop's Lacey or Hinley?"

"What do you mean? Talk sense, you little fool."

"Bishop's Lacey or Hinley," I repeated. "There's only a one-room police station at Bishop's Lacey, so I don't expect he's been taken there. The County Constabulary is at Hinley. So they've likely taken him to Hinley."

"They'll charge him with murder," Ophelia said, "and then he'll be hanged!" She burst into tears again and turned away. For a moment I almost felt sorry for her.

I CAME OUT OF THE DRAWING ROOM and into the hallway and saw Dogger halfway up the west staircase, plodding slowly, step by step, like a condemned man ascending the steps of the scaffold.

Now was my chance!

I waited until he was out of sight at the top of the stairs, then slipped into Father's study and quietly locked the door behind me. It was the first time in my life I had ever been alone in the room.

One full wall was given over to Father's stamp albums, fat leather volumes whose colors indicated the reign of each monarch: black for Queen Victoria, red for Edward the Seventh, green for George the Fifth, and blue for our present monarch, George the Sixth. I remembered that a slim scarlet volume tucked between the green book and the blue contained only a few items—one each of the nine known variations of the four stamps issued bearing the head of Edward the Eighth before he decamped with that American woman.

I knew that Father derived endless pleasure from the countless and minute variations in his bits of confetti, but I did not know the details. Only when he became excited enough over some new tidbit of trivia in the latest issue of *The London Philatelist* to rhapsodize aloud at breakfast would we learn a little more about his happy, insulated world. Apart from those rare occasions, we were all of us, my sisters and me, babes in the wood when it came to postage stamps, while Father puttered on, mounting bits of colored paper with more fearsome relish than some men mount the heads of stags and tigers.

On the wall opposite the books stood a Jacobean sideboard whose top surface and drawers overflowed with what seemed to be no end of philatelic supplies: stamp hinges, perforation gauges, enameled trays for soaking, bottles of fluid for revealing watermarks, gum erasers, stock envelopes, page reinforcements, stamp tweezers, and a hooded ultraviolet lamp.

At the end of the room, in front of the French doors that opened onto the terrace, was Father's desk: a partner's desk the size of a playing field, which might once have seen service in Scrooge and Marley's counting house. I knew at once that its drawers would be locked—and I was right.

Where, I wondered, would Father hide a stamp in a room full of stamps? There wasn't a doubt in my mind that he *had* hidden it—as I would have done. Father and I shared a passion for privacy, and I realized he would never be so foolish as to put it in an obvious place.

Rather than look on top of things, or inside things, I lay flat on the floor like a mechanic inspecting a motorcar's undercarriage, and slid round the room on my back examining the underside of things. I looked at the bottoms of the desk, the table, the wastepaper basket, and Father's

Windsor chair. I looked under the Turkey carpet and behind the curtains. I looked at the back of the clock and turned over the prints on the wall.

There were far too many books to search, so I tried to think of which of them would be least likely to be looked into. Of course! The Bible!

But a quick riffle through King James produced no more than an old church leaflet and a mourning card for some dead de Luce from the time of the Great Exhibition.

Then suddenly I remembered that Father had plucked the Penny Black from the bill of the dead snipe and put it in his waistcoat pocket. Perhaps he had left it there, meaning to dispose of it later.

Yes, that was it! The stamp wasn't here at all. What an idiot I was to think it would be. The entire study, of course, would be at the very top of the list of too-obvious hiding places. A wave of certainty washed over me and I knew, with what Feely and Daffy incorrectly call "female intuition," that the stamp was somewhere else.

Trying not to make a sound, I turned the key and stepped out into the hall. The Weird Sisters were still going at it in the drawing room, their voices rising and falling between notes of anger and grief. I could have listened at the door, but I chose not to. I had more important things to do.

I went, silent as a shadow, up the west staircase and into the south wing.

As I expected, Father's room was in near-darkness as I stepped inside. I had often glanced up at his windows from the lawn and seen the heavy drapes pulled tightly shut.

From inside, it possessed all the gloom of a museum after hours. The strong scent of Father's colognes and shaving lotions suggested open sarcophagi and canopic jars that had once been packed with ancient spices. The finely curved legs of a Queen Anne washstand seemed almost indecent beside the gloomy Gothic bed in the corner, as if some sour old chamberlain were looking on dyspeptically as his mistress unfurled silk stockings over her long, youthful legs.

Even the room's two clocks suggested times long past. On the chimneypiece, an ormolu monstrosity, its brass pendulum, like the curved blade in "The Pit and the Pendulum," tock-tocking away the time and flashing dully at the end of each swing in the subdued lighting of the room. On the bedside table, an exquisite little Georgian clock stood in silent disagreement: Her hands were at 3:15, his at 3:12.

I walked down the long room to the far end, and stopped.

Harriet's dressing room—which could be entered only through Father's bedroom—was forbidden territory. Father had brought us up to respect the shrine that he had made of it the day he learned of her death. He had done this by making us believe, even if we were not told so outright, that any violation of his rule would result in our being marched off in single file to the end of the garden, where we would be lined up against the brick wall and summarily shot.

The door to Harriet's room was covered with green baize, rather like a billiard table stood on end. I gave it a push and it swung open with an uneasy silence.

The room was awash in light. Through the tall windowpanes on three of its sides poured torrents of sunshine, diffused by endless swags of Italian lace, into a chamber that might have been a stage-setting for a play about the Duke and Duchess of Windsor. The dresser top was laid out with brushes and combs by Fabergé, as if Harriet had just stepped into the adjoining room for a bath. Lalique scent bottles were ringed with colorful bracelets of Bakelite and amber, while a charming little hotplate and a silver kettle stood ready to make her early morning tea. A single yellow rose was wilting in a vase of slender glass.

On an oval tray stood a tiny crystal bottle containing no more than a drop or two of scent. I picked it up, removed the stopper, and waved it languidly under my nose.

The scent was one of small blue flowers, of mountain meadows, and of ice.

A peculiar feeling passed over me—or, rather, through me, as if I were an umbrella remembering what it felt like to pop open in the rain. I looked at the label and saw that it bore a single word: *Miratrix*.

A silver cigarette case with the initials H. de L. lay beside a hand mirror whose back was embossed with the image of Flora, from Botticelli's painting *Primavera*. I had never noticed this before in prints from the original, but Flora looked hugely and happily pregnant. Could this mirror have been a gift from Father to Harriet while she was pregnant with one of us? And if so, which one: Feely? Daffy? Me? I thought it unlikely that it was me: A third girl would hardly have been a gift from the gods—at least so far as Father was concerned.

No, it was probably Ophelia the Firstborn—she who seemed to have arrived on earth with a mirror in her hand . . . perhaps this very one.

A basket chair at one of the windows made a perfect spot for reading and here, within arm's reach, was Harriet's own little library. She had brought the books back from her school days in Canada and summers with an aunt in Boston: *Anne of Green Gables* and *Jane of Lantern Hill* were next-door neighbors to *Penrod* and *Merton of the Movies*, while at the far end of the shelf leaned a dog-eared copy of *The Awful Disclosures of Maria Monk*. I had not read any of them, but from what I knew of Harriet, they were probably all of them books about free spirits and renegades.

Nearby, on a small round table, was a photo album. I lifted the cover and saw that its pages were of black pulpy paper, the captions handwritten below each black-and-white snapshot in chalky ink: Harriet (Age 2) at Morris House; Harriet (Age 15) at Miss Bodycote's Female Academy (1930—Toronto, Canada); Harriet with *Blithe Spirit*, her de Havilland Gypsy Moth (1938); Harriet in Tibet (1939).

The photos showed Harriet growing from a fat cherub with a mop of golden hair, through a tall, skinny, laughing girl (with no perceptible breasts) dressed in hockey gear, to a film star with blond bangs, standing, like Amelia Earhart, with one hand resting negligently on the rim of *Blithe Spirit*'s cockpit. There were no photographs of Father. Nor were there any of us.

In every photograph, Harriet's features were those of a woman whose design has been arrived at by taking those of Feely, Daffy, and me and shaking them in a jar before reassembling them into this grinning, confident, yet endearingly shy adventuress.

As I stared at her face, trying to see through the photographic paper to Harriet's soul, there was a light tapping at the door.

A pause—and then another tapping. And the door began to open.

It was Dogger. He stuck his head slowly into the room. "Colonel de Luce?" he said. "Are you here?"

I froze, hardly daring even to breathe. Dogger didn't move a muscle, but gazed straight ahead in the expectant way of a well-trained servant who knows his place, relying on his ears to tell him if he was intruding.

But what was he playing at? Hadn't he just told me that the police had taken Father away? Why on earth, then, would he expect to find him here in Harriet's dressing room? Was Dogger so addled as that? Or could it be that he was shadowing me?

I parted my lips slightly and breathed in slowly through my mouth so that a wayward nose-whistle wouldn't give me away, at the same time offering up a silent prayer that I wouldn't sneeze.

Dogger stood there for the longest time, like a *tableau vivant*. I had seen etchings in the library of those ancient entertainments in which the actors were plastered with whitewash and powder before arranging themselves in motionless poses, often of a titillating nature, each supposedly representing a scene from the lives of the gods.

After a time, just as I was beginning to realize how a rabbit must feel when it "freezes," Dogger slowly withdrew his head and the door closed without a sound.

Had he seen me? And if he had, was he pretending he hadn't?

I waited, listening, but there wasn't a sound from the room next door. I knew Dogger would not linger for long, and when I judged that time enough had passed, I opened the door and peeked out.

Father's room was as I had left it, the two clocks ticking away, but now, because of my fright, they seemed louder than they had before. Realizing this was an opportunity that would never come again, I began my search using the same method as I had in Father's study, but because his bedroom was as spartan as the campaign tent of Leonidas must have been, it did not take very long.

The only book in the room was a sale catalogue from Stanley Gibbons for a stamp auction to be held in three months' time. I turned it over and flipped eagerly through its pages, but nothing tumbled out.

There were shockingly few clothes in Father's closet: a couple of old tweed jackets with leather patches at their elbows (their pockets empty), two wool sweaters, and some shirts. I dug inside his shoes and an ancient pair of regimental half-Wellingtons but found nothing.

I realized with a twinge that Father's only other clothing was his Sunday suit, which he must still have been wearing when Inspector Hewitt took him away. (I would not allow myself to use the word *arrested*.)

Perhaps he had hidden the pierced Penny Black somewhere else—in the glove box of Harriet's Rolls-Royce, for instance. For all I knew, he might already have destroyed it. Now that I stopped to think about it, that would have made most sense. The stamp itself was damaged, and therefore of no value. Something about it, though, had upset Father, and it seemed logical that as soon as he had gone to his room on Friday, he would have put a match to it at once.

That, of course, would have left its traces: paper ash in the ashtray and a burnt-out match in the wastepaper basket. It was easy enough to check since both of these were right there in front of me—and both were empty.

Perhaps he had flushed away the evidence.

Now I knew that I was clutching at straws.

Give it up, I thought; leave it to the police. Go back to your cozy lab and get on with your life's work.

I thought—but only for a moment, and with a little thrill—what lethal drops could be distilled from the entries at the Spring Flower Show; what a jolly poison could be extracted from the jonquil and what deadly liquors from the daffodil. Even the common churchyard yew, so loved by poets and by courting couples, contained within its seeds and leaves enough taxine to put paid to half the population of England.

But these pleasures would have to wait. My duty was to Father, and it had fallen upon my shoulders to help him, particularly now that he couldn't help himself. I knew that I should go to him, wherever he was, and lay my sword at his feet in the way that a medieval squire vows service to his knight. Even if I couldn't help him, I could still sit beside him, and I realized with a sudden piercing pang that I missed him dreadfully.

I was seized with a sudden idea: How many miles was it to Hinley? Could I reach there before dark? And even if I did, would I be allowed to see him?

My heart began to pound as if someone had slipped me a cup of foxglove tea.

Time to go. I had been here long enough. I glanced at the bedside clock—3:40, it now said. The chimneypiece clock ticked solemnly on, its hands at 3:37.

Father must have been too distraught to notice, I supposed, since generally, when it came to the time of day, he was a martinet. I remembered his way of giving orders to Dogger (although not to us) in military fashion:

"Take the gladioli along to the Vicar at thirteen hundred hours, Dogger," he'd say. "He'll be expecting you. Be back by thirteen forty-five and we'll decide what to do with the duckweed."

I stared at the two clocks, hoping that something would come to me. Father had told us once, in one of his rare expansive moods, that what made him fall in love with Harriet was her ability to cogitate. "Remarkable thing in a woman, really, when you come to think of it," he had said.

And suddenly I saw. One of his clocks had been stopped—stopped for precisely three minutes. The clock on the chimneypiece.

I moved slowly towards it, as one would stalk a bird. Its dark funereal case gave it the look of a Victorian horse-drawn hearse: all knobs and glass and black shellac.

I saw my hand reaching out, small and white in the shadowed room; felt my fingers touch its cold face; felt my thumb pop open the silver catch. Now the brass pendulum was right at my fingertips, swinging to and fro, to and fro with its ghastly tock-tocking. I was almost afraid to touch the thing. I took a deep breath and grabbed the pulsing pendulum. Its inertia made it squirm heavily in my hand for a moment, like a goldfish suddenly seized; like the tell-tale heart before it fell still.

I felt round the back of the weighted brass. Something was fastened there; something taped behind it: a tiny packet. I pulled at it with my fingers, felt it come free and drop into my hand. Even as I withdrew my fingers from the clock's internal organs I guessed what I was about to see... and I was right. There in my palm lay a little glassine envelope inside which, clearly visible, was a Penny Black postage stamp. A Penny Black with a hole in its center, such as might have been produced by the bill of a dead jack snipe. What was there about it that had frightened Father so?

I fished the stamp out for a better look. In the first place, there was Queen Victoria with a hole in her head. Unpatriotic, perhaps, but hardly enough to shake a grown man to his roots. No, there must be more.

What was it that set this stamp apart from any other of its kind? After all, hadn't the things been printed by the tens of millions, and all of them alike? Or were they?

I thought of the time that Father—in the interests of broadening our outlook—had suddenly announced that Wednesday evenings would henceforth be given over to a series of compulsory lectures (delivered by him) on various aspects of British Government. "Series A," as he called it, was to be, predictably enough, on the topic "The History of the Penny Post."

Daffy, Feely, and I had all brought notebooks to the drawing room and pretended to take notes while passing scraps of paper back and forth with scribbled messages to one another such as "Stamp Out Lectures" and "Let's Lick Boredom!"

Postage stamps, Father had explained, were printed in sheets of two hundred and forty; twenty horizontal rows of twelve, which was easy enough for me to remember since 20 is the atomic number for Calcium and 12 the number for Magnesium—all I had to do was think of CaMg. Each stamp on the sheet carried a unique two-letter identifier beginning with "AA" on the upper left stamp and progressing alphabetically from left to right until "TL" was reached at the right end of the twentieth, or bottom, row.

This scheme, Father told us, had been implemented by the Post Office to prevent forgeries, although it was not perfectly clear how this was to work. There had been rampant paranoia, he said, that dens of forgers would be toiling away day and night, from Land's End to John o'Groats, producing copies to bilk Her Victorian Majesty out of a penny per time.

I looked closely at the stamp in my hand. At the bottom, below Queen Victoria's head, was written its value: ONE PENNY. To the left of these words was the letter B, to their right, the letter H.

It looked like this: **B   ONE PENNY.   H**

"BH." The stamp had come from the second row on the printed sheet, eighth column to the right. Two-eight. Was that significant? Aside from the fact that 28 was the atomic number for Nickel, I could think of nothing.

And then I saw it! It wasn't a number at all: It was a word!

Bonepenny! Not just Bonepenny, but Bonepenny, H.! Horace Bonepenny!

Impaled on the jack snipe's bill (Yes! Father's schoolboy nickname had been "Jacko"!), the stamp had served as calling card and death threat. A threat that Father had taken in and understood at first glance.

The bird's bill had pierced the Queen's head, but left the name of its sender in clear view for anyone who had the eyes to see.

Horace Bonepenny. The *late* Horace Bonepenny.

I returned the stamp to its hiding place.

AT THE TOP OF THE HILL, a rotted wooden post—all that remained of an eighteenth-century gibbet—pointed two fingers in opposing directions. I could reach Hinley, I knew, by either taking the road to Doddingsley, or by following a somewhat longer, less traveled road that would take me through the village of St. Elfrieda's. The former would get me there more quickly; the latter, being more sparsely traveled, would offer less risk of being spotted in case someone reported me missing.

"Har-har-har!" I said, with vast irony. Who could care enough?

Still, I took the road to the right and pointed Gladys towards St. Elfrieda's. It was downhill all the way, and I made good speed. When I backpedaled, the Sturmey-Archer three-speed hub on Gladys's rear wheel gave off a noise like a den of enraged, venom-dripping rattlesnakes. I pretended they were right there behind me, striking at my heels. It was glorious! I hadn't felt in such fine form since the day I first produced, by successive extraction and evaporation, a synthetic curare from the bog arum in the Vicar's lily pond.

I put my feet up on the handlebars and gave Gladys her head. As we shot down the dusty hill, I yodeled a song into the wind:

> " 'They call her the lass
> With the delicate air! . . .' "

thirteen

AT THE BOTTOM OF OAKSHOTT HILL I SUDDENLY
thought of Father and sadness came creeping back. Did
they honestly believe he had murdered Horace Bonepenny?
And if so, how? If Father had murdered him beneath my
bedroom window, the deed had been done in utter silence.
I could hardly imagine Father killing someone without
raising his voice.

But before I could speculate further, the road leveled
out before twisting off to Cottesmore and to Doddingsley
Magna. In the shade of an ancient oak was a bus stop
bench, upon which sat a familiar figure: an ancient gnome
in plus fours, looking like a George Bernard Shaw who
had shrunk in the wash. He sat there so placidly, his
feet dangling four inches above the ground, that he
might have been born on the bench and lived there all
his life.

It was Maximilian Brock, one of our Buckshaw neighbors, and I prayed he hadn't seen me. It was whispered in Bishop's Lacey that Max, retired from the world of music, was now earning a secret living by writing—under feminine pseudonyms (such as Lala Dupree)—scandalous stories for American magazines with titles like *Confidential Confessions* and *Red Hot Romances*.

Because of the way he pried into the affairs of everyone he met, then spun what he was told in confidence into news-seller's gold, Max was called, at least behind his back, "The Village Pump." But as Feely's onetime piano teacher, he was someone whom I could not politely ignore.

I pulled off into the shallow ditch, pretending I hadn't seen him as I fiddled with Gladys's chain. With any luck, he'd keep looking the other way and I could hide out behind the hedge until he was gone.

"Flavia! *Haroo, mon vieux.*"

Curses! I'd been spotted. To ignore a "haroo" from Maximilian—even one from a bus stop bench—was to ignore the eleventh commandment. I pretended I had just noticed him, and laid on a bogus grin as I wheeled Gladys towards him through the weeds.

Maximilian had lived for many years in the Channel Islands, where he had been pianist with the Alderney Symphony, a position—he said—which required a great deal of patience and a good supply of detective novels.

On Alderney, it was only necessary (or so he had told me once while chatting about crime, at St. Tancred's annual Flower Show), in order to bring down the full power of the law, to stand in the middle of the town square and cry "*Haroo, haroo, mon prince. On me fait tort!*" This was called the "hue and cry," and meant, in essence, "Attention, my Prince, someone is torting me!" Or, in other words, committing a crime against me.

"And how are you, my little pelican?" Max asked, canting his head like a magpie awaiting a crumb of response even before it was offered.

"I'm all right," I said warily, remembering that Daffy had once told me that Max was like one of those spiders that paralyzed you with a bite, and didn't quit until he had sucked the last drop of juice from your life—and from the life of your family.

"And your father, the good Colonel?"

"He's keeping busy, what with one thing and another," I said. I felt my heart give a flip-flop in my breast.

"That Miss Ophelia, now," he asked. "Is she still painting her face like Jezebel and admiring herself in the tea service?"

This was too close to home, even for me. It was none of his business, but I knew that Maximilian could fly into a towering rage at the drop of a hat. Feely sometimes referred to him behind his back as "Rumpelstiltskin," and Daffy as "Alexander Pope—or lower."

Still, I had found Maximilian, in spite of his repellent habits, and perhaps because of our similarity in stature, occasionally to be an interesting and informative conversationalist—just so long as you didn't mistake his diminutive size for weakness.

"She's very well, thank you," I said. "Her complexion was quite lovely this morning."

I did not add "maddeningly."

"Max," I asked, before he could wedge in another question, "do you think I could ever learn to play that little toccata by Paradisi?"

"No," he said, without an instant's hesitation. "Your hands are not the hands of a great artist. They are the hands of a poisoner."

I grinned. This was our little joke. And it was obvious that he had not yet learned of the murder at Buckshaw.

"And the other one?" he asked. "Daphne . . . the slow sister?"

"Slow" was a reference to Daffy's prowess, or lack of it, at the piano: an endless, painful quest to place unwilling fingers upon keys that seemed to shy away from her touch. Daffy's battle with the instrument was one of the hen pitted against the fox, a losing battle that always ended in tears. And yet, because Father insisted upon it, the war went on.

One day when I found her sobbing on the bench with her head on the closed piano lid, I had whispered, "Give it up, Daff," and she had flown at me like a fighting cock.

I had even tried encouragement. Whenever I heard her at the Broadwood, I would drift into the drawing room, lean against the piano, and gaze off into the distance as if her playing had enchanted me. Usually she ignored me, but once when I said, "What a lovely piece that is! What's it called?" she had almost slammed the lid on my fingers.

"The scale of G major!" she had shrieked, and fled the room.

Buckshaw was not an easy place in which to live.

"She's well," I said. "Reading Dickens like billy-ho. Can't get a word out of her."

"Ah," Maximilian said. "Dear old Dickens."

He didn't seem to be able to think of anything further on that topic, and I dived into the momentary silence.

"Max," I said. "You're a man of the world—"

At this he preened himself, and puffed up to whatever little height he could muster.

"Not just a man of the world—a boulevardier," he said.

"Exactly," I said, wondering what the word meant. "Have you ever visited Stavanger?" It would save me looking it up in the atlas.

"What? Stavanger in Norway?"

"SNAP!" I almost shouted aloud. Horace Bonepenny had been in Norway! I took a deep breath to recover myself, hoping it would be mistaken for impatience.

"Of course in Norway," I said condescendingly. "Are there other Stavangers?"

For a moment I thought he was onto me. His eyes narrowed and I felt a chill as the thunderclouds of a Maximilian tantrum blew across the sun. But then he gave a tiny giggle, like springwater gurgling into a glass.

"Stavanger is the first stepping-stone on the Road to Hell...which is a railway station," he said. "I traveled over it to Trondheim, and then on to Hell, which, believe it or not, is a very small village in Norway, from which tourists often dispatch picture postcards to their friends with the message, 'Wish you were here!' and where I performed Grieg's Piano Concerto in A Minor. Grieg, incidentally, was as much a Scot as a Norwegian. Grandfather from Aberdeen, left in disgust after Culloden—must have had second thoughts, though, when he realized he'd done no more than trade the firths for the fjords.

"Trondheim was a great success, I must say...critics kind, public polite. But those people, they never understand their own music, you know. Played Scarlatti as well, to bring a glimpse of Italian sunshine to those snowy northern climes. Still, at the intermission I happened to hear a commercial traveler from Dublin whispering to a friend, 'It's all Grieg to me, Thor.'"

I smiled dutifully, although I had heard this ancient jest about forty-five times before.

"That was in the old days, of course, before the war. Stavanger! Yes, of course I've been there. But why do you ask?"

"How did you get there? By ship?"

Horace Bonepenny had been alive in Stavanger and now he was dead in England and I wanted to know where he had been in between.

"Of course by ship. You're not thinking of running away from home, are you, Flavia?"

"We were having a discussion—actually a row—about it last night at supper."

This was one of the ways to optimize a lie: shovel on the old frankness.

"Ophelia thought one would embark from London; Father insisted it was Hull; Daphne voted for Scarborough, but only because Anne Brontë is buried there."

"Newcastle-upon-Tyne," Maximilian said. "Actually, it's Newcastle-upon-Tyne."

There was a rumble in the distance as the Cottesmore bus approached, waddling along the lane between the hedgerows like a chicken walking a tightrope. It stopped in front of the bench, wheezing heavily as it subsided from the effort of its hard life among the hills. The door swung open with an iron groan.

"Ernie, *mon vieux*," Maximilian said. "How fares the transportation industry?"

"Board," Ernie said, looking straight ahead through the windscreen. If he caught the joke he chose to ignore it.

"No ride today, Ernie. Just using your bench to rest my kidneys."

"Benches are for the sole use of travelers awaiting a coach. It's in the rule book, Max. You know that as well as I do."

"Indeed I do, Ernie. Thank you for reminding me."

Max slid off the bench and dropped to the ground.

"Cheerio, then," he said, and tipping his hat, he set off along the road like Charlie Chaplin.

The door of the bus squealed shut as Ernie engaged the juddering gears and the coach whined into reluctant forward motion. And so we all went our separate ways: Ernie and his bus to Cottesmore, Max to his cottage, Gladys and I resuming our ride to Hinley.

THE POLICE STATION IN HINLEY was housed in a building that had once been a coaching inn. Uncomfortably hemmed in between a small park and a cinema, its half-timbered front jutted beetle-brow out over the street, the blue lamp suspended from its overhang. A cinder-block addition, painted a nondescript brown, adhered to the side of the building like cow muck to a passing railway carriage. This, I suspected, was where the cells were located.

Leaving Gladys to graze in a bicycle stand that was more than half full of official-looking black Raleighs, I went up the worn steps and in the front door.

A uniformed sergeant sat at a desk shuffling bits of paper and scratching his sparse hair with the sharpened end of a pencil. I smiled and walked on past.

" 'Old on, 'old on," he rumbled. "Where do you think you're goin', miss?" he asked.

It seems to be a trait of policemen to speak in questions. I smiled as if I hadn't understood and moved towards an open door, beyond which I could see a dark passageway. More quickly than I would have believed, the sergeant was on his feet and had seized me by the arm. I was nabbed. There was nothing else to do but burst into tears.

I hated to do it, but it was the only tool I had with me.

TEN MINUTES LATER, we were sipping cocoa in the station tearoom, P. C. Glossop and I. He had told me that he had a girl just like me at home (which, somehow, I doubted), name of Elizabeth.

"She's a great 'elp to her poor mother, our Lizzie is," he said, "seeing as 'ow Missus Glossop, the wife, that is, 'ad a fall from a ladder in the happle horchard and broke 'er leg two weeks ago come Saturday."

My first thought was that he had read too many issues of *The Beano* or *The Dandy*; that he was laying it on a bit thick for entertainment purposes. But the earnest look on his face and the furrowed brow quickly told me otherwise: This was the real Constable Glossop and I would have to deal with him on his own terms.

Accordingly, I began to sob again and told him I had no mother and that she had died in far-off Tibet in a mountaineering accident and that I missed her dreadfully.

" 'Ere, 'ere, miss," he said. "Cryin's not allowed in these 'ere premises. Takes away from the natural dignity of the surroundin's, so to speak. You'd best dry up now 'fore I 'ave to toss you in the clink."

I managed a pale smile, which he returned with interest.

Several detectives had slipped in for tea and a bun during my performance, each one of them giving me a silent thumbs-up smile. At least they hadn't asked any questions.

"May I see my father, please?" I asked. "His name is Colonel de Luce, and I believe you're holding him here."

Constable Glossop's face went suddenly blank and I saw that I had played my hand too quickly; that I was now up against officialdom.

"Wait 'ere," he said, and stepped out into a narrow passageway at the end of which there appeared to be a wall of black steel bars.

As soon as he was gone I had a quick look at my surroundings. I was in a dismal little room with sticks of furniture so shabby that they might have been bought directly off the tailgate of a peddler's cart, their legs chipped and dented as if they had suffered a century of kicks in the shin from government regulation boots.

In a vain attempt to cheer things up, a tiny wooden cupboard had been painted apple green, but the sink was a rust-stained relic that might have been on loan from Wormwood Scrubs. Cracked cups and crazed saucers stood sadly cheek by jowl on a draining board, and I noticed for the first time that the mullions of the window were, in fact, iron bars only halfheartedly disguised. The whole place had an odd, sharp odor that I had noticed when I first came in: It smelled as if a jar of gentleman's relish, forgotten years ago at the back of a drawer, had gone off.

Snatches of a song from *The Pirates of Penzance* flashed into my mind. "A policeman's lot is not a happy one," the

D'Oyly Carte Opera Company had sung on the wireless and, as usual, Gilbert and Sullivan were right.

Suddenly I found myself thinking about leaving. This whole mission was foolhardy, no more than an impulse to save Father; something thrown up from the prehistoric part of my brain. Just get up and walk to the door, I said to myself. No one will even notice you've gone.

I listened for a moment, cocking my head like Maximilian to turn up my already acute hearing. Somewhere in the distance bass voices buzzed like bees in a far-off hive.

I slid my feet slowly one in front of the other, like some sensuous señorita doing the tango, and stopped abruptly at the door. From where I stood, I could see only one corner of the sergeant's desk outside in the hall-way and, mercifully, there was no official elbow resting upon it.

I ventured a peep. The corridor was empty, and I tan-goed unhindered all the way to the door and stepped out-side into the daylight.

Even though I was not a prisoner, my sense of escape was immense.

I strolled casually over to the bicycle stand. Ten sec-onds more and I'd be on my way. And then, as if someone had thrown a pail of ice water into my face, I froze in shock: Gladys was gone! I almost screamed it aloud.

There rested all the official bicycles with their officious little lamps and government-issue carriers—but Gladys was gone!

I looked this way and that, and somehow, frighten-ingly, the streets seemed suddenly different now that I was on foot. Which way was home? Which way to the open road?

As if I hadn't problems enough, there was a storm coming. Black clouds were boiling in the western sky, while those scudding directly overhead were already unpleasantly purple and bruised.

Fear filled me, and then anger. How could I have been so stupid as to leave Gladys unlocked in a strange place? How would I get home? What was to become of poor Flavia?

Feely had once told me never to look vulnerable in unfamiliar surroundings, but how, I found myself wondering, does one actually go about doing that?

That was what I was thinking about when a heavy hand fell onto my shoulder and a voice said, "I think you'd better come with me."

It was Inspector Hewitt.

"THAT WOULD BE HIGHLY IRREGULAR," the Inspector said. "Most improper."

We were sitting in his office: a long narrow room that had been the saloon bar of this onetime coaching inn. It was impressively neat, a room that needed only a potted aspidistra and a piano.

A file cabinet and a desk of quite-ordinary design; a chair, a telephone, and a small bookshelf, atop which was a framed photograph of a woman in a camel-hair coat perching on the rail of a quaint stone bridge. Somehow I had expected more.

"Your father is being detained here until we are in receipt of certain information. At that time he will likely be taken elsewhere, a place which I'm not at liberty to disclose. I'm sorry, Flavia, but seeing him is out of the question."

"Is he under arrest?" I asked.

"I'm afraid so," he answered.

"But why?" This was a bad question, and I knew it as soon as it was out of my mouth. He was looking at me as if I were a child.

"Look, Flavia," he said, "I know you're upset. That's understandable. You didn't have a chance to see your father before . . . well, you were away from Buckshaw when we brought him here. These things are always very difficult for a police officer, you know, but you must understand that there are sometimes things which I would very much like to do as a friend, but which, as a representative of His Majesty, I am forbidden to do."

"I know," I said. "King George the Sixth is not a frivolous man."

Inspector Hewitt looked at me sadly. He got up from his desk and went to the window where he stood looking out at the gathering clouds, his hands clasped behind his back.

"No," he said at last, "King George is not a frivolous man."

Then suddenly, I had an idea. Like the proverbial bolt of lightning, everything fell into place as smoothly as one of those backwards cinema films in which the pieces of a jigsaw puzzle jump each into its proper place, completing itself before your very eyes.

"May I be frank with you, Inspector?" I asked.

"Of course," he said. "Please do."

"The body at Buckshaw was that of a man who arrived in Bishop's Lacey on Friday after a journey from Stavanger, in Norway. You must release Father at once, Inspector, because, you see, he didn't do it."

Although he was a little taken aback, the Inspector recovered quickly and gave me an indulgent smile.

"He didn't?"

"No," I said. "I did. I killed Horace Bonepenny."

fourteen

IT WAS ABSOLUTELY PERFECT. THERE WAS NO ONE who could prove otherwise.

I had been awakened in the night, I would claim, by a peculiar sound outside the house. I had gone downstairs and then into the garden, where I had been put upon by a prowler: a burglar, perhaps, bent on stealing Father's stamps. After a brief struggle I had overpowered him.

Hold on, Flave, that last bit seemed a little far-fetched: Horace Bonepenny was more than six feet tall and could have strangled me between his thumb and forefinger. No, we had struggled and he had died—a dicky heart perhaps, the result of some long-forgotten childhood illness. Rheumatic fever, let's say. Yes, that was it. Delayed congestive heart failure, like Beth in *Little Women*. I sent up a silent prayer to Saint Tancred to work a miracle: Please, dear Saint Tancred, let Bonepenny's autopsy confirm my fib.

"*I* killed Horace Bonepenny," I repeated, as if saying it twice would make it seem more credible.

Inspector Hewitt drew in a deep breath and let it out through his nose. "Tell me about it," he said.

"I heard a noise in the night, I went out into the garden, someone jumped out at me from the shadows—"

"Hold on," he said, "what part of the shadows?"

"The shadows behind the potting shed. I was struggling to get free when there was a sudden gurgle in his throat, almost as if he had suffered congestive heart failure due to a bout of rheumatic fever he suffered as a child—or something like that."

"I see," Inspector Hewitt said. "And what did you do then?"

"I went back into the house and fetched Dogger. The rest, I believe, you know."

But wait—I knew that Dogger had not told him about our joint eavesdropping on Father's quarrel with Horace Bonepenny; still, it was unlikely that Dogger would tell the Inspector I had awakened him at four in the morning without mentioning the fact that I had killed the man. Or was it?

I needed time to think this through.

"Struggling with an attacker is hardly murder," the Inspector said.

"No," I said, "but I haven't told you everything."

I riffled at lightning speed through my mental index cards: poisons unknown to science (too slow); fatal hypnotism (ditto); the secret and forbidden blows of jujitsu (unlikely; too obscure to explain). Suddenly, it began to dawn on me that martyrdom required real inventive genius—a glib tongue was not enough.

"I'm ashamed to," I added.

When in doubt, I thought, fall back on feelings. I was proud of myself for having thought of this.

"Hmm," the Inspector said. "Let's leave it for now. Did you tell Dogger you had killed this prowler?"

"No, I don't believe I did. I was too upset by it all, you see."

"Did you tell him later?"

"No, I didn't think his nerves were up to it."

"Well, this is all very interesting," Inspector Hewitt said, "but the details seem a bit sparse."

I knew that I was standing at the edge of a precipice: one step more and there would be no turning back.

"There's more," I said, "but—"

"But?"

"I'm not saying another word until you let me speak to Father."

Inspector Hewitt seemed to be trying to swallow something that wouldn't go down. He opened his mouth as if some obstruction had suddenly materialized in his throat, then closed it again. He gulped, and then did something that I had to admire, something I made a mental note to add to my own bag of tricks: He grabbed for his pocket handkerchief and transformed his astonishment into a sneeze.

"Privately," I added.

The Inspector blew his nose loudly and went back to the window, where he stood gazing out at nothing in particular, his hands again behind his back. I was beginning to learn that this meant he was thinking deeply.

"All right," he said abruptly. "Come along."

I jumped up eagerly from my chair and followed him. At the door he barred the way into the corridor with one arm and turned, his other hand floating down as gently as a feather onto my shoulder.

"I'm about to do something which I may have grave cause to regret," he said. "I'm risking my career. Don't let me down, Flavia . . . please don't let me down."

"FLAVIA!" Father said. I could tell he was amazed to see me there. And then he spoiled it by adding, "Take this child away, Inspector. I beg of you, remove her."

He turned away from me and faced towards the wall.

Although the door of the room had been painted over with yellowish cream enamel, it was obvious that it was clad with steel. When the Inspector had unlocked it, I had seen that the chamber itself was little more than a small office with a fold-down cot and a surprisingly clean sink. Mercifully they had not put Father into one of the barred cages I'd glimpsed earlier.

Inspector Hewitt gave me a curt nod, as if to say, "It's up to you," then stepped outside and closed the door as quietly as possible. There was no sound of a key turning in the lock, or of a bolt shooting home, although a bright flash outside and the sudden crash of thunder might well have masked the sound.

Father must have thought that I'd gone out with the Inspector, because he gave a nervous start as he turned round and saw that I was still there.

"Go home, Flavia," he said.

Although he stood stiffly and perfectly erect, his voice was old and tired. I could see that he was trying to play the stolid English gentleman, fearless in the face of danger, and I realized with a pang that I loved him and hated him for it at the same time.

"It's raining," I said, pointing to the window. The clouds had torn themselves apart as they had done earlier at the Folly, and the rain was falling heavily once again, the fat drops clearly audible as they bounced like shot from the ledge outside the window. In a tree across the road, a solitary rook shook itself out like a wet umbrella.

"I can't go home until it stops. And someone's pinched Gladys."

"Gladys?" he said, his eyes like those of an extinct sea creature swimming up from unknown depths.

"My bicycle," I told him.

He nodded absently, and I knew he hadn't heard me.

"Who brought you here?" Father asked. "Him?" He jerked his thumb towards the door to indicate Inspector Hewitt.

"I came by myself."

"By yourself? From Buckshaw?"

"Yes," I said.

This seemed to be more than he could grasp, and he turned back to the window. I couldn't help noticing that he took up the same stance as Inspector Hewitt, with his hands clasped behind his back.

"By yourself. From Buckshaw," he said at last, as if he had just worked it out.

"Yes."

"And Daphne and Ophelia?"

"They are both well," I assured him. "Missing you terribly, of course, but they're looking after things until you come home."

If I tell a lie, my mother will die.

That was what the little girls sometimes chanted as they skipped rope in the churchyard. Well, my mother was already dead, wasn't she, so what harm could it possibly do? And who knows? Because of it, I might even have a credit in Heaven.

"Come home?" Father said at last, as something like a sigh escaped him. "That might not be for some time. No . . . that might not be for quite some time."

On the wall, beside a barred window, was pasted up a calendar from a Hinley greengrocer, bearing a picture of King George and Queen Elizabeth, each hermetically sealed in his or her own private bubble, and dressed in a way that made me think the photographer had caught them by chance on their way to a costume ball at the castle of some Bavarian princeling.

Father gave the calendar a furtive glance and began pacing restlessly back and forth in the little room, studiously avoiding my gaze. He seemed to have forgotten I was there, and had now begun making irregular little humming noises punctuated with an occasional indignant sniff as if he were defending himself before an invisible tribunal.

"I confessed just now," I said.

"Yes, yes," Father said, and went on pacing and mumbling to himself.

"I told Inspector Hewitt that *I* killed Horace Bonepenny."

Father came to as dead a stop as if he had run onto a sword. He turned and fixed me with that dreaded blue stare which was so often his weapon of choice when dealing with his daughters.

"What do you know about Horace Bonepenny?" he asked in a chill tone.

"Quite a lot, actually," I said.

Then, surprisingly, the fight went out of him all at once, just like that. One moment his cheeks were puffed out like the face of the winds that blow across medieval maps, and the next they were as hollow as a horse trader's. He sat down on the edge of the bunk, spreading out the fingers of one hand to steady himself.

"I overheard your disagreement in the study," I said. "I'm sorry if I eavesdropped. I didn't mean to, but I heard voices in the night and came downstairs. I know that he tried to blackmail you . . . I heard the quarrel. That's why I told Inspector Hewitt that I killed him."

This time it filtered through to Father.

"Killed him?" he asked. "What do you mean, killed him?"

"I didn't want them to know it was you," I said.

"Me?" Father said, rocketing up off the bed. "Good Lord! Whatever makes you think I killed the man?"

"It's all right," I said. "He most likely deserved it. I'll never tell anyone. I promise."

With my right hand I crossed my heart and hoped to die, and Father stared at me as if I were some monstrous wet creature that had just flopped out of a painting by Hieronymus Bosch.

"Flavia," he said. "Please understand this: Much as I should have liked to, I did not kill Horace Bonepenny."

"You didn't?"

I could scarcely believe it. I had already come to the conclusion that Father must have committed murder, and I could see that it was going to be hard cheese admitting I was wrong.

Still, I remembered that Feely had once told me that confession was good for the soul—this while she had my arm bent behind my back trying to force me to tell her what I had done with her diary.

"I overheard what you said about killing your house-master, Mr. Twining. I went to the library and looked it up in the newspaper archives. I talked to Miss Mountjoy—she's Mr. Twining's niece. She remembered the names Jacko and Horace Bonepenny from the inquest. I know that he stayed at the Thirteen Drakes and that he brought a dead jack snipe from Norway hidden in a pie."

Father shook his head slowly and sadly from side to side, not in admiration of my detective skills, but like an old bear that has been shot yet refuses to lie down.

"It's true," he said. "But do you really believe your father capable of cold-blooded murder?"

When I thought about it for a moment—actually thought about it—I saw how foolish I had been. Why had I not realized this before? Cold-blooded murder was just one of the many things Father was incapable of.

"Well . . . no," I ventured.

"Flavia, look at me," he said, but when I looked up and into his eyes, I saw, for an unnerving instant, my own eyes staring back at me and I had to look away.

"Horace Bonepenny was not particularly a decent man, but he did not deserve to die. No one deserves to die," Father said, his voice fading out like a distant broadcast on the shortwave, and I knew that he was no longer speaking only to me.

"There is already so much death in the world," he added.

He sat, looking at his hands, each thumb stroking

the other, his fingers engaging like the cogs of an old clock.

After a time he said, "What about Dogger?"

"He was there too," I admitted. "Outside your study..."

Father gave a groan.

"That is what I feared," he whispered. "That is what I feared more than anything."

And then, as the rain swept in sheets across the windowpane, Father began to talk.

fifteen

AT FIRST FATHER'S UNACCUSTOMED WORDS CAME slowly and hesitantly—jerking into reluctant motion like rusty freight cars on the railway. But then, picking up speed, they soon smoothed out into a steady flow.

"My father was not an easy man to like," he said. "He sent me away to boarding school when I was eleven. I seldom saw him again. It's odd, you know: I never knew what interested him until someone at his funeral, one of the pallbearers, chanced to remark that his passion had been netsuke. I had to look it up in the dictionary."

"It's a small Japanese carving in ivory," I said. "It's in one of Austin Freeman's Dr. Thorndyke stories."

Father ignored me and went on. "Although Greyminster was no more than a few miles from Buckshaw, in those days it might just as well have been on the moon. We were fortunate indeed in our headmaster, Dr. Kissing, a gentle soul who believed no harm could ever come to the boy who was administered daily doses of Latin, rugger, cricket, and history, and on the whole, we were treated well.

"Like most, I was a solitary boy at first, keeping to my books and weeping in the hedgerows whenever I could get away on my own. Surely, I thought, I must be the saddest child in the world; that there must be something innately horrid about me to cause my father to cast me off so heartlessly. I believed that if I could discover what it was, there might be a chance of putting things right, of somehow making it up to him.

"At night in the dorm I would tunnel under the blankets with an electric torch and examine my face in a stolen shaving mirror. I couldn't see anything particularly wrong, but then I was only a child and not really equipped to judge these things.

"But time went on, as time does, and I found myself being swept up into the life of the school. I was good at history but quite hopeless when it came to the books of Euclid, which put me somewhere in the middle ranks: neither so proficient nor so stupid as to draw attention to myself.

"Mediocrity, I discovered, was the great camouflage; the great protective coloring. Those boys who did not fail, yet did not excel, were left alone, free of the demands of the master who might wish to groom them for glory and of the school bully who might make them his scapegoat. That simple fact was the first great discovery of my life.

"It was in the fourth form, I think, that I finally began to take an interest in the things around me and, like all boys of that age, I had an insatiable taste for mystification, so that when Mr. Twining, my housemaster, proposed the founding of a conjuring circle, I found myself suddenly ablaze with new enthusiasm.

"Mr. Twining was more kindly than adept; not a very polished performer, I must admit, but he carried off his tricks with such ebullience, such good-hearted enthusiasm, that it would have been churlish of us to withhold our noisy schoolboy applause.

"He taught us, in the evenings, to turn wine into water using no more than a handkerchief and a bit of colored blotting paper; how to make a marked shilling vanish from a covered drinking glass before being extracted from Simpkins's ear. We learned the importance of 'patter,' the conjurer's line of talk, as it were; and he drilled us in spectacular shuffles which left the ace of hearts always at the bottom of the pack.

"It goes without saying that Mr. Twining was popular; *loved* might be a better word, although few of us at the time had seen enough of that emotion to recognize it for what it was.

"His greatest recognition came when the headmaster, Dr. Kissing, asked him to get up a conjuring show for Parents' Day, a happy scheme into which he threw himself wholeheartedly.

"Because of my prowess with an illusion called 'The Resurrection of Tchang Fu,' Mr. Twining was keen to have me perform it as the grand finale of the show. The stunt required two operators, and for that reason he allowed me to choose any assistant I wanted; that was how I came to know Horace Bonepenny.

"Horace had come to us from St. Cuthbert's after a fuss at that school about some missing money—just a couple of pounds, I believe it was, although at the time it seemed a fortune. I felt sorry for him, I admit. I felt he had been mis-used, particularly when he confided to me that his father was the cruelest of men and had done unspeakable things in the name of discipline. I hope this is not too coarse for your ears, Flavia."

"No, of course not," I said, pulling my chair closer. "Please go on."

"Horace was an extraordinarily tall boy even then, with a shock of flaming red hair. His arms were so long in the school jacket that his wrists stuck out like bare twigs beyond the cuffs. 'Bony,' the boys called him, and they ragged him without mercy about his appearance.

"To make matters worse, his fingers were impossibly long and thin and white, like the tentacles of an albino oc-topus, and he had that pale bleached skin one sometimes sees in redheads. It was whispered that his touch was poi-son. He played this up a bit, of course, snatching with pre-tended clumsiness at the jeering boys who danced round him, always just out of reach.

"One evening after a game of hare and hounds he was resting at a stile, panting like a fox, when a small boy named Potts danced in on tiptoe and delivered him a stinging blow across the face. It was meant to be no more than a touch, like tagging the runner, but it soon turned into something else.

"When they saw that the fearful monster, Bonepenny, was stunned, and his nose bleeding, the other boys began to pile on, and Bony was soon down, being pummeled, kicked, and savagely beaten. It was just then that I hap-pened along.

"'Hold up!' I shouted, as loudly as I could, and to my amazement, the scuffle stopped at once. The boys began extricating themselves, one by one, from the tangle of arms and legs. There must have been something in my voice that made them obey instantly. Perhaps the fact that they had seen me perform mystifying tricks lent me some invisible air of authority, I don't know, but I do know that when I ordered them to get themselves back to Greyminster, they faded like a pack of wolves into the dusk.

" 'Are you all right?' I asked Bony, helping him to his feet.

" 'Faintly tender, but only in one or two widely separated spots—like Carnforth's beef,' he said, and we both laughed. Carnforth was the notorious Hinley butcher whose family had been supplying Greyminster with its boot-leather Sunday roasts of beef since the Napoleonic Wars.

"I could see that Bony was more badly beaten than he was willing to let on, but he put a brave face on it. I gave him my shoulder to lean upon, and helped him hobble back to Greyminster.

"From that day on, Bony was my shadow. He adopted my enthusiasms, and in doing so seemed almost to become a different person. There were times, in fact, when I fancied he was *becoming* me; that here before me was the part of myself for which I had been searching in the midnight mirror.

"What I do know is that we were never in better form than when we were together; what one of us couldn't do, the other could accomplish with ease. Bony seemed to have been born with a fully formed mathematical ability, and he was soon unveiling for me the mysteries of geometry and trigonometry. He made a game of it, and we spent many a happy hour calculating upon whose study the clock tower of Anson House would fall when we toppled it with a gigantic steam lever of our own invention. Another time, we worked out by triangulation an ingenious series of tunnels which, at a given signal, would collapse simultaneously, causing Greyminster and all its inhabitants to plunge into a Dantean abyss, where they would be attacked by the wasps, hornets, bees, and maggots with which we planned to stock the place."

Wasps, hornets, bees, and maggots? Could this be Father speaking? I suddenly found myself listening to him with new respect.

"How this was to be achieved," he went on, "we never really thought through, but the upshot of it all was that while I was getting chummy with old Euclid and his books of propositions, Bony, with a bit of coaching, was turning out to be a natural conjurer.

"It was the fingers, of course. Those long white appendages seemed to have a life of their own, and it wasn't long before Bony had mastered completely the arts of prestidigitation. Various objects appeared and vanished at his fingertips with such fluid grace that even I, who knew perfectly well how each illusion was done, could scarcely believe my eyes.

"And as his conjuring skill grew, so did his sense of self-worth. With a bit of magic in hand, he became a new Bony, confident, smooth, and perhaps even brash. His voice changed too. Where yesterday he had sounded like a raucous schoolboy, he seemed now, suddenly—at least, when he was performing—to possess a voice box of polished mahogany: a hypnotic professional voice which never failed to convince its hearers.

"'The Resurrection of Tchang Fu' worked like this: I decked myself out in an oversized silk kimono I had found at a church jumble sale, a beautiful bloodred thing covered with Chinese dragons and mystical markings. I plastered my face with yellow chalk and stretched a thin elastic round my head to pull my eyes up at the corners. A couple of sausage casings from Carnforth's, varnished and cut into long, curving fingernails, added a disgusting detail. All that was needed to complete my getup was a bit of burnt cork, a few wisps of frayed string for a beard, and a frightful theatrical wig.

"I would call for a volunteer from the audience—a confederate, of course, who had been rehearsed beforehand. I would bring him onstage and explain, in a comic singsong Mandarin voice, that I was about to kill him, to send him off to the Land of the Happy Ancestors. This matter-of-fact announcement never failed to fetch a gasp from the audience, and before they could recover themselves, I would pull a pistol from the folds of my robe, point it at my confederate's heart, and pull the trigger.

"A starter's pistol can make a frightful din when it's fired indoors, and the thing would go off with the most dreadful bang. My assistant would clasp his chest, squeezing in his hand a concealed paper twist of ketchup, which would ooze out horribly between his fingers. Then he would look down at the mess on his chest and gape in disbelief.

"'Help me, Jacko!' he would shriek. 'The trick's gone wrong! I'm shot!' and fall dead flat on his back.

"The audience would, by now, be sitting bolt upright in shock; several would be on their feet, and a few in tears. I would hold up a hand to quiet them.

" 'Sirence!' I would hiss, fixing them with an awful stare. 'Ancestahs lequire sirence.'

"There might be a few titters of nervous laughter, but generally there was a shocked hush. I would fetch a rolled-up sheet from the shadows and drape it over my apparently dead assistant, leaving only his upturned face visible.

"Now this sheet was quite a remarkable object; one which I had manufactured in great secrecy. It was divided lengthwise into thirds by a pair of slender wooden dowels sewn into two narrow pockets that ran the length of the sheet and were, of course, invisible when the thing was rolled up.

"Squatting down and using my robe as cover, I would slip my assistant's shoes from his feet (this was easily done, since he had secretly loosened his laces just before I chose him from the audience) and stick them, toes up, on the end of the dowels.

"The shoes, you see, had been specially prepared by having a hole drilled up through each heel into which a penny nail could be inserted and pushed through to pierce the end of the dowel. The result was most convincing: a gaping corpse lying dead on the floor, its head sticking out at one end of the draped sheet and its upturned shoes at the other.

"If everything went according to plan, great red stains would by now have begun to seep through the sheet above the 'corpse's' chest, and if not, I could always add a bit from a second twist of paper sewn into my sleeve.

"Now came the important part. I would call for the lights to be lowered ('Honabuh ancestahs lequire comprete dahkness!') and in the gloom I would set off a couple of flashes of magnesium paper. This had the effect of blinding the audience for a moment: just enough time for my assistant to arch his back and, as I adjusted the sheet, get his feet firmly on the floor in a squatting position. His shoes, of course, protruding from the bottom of the sheet, made it seem as if he were still lying perfectly horizontal.

"Now I would go into my Oriental mumbo jumbo, waving my hands about, summoning him back from the land of the dead. As I jabbered away in made-up incantations, my assistant would very slowly begin to raise himself from a squat until he was standing upright, supporting the projecting dowels on his shoulders, his shoes sticking out at the far end of the sheet.

"What the audience saw, of course, was a sheet-draped body that rose straight up into the air and hung floating there five feet above the floor.

"Then I would beg the happy ancestors to restore him to the Land of the Living Spirits. This would be done with many mystifying passes of my hands, after which I would set off a final flash of magnesium paper and my assistant would throw off the sheet as he leaped into the air and landed on his feet.

"The sheet, with its nailed-on shoes and its sewn-in dowels, would be thrown aside in the darkness, and we would be left to take our bows amid a storm of thunderous applause. And because he wore black socks, no one ever seemed to notice that the 'dead man' had lost his shoes.

"This was 'The Resurrection of Tchang Fu,' and that was the way I planned to stage it for Parents' Day. Bony and I would sneak off to the washhouse with our gear, where I would drill him in the niceties of the illusion.

"But it soon became apparent that Bony was not the ideal confederate. In spite of his enthusiasm, he was simply too tall. His head and feet stuck out too far beyond my doctored sheet, and it was too late to fabricate a new one. And there was the inescapable fact that while Bony was a marvel with his hands, his body and limbs were still those of an awkward and ungainly schoolboy. His stork-like knees would tremble when he was supposed to be levitating, and at one rehearsal he fell flat on his behind, bringing the whole illusion—sheet, shoes, and all—down with a crash.

"I couldn't think what to do. Bony would be devastated if I chose another assistant, and yet it was too much to hope that he would master his role in the few days remaining before the performance. I was on the verge of despair.

"It was Bony who came up with the solution.

"'Why not swap roles?' he suggested after one particularly embarrassing collapse of our props. 'Let me have a go. I'll put on the old sorcerer's robe and you shall be the floater.'

"I have to admit it was brilliant. With his face a chalky yellow, and his long thin hands projecting from the sleeves of the red kimono (made even more ghastly by three inches of sausage-skin fingernails), Bony made as remarkable a figure as has ever stalked the stage.

"And because he was a natural mimic, he had no trouble in picking up the cracked, piping voice of an ancient Mandarin. His Oriental double-talk was, if anything, better than my own, and those long twiggy fingers waving in the air like stick insects were a sight not soon to be forgotten.

"The performance itself was brilliant. With the entire school and the visiting parents as onlookers, Bony put on a show that none of them will ever forget. He was, by turns, exotic and sinister. When he called me up from the audience as his assistant, even I shivered a little at this menacing figure who was beckoning from beyond the footlights.

"And when he fired the pistol and shot me in the chest, there was pandemonium! I had taken the precaution of warming up and watering down my reservoir of ketchup blood, and the resulting stain was all too horridly real.

"One of the parents—the father of Giddings Minor— had to be physically restrained by Mr. Twining, who had foreseen that some gullible onlooker might rush the stage.

"'Steady on, dear sir,' Twining whispered in Mr. Giddings's ear, 'It's simply an illusion. These boys have done it many a time before.'

"Mr. Giddings was escorted reluctantly back to his seat, his face still burning red. Yet in spite of it, he was man enough to come up after the show and give both our hands a good cranking.

"After such a bath of gore at the death, my levitation at the resurrection was almost a letdown, if I may use the phrase, although it brought round after round of ringing applause from an audience of kind hearts who were relieved to see the hapless volunteer restored to life. At the end, we were made to come back for seven curtain calls, although I knew perfectly well that at least six of them were for my partner.

"Bony soaked up the adulation like a parched sponge. An hour after the show he was still shaking hands and being patted on the back by a tidal wave of admiring mothers and fathers who seemed to want only to touch him, although when I threw my arm across his shoulders, he gave me rather an odd look: a look which suggested, for a fleeting instant, that he had never seen me before.

"In the days that followed, I saw that a transformation had come over him. Bony had become the confident conjurer, and I was now no more than his simple assistant. He began speaking to me in a new way, and adopted a rather offhand manner, as if his earlier timidity had never existed.

"I suppose I could say he dropped me—or that was how it seemed. I often saw him with an older boy, Bob Stanley, who was someone I had never much fancied. Stanley had one of those angular, square-jawed faces that photographs well but seems hard in real life. As he had done with me, Bony seemed to take on some of Stanley's traits, in much the same way a bit of blotting paper absorbs the handwriting from a letter. I know that it was at about this time that Bony began smoking and, I suspect, tippling a bit as well.

"One day, I realized with a bit of a shock that I no longer liked him. Something had changed inside Bony or, perhaps, had crawled out. There were times when I caught him staring at me in the classroom when his eyes would seem to be at first the eyes of an aged Mandarin, and then, as they regarded me, would become cold and reptilian. I began to feel as if, in some unknowable way, something had been stolen from me.

"But there was worse to come."

Father fell silent and I waited for him to go on with his story, but instead he sat gazing out sightlessly into the falling rain. It seemed best to keep quiet and leave him to his thoughts, whatever those might be.

But I knew that, as with Horace Bonepenny, something had changed between us.

Here we were, Father and I, shut up in a plain little room, and for the first time in my life having something that might pass for a conversation. We were talking to one another almost like adults; almost like one human being to another; almost like father and daughter. And even though I couldn't think of anything to say, I felt myself wanting it to go on and on until the last star blinked out.

I wished I could hug him, but I couldn't. For some time now I had been aware that there was something in the de Luce character which discouraged any outward show of affection towards one another; any spoken statement of love. It was something in our blood.

And so we sat, Father and I, primly, like two old women at a parish tea. It was not a perfect way to live one's life, but it would have to do.

sixteen

A FLASH OF LIGHTNING BLEACHED EVERY TRACE OF color from the room, and with it came a deafening crack of thunder. We both of us flinched.

"The storm is directly overhead," Father said.

Nodding to reassure him that we were in it together, I looked about at my surroundings. The brightly lighted little cubicle—its naked bulb overhead, its steel door, and its .cot—the rain pouring down outside, was oddly like the control room of the submarine in *We Dive at Dawn*. I imagined the rolling thunder of the storm to be the sound of depth charges exploding immediately above our heads, and suddenly I was not quite so fearful for Father. We two, at least, were allies. I would pretend that as long as we kept still and I remained silent, nothing on earth could harm us.

Father went on as if there had been no interruption.

"We became rather strangers, Bony and I," he said.

"Although we continued as members of Mr. Twining's Magic Circle, each of us pursued his own particular interests. I developed a passion for the great stage tricks: sawing a lady in half, vanishing a cage of singing canaries, that sort of thing. Of course, most of these effects were beyond my schoolboy budget, but as time went on, it seemed enough simply to read about them and learn how each one was executed.

"Bony, however, progressed to tricks which required an ever-greater degree of manual dexterity: simple effects which could be done under the spectator's nose with a minimal amount of gadgetry. He could make a nickel-plated alarm clock disappear from one hand and appear in the other before your very eyes. He never would show me how it was done.

"It was about that time that Mr. Twining had the idea of organizing a Philatelic Society, another of his great enthusiasms. He felt that in learning to collect, catalogue, and mount postage stamps from round the world, we would learn a great deal about history, geography, and neatness, to say nothing of the fact that regular discussions would promote confidence among the more shy members of the club. And since he was himself a devoted collector, he saw no reason why every one of his boys should be any less enthusiastic.

"His own collection was the eighth wonder of the world, or so it seemed to me. He specialized in British stamps, with particular attention to color variations in the printing inks. He had the uncanny ability of being able to deduce the day—sometimes the very hour—a given specimen was printed. By comparing the ever-changing microscopic cracks and variations produced by wear and stress upon the engraved printing plates, he was able to deduce an astonishing amount of detail.

"The leaves of his albums were masterpieces. The colors! And the way in which they ranged across the page, each one a dab from the palette of a Turner.

"They began, of course, with the black issues of 1840. But soon the black warms to brown, the brown to red, the red to orange, the orange to bright carmine; on to indigo, and Venetian red—a bright blossoming of color, as if to paint the bursting into bloom of the Empire itself. There's glory for you!"

I had never seen Father so alive. He was suddenly a schoolboy again, his face transformed, and shining like a polished apple.

But those words about glory: Hadn't I heard them before? Weren't they the ones spoken to Alice by Humpty Dumpty?

I sat quietly, trying to work out the connections his mind must be making.

"For all that," he went on, "Mr. Twining was not in possession of the most valuable philatelic collection at Greyminster. That honor belonged to Dr. Kissing, whose collection, although not extensive, was choice—perhaps even priceless.

"Dr. Kissing was not, as one might expect of the head of one of our great public schools, a man born either to wealth or to privilege. He was orphaned at birth and brought up by his grandfather, a bell-foundry worker in London's East End which, in those days, was better known for its crushing living conditions than for its charity, and for its crime rather than its educational opportunities.

"When he was forty-eight, the grandfather lost his right arm in a ghastly accident involving molten metal. Now no longer able to work at his trade, there was nothing for it but take to the streets as a beggar; a predicament in which he remained sunk for nearly three years.

"Five years earlier, in 1840, the London firm of Messrs. Perkins, Bacon and Petch had been appointed by the Lords of the Treasury as the sole printers of British postage stamps.

"Business prospered. In the first twelve years alone of their appointment some two billion stamps were printed, most of which eventually found their way into the dust-bins of the world. Even Charles Dickens referred to their prodigious output of Queens' heads.

"Happily it was in the Fleet Street printing plant of this very firm that Dr. Kissing's grandfather found employment at last—as a sweeper. He taught himself to push a broom with one hand better than most men did with two, and because he was a firm believer in deference, punctuality, and reliability, he soon found himself one of the firm's most valued employees. Indeed, Dr. Kissing himself once told me that the senior partner, old Joshua Butters Bacon himself, always called his grandfather 'Ringer' out of respect to his former trade.

"When Dr. Kissing was still a child, his grandfather often brought home stamps that had been rejected and discarded because of irregularities in printing. These 'pretty bits of paper,' as he called them, were often his only playthings. He would spend hours arranging and rearranging the colorful scraps by shade, by variation too subtle for the human eye unaided. His greatest gift, he said, was a magnifying glass, which his grandfather bargained away from a street-seller after pawning his own mother's wedding ring for a shilling.

"Each day, on his way to and from the board school, the boy called upon as many shops and offices as he was able, offering to sweep their pavements clear of rubbish in exchange for the stamped envelopes from their wastepaper baskets.

"In time, those pretty bits of paper became the nucleus of a collection which was to be the envy of Royalty, and even when he had risen to become headmaster of Greyminster, he still possessed the little magnifying glass his grandfather had given him.

"'Simple pleasures are best,' he used to tell us.

"The young Kissing built upon the tenacity with which life had favored him as a boy and went on from scholarship to scholarship, until there came the day when old 'Ringer' was on hand in tears to see his grandson graduate with a double first at Oxford.

"Now, there is a belief among those who should know better, that the rarest of postage stamps are those freaks and mutilations that are inevitably produced as by-products of the printing process, but this is simply not so. No matter what sums such monstrosities might fetch if they are leaked upon the market, to the true collector they are never more than salvage.

"No, the real scarcities are those stamps which have been put into official circulation, legitimately or otherwise, but in very limited numbers. Sometimes a few thousand stamps may be released before a problem is noticed; sometimes a few hundred, as is the case when a single sheet manages to effect its escape from the Treasury.

"But in the entire history of the British Post Office, there has been one occasion—and one occasion only—when a single sheet of stamps was so dramatically different from its millions of fellows. This is how it came about.

"In June of 1840, a crazy potboy named Edward Oxford had fired two pistols at nearly point-blank range at Queen Victoria and Prince Albert as they rode in an open carriage. Mercifully, both shots missed their target, and the Queen, who was then four months pregnant with her first child, was unharmed.

"The attempted assassination was thought by some to be a Chartist plot, while others believed it to be a conspiracy of Orangemen who wished to set the Duke of Cumberland upon the throne of England. There was more truth in the latter than the government believed, or perhaps than they were prepared to admit. Although Oxford would pay for his crime by spending the next twenty-seven years of his life confined to Bedlam—where he seemed more sane than most of the inhabitants and many of the doctors—his handlers would remain at large, invisible in the metropolis. They had other hares to run.

"In the autumn of 1840, an apprentice pressman named Jacob Tingle was employed at the firm of Perkins, Bacon and Petch. Because he was, above all else, a creature of ambition, young Jacob was soon progressing in his trade by leaps and bounds.

"What his employers did not yet know was that Jacob Tingle was the pawn in a deadly serious game, a game to which only his shadowy masters were privy."

If there was anything that surprised me about this tale, it was the way in which Father brought it to life. I could almost reach out and touch the gentlemen in their high starched collars and stovepipe hats; the ladies in their bustled skirts and bonnets. And as the characters in his tale came to life, so did Father.

"Jacob Tingle's mission was a most secret one: He was, by whatever means were at hand, to print one sheet, and one sheet only, of Penny Black stamps, using a bright orange ink which had been provided for his mission. The vial had been handed to him, along with a retaining fee, in an alehouse adjoining St. Paul's Churchyard by a man with a broad-brimmed hat who had sat in the tavern's shadows and spoken in a stony whisper.

"When he had secretly printed this bastard sheet, he was to conceal it in a ream of ordinary Penny Blacks which were awaiting dispatch to the post offices of England. With this accomplished, Jacob's work was done. Fate would see to the rest.

"Sooner or later, somewhere in England, a sheet of orange stamps would surface, and their message would be plain enough to those with eyes to see. 'We are in your midst,' they would declare. 'We move amongst you freely and unseen.'

"The unsuspecting Post Office would have no opportunity to recall the inflammatory stamps. And once they came to light, word of their existence would spread like wildfire. Not even Her Majesty's Government could keep it quiet. The result would be terror at the highest levels.

"You see," Father went on, "although his message came too late, a secret agent had infiltrated the ranks of the conspirators and sent back word that discovery of the orange stamps was to serve as a signal to conspirators everywhere to begin a new wave of personal attacks upon the Royal Family.

"It seemed the perfect scheme. Had it failed, the perpetrators would simply have bided their time and tried again another day. But there was no need to try again; the thing went off like clockwork.

"The day after he met the stranger in St. Paul's Churchyard, there was a spectacular, and suspicious, conflagration in an alley directly behind Perkins, Bacon and Petch. As the printers and clerical staff dashed outside for a better view of the fire, Jacob coolly pulled the vial of orange ink from his pocket, inked the plate with a spare roller he had hidden behind a row of chemical bottles on a shelf, applied a damped sheet of watermarked paper, and printed the sheet. It was almost too easy.

"Before the other workers returned to their posts, Jacob had already tucked the orange sheet among its black sisters, cleaned the plate, hidden the soiled rags, and was setting up for the next run of ordinary stamps when old Joshua Butters Bacon himself strolled by and congratulated the young man on his coolness in the face of danger. He would go far in his chosen trade, the old man told him.

"And then Fate, as Fate so often does, threw a wrench into the works. What the plotters could not foresee was that the man in the broad-brimmed hat would, that very night, be struck down in the rain in Fleet Street by a runaway cart-horse, and that with his dying breath, he would revert to the faith into which he had been born and confess the plot—Jacob Tingle and all—to a rain-caped bobby whom he mistook for a cassocked Catholic priest.

"But by that time, Jacob had done his dirty work, and the sheet of orange stamps was already flying, via the night mail, to some unknown corner of England. I hope you are not finding this too boring, Harriet?"

Harriet? Had Father called me "Harriet"?

It is not unknown for fathers with a brace of daughters to reel off their names in order of birth when summoning the youngest, and I had long ago become accustomed to being called "Ophelia Daphne Flavia, damn it." But Harriet? Never! Was this a slip of the tongue, or did Father actually believe he was telling his tale to Harriet?

I wanted to shake the stuffing out of him; I wanted to hug him; I wanted to die.

I realized that the sound of my voice might break the spell, and I turned my head slowly from side to side as if it were in danger of falling off.

Outside, the wind was tearing at the vines that fringed the window as the wild rain came pelting down.

"The hue and cry was raised," Father went on at last, and I stopped holding my breath.

"Telegraphs were sent to every postmaster in the realm. To whatever corner of England the orange stamps might make their way, they were to be placed at once under lock and key, and the Treasury notified, posthaste, of their whereabouts.

"Because larger shipments of the Penny Blacks had been sent to the cities, it was thought that they would most likely make their appearance in London or Manchester; perhaps Sheffield or Bristol. As it turned out, in fact, it was none of these.

"Tucked away in one of the farthest pockets of Cornwall is the village of St. Mary-in-the-Marsh. It is a place where nothing had ever happened, and nothing was ever expected to.

"The postmaster there was one Melville Brown, an elderly gentleman who was already some years past the usual retirement age, and was trying, with little luck, to put away a bit of his small salary to 'tide him over to the churchyard,' as he told anyone who would listen.

"As it happened—since St. Mary-in-the-Marsh was off the beaten track in more ways than one—Postmaster Brown did not receive the telegraphed directive from the Treasury, and so it was with complete surprise that, some days later, after he had unwrapped a small shipment of Penny Blacks and was counting them to see that the tally was correct, he found the missing stamps literally at his fingertips.

"Of course he spotted the orange stamps at once. Someone had made a dreadful mistake! There had not been, as there normally should have been, an official 'Instructions to Postmasters' pamphlet announcing a new color for the penny stamp. No, this was something of vast import, even though he could not say what it was.

"For a moment—but only a moment, mind you—he thought that this oddly colored sheet of stamps might be worth more than its face value. Less than half a year after their introduction, some people, most likely people up in London, he believed, who had nothing better to do with their time, had already begun collecting self-adhesive postage stamps, and putting them in little books. A stamp printed off-register or with inverted check numbers might even fetch a quid or two, and as for a whole sheet of them, why . . .

"But Melville Brown was one of those human beings who seem to be as scarce as archangels: He was an honest man. Accordingly, he at once sent off a telegraph to the

Treasury, and within the hour a ministerial courier was dispatched from Paddington to retrieve the stamps and convey them back to London.

"The Government intended that the rogue sheet be destroyed at once, with all the official solemnity of a Pontifical Requiem Mass. Joshua Butters Bacon suggested rather that the stamps be placed in the printing house archive, or perhaps in the British Museum, where they could be studied by future generations.

"Queen Victoria, however, who was, as the Americans say, more than a bit of a pack rat, had her own ideas: She asked to be given a single stamp as a memento of the day she was spared an assassin's bullet; the remainder were to be destroyed by the highest-ranking officer of the firm that had printed them.

"And who could deny the Queen? By now, with British troops about to invade Beirut, the Prime Minister, Viscount Melbourne (whose name had been once linked romantically with Her Majesty's), had other things on his mind. And there the matter was allowed to rest.

"So it was that the world's only sheet of orange penny stamps was burned in a cruet on the desk of the managing director of Perkins, Bacon and Petch. But before he lit the match, Joshua Butters Bacon had, with surgical precision, snipped off two specimens—this was some years before perforations were introduced, you see: the stamp marked 'AA' from one corner, for Queen Victoria and, in great secrecy, another marked 'TL,' from the opposite corner, for himself.

"These were the stamps which would one day be known to collectors as the Ulster Avengers, although for many

years before they were given that name, their very existence was a state secret.

"Years later, when Bacon's desk was moved after his
death, an envelope which had somehow become lodged
behind it fell to the floor. As you may have guessed, the
sweeper who found it was Dr. Kissing's grandfather, Ringer.
With old Bacon dead, he thought, what harm could there
be in his taking home as a plaything for his three-year-old
grandson the single bright-orange postage stamp which lay
nestled within it?"

I felt a flush rising to my cheek, and prayed desperately
that Father was too distracted to notice. How, without
making the situation even worse than it was, could I tell
him that both of the Ulster Avengers, one marked "AA"
and the other "TL," were, at that very moment, stuffed
carelessly into the bottom of my pocket?

seventeen

PART OF ME WAS POSITIVELY TWITCHING TO PULL out the blasted stamps and press them into his hand, but Inspector Hewitt had put me on my honor. I could not possibly put into Father's hands anything which might have been stolen; anything which might further incriminate him.

Fortunately Father was oblivious. Even another sudden flash of lightning, followed by a sharp crack and a long roll of thunder, did not pull him back to the present.

"The Ulster Avenger marked TL, of course," he went on, "became the cornerstone of Dr. Kissing's collection. It was a well-known fact that only two such stamps were in existence. The other one—the specimen marked AA—having passed upon the death of Queen Victoria to her son, Edward the Seventh, and upon his death, to his son, George the Fifth, in whose collection it remained until recently—was stolen in broad daylight from a stamp exhibition. It has not been recovered."

"Ha!" I thought. "What about the TL?" I said aloud.

"TL, as we have seen, was tucked safely away in the safe of the headmaster's study at Greyminster. Dr. Kissing brought it out from time to time, 'in part to gloat,' he once told us, 'and in part to remember my humble beginnings in case I should ever show signs of rising above myself.'

"The Ulster Avenger was seldom shown to others, though; perhaps only to a few of the most serious philatelists. It was said that the King himself had once offered to buy the stamp, an offer that was politely but firmly declined. When that failed, the King begged, through his private secretary, special permission to view 'this marmalade phenomenon' as he called it: a request which was speedily granted and which ended with a secret after-dark visit to Greyminster by his late Royal Highness. One wonders, of course, whether he brought AA with him so that the two great stamps might be once more, if only for a few hours, reunited. That, perhaps, will forever remain one of the great mysteries of philately."

I touched my pocket lightly, and my fingertips tingled at the slight rustle of paper.

"Our old housemaster, Mr. Twining, clearly recalled the occasion, and remembered, most poignantly, how the lights in the headmaster's study burned long into that winter night.

"Which brings me back, alas, to Horace Bonepenny."

I could tell by the changed tone of his voice that Father had once more retreated into his personal past. A chill of excitement ran up my spine. I was about to get at the truth.

"Bony had, by this time, become more than an accomplished conjurer. He was now a forward, pushy young man with a brazen manner, who generally got his own way by the simple expedient of shoving harder than the other fellow.

"Besides the allowance he received from his father's solicitors, he was earning a good bit extra by performing in and around Greyminster, first at children's parties and then later, as his confidence grew, at smoking concerts and political dinners. By then he had taken on Bob Stanley as his sole confederate, and one heard tales of some of their more extravagant performances.

"But outside of the classroom I seldom saw him in those days. Having risen above the abilities of the Magic Circle, he dropped out of it, and was heard to make disparaging remarks about those 'amateur noodles' who kept up their membership.

"With its dwindling attendance, Mr. Twining finally announced that he was giving up the halls of illusion, as he called the Magic Circle, to concentrate more fully upon the Stamp Society.

"I remember the night—it was in early autumn, the first meeting of the year—that Bony suddenly showed up, all teeth and laughter and false good-fellowship. I had not seen him since the end of the last term, and he now seemed to me somehow alien and too large for the room.

" 'Ah, Bonepenny,' Mr. Twining said, 'what an unexpected delight. What brings you back to these humble chambers?'

" 'My feet!' Bony shouted, and most of us laughed.

"And then suddenly he dropped the pose. In an instant

he was all schoolboy again, deferential and filled with humility.

" 'I say, sir,' he said, 'I've been thinking all during the hols about what a jolly treat it would be if you could persuade the Head to show us that freakish stamp of his.'

"Mr. Twining's brow darkened. 'That freakish stamp, as you put it, Bonepenny, is one of the crown jewels of British philately, and I should certainly never suggest that it be trotted out for viewing by such a saucy scallywag as yourself.'

" 'But, sir! Think of the future! When we lads are grown ... have families of our own ...'

"At that we grinned at one another and traced patterns in the carpet with our toes.

" 'It will be like that scene in *Henry the Fifth*, sir,' Bony went on. 'Those families back in England home abed will count themselves accursed they were not at Greyminster to have a squint at the great Ulster Avenger! Oh please, sir! Please!'

" 'I shall give you an alpha-plus for boldness, young Bonepenny, and a goose egg for your travesty of Shakespeare. Still ...'

"We could see that Mr. Twining was softening. One corner of his mustache lifted ever so slightly.

" 'Oh please, sir,' we all chimed in.

" 'Well ...' Mr. Twining said.

"And so it was arranged. Mr. Twining spoke to Dr. Kissing, and that worthy, flattered that his boys would take an interest in such an arcane object, readily assented. The viewing was set for the following Sunday evening after Chapel, and would be conducted in the headmaster's private apartments. Invitation was by membership in the

Stamp Society only, and Mrs. Kissing would cap the evening with cocoa and biscuits.

"The room was filled with smoke. Bob Stanley, who had come with Bony, was openly smoking a gasper and nobody seemed to mind. Although the sixth-form boys had privileges, this was the first time I had seen one of them light up in front of the Head. I was the last to arrive, and Mr. Twining had already filled the ashtray with the stubs of the Wills's Gold Flake cigarettes which, outside of the classroom, he smoked incessantly.

"Dr. Kissing was, as are all of the truly great headmasters, no mean showman himself. He chatted away about this and that: the weather, the cricket scores, the Old Boys' Fund, the shocking condition of the tiles on Anson House; keeping us in suspense, you know.

"Only when he had us all twitching like crickets did he say, 'Dear me, I had quite forgotten—you've come to have a look at my famous snippet.'

"By now we were boiling over like a room full of teakettles. Dr. Kissing went to his wall safe and twirled his fingertips in an elaborate dance on the dial of the combination lock.

"With a couple of clicks the thing swung open. He reached in and brought out a cigarette tin—an ordinary Gold Flake cigarette tin! That fetched a bit of a laugh, I can tell you. I couldn't help wondering if he'd had the cheek to pull out the same old container in front of the King.

"There was a bit of a hubbub, and then a hush fell over the room as he opened the lid. There inside, nestled on a bed of absorbent blotting paper, was a tiny envelope: too small, too insignificant, one would say, to hold a treasure of such great magnitude.

"With a flourish Dr. Kissing produced a pair of stamp tweezers from his waistcoat pocket and, removing the stamp as carefully as a sapper extracting a fuse from an unexploded bomb, laid it on the paper.

"We crowded round, pushing and shoving for a better view.

"'Careful, boys,' said Dr. Kissing. 'Remember your manners; gentlemen always.'

"And there it was, that storied stamp, looking just as one always knew it would look, and yet so much more . . . so much more spellbinding. We could hardly believe we were in the same room as the Ulster Avenger.

"Bony was directly behind me, leaning over my shoulder. I could feel his hot breath on my cheek, and thought I caught a whiff of pork pie and claret. Had he been drinking? I wondered.

"And then something happened which I will not forget until my dying day—and perhaps not even then. Bony darted in, snatched up the stamp, and held it high in the air between his thumb and forefinger like a priest elevating the host.

"'Watch this, sir!' he shouted. 'It's a trick!'

"We were all of us too numb to move. Before anyone could bat an eye, Bony had pulled a wooden match from his pocket, flicked it alight with his thumbnail, and held it to the corner of the Ulster Avenger.

"The stamp began blackening, then curled; a little wave of flame passed across its surface, and a moment later, there was nothing left of it but a smudge of black ash in

Bony's palm. Bony lifted up his hands and in an awful voice, chanted:

> 'Ashes to ashes, dust to dust,
>   If the King can't have you, the Devil must!'

"It was appalling. There was a shocked silence. Dr. Kissing stood there with his mouth open, and Mr. Twining, who had brought us there, looked as if he had been shot in the heart.

"'It's a trick, sir,' Bony shouted, with that charnel-house grin of his. 'Now help me get it back, all of you. If we all join hands and pray together—'

"He grabbed my hand with his right, and with his left, he seized Bob Stanley's.

"'Form a circle,' he ordered. 'Join hands and form a prayer circle!'

"'Stop it!' Dr. Kissing commanded. 'Stop this insolence at once. Return the stamp to its box, Bonepenny.'

"'But, sir,' Bony said—and I swear I saw his teeth glint in the light of the flames from the fireplace—'if we don't pull together, the magic can't work. That's how magic is, you see.'

"'Put ... the ... stamp ... back ... in ... the ... box,' Dr. Kissing said, slowly and deliberately, his face like one of those ghastly things one finds in a trench after a battle.

"'All right then, I'll have to go it alone,' Bony said. 'But it's only fair to warn you it's much more difficult this way.'

"Never had I seen him so confident; never had I seen him so full of himself.

"He rolled up his sleeve and held those long white pointed fingers upright in the air as high as he could reach.

> 'Come back, come back, O Orange Queen,
> Come back and tell us where you've been!'

"At this, he snapped his fingers, and suddenly there was a stamp where no stamp had been a moment earlier. An orange stamp.

"Dr. Kissing's grim face relaxed a little. He almost smiled. Mr. Twining's fingers dug deeply into my shoulder blade, and I realized for the first time that he had been hanging on to me for dear life.

"Bony reeled the stamp in for a closer look until it was almost touching the tip of his nose. At the same time he whipped an indecently large magnifying glass from his hip pocket and examined the newly materialized stamp with pursed lips.

"Then suddenly his voice was the voice of Tchang Fu, the ancient Mandarin, and I swear that even though he wore no makeup, I could clearly see the yellow skin, the long fingernails, the red dragon kimono.

"'Uh-oh! Honabuh ancestahs send long stamp!' he said, holding it out to us for our inspection. It was an ordinary Internal Revenue issue from America: a common Civil War vintage stamp which most of us had aplenty in our albums.

"He let it flutter to the floor, then gave a shrug and rolled his eyes heavenward.

> 'Come back, come back, O Orange Queen—'

he began again, but Dr. Kissing had seized him by the shoulders and was shaking him like a tin of paint.

" 'The stamp,' he demanded, holding out his hand. 'At once.'

"Bony turned out his trouser pockets, one after another.

" 'I can't seem to find it, sir,' he said. 'Something seems to have gone wrong.'

"He looked up each of his sleeves, ran a long finger round the inside of his collar, and a sudden transformation came over his face. In an instant he was a frightened schoolboy who looked as if he'd like nothing better than to make a bolt for it.

" 'It's worked before, sir,' he stammered. 'Lots and lots of times.'

"His face was growing red, and I thought he was about to cry.

" 'Search him,' Dr. Kissing snapped, and several of the boys, under the direction of Mr. Twining, took Bony into the lavatory where they turned him upside down and searched him from his red hair to his brown shoes.

" 'It's as the boy says,' Mr. Twining said when they returned at last. 'The stamp seems to have vanished.'

" 'Vanished?' Dr. Kissing said. 'Vanished? How can the bloody thing have *vanished*? Are you quite sure?'

" '*Quite* sure,' Mr. Twining said.

"A search was made of the entire room: The carpet was lifted, tables were moved, ornaments turned upside down, but all to no avail. At last Dr. Kissing crossed the room to the corner where Bony was sitting with his head sunk deeply in his hands.

" 'Explain yourself, Bonepenny,' he demanded.

"'I—I can't, sir. It must have burned up. It was supposed to be switched, you see, but I must have . . . I don't . . . I can't . . .'

"And he burst into tears.

"'Go to bed, boy!' Dr. Kissing shouted. 'Leave this house and go to bed!'

"It was the first time any of us had ever heard him raise his voice above the level of pleasant conversation, and it shook us to the core.

"I glanced over at Bob Stanley and noticed that he was rocking back and forth on his toes, staring at the floor as unconcernedly as if he were waiting for a tram.

"Bony stood up and walked slowly across the room towards me. His eyes were rimmed with red as he reached out and took my hand. He gave it a flaccid shake, but it was a gesture I found myself unable to return.

"'I'm sorry, Jacko,' he said, as if I, and not Bob Stanley, were his confederate.

"I could not look him in the eye. I turned my head away until I knew that he was no longer near me.

"When Bony had slunk from the room, looking back over his shoulder, his face bloodless, Mr. Twining tried to apologize to the headmaster, but that seemed only to make matters worse.

"'Perhaps I should ring up his parents, sir,' he said.

"'Parents? No, Mr. Twining. I think it is not the parents who should be brought in.'

"Mr. Twining stood in the middle of the room wringing his hands. God knows what thoughts were racing through the poor man's mind. I can't even remember my own.

"The next morning was Monday. I was crossing the quad, tacking into the stiff breeze with Simpkins, who was prattling on about the Ulster Avenger. The word had spread like wildfire and everywhere one looked knots of boys stood with their heads together, hands waving excitedly as they swapped the latest—and almost entirely false—rumors.

"When we were about fifty yards from Anson House, someone shouted, 'Look! Up there! On the tower! It's Mr. Twining!'

"I looked up to see the poor soul on the roof of the bell tower. He was clinging to the parapet like a tattered bat, his gown snapping in the wind. A beam of sunlight broke through between the flying clouds like a theatrical spotlight, illuminating him from behind. His whole body seemed to be aglow, and the hair sticking out from beneath his cap resembled a disk of beaten copper in the rising sun like the halo of a saint in an illuminated manuscript.

" 'Careful, sir,' Simpkins shouted. 'The tiles are in shocking shape!'

"Mr. Twining looked down at his feet, as if awakening from a dream, as if bemused to find himself suddenly transported eighty feet into the air. He glanced down at the tiles and for a moment was perfectly still.

"And then he drew himself up to his full stature, holding on only with his fingertips. He raised his right arm in the Roman salute, his gown fluttering about him like the toga of some ancient Caesar on the ramparts.

" '*Vale!*' he shouted. Farewell.

"For a moment, I thought he had stepped back from the parapet. Perhaps he had changed his mind; perhaps the sun behind him dazzled my eyes. But then he was in the air, tumbling. One of the boys later told a newspaper reporter that he looked like an angel falling from Heaven, but he did not. He plummeted straight down to the ground like a stone in a sock. There is no more pleasant way of describing it."

Father paused for a long while, as if words failed him. I held my breath.

"The sound his body made when it hit the cobbles," he said at last, "has haunted my dreams from that day to this. I've seen and heard things in the war, but nothing like this. Nothing like this at all.

"He was a dear man and we murdered him. Horace Bonepenny and I murdered him as surely as if we had flung him from the tower with our own hands."

"No!" I said, reaching out and touching Father's hand. "It was nothing to do with you!"

"Ah, but it was, Flavia."

"No!" I repeated, although I was a little taken aback by my own boldness. Was I actually talking to Father like this? "It was nothing to do with you. Horace Bonepenny destroyed the Ulster Avenger!"

Father smiled a sad smile. "No, he didn't, my dear. You see, when I got back to my study that Sunday night and removed my jacket, I found an oddly sticky spot on my shirt cuff. I knew instantly what it was: While joining hands to form his distracting prayer circle, Bony had pushed his forefinger inside the sleeve of my jacket and stuck the Ulster Avenger to my cuff. But why me? Why not Bob Stanley? For a very good reason: If they had searched us all, the stamp would have been found in my sleeve and Bony'd have cried innocence. No wonder they couldn't find it when they turned him inside out!

"Of course, he retrieved the stamp as he shook my

hand before leaving. Bony was a master of prestidigitation, remember, and because I had once been his accomplice, it stood to reason that I should have been so again. Who would ever have believed otherwise?"

"No!" I said.

"Yes." Father smiled. "And now there's little more to tell.

"Although nothing was ever proved against him, Bony did not return to Greyminster after that term. Someone told me he had gone abroad to escape some later unpleasantness, and I can't say I was surprised. Nor was I surprised to hear, years later, that Bob Stanley, after being ejected from medical school, had ended up in America where he had set up a philatelic shop: one of those mail-order companies that place advertisements in the comic papers and sell packets of stamps on approval to adolescent boys. The whole business, though, seems to have been little more than a front for his more sinister dealings with wealthy collectors.

"As for Bony, I didn't see him again for thirty years. And then, just last month, I went up to London to attend an international exhibition of stamps put on by the Royal Philatelic Society. You might remember the occasion. One of the highlights of the show was the public display of a few choice items from our present Majesty the King's collection, including the rare Ulster Avenger: AA—the twin of Dr. Kissing's stamp.

"I gave it little more than a glance; the memories it brought back were not pleasant ones. There were other exhibits I wished to see, and consequently the King's Ulster Avenger occupied no more than a few seconds of my time.

"Just before the exhibit was to close for the day, I was at

the far side of the exhibition hall examining a mint sheet to which I thought I might treat myself, when I happened to glance across and catch a glimpse of shocking red hair, hair that could belong to only one person.

"It was Bony, of course. He was holding forth for the benefit of a small crowd of collectors who had gathered in front of the King's stamp. Even as I looked on, the debate became more heated, and it seemed that something Bony had said was agitating one of the curators, who shook his head vehemently as their voices rose.

"I didn't think that Bony had seen me—nor did I want him to.

"It was fortuitous that an old army friend, Jumbo Higginson, happened along at that very moment and dragged me off for a late dinner and a drink. Good old Jumbo... it's not the first instance where he's turned up just in the nick of time."

Something came over Father's eyes, and I saw that he had vanished down one of those personal rabbit holes which so often engulfed him. I sometimes wondered if I would ever learn to live with his sudden silences. But then, like a jammed clockwork toy that jerks abruptly back to life when it's flicked with a finger, he went on with his story as if there had been no interruption.

"When I opened the newspaper on the train home that night, and read that the King's Ulster Avenger had been switched for a counterfeit—this apparently done in full view of the general public, several irreproachable philatelists, and a pair of security guards—I knew not only who had carried off the theft, but also, at least in general terms, how the thing had been accomplished.

"Then, last Friday, when the jack snipe turned up dead

on our doorstep, I knew at once that Bony had been there. 'Jack Snipe' was my nickname at Greyminster, 'Jacko' for short. The letters at the corner of the Penny Black spelled out his name. It's very complicated."

"B One Penny H," I said. "Bonepenny, Horace. At Greyminster, he was called Bony and you were Jacko, for short. Yes, I figured that out quite some time ago."

Father looked at me as if I were an asp which he was torn between pressing to his breast and flinging out the window. He rubbed his upper lip with his forefinger several times, as if to form an airtight seal, but then went on.

"Even knowing that he was somewhere nearby did not prepare me for the dreadful shock of seeing that white cadaverous face which appeared suddenly from out of the darkness at the window of my study. It was after midnight. I should have refused to speak with him, of course, but he made certain threats . . .

"He demanded I buy both of the Ulster Avengers from him: the one he had stolen recently and the one he had made to vanish years ago from Dr. Kissing's collection.

"He had it in his head, you see, that I was a wealthy man. 'It's the investment opportunity of a lifetime,' he told me.

"When I replied that I had no money, he threatened to tell the authorities that I had planned the theft of the first Ulster Avenger and commissioned the second. And Bob Stanley would back up his claim. After all, it was I who was the stamp collector, not he.

"And hadn't I been present when both of the stamps were stolen? The devil even hinted that he may have already—*may* have, mind!—planted the Ulster Avengers somewhere in my collections.

"After our quarrel, I was too upset to go to bed. When Bony had gone, I paced up and down in my study for hours, agonizing, going over and over the situation in my mind. I had always felt responsible in part for Mr. Twining's death. It's a terrible thing to admit, but it's true. It was my silence that led directly to that dear old man's suicide. If only I'd had the intestinal fortitude, as a schoolboy, to voice my suspicions, Bonepenny and Stanley should never have gotten away with it and Mr. Twining would not have been driven to take his own life. You see, Flavia, silence is sometimes the most costly of commodities.

"After a very long time and a great deal of thought, I decided—against everything I believe in—to give in to his blackmail. I would sell my collections, everything I owned, to buy his silence, and I must tell you, Flavia, that I am more ashamed of that decision than anything I have ever done in my life. Anything."

I wish I had known the right thing to say, but for once my tongue failed me, and I sat there like a mop, not able, even, to look my father in the face.

"Sometime in the small hours—it must have been four o'clock, perhaps, since it was already becoming light outside—I turned out the lamp, with the full intention of walking into the village, rousing Bonepenny from his room at the inn, and agreeing to his demands.

"But something stopped me. I can't explain it, but it's true. I stepped out onto the terrace, but rather than going round to the front of the house to the drive as I had determined to do, I found myself being drawn like a magnet to the coach house."

So! I thought. It wasn't Father who had gone out through the kitchen door. He had walked from the terrace outside his study, along the outside of the garden wall to the coach house. He had not set foot in the garden. He had not walked past the dying Horace Bonepenny.

"I needed to think," Father went on, "but I couldn't seem to bring my mind into proper focus."

"And you got into Harriet's Rolls," I blurted. Sometimes I could shoot myself.

Father stared at me with the sad kind of look the worm must give the early bird the instant before its beak snaps shut.

"Yes," he said softly. "I was tired. The last thing I remember thinking was that once Bony and Bob Stanley found I was a bankrupt, they'd give up the game for someone more promising. Not that I would ever wish this predicament on another . . .

"And then I must have fallen asleep. I don't know. It doesn't really matter. I was still there when the police found me."

"A bankrupt?" I said, astonished. I couldn't help myself. "But, Father, you have Buckshaw."

Father looked at me, his eyes moist: eyes that I had never before seen looking out of his face.

"Buckshaw belonged to Harriet, you see, and when she died, she died intestate. She didn't leave a will. The death duties—well, the death duties shall most likely consume us."

"But Buckshaw is yours!" I said. "It's been in the family for centuries."

"No," Father said sadly. "It is not mine, not mine at all. You see, Harriet was a de Luce before I married her. She was my third cousin. Buckshaw was hers. I have nothing left to invest in the place, not a sou. I am, as I have said, a virtual bankrupt."

There was a metallic tapping at the door and Inspector Hewitt stepped into the room.

"I'm sorry, Colonel de Luce," he said. "The Chief Constable, as you are undoubtedly aware, is most particular that the very shadow of the law be observed. I've allowed you as much time as I can and still escape with my skin."

Father nodded sadly.

"Come along, Flavia," the Inspector said to me. "I'll take you home."

"I can't go home yet," I said. "Someone's pinched my bicycle. I'd like to file a complaint."

"Your bicycle is in the backseat of my car."

"You've found it already?" I asked. Hallelujah! Gladys was safe and sound!

"It was never missing," he said. "I saw you park it out front and had Constable Glossop put it away for safekeeping."

"So that I couldn't escape?"

Father lifted an eyebrow at this impertinence, but said nothing.

"In part, yes," Inspector Hewitt said, "but largely because it's still raining buckets outside and it's a long old pedal uphill to Buckshaw."

I gave Father a silent hug to which, although he remained rigid as an oak, he did not seem to object.

"Try to be a good girl, Flavia," he said.

Try to be a good girl? Was that all he could think of? It was evident that our submarine had surfaced, its occupants hauled up from the vasty deeps and all the magic left below.

"I'll do my best," I said, turning away. "I'll do my very best."

"YOU MUSTN'T BE TOO HARD on your father, you know," Inspector Hewitt said as he slowed to negotiate the turn at the fingerpost which pointed to Bishop's Lacey. I glanced at him, his face lit from below by the soft glow of the Vauxhall's instrument panel. The windscreen wipers, like black scythes, swashed back and forth across the glass in the strange light of the storm.

"Do you honestly believe he murdered Horace Bonepenny?" I asked.

His reply was ages in coming, and when it did, it was burdened with a heavy sadness.

"Who else *was* there, Flavia?" he said.

"Me," I said, ". . . for instance."

Inspector Hewitt flicked on the defroster to evaporate the condensation our words were forming on the windscreen.

"You don't expect me to believe that story about the struggle and the dicky heart, do you? Because I don't. That isn't what killed Horace Bonepenny."

"It was the pie, then!" I blurted out with sudden inspiration. "He was poisoned by the pie!"

"Did you poison the pie?" he asked, almost grinning.

"No," I admitted. "But I wish I had."

"It was quite an ordinary pie," the Inspector said. "I've already had the analyst's report."

Quite an ordinary pie? This was the highest praise Mrs. Mullet's confections were ever likely to receive.

"As you've deduced," he went on, "Bonepenny did indeed indulge in a slice of pie several hours before his death. But how could you know that?"

"Who but a stranger would eat the stuff?" I asked, with just enough of a scoff in my voice to mask the sudden realization that I had made a mistake: Bonepenny hadn't been poisoned by Mrs. Mullet's pie after all. It was childish to have pretended that he had.

"I'm sorry I said that," I told him. "It just popped out. You must think me a complete bloody fool."

Inspector Hewitt didn't reply for far too long. At last he said:

> " 'Unless some sweetness at the bottom lie,
> Who cares for all the crinkling of the pie?'

"My grandmother used to say that," he added.

"What does it mean?" I asked.

"It means—well, here we are at Buckshaw. They're probably worried about you."

"OH," said Ophelia in her careless voice. "Have you been gone? We hadn't noticed, had we, Daff?"

Daffy was showing the prominent equine whites of her eyes. She was definitely spooked but trying not to let on.

"No," she muttered, and plunged back into *Bleak House*. Daffy was, if nothing else, a rapid reader.

Had they asked, I should have told them gladly about my visit with Father, but they did not. If there was to be any grieving for his predicament, I was not to be a part of it; that much was clear. Feely and Daffy and I were like three grubs in three distinct cocoons, and sometimes I wondered why. Charles Darwin had once pointed out that the fiercest competition for survival came from one's own tribe, and as the fifth of six children—and with three older sisters—he was obviously in a position to know what he was talking about.

To me it seemed a matter of elementary chemistry: I knew that a substance tends to be dissolved by solvents that are chemically similar to it. There was no rational explanation for this; it was simply the way of Nature.

It had been a long day, and my eyelids felt as if they'd been used for oyster rakes.

"I think I'll go to bed," I said. "G'night, Feely. G'night, Daffy."

My attempt at sociability was greeted with silence and a grunt. As I was making my way up the stairs, Dogger materialized suddenly above me on the landing with a candleholder that might have been snapped up at an estate sale at Manderley.

"Colonel de Luce?" he whispered.

"He is well, Dogger," I said.

Dogger nodded a troubled nod, and we each of us trudged off to our respective quarters.

eighteen

GREYMINSTER SCHOOL LAY DOZING IN THE SUN, AS if it were dreaming of past glories. The place was precisely as I had imagined it: magnificent old stone buildings, tidy green lawns running down to the lazy river, and vast, empty playing fields that seemed to give off silent echoes of cricket matches whose players were long dead.

I leaned Gladys against a tree in the side lane by which I had entered the grounds. Behind a hedgerow, a tractor stood ticking idly, its driver nowhere in sight.

The voices of choirboys came floating across the lawns from the chapel. In spite of the bright morning sunshine, they were singing:

> "Softly now the light of day
> Fades upon my sight away—"

I stood listening for a moment until suddenly they broke off. Then, after a pause, the organ started up again, peevishly, and the singers went back to the beginning.

As I walked slowly across the grass of what I'm sure Father would have called "the Quad," the tall blank windows of the school stared down at me coldly and I had the sudden queer feeling an insect must have when it's placed under a microscope—the feeling of an invisible lens hovering, and something strange, perhaps, about the light.

Except for a single schoolboy dashing along and two black-gowned masters walking and talking with their heads together, the broad lawns and winding walkways of Greyminster were empty beneath a sky of deepest blue. The whole place seemed slightly unreal, like a grossly enlarged Agfacolor print: something you might see in one of those books with a name such as *Picturesque Britain*.

That limestone pile on the east side of the Quad—the one with the clock tower—must be Anson House, I thought: Father's old digs.

As I approached it, I raised my hand to shield my eyes against the glare of the sky. It was from somewhere up there among the battlements and tiles that Mr. Twining had plummeted to his death on the cobbles below; those ancient cobbles which now lay no more than a hundred feet from where I was standing.

I strolled across the grass to have a look.

Disappointingly, there were no bloodstains. Of course there wouldn't be, not after all these years. Those would have been washed away as soon as was decently possible— quite likely even before Mr. Twining's broken body had been laid to whatever passed for rest.

Other than of their constant wearing down by two hundred years of privileged feet, these cobbles told no tales. Tucked tightly in along the stone walls of Anson House, the walk was scarcely six feet wide.

I threw back my head and gazed straight up at the tower. Viewed from this angle, it rose dizzily in a sheer wall of stone that ended far, far above me in a filigree of airy ornamental stonework where fat white clouds, drifting lazily past the parapets, created the peculiar sensation that the whole structure was leaning...falling...toppling towards me. The illusion made my stomach go all queasy, and I had to look away.

Worn stone steps led enticingly from the cobbled walk, through an arched entrance, to a double door. To my left was the porter's lodge, its occupant huddled over a telephone. He did not even look up as I slipped inside.

A cool, dim corridor stretched away in front of me, to infinity it seemed, and I set out along it, lifting my feet carefully to keep from making scuffing noises on the slate floor.

On either side, a long gallery of smiling faces—some of them schoolboys and some masters—receded into the darkness, each one a Greyminsterian who had given his life for his country, and each in his own black-lacquered frame: "That Others Might Live," it said on a gilded scroll. At the end of the corridor, set apart from the others, were photographs of three boys, their names engraved in red on little brass rectangles. Under each name were the words *Missing in Action*.

"Missing in Action?" Why wasn't Father's photo hanging there? I wondered.

Father was generally as absent as these young men whose bones were somewhere in France. I felt a little guilty at the thought, but it was true.

I think it was at that moment, there in the shadowy hall at Greyminster, that I began to realize the full extent of Father's distant nature. Yesterday I had been all too ready to throw my arms around him and hug him to jelly, but now I understood that yesterday's cozy prison scene had not been a dialogue, but a troubled monologue. It had not been me, but Harriet to whom he was speaking. And, as with the dying Horace Bonepenny, I had been no more than an unwitting confessor.

Now, just being here at Greyminster where Father's troubles had begun, it seemed all the more cold and remote and inhospitable a place.

In the gloom beyond the photos, a staircase led up to the first floor, and I climbed up it to a hallway which, like the one I had left below, also ran the length of the building. Although the doors on either side were closed, each one was fitted with a small pane of glass, which allowed me a peek into the room. They were classrooms, and all alike.

At the end of the corridor, a large corner room promised something more: A sign on its door read Chemistry Lab.

I tried the door and it opened at once. The curse was broken!

I don't know what I was expecting, but I wasn't expecting this: stained wooden tables, boring flasks, cloudy retorts, chipped test tubes, inferior Bunsen burners, and a colored wall chart of the elements containing a laughable printing error in which the positions of arsenic and selenium were interchanged. I spotted this at once and— with a nub of blue chalk from the ledge beneath the blackboard—took the liberty of correcting the mistake by drawing in a two-headed arrow. "WRONG!" I wrote beneath it, and underlined the word twice.

This so-called lab was nothing compared with my own at Buckshaw, and at the thought, my chest swelled with pride. I wanted nothing more than to bolt for home at once, just to be there, to touch my own gleaming glassware; to concoct the perfect poison just for the thrill of it.

But that pleasure would have to wait. There was work to be done.

BACK OUTSIDE IN THE CORRIDOR, I retraced my steps to the center of the building. If I had guessed accurately, I should now be directly under the tower, and the entrance to it could not be far away.

A small door in the paneling, which I had taken at first to be a broom closet, swung open to reveal a steep stone staircase. My heart skipped a beat.

And then I saw the sign. A few steps up from the bottom, a length of chain was draped across the steps, with a hand-printed card: *Tower Off Limits—Strictly Enforced.*

I was up them like a shot.

It was like being inside a nautilus shell. The stairs twisted round and round, winding their narrow way upwards in echoing sameness. There was no possible way of seeing what lay ahead or, for that matter, what lay behind. Only the few steps immediately above and below me were visible.

For a while, I counted them in a whisper as I climbed, but after a time I found that I needed my breath to fuel my legs. It was a steep ascent and I was getting a stitch in my side. I stopped for a moment to rest.

What little light there was appeared to be coming from tiny slit windows, one positioned at each complete turn of the staircase. On that side of the tower, I guessed, lay the Quad. Still short of breath, I resumed my ascent.

Then suddenly and unexpectedly the staircase ended— just like that—at a little timbered door.

It was a door such as a dwarf might pop into in the side of a forest oak: a half-rounded hatch with an iron opening for a skeleton key. And, needless to say, the stupid thing was locked.

I let out a hiss of frustration and sat down on the top step, breathing heavily.

"Damnation!" I said, and the word echoed back with startling volume from the walls.

"Hallo up there!" came a hollow, stony voice, followed by the scraping of footsteps far below.

"Damnation!" I said again, this time under my breath. I had been spotted.

"Who's up there?" the voice demanded. I put my hand over my mouth to stifle the urge to reply.

As my fingers touched my teeth, I had an idea. Father had once said there would come a time when I was grateful for the braces I had been made to wear, and he had been right. This was it.

Using my thumbs and forefingers as a dual pair of pincers, I yanked down on the braces with all the strength I could muster, and with a satisfying "click" the things popped out of my mouth and into my hand.

As the footsteps came closer and closer, climbing relentlessly up to where I was trapped against the locked door, I twisted the wire into an "L" with a loop on the end and jammed the ruined braces into the keyhole.

Father would have me horsewhipped, but I had no other choice.

The lock was old and unsophisticated, and I knew I could crack it—if only I had enough time.

"Who is it?" the voice demanded. "I know you're up there. I can hear you. The tower is off limits. Come down at once, boy."

Boy? I thought. So he hadn't actually seen me.

I eased in and out on the wire and twisted it to the left. As if it had been oiled this morning, the bolt slid smoothly back. I opened the door and stepped through, pulling it silently closed behind me. There was no time to try locking it from the inside. Besides, whoever was coming up the stairs would likely have a key.

I was in a space as dark as a coal cellar. The slit windows had ended at the top of the stairs.

The footsteps stopped outside the door. I stepped soundlessly to one side and flattened myself against the stone wall.

"Who's up here?" the voice asked. "Who is it?" And then a key was inserted, the latch clicked, the door opened, and a man stuck his head in through the opening.

The beam from his torch shot here and there, illuminating a crazy maze of ladders that twisted up into the darkness. He shone the light on each ladder, allowing his beam to climb it, rung by rung, until it vanished in the blackness far above.

I didn't move a muscle: not even my eyes. In my peripheral vision I had an impression of the man silhouetted against the open door: white hair and a fearsome mustache. He was so close I could have reached out and touched him.

There was a pause that seemed an eternity.

"Bloody rats again," he said to himself at last, and the door slammed shut, leaving me in darkness. There was the jingle of a ring of keys and then the bolt shot home.

I was locked in.

I suppose I should have let out a shout, but I didn't. I was nowhere near my wits' end. In fact, I was rather beginning to enjoy myself.

I knew that I could try picking the lock again, and creep back down the stairs, but quite possibly I'd creep straight into the porter's clutches.

Since I couldn't stay where I was forever, the only other option was up. Sticking my arms out like a sleepwalker, I slid my feet slowly one in front of the other, until my fingers touched the closest of the ladders I had seen illuminated by his torch—and up I went.

There's no real trick to climbing a ladder in the dark. In many ways, it's preferable to seeing the abyss that's always there below you. But as I climbed, my eyes became more and more accustomed to the darkness—or near-darkness. Tiny chinks in the stone and timbers were letting in pinpricks of light here and there, and I soon found I was able to make out the general outline of the ladder, black on black in the tower's gray light.

The rungs ended suddenly, and I found myself on a small wooden platform, like a sailor in the rigging. To my left, another ladder led up into the gloom.

I gave it a good shaking, and although it creaked fearsomely, it seemed solid enough. I took a deep breath, stepped onto the bottom rung, and up I went.

A minute later I had reached the top, and a smaller, shakier platform. Still another ladder, this one more narrow and spindly than the others, trembled alarmingly as I set foot upon it and began my slow, creeping ascent. Halfway up I began counting the rungs:

"Ten (approximately)...eleven...twelve...thirteen—"

My head smashed against something and for a moment I could see nothing but spinning stars. I hung on to the rungs for dear life, my head aching like a burst melon and the matchstick ladder vibrating in my hands like a plucked bowstring. I felt as if someone had scalped me.

As I reached up with one hand and felt above my broken head, my fingers closed around a wooden handle. I pushed up on it with all my remaining strength, and the trapdoor lifted.

In a flash I had scrambled out onto the roof of the tower, blinking like an owl in the sudden sunshine. From a square platform in its center, slate tiles sloped gently outwards to each of the four points of the compass.

The view was nothing short of magnificent. Across the Quad, beyond the slates of the chapel, vistas of different greens folded away into the hazy distance.

Still squinting, I stepped a little closer to the parapet, and I almost lost my life.

There was a sudden yawning hole at my feet, and I had to windmill my arms to keep from falling into it. As I teetered on the edge, I had a sickening glimpse of the cobbles far below shining blackly in the sun.

The gap was perhaps eighteen inches wide, with a half-inch raised lip around it, bridged every ten feet or so by a narrow finger of stone that joined the jutting parapet to the roof. This opening had evidently been designed to provide emergency drainage in case of unusually heavy rainfall.

I jumped carefully across the opening and looked over the waist-high battlements. Far below, the grass of the Quad spread off in three directions.

Tucked in tightly as it was against the wall of Anson House, the cobbled walk was not visible below the jutting battlements. How odd, I thought. If Mr. Twining had leapt out from these battlements, he could only have landed in the grass.

Unless, of course, in the thirty years that had gone by since the day of his death, the Quad had undergone substantial landscaping changes. Another dizzying look down through the opening behind me made it obvious that they had not: the cobbles below and the linden trees that lined them were positively ancient. Mr. Twining had fallen through this hole. Without a doubt.

There was a sudden noise behind me and I spun round. In the center of the roof a corpse hung, dangling from a gibbet. I had to fight to keep from crying out.

Like the bound body of a highwayman I had seen in the pages of the *Newgate Calendar*, the thing was twisting and turning in the sudden breeze. Then, without warning, its belly seemed to explode, and its guts flew up into the air in a twisted and sickening rope of scarlet, white, and blue.

With a loud *crack!* the entrails unfurled themselves, and suddenly, high above my head, at the top of the pole, the Union Jack was flapping in the wind.

As I recovered from my fright, I saw that the flag was rigged so that it could be raised and lowered from below, perhaps from the porter's lodge, by an ingenious series of cables and pulleys that terminated in the weatherproof canvas casing. It was this I had mistaken for corpse and gibbet.

I grinned stupidly at my foolishness and edged cautiously closer to the mechanism for a better look. But aside from the mechanical ingenuity of the device, there was little else of interest about it.

I had just turned and was moving back towards the open gap when I tripped and fell flat on my face, my head sticking out over the edge of the abyss.

I might have broken every bone in my body but I was afraid to move. A million miles below, or so it seemed, a pair of ant-like figures emerged from Anson House and set out across the Quad.

My first thought was that I was still alive. But then as my terror subsided, anger rushed in to take its place: anger at my own stupidity and clumsiness, anger at whatever invisible witch was blighting my life with an endless chain of locked doors, barked shins, and skinned elbows.

I got slowly to my feet and dusted myself off. Not only was my dress filthy, but I had also managed somehow to rip the sole half off my left shoe. The cause of the damage was not hard to spot: I had tripped on the sharp edge of a jutting tile which, torn from its place, now lay loose on the roof looking like one of the tablets upon which Moses had been given the Ten Commandments.

I'd better replace the slate, I thought. Otherwise the inhabitants of Anson House will find rainwater showering down on their heads and it will be no one's fault but mine.

The tile was heavier than it looked, and I had to drop to my knees as I tried to shove it back into place. Perhaps the thing had rotated, or maybe the adjoining tiles had sagged. Whatever the reason, it simply would not slide back into the dark socket from which my foot had yanked it.

I could easily slip my hand into the opening to see if there was any obstruction—but then I remembered the spiders and scorpions that are known to inhabit such grottoes.

I closed my eyes and shoved my fingers in. At the back of the cavity they encountered something—something soft.

I jerked back my hand and bent over to peer inside. There was nothing in the hole but darkness.

Carefully, I stuck my fingers in again and, with my thumb and forefinger, plucked at whatever was in there at the back of the hole.

In the end, it came out almost effortlessly, unfolding as it emerged, like the flag that fluttered above my head. It was a length of rusty black cloth—Russell cord, I think the stuff is called—sour with mold: a schoolmaster's gown. And rolled up tightly inside it, crushed beyond repair, was a black, square-topped mortarboard cap.

And in that instant I knew, as sure as a shilling, that these things had played a part in Mr. Twining's death. I didn't know what it was, but I would jolly well find out.

I ought to have left the things there, I know. I ought to have gone to the nearest telephone and rung up Inspector Hewitt. Instead, the first thought that popped into my mind was this: How was I going to get away from Greyminster without being noticed?

And, as it so often does when you're in a jam, the answer came at once.

I shoved my arms into the sleeves of the moldy gown, straightened the bent crown of the mortarboard and jammed it on my head, and like a large black bat, flapped my way slowly and precariously back down the cascades of trembling ladders to the locked door.

The pick I had fashioned from my braces had worked before, and now I needed it to work again. As I fidgeted the wire in the keyhole, I offered up a silent prayer to the god who governs such things.

After a great deal of scraping, a bent wire, and a couple of minor curses, my prayer was finally heard, and the bolt slid back with a sullen croak.

Before you could say "Scat!" I was down the stairs, listening at the bottom door, peering out through a crack at the long hall. The place was in empty silence.

I eased the door open, stepped quietly out into the corridor, and made my way swiftly down the gallery of lost boys, past the empty porter's lodge, and out into the sunshine.

There were schoolboys everywhere—or so it seemed—talking, lounging, strolling, laughing. Glorying in the outdoors with the end of term at hand.

My instinct was to hunch over in my cap and cape and skulk crabwise away across the Quad. Would I be noticed? Of course I would; to these wolfish boys I would stand out like the wounded reindeer at the back of the herd.

No! I would throw my shoulders back and, like a boy late for the hurdles, lope off, head held high, in the direction of the lane. I could only hope that no one would notice that underneath the gown I was wearing a dress.

And nobody did; no one gave me so much as a second glance.

The farther I got from the Quad, the safer I felt, but I knew that, alone in the open, I would be far more conspicuous.

Just a few feet ahead, an ancient oak squatted comfortably on the lawn as if it had been resting there since the days of Robin Hood. As I reached out to touch it (home free!), an arm shot out from behind the trunk and grabbed my wrist.

"Ow! Let go! You're hurting me!" I yelped automatically, and my arm was released at once, even as I was still spinning round to face my assailant.

It was Detective Sergeant Graves, and he seemed every bit as surprised as I was.

"Well, well," he said with a slow grin. "Well, well, well, well, well."

I was going to make a cutting remark, but thought better of it. I knew the sergeant liked me, and I might need all the help I could get.

"The Inspector'd like the pleasure of your company," he said, pointing to a group of people who stood talking in the lane where I had left Gladys.

Sergeant Graves said no more, but as we approached, he pushed me gently in front of him towards Inspector Hewitt like a friendly terrier presenting its master with a dead rat. The torn sole of my shoe was flapping like Charlie Chaplin's Little Tramp, but although the Inspector glanced at it, he was considerate enough to keep his thoughts to himself.

Sergeant Woolmer stood towering above the blue Vauxhall, his face as large and craggy as the Matterhorn. In his shadow were a sinewy, darkly tanned man in overalls and a wizened little gentleman with a white mustache who, when he saw me, jabbed at the air excitedly with his finger.

"That's him!" he said. "That's the one!"

"Is it, indeed?" Inspector Hewitt asked, as he lifted the

cap from my head and took the gown from my shoulders with the gentle deference of a valet.

The little man's pale blue eyes bulged visibly in their sockets.

"Why, it's only a girl!" he said.

I could have slapped his face.

"Ay, that's her," said the suntanned one.

"Mr. Ruggles here has reason to believe that you were up in the tower," the Inspector said, with a nod at the white mustache.

"What if I was?" I said. "I was just having a look round."

"That tower's off limits," Mr. Ruggles said loudly. "Off limits! And so it says on the sign. Can't you read?"

I gave him a graceful shrug.

"I'd have come up the ladders after you if I knew you were just a girl." And he added, in an aside to Inspector Hewitt, "Not what they used to be, my old knees.

"I knew you were up there," he went on. "I made out like I didn't so's I could ring up the police. And don't pretend you didn't pick the lock. That lock's my business, and I know it was locked as sure as I'm standing here in Fludd's Lane.

"Imagine! A girl! Tsk, tsk," he remarked, with a disbelieving shake of his head.

"Picked the lock, did you?" the Inspector asked. Even though he acted like he wasn't, I could see that he was taken aback. "Wherever did you learn a trick like that?"

I couldn't tell him, of course. Dogger was to be protected at all costs.

"Long ago and far away," I said.

The Inspector fixed me with a steely gaze. "There might

be those who are satisfied with that kind of answer, Flavia, but I am not among them."

Here comes that old "King George is not a frivolous man" speech again, I thought, but Inspector Hewitt had decided to wait for my answer, no matter how long it was in coming.

"There isn't much to do at Buckshaw," I said. "Sometimes I do things just to keep from getting bored."

He held out the black gown and cap. "And that's why you're wearing this costume? To keep from getting bored?"

"It's not a costume," I said. "If you must know, I found them under a loose tile on the tower roof. They have something to do with Mr. Twining's death. I'm sure of it."

If Mr. Ruggles's eyes had bulged before, they now almost popped out of his head.

"Mr. Twining?" he said. "Mr. Twining as jumped off the tower?"

"Mr. Twining didn't jump," I said. I couldn't resist the temptation to get even with this nasty little man. "He was—"

"Thank you, Flavia," Inspector Hewitt said. "That will do. And we'll take up no more of your time, Mr. Ruggles. I know you're a busy man."

Ruggles puffed himself up like a courting pigeon, and with a nod to the Inspector and an impertinent smile at me, he set off across the lawn towards his quarters.

"Thank you for your report, Mr. Plover," the Inspector said, turning to the man in overalls, who had been standing silently by.

Mr. Plover tugged at his forelock and returned to his tractor without a word.

"Our great public schools are cities in miniature," the Inspector said, with a wave of his hand. "Mr. Plover spotted you as an intruder the instant you turned into the lane. He wasted no time in getting to the porter's lodge."

Damn the man! And damn old Ruggles too! I'd have to remember when I got home to send them a jug of pink lemonade, just to show that there were no hard feelings. It was too late in the season for anemones, so *anemonin* was out of the question. Deadly nightshade, on the other hand, although uncommon, could be found if you knew exactly where to look.

Inspector Hewitt handed the cap and gown to Sergeant Graves, who had already produced several sheets of tissue paper from his kit.

"Smashing," the sergeant said. "She might just have saved us a crawl across the slates."

The Inspector shot him a look that could have stopped a runaway horse.

"Sorry, sir," the sergeant said, his face suddenly aflame as he turned to his wrapping.

"Tell me, in detail, how you found these things," Inspector Hewitt said, as if nothing had happened. "Don't leave anything out—and don't add anything."

As I spoke he wrote it all down in his quick, minuscule hand. Because of sitting across from Feely as she wrote in her diary at breakfast, I had become rather good at reading upside down, but Inspector Hewitt's notes were no more than tiny ants marching across the page.

I told him everything: from the creak of the ladders to my near-fatal slip; from the loose tile and what lay behind it to my clever escape.

When I had finished, I saw him scribble a couple of characters beside my account, although what they were, I could not tell. He snapped the notebook shut.

"Thank you, Flavia," he said. "You've been a great help."

Well, at least he had the decency to admit it. I stood there expectantly, waiting for more.

"I'm afraid King George's coffers are not deep enough to ferry you home twice in twenty-four hours," he said, "so we'll see you on your way."

"And shall I come back with tea?" I asked.

He stood there with his feet planted in the grass, and a look on his face that might have meant anything. A minute later, Gladys's Dunlop tires were humming happily along the tarmac, leaving Inspector Hewitt—"and his ilk" as Daffy would have said—farther and farther behind.

Before I had gone a quarter of a mile, the Vauxhall overtook, and then passed me. I waved like mad as it went by, but the faces that stared out at me from its windows were grim.

A hundred feet farther on, the brake lights flashed and the car pulled over onto the verge. As I came alongside, the Inspector rolled the window down.

"We're taking you home. Sergeant Graves will load your bicycle into the boot."

"Has King George changed his mind, Inspector?" I asked haughtily.

A look crossed his face that I had never seen there before. I could almost swear it was worry.

"No," he said, "King George has not changed his mind. But I have."

nineteen

NOT TO BE TOO DRAMATIC ABOUT IT, THAT NIGHT I slept the sleep of the damned. I dreamt of turrets and craggy ledges where the windswept rain blew in from the ocean with the odor of violets. A pale woman in Elizabethan dress stood beside my bed and whispered in my ear that the bells would ring. An old salt in an oilcloth jacket sat atop a piling, mending nets with an awl, while far out at sea a tiny aeroplane winged its way towards the setting sun.

When at last I awoke, the sun was at the window and I had a perfectly wretched cold. Even before I went down to breakfast I had used up all the handkerchiefs from my drawer and put paid to a perfectly good bath towel. Needless to say, I was not in a good humor.

"Don't come near me," Feely said as I groped my way to the far end of the table, snuffling like a grampus.

"Die, witch," I managed, making a cross of my fore-fingers.

"Flavia!"

I poked at my cereal, giving it a stir with a corner of my toast. In spite of the burnt bits of crust to liven it up, the soggy muck in the bowl still tasted like cardboard.

There was a jerk, a jump in my consciousness like a badly spliced cinema film. I had fallen asleep at the table.

"What's wrong?" I heard Feely ask. "Are you all right?"

"She is stuck in her 'enervating slumbers, from the hesternal dissipation or debauch,'" Daffy said.

Daffy had recently been reading Bulwer-Lytton's *Pelham*, a few pages each night for her bedtime book, and until she finished it, we were likely to be lashed daily at breakfast with obscure phrases in a style of prose as stiff and inflexible as a parlor poker.

Hesternal, I remembered, meant, "pertaining to yesterday." I was nodding over the rest of the phrase when suddenly Feely leapt up from the table.

"Good God!" she exclaimed, quickly wrapping her dressing gown round her like a winding-sheet. "Who on earth is that?"

Someone stood silhouetted at the French doors, peering in at us through hands cupped against the glass.

"It's that writer," I said. "The country house man. Pemberton."

Feely gave a squeak and fled upstairs where I knew she would throw on her tight blue sweater set, dab powder on her morning blemishes, and float down the staircase pretending she was someone else: Olivia de Havilland, for instance. She always did that when there was a strange man on the property.

Daffy glanced up disinterestedly, and then went on reading. As usual, it was up to me.

I stepped out onto the terrace, pulling the door closed behind me.

"Good morning, Flavia," Pemberton said with a grin. "Did you sleep well?"

Did I sleep well? What kind of question was that? Here I was on the terrace, sleep in my eyes, my hair a den of nesting rats, and my nose running like a trout stream. Besides, wasn't a question about the quality of one's sleep reserved for those who had spent a night under the same roof? I wasn't sure; I'd have to look it up in *Beeton's Complete Etiquette for Ladies*. Feely had given me a copy for my last birthday, but it was still propping up the short leg of my bed.

"Not awfully," I said. "I've caught cold."

"I'm sorry to hear that. I was hoping to be able to interview your father about Buckshaw. I don't like to be a pest, but my time here is limited. Since the war, the cost of accommodation away from home, even in the most humble hostelry, such as the Thirteen Drakes, is simply shocking. One doesn't like to plead poverty, but we poor scholars still dine mostly upon bread and cheese, you know."

"Have you had breakfast, Mr. Pemberton?" I asked. "I'm sure Mrs. Mullet could manage something."

"That's very kind of you, Flavia," he said, "but Landlord Stoker laid on a veritable feast of two bangers and an egg and I live in fear for my waistcoat buttons."

I wasn't quite sure how to take this, and my cold was making me too grumpy to ask.

"Perhaps I can answer your questions," I said. "Father has been detained—"

Yes, that was it! You sly little fox, Flavia!

"Father has been detained in town."

"Oh, I don't think they're matters that would much interest you: a few knotty questions about drains and the Enclosure Acts—that sort of thing. I was hoping to put in an appendix about the architectural changes made by Antony and William de Luce in the nineteenth century. 'A House Divided' and all that."

"I've heard of an appendix being taken out," I blurted, "but this is the first time I've heard of one being put in."

Even with my nose running I could still thrust and parry with the best of them. A wet, explosive sneeze ruined the effect.

"P'raps I could just step in and have a quick look round. Make a few notes. I shan't disturb anyone."

I was trying to think of synonyms for "no" when I heard the growl of an engine, and Dogger, at the wheel of our old tractor, appeared between the trees at the end of the avenue, hauling a load of compost to the garden. Mr. Pemberton, who noticed at once that I was staring over his shoulder, turned to see what I was looking at. When he spotted Dogger coming our way, he gave a friendly wave.

"That's old Dogger, isn't it? The faithful family retainer?"

Dogger had braked, looking round to see who Pemberton might be waving at. When he saw no one, he raised his hat as if in greeting, then gave his head a scratch. He climbed down from the wheel and shambled across the lawn towards us.

"I say, Flavia," Pemberton said, glancing at his wristwatch, "I'd quite lost track of the time. I promised to meet my publisher at Nether Eaton to have a look over a shroud tomb, quite a rare one: both hands exposed and all that. Extraordinary railings. He's got a thing about tombs, has old Quarrington, so I'd better not stand him up. If I do, why, *Pemberton's Tombs and Traceries* might never be anything more than a twinkle in its author's eye."

He hitched up his artist's knapsack and strolled down the steps, pausing at the corner of the house to close his eyes and draw in a deep, bracing lungful of the morning air.

"My regards to Colonel de Luce," he said, and then he was gone.

Dogger shuffled up the steps as if he hadn't slept. "Visitors, Miss Flavia?" he asked, removing his hat and wiping his forehead on his sleeve.

"A Mr. Pemberton," I said. "He's writing a book about country houses or tombs or something. He wanted to interview Father about Buckshaw."

"I don't believe I've heard his name," Dogger said. "But then I'm not much of a reader. Still and all, Miss Flavia..."

I knew that he was going to give me a homily, complete with parables and bloodcurdling instances, about talking to strangers, but he didn't. Instead he settled for touching the brim of his hat with his forefinger, and we both of us stood there gazing out across the lawn like a couple of cows. Message sent; message received. Dear old Dogger. Such was his way of teaching.

It had been Dogger, for instance, who had patiently taught me to pick locks when I had come upon him one day fiddling with the greenhouse door. He had lost the key during one of his "episodes," and was busily at work with the bent tines of a retired kitchen fork he'd found in a flowerpot.

His hands were shaking badly. Whenever Dogger was like that, you always had the feeling that if you stuck out a finger and touched him, you'd be instantly electrocuted. But in spite of that, I had offered to help, and a few minutes later he was showing me how the thing was done.

"It's easy enough, Miss Flavia," he'd said after my third try. "Just keep in mind the three *T*s: torque, tension, and tenacity. Imagine you live inside the lock. Listen to your fingertips."

"Where did you learn to do this?" I asked, marveling as the thing clicked open. It was laughably easy once you'd got the hang of it.

"Long ago and far away," Dogger had said as he stepped into the greenhouse and made himself too busy for further questioning.

ALTHOUGH SUNLIGHT WAS FLOODING in through the windows of my laboratory, I could not seem to think properly. My mind was swarming with the things Father had told me and what I had ferreted out on my own: the deaths of Mr. Twining and Horace Bonepenny.

What was the meaning of the cap and gown I had found hidden in the tiles of Anson House? Whom did they belong to, and why had they been left there?

Both Father's account, and that in the pages of *The Hinley Chronicle*, had stated that Mr. Twining was wearing his gown when he tumbled to his death. That both of them could be mistaken seemed most unlikely.

Then, too, there were the thefts of His Majesty's Ulster Avenger and its twin, which had belonged to Dr. Kissing.

Where was Dr. Kissing now? I wondered. Would Miss Mountjoy know? She seemed to know everything else. Could he possibly still be alive? Somehow it seemed doubtful. It had been thirty years since he thought he saw his precious stamp going up in smoke.

But my mind was swirling, my brain addled, and I couldn't think clearly. My sinuses were plugged, my eyes were watering, and I felt a splitting headache coming on. I needed to clear my head.

It was my own fault: I never should have let my feet get cold. Mrs. Mullet was fond of saying, "Keep warm feet and a cool head, and you'll ne'er find yourself sneezing in bed." If one did come down with a cold, there was only one thing for it, so down to the kitchen I shuffled where I found Mrs. Mullet making pastry.

"You're sniffling, dear," she said, without looking up from her rolling pin. "Let me fix you a nice mug of chicken broth." The woman could be maddeningly perceptive.

At the words *chicken broth*, she dropped her voice to a near-whisper and shot a conspiratorial look over her shoulder.

"Hot chicken broth," she said. "It's a secret Mrs. Jacobson told me at a Women's Institute tea. Been in her family since the Exodus. Mind you, I've said nothing."

Mrs. Mullet's other favorite bit of village wisdom had to do with eucalyptus. She forced Dogger to grow it for her in the greenhouse, and assiduously concealed sprigs of the stuff here and there about Buckshaw as talismans against the cold or grippe.

"Eucalyptus in the hall, no grippe or colds shall you

befall," she used to crow triumphantly. And it was true. Since she had been secreting the dark waxy green leaves in unsuspected places around the house, none of us had suffered so much as a sniffle.

Until now. Something had obviously failed.

"No, thank you, Mrs. Mullet," I said. "I've just brushed my teeth."

It was a lie, but it was the best I could come up with at short notice. Besides having a whiff of martyrdom about it, my reply had the added advantage of bucking up my image in the personal cleanliness department. On my way out, I filched from the pantry a bottle of yellow granules labeled Partington's Essence of Chicken, and from a wall sconce in the hall I helped myself to a handful of eucalyptus leaves.

Upstairs in the laboratory, I took down a bottle of sodium bicarbonate which Uncle Tar, in his spidery copperplate script, had marked *sal aeratus*, as well as, in his usual meticulous manner, Sod. Bicarb. to distinguish it from potassium bicarbonate, which also was sometimes called *sal aeratus*. Pot. Bicarb. was more at home in fire extinguishers than in the tummy.

I knew the stuff as $NaHCO_3$, which the cottagers called baking soda. Somewhere I remembered hearing that the same rustics believed in the power of a good old dosing of alkali salts to flush out even the fiercest case of the common cold.

It made good chemical sense, I reasoned: If salts were a cure, and chicken broth were a cure, think of the magnificent restorative power of a glass of effervescent chicken broth! It boggled the mind. I'd patent the thing; it would be the world's first antidote against the common cold: *De Luce's Deliquescence, Flavia's Foup Formula!*

I even managed a moderately happy hum as I measured eight ounces of drinking water into a beaker, and set it over the flame to heat. Meanwhile, in a stoppered flask I boiled the torn shreds of eucalyptus leaves and watched as straw-colored drops of oil began to form at the end of the distillation coil.

When the water was at a rolling boil, I removed it from the heat and let it cool for several minutes, then dropped in two heaped teaspoons of Partington's Chicken Essence and a tablespoon of good old $NaHCO_3$.

I gave it a jolly good stir and let it foam like Vesuvius over the lip of the beaker. I pinched my nostrils shut and tossed back half of the concoction chug-a-lug.

Chicken fizz! O Lord, protect all of us who toil in the vineyards of experimental chemistry!

I unstoppered the flask and dumped the eucalyptus water, leaves and all, into the remains of the yellow soup. Then, peeling off my sweater and draping it over my head as a fume hood, I inhaled the camphoraceous steam of poultry eucalyptus, and somewhere up inside the sticky caverns of my head I thought I felt my sinuses throw their hands up into the air and surrender. I was feeling better already.

There was a sharp knock on the door and I nearly jumped out of my skin. So seldom did anyone come into this part of the house that a tap at the door was as unexpected as one of those sudden heart-clutching organ chords in a horror film when a door swings open upon a gallery of corpses. I shot back the bolt and there stood Dogger, wringing his hat like the Irish washerwoman. I could see that he had been having one of his episodes.

I reached out and touched his hands and they stilled at

once. I had observed—although I did not often make use of the fact—that there were times when a touch could say things that words could not.

"What's the password?" I asked, linking my fingers together and placing both hands atop my head.

For about five and a half seconds Dogger looked blank, and then his tense jaw muscles relaxed slowly and he almost smiled. Like an automaton he meshed his fingers and copied my gesture.

"It's on the tip of my tongue," he said haltingly. Then, "I remember now: It's 'arsenic.'"

"Careful you don't swallow it," I replied. "It's poison."

With a remarkable display of sheer willpower, Dogger made himself smile. The ritual had been properly observed.

"Enter, friend," I said, and swung the door wide.

Dogger stepped inside and looked round in wonder, as if he had suddenly found himself transported to an alchemist's lab in ancient Sumer. It had been so long since he had been in this part of the house that he had forgotten the room.

"So much glass," he said shakily.

I pulled out Tar's old Windsor chair from the desk, steadying it until Dogger had folded himself between its wooden arms.

"Have a sit. I'll fix you something."

I filled a clean flask with water and set it atop a wire mesh. Dogger started at the little "pop" of the Bunsen burner as I applied the match.

"Coming up," I said. "Ready in a jiff."

The fortunate thing about lab glassware is that it boils water at the speed of light. I threw a spoonful of black leaves into a beaker. When it had gone a deep red I handed it to Dogger, who stared at it skeptically.

"It's all right," I said. "It's Tetley's."

He sipped at the tea gingerly, blowing on the surface of the drink to cool it. As he drank, I remembered that there's a reason we English are ruled more by tea than by Buckingham Palace or His Majesty's Government: Apart from the soul, the brewing of tea is the only thing that sets us apart from the great apes—or so the Vicar had remarked to Father, who had told Feely, who had told Daffy, who had told me.

"Thank you," Dogger said. "I feel quite myself now. But there's something I must tell you, Miss Flavia."

I perched on the edge of the desk, trying to look chummy.

"Fire away," I said.

"Well," Dogger began, "you know that there are occasions when I have sometimes—that is, now and then, I have times when I—"

"Of course I do, Dogger," I said. "Don't we all?"

"I don't know. I don't remember. You see, the thing of it is that, when I was—" His eyes rolled like those of a cow in the killing-pen. "I think I might have done something to someone. And now they've gone and arrested the Colonel for it."

"Are you referring to Horace Bonepenny?"

There was a crash of glassware as Dogger dropped the beaker of tea on the floor. I scrambled for a cloth and for some stupid reason dabbed at his hands, which were quite dry.

"What do you know about Horace Bonepenny?" he

demanded, clamping my wrist in a steely grip. If it hadn't been Dogger I should have been terrified.

"I know all about him," I said, gently prying his fingers loose. "I looked him up at the library. I talked to Miss Mountjoy, and Father told me the whole story Sunday evening."

"You saw Colonel de Luce Sunday evening? In Hinley?"

"Yes," I said. "I bicycled over. I told you he was well. Don't you remember?"

"No," Dogger said, shaking his head. "Sometimes I don't remember."

Could this be possible? Could Dogger have encountered Horace Bonepenny somewhere inside the house, or in the garden, then grappled with him and brought about his death? Had it been an accident? Or was there more to it than that?

"Tell me what happened," I said. "Tell me as much as you can remember."

"I was sleeping," Dogger said. "I heard voices—loud voices. I got up and went along to the Colonel's study. There was someone standing in the hall."

"That was me," I said. "I was in the hall."

"That was you," Dogger said. "You were in the hall."

"Yes. You told me to buzz off."

"I did?" Dogger seemed shocked.

"Yes, you told me to go back to bed."

"A man came out of the study," Dogger said suddenly. "I ducked in beside the clock and he walked right past me. I could have reached out and touched him."

It was clear he had jumped to a point in time after I had gone back to bed.

"But you didn't—touch him, I mean."

"Not then, no. I followed him into the garden. He didn't see me. I kept to the wall behind the greenhouse. He was standing in the cucumbers...eating something... agitated...talking to himself...foulest language...didn't seem to notice he was off the path. And then there were the fireworks."

"Fireworks?" I asked.

"You know, Catherine wheels, skyrockets, and all that. I thought there must be a fête in the village. It's June, you know. They often have a fête in June."

There had been no fête; of that I was sure. I'd rather slog the entire length of the Amazon in perforated tennis shoes than miss a chance to pitch coconuts at the Aunt Sally and gorge myself on rock cakes and strawberries-and-cream. No, I was well up on the dates of the fêtes.

"And then what happened?" I asked. We would sort out the details later.

"I must have fallen asleep," Dogger said. "When I woke up I was lying in the grass. It was wet. I got up and went in to bed. I didn't feel well. I must have had one of my bad turns. I don't remember."

"And you think that, during your bad turn, you might have killed Horace Bonepenny?"

Dogger nodded glumly. He touched the back of his head.

"Who else *was* there?" he asked.

Who else was there? Where had I heard that before? Of course! Hadn't Inspector Hewitt used those very words about Father?

"Bow your head, Dogger," I said.

"I'm sorry, Miss Flavia. If I killed someone I didn't mean to."

"Bend down your head."

Dogger slumped down in the chair and leaned forward. As I lifted his collar he winced.

On his neck, below and behind his ear, was a filthy great purple bruise the size and shape of a shoe heel. He winced when I touched it.

I let out a low whistle.

"Fireworks, my eye!" I said. "Those were no fireworks, Dogger. You've been well and truly nobbled. And you've been walking around with this mouse on your neck for two days? It must hurt like anything."

"It does, Miss Flavia, but I've had worse."

I must have looked at him in disbelief.

"I had a look at my eyes in the mirror," he added. "Pupils the same size. Bit of concussion—but not too bad. I'll soon be over it."

I was about to ask him where he had picked up this bit of lore when he added quickly: "But that's just something I read somewhere."

I suddenly thought of a more important question.

"Dogger, how could you have killed someone if you were knocked unconscious?"

He stood there, looking like a small boy hauled in for a caning. His mouth was opening and closing but nothing was coming out.

"You were attacked!" I said. "Someone clubbed you with a shoe!"

"No, I think not, miss," he said sadly. "You see, aside from Horace Bonepenny, I was alone in the garden."

twenty

I HAD SPENT THE PAST THREE QUARTERS OF AN HOUR
trying to talk Dogger into letting me put an ice pack on the
back of his neck, but he would not allow it. Rest, he assured
me, was the only thing for it, and he had wandered off to
his room.

From my window, I could see Feely stretched out on a
blanket on the south lawn trying to reflect sunshine onto
both sides of her face with a couple of issues of the *Picture
Post*. I fetched a pair of Father's old army binoculars and
took a close look at her complexion. When I'd had a good
squint I opened my notebook and wrote:

Tuesday, 6th of June 1950, 9:15 A.M. Subject's appearance remains normal. 96 hours since administration.
Solution too weak? Subject immune? Common knowledge that Eskimos of Baffin Island immune to poison
ivy. Could this mean what I think it might?

But my heart wasn't in it. It was difficult to study Feely when Father and Dogger were so much on my mind. I needed to collect my thoughts.

I turned to a fresh page and wrote:

Possible Suspects

FATHER: Best motive of all. Has known dead man for most of life; has been threatened with exposure; was heard quarreling with victim shortly before murder. No one knows whereabouts at the time crime was committed. Insp. Hewitt has already arrested him and charged him with murder, so we know where the Inspector's suspicions lie!

DOGGER: Bit of a dark horse. Don't know much about his past, but do know he is fiercely loyal to Father. Overheard Father's quarrel with Bonepenny (but so did I) and may have decided to eliminate threat of exposure. Dogger subject to "episodes" during and after which memory is affected. Might he have killed Bonepenny during one of these? Could it have been an accident? But if so, who bashed Dogger on the head?

MRS. MULLET: No motive, unless to wreak vengeance upon person who left dead snipe on her kitchen doorstep. Too old.

DAPHNE de LUCE and OPHELIA GERTRUDE de LUCE: (Your secret is out, Gertie!) Don't make me laugh! These two so absorbed in book and looking-glass that they wouldn't kill cockroach on own dinner plate. Did not know deceased, had no motive, and were snoring with mouths open when Bonepenny met his end. Case closed, as far these two dimwits concerned.

MARY STOKER: Motive: Bonepenny made improper advances to her at Thirteen Drakes. Could she have followed him to Buckshaw and dispatched him in cucumbers? Seems unlikely.

TULLY STOKER: Bonepenny was guest at Thirteen Drakes. Did Tully hear what happened with Mary? Decide to seek revenge? Or is a paying guest more important than daughter's honor?

NED CROPPER: Ned sweet on Mary (plus others). Knew what happened between Mary and Bonepenny. May have decided to do him in. Good motive, but no evidence he was at Buckshaw that night. Could have killed Bonepenny somewhere else and brought him here in wheelbarrow? But so could Tully. Or Mary!

MISS MOUNTJOY: Perfect motive: Believes Bonepenny (and Father) killed her uncle, Mr. Twining. Problem is age: Can't see Mountjoy grappling with someone Bonepenny's height and strength. Unless she used some kind of poison. Query: What was the official cause of death? Would Insp. Hewitt tell me?

INSPECTOR HEWITT: Police officer. Must include only in order to be fair, complete, and objective. Was not at Buckshaw at time of the crime, and has no known motive. (But did he attend Greyminster?)

DETECTIVE SERGEANTS WOOLMER & GRAVES: Ditto.

FRANK PEMBERTON: Didn't arrive in Bishop's Lacey until after the murder.

MAXIMILIAN BROCK: Gaga; too old; no motive.

I read through this list three times, hoping nothing had escaped me. And then I saw it: something that set my mind to racing. Hadn't Horace Bonepenny been a diabetic? I had found his vials of insulin in the kit at the Thirteen Drakes with the syringe missing. Had he lost it? Had it been stolen?

He had traveled, most likely by ferry, from Stavanger in Norway to Newcastle-upon-Tyne, and from there by rail to York, where he'd have changed trains for Doddingsley. From Doddingsley he'd have taken a bus or taxi to Bishop's Lacey.

And, as far as I knew, in all that time, he had not eaten! The pie shell in his room (as evidenced by the embedded feather) had been the one in which he secreted the dead jack snipe to smuggle it into England. Hadn't Tully Stoker told the Inspector that his guest had a drink in the saloon bar? Yes—but there had been no mention of food!

What if, after coming to Buckshaw and threatening Father, he had walked out of the house through the kitchen—which he almost certainly had—and had spied the custard pie on the windowsill? What if he had helped himself to a slice, wolfed it down, stepped outside, and gone into shock? Mrs. M's custard pies had that effect on all of us at Buckshaw, and none of us were even diabetics!

What if it had been Mrs. Mullet's pie after all? No more than a stupid accident? What if everyone on my list was innocent? What if Bonepenny had not been murdered?

But if that was true, Flavia, a sad and quiet little voice inside me said, why would Inspector Hewitt have arrested Father and laid charges against him?

Although my nose was still running and my eyes still watering, I thought perhaps my chicken draught was beginning to have an effect. I read again through my list of suspects and thought until my head throbbed.

I was getting nowhere. I decided at last to go outside, sit in the grass, inhale some fresh air, and turn my mind to something entirely different: I would think about nitrous oxide, for example, N_2O, or laughing gas: something that Buckshaw and its inhabitants were sorely in need of.

Laughing gas and murder seemed strange bedfellows indeed, but were they really?

I thought of my heroine, Marie-Anne Paulze Lavoisier, one of the giants of chemistry, whose portrait, with those other immortals, was stuck up on the mirror in my bedroom, her hair like a hot-air balloon, her husband looking on adoringly, not seeming to mind her silly coiffure. Marie was a woman who knew that sadness and silliness often go hand in hand. I remembered that it was during the French Revolution, in her husband Antoine's laboratory—just as they had sealed all of their assistant's bodily orifices with pitch and beeswax, rolled him up in a tube of varnished silk, and made him breathe through a straw into Lavoisier's measuring instruments—at that very moment, with Marie-Anne standing by making sketches of the proceedings, the authorities kicked down the door, burst into the room, and hauled her husband off to the guillotine.

I had once told this grimly amusing story to Feely.

"The need for heroines is generally to be found in the sort of persons who live in cottages," she had said with a haughty sniff.

But this was getting nowhere. My thoughts were all higgledy-piggledy, like straws in a haystack. I needed to find a catalyst of some description as, for example, Kirchoff had. He had discovered that starch boiled in water remained starch but when just a few drops of sulphuric acid were added, the starch was transformed into glucose. I had once repeated the experiment to reassure myself that this was so, and it was. Ashes to ashes; starch to sugar. A little window into the Creation.

I went back into the house, which now seemed strangely silent. I stopped at the drawing room door and listened, but there was no sound of Feely at the piano or of Daffy flipping pages. I opened the door.

The room was empty. And then I remembered that my sisters had talked at breakfast about walking into Bishop's Lacey to post Father the letters that each of them had written. Aside from Mrs. Mullet, who was off in the depths of the kitchen, and Dogger, who was upstairs resting, I was, perhaps for the first time in my life, alone in the halls of Buckshaw.

I switched on the wireless for company, and as the valves warmed up, the room was filled with the sound of an operetta. It was Gilbert and Sullivan's *Mikado*, one of my favorites. Wouldn't it be lovely, I had once thought, if Feely, Daffy, and I could be as happy and carefree as Yum-Yum and her two sisters?

> "Three little maids from school are we,
> Pert as a schoolgirl well can be,
> Filled to the brim with girlish glee,
> Three little maids from school!"

I smiled as the three of them sang:

"Everything is a source of fun.
Nobody's safe, for we care for none!
Life is a joke that's just begun!
Three little maids from school!"

Wrapped up in the music, I threw myself into an over-stuffed chair and let my legs dangle over the arm, the position in which Nature intended music to be listened to, and for the first time in days I felt the muscles in my neck relaxing.

I must have fallen into a brief sleep, or perhaps only a reverie—I don't know—but when I snapped out of it, Ko-Ko, the Lord High Executioner, was singing:

"He's made to dwell
In a dungeon cell—"

The words made me think at once of Father, and tears sprang up in my eyes. This was no operetta, I thought. Life was not a joke that's just begun, and Feely and Daffy and I were not three little maids from school. We were three girls whose father was charged with murder. I leaped up from the chair to switch off the wireless, but as I reached for the switch, the voice of the Lord High Executioner floated grimly from the loudspeaker:

"My object all sublime
I shall achieve in time
To let the punishment fit the crime—
The punishment fit the crime . . ."

Let the punishment fit the crime. Of course! Flavia, Flavia, Flavia! How could you not have seen?

Like a steel ball bearing dropping into a cut-glass vase, something in my mind went *click*, and I knew as surely as I knew my own name how Horace Bonepenny had been murdered.

Only one thing more (well, two things, actually; three at most) were needed to wrap this whole thing up like a box of birthday sweets and present it, red ribbons and all, to Inspector Hewitt. Once he heard my story, he would have Father out of the clink before you could say Jack Robinson.

MRS. MULLET WAS STILL IN THE KITCHEN with her hand up a chicken.

"Mrs. M," I said, "may I speak frankly with you?"

She looked up at me and wiped her hands on her apron.

"Of course, dear," she said. "Don't you always?"

"It's about Dogger."

The smile on her face congealed as she turned away and began fussing with a ball of butcher's twine with which she was trussing the bird.

"They don't make things the way they used to," she said as it snapped. "Not even string. Why, just last week I said to Alf, I said, 'That string as you brang home from the stationer's—'"

"Please, Mrs. Mullet," I begged. "There's something I need to know. It's a matter of life and death! Please!"

She looked at me over her spectacles like a churchwarden, and for the first time ever in her presence, I felt like a little girl.

"You said once that Dogger had been in prison, that he had been made to eat rats, that he was tortured."

"That's so, dear," she said. "My Alf says I ought not to have let it slip. But we mustn't ever speak of it. Poor Dogger's nerves are all in tatters."

"How do you know that? About the prison, I mean?"

"My Alf was in the army too, you know. He served for a time with the Colonel, and with Dogger. He doesn't talk about it. Most of 'em don't. My Alf got home safely with no more harm than troubled dreams, but a lot of them didn't. It's like a brotherhood, you know, the army; like one man spread out thin as a layer of jam across the whole face of the globe. They always know where all their old mates are and what's happened to 'em. It's eerie—psychic, like."

"Did Dogger kill someone?" I asked, point-blank.

"I'm sure he did, dear. They all did. It was their job, wasn't it?"

"Besides the enemy."

"Dogger saved your father's life," she said. "In more ways than one. He was a medical orderly, or some such thing, was Dogger, and a good one. They say he fished a bullet out of your father's chest, right next to the heart. Just as he was sewin' him up, some RAF bloke went off his head from shell shock. Tried to machete everyone in the tent. Dogger stopped him."

Mrs. Mullet pulled tight the final knot and used a pair of scissors to snip off the end of the string.

"Stopped him?"

"Yes, dear. Stopped him."

"You mean he killed him."

"Afterwards, Dogger couldn't remember. He'd been having one of his moments, you see, and—"

"And Father thinks it's happened again; that Dogger

has saved his life again by killing Horace Bonepenny! That's why he's taking the blame!"

"I don't know, dear, I'm sure. But if he did, it would be very like the Colonel."

That had to be it; there was no other explanation. What was it Father had said when I told him Dogger, too, had overheard his quarrel with Bonepenny? "That is what I fear more than anything." His exact words.

It was odd, really—almost ludicrous—like something out of Gilbert and Sullivan. I had tried to take the blame to protect Father. Father was taking the blame to protect Dogger. The question was this: Whom was Dogger protecting?

"Thank you, Mrs. M," I said. "I'll keep our conversation confidential. Strictly on the q.t."

"Girl to girl, like," she said, with a horrible smirking leer.

The "girl to girl" was too much. Too chummy, too belittling. Something in me that was less than noble rose up out of the depths, and I was transformed in the blink of an eye into Flavia the Pigtailed Avenger, whose assignment was to throw a wrench into this fearsome and unstoppable pie machine.

"Yes," I said. "Girl to girl. And while we're speaking girl to girl, it's probably as good a time as any to tell you that we none of us at Buckshaw really care for custard pie. In fact, we hate it."

"Oh piff, I know that well enough," she said.

"You do?" I was too taken aback to think of more than two words.

" 'Course I do. Cooks know all, they say, and I'm no dif-

ferent than the next one. I've known that de Luces and
custard don't mix since Miss Harriet was alive."

"But—"

"Why do I make them? Because Alf fancies a nice custard pie now and again. Miss Harriet used to tell me, 'The
de Luces are all lofty rhubarbs and prickly gooseberries,
Mrs. M, whereas your Alf's a smooth, sweet custard man. I
should like you to bake an occasional custard pie to remind us of our haughty ways, and when we turn up our
noses at it, why, you must take it home to your Alf as a
sweet apology.' And I don't mind sayin' I've taken home a
goodly number of apologies these more than twenty years
past."

"Then you'll not need another," I said.

And then I fled. You couldn't see my bottom for dust.

twenty-one

I PAUSED IN THE HALLWAY, STOOD PERFECTLY STILL, and listened. Because of its parquet floors and hardwood paneling, Buckshaw transmitted sound as perfectly as if it were the Royal Albert Hall. Even in complete silence, Buckshaw had its own unique silence; a silence I would recognize anywhere.

As quietly as I could, I picked up the telephone and gave the cradle a couple of clicks with my finger. "I'd like to place a trunk call to Doddingsley. I'm sorry, I don't have the number, but it's the inn there: the Red Fox or the Ring and Funnel. I've forgotten its name, but I think it has an R and an F in it."

"One moment, please," said the bored but efficient voice at the other end of the crackling line.

This shouldn't be too difficult, I thought. Being located across the street from the railway platform, the "RF," or whatever it was called, was the closest inn to the station and Doddingsley, after all, was no metropolis.

"The only listings I have are for the Grapes and the Jolly Coachman."

"That's it," I said. "The Jolly Coachman!"

The "RF" must have bubbled up from the sludge at the bottom of my mind.

"The number is Doddingsley two three," the voice said. "For future reference."

"Thank you," I mumbled, as the ringing at the other end began its little jig.

"Doddingsley two three. Jolly Coachman. Are you there? Cleaver, here." Cleaver, I assumed, was the proprietor.

"Yes, I'd like to speak with Mr. Pemberton, please. It's rather important."

Any barrier, I had learned—even a potential one—was best breached by pretending urgency.

"He's not here," said Cleaver.

"Oh dear," I said, laying it on a bit thick. "I'm sorry I missed him. Could you tell me when he left? Perhaps then I'll know what time to expect him."

Flave, I thought, you ought to be in Parliament.

"He left Saturday morning. Three days ago."

"Oh, thank you!" I breathed throatily, in a voice I hoped would fool the Pope. "You're awfully kind."

I rang off and returned the receiver to its cradle as gently as if it were a newly hatched chick.

"What do you think you're doing?" demanded a muffled voice.

I spun round and there was Feely, a winter scarf wrapped round the bottom part of her face.

"What are you doing?" she repeated. "You know perfectly well you're not to use the instrument."

"What are *you* doing?" I parried. "Going tobogganing?"

Feely made a grab for me and the scarf fell away to reveal a pair of red swollen lips which were the spitting image of a Cameroon mandrill's south pole.

I was too in awe to laugh. The poison ivy I had injected into her lipstick had left her mouth a blistered crater that might have done credit to Mount Popocatepetl. My experiment had succeeded after all. Loud fanfare of trumpets!

Unfortunately, I had no time to write it up; my notebook would have to wait.

MAXIMILIAN, IN MUSTARD CHECKS, was perched on the edge of the stone horse trough which lay in the shadow of the market cross, his tiny feet dangling in the air like Humpty Dumpty. He was so small I almost hadn't seen him.

"*Haroo, mon vieux*, Flavia!" he shouted, and I brought Gladys to a sliding stop at the very toes of his patent leather shoes. Trapped again! I'd better make the best of it.

"Hullo, Max," I said. "I have a question for you."

"Ho-ho!" he said. "Just like that! A question! No preliminaries? No talk of the sisters? No gossip from the great concert halls of the world?"

"Well," I said, a little embarrassed, "I did listen to *The Mikado* on the wireless."

"And how was it? Dynamically speaking? They always have an alarming tendency to shout Gilbert and Sullivan, you know."

"Enlightening," I said.

"Aha! You must tell me in what fashion. Dear Arthur composed some of the most sublime music ever written in this sceptered isle: 'The Lost Chord,' for instance. G and S fascinate me to no end. Did you know that their immortal partnership was shattered by a disagreement about the cost of a carpet?"

I looked closely at him to see if he was pulling my leg, but he seemed in earnest.

"Of course I'm simply dying to pump you about the recent unpleasantness at Buckshaw, Flavia dear, but I know your lips are thrice sealed by modesty, loyalty, and legality—and not necessarily in that order, am I correct?"

I nodded my head.

"Your question of the oracle, then?"

"Were you at Greyminster?"

Max tittered like a little yellow bird. "Oh dear, no. Nowhere quite so grand, I'm afraid. My schooling was on the Continent, Paris to be precise, and not necessarily indoors. My cousin Lombard, though, is an old Greyminsterian. He always speaks highly enough of the place—whenever he's not at the races or playing Oh Hell at Montfort's."

"Has he ever mentioned the head, Dr. Kissing?"

"The stamp wallah? Why, dear girl, he seldom speaks of anything else. He idolized the old gentleman. Claims old Kissing made him what he is today—which isn't much, but still..."

"I shouldn't think he's still alive? Dr. Kissing, I mean. He'd be very old, though, wouldn't he? I'm willing to bet everything I have that he's been dead for ages."

"Then you shall lose all your money!" said Max with a whoop. "Every blessed penny of it!"

ROOK'S END WAS TUCKED into the folds of a cozy bed formed by Squires Hill and the Jack O'Lantern, the latter a curious outcropping of the landscape which, from a distance, appeared to be an Iron Age tumulus but, upon approach, proved to be substantially larger and shaped like a skull.

I steered Gladys into Pooker's Lane, which ran along its jaw, or eastern edge. At the end of the lane, dense hedges bracketed the entrance to Rook's End.

Once past these ragged remnants of an earlier day, the lawns spread off to the east, west, and south, neglected and spiky. In spite of the sun, fingers of mist still floated in the shadows above the unkempt grass. Here and there the broad expanse of lawn was broken by one of those huge, sad beech trees whose massive boles and drooping branches always reminded me of a family of despondent elephants wandering lonely on the African veld.

Beneath the beeches, two antique ladies drifted in animated dialogue, as if competing for the role of Lady Macbeth. One was dressed in a diaphanous muslin nightgown, and a mobcap which seemed somehow to have escaped the eighteenth century, while her companion, enveloped in a cyanide blue tent dress, was wearing brass earrings the size of soup plates.

The house itself was what is often called romantically "a pile." Once the ancestral home of the de Lacey family, from whom Bishop's Lacey took its name (and who were said to be very distantly related to the de Luces), the place had come down in the world in stages: from being the country house of an inventive and successful Huguenot linen merchant to what it was today, a private hospital to which Daffy would instantly have assigned the name *Bleak House*. I almost wished she were here.

Two dusty motorcars huddling together in the forecourt testified to the shortage of both staff and visitors. Dumping Gladys beside an ancient monkey puzzle tree, I picked my way up the mossy, pitted steps to the front door.

A hand-inked sign said *Ring Plse.*, and I gave the enameled handle a pull. Somewhere inside the place a hollow clanking, like a cowbell Angelus, announced my arrival to persons unknown.

When nothing happened I rang again. Across the lawn, the two old ladies had begun to feign a tea party, with elaborate mincing curtsies, crooked fingers, and invisible cups and saucers.

I pressed an ear to the massive door, but other than an undertone, which must have been the sound of the building's breathing, I could hear nothing. I pushed the door open and stepped inside.

The first thing that struck me was the smell of the place: a mixture of cabbage, rubber cushions, dishwater, and death. Underlying that, like a groundsheet, was the sharp tang of the disinfectant used to swab the floors— dimethyl benzyl ammonium chloride, by the smell of it— a faint whiff of bitter almonds which was uncommonly like that of hydrogen cyanide, the gas that was used to exterminate killers in American gas chambers.

The entrance hall was painted a madhouse apple green: green walls, green woodwork, and green ceilings. The floors were covered with cheap brown linoleum so pitted with gladiatorial gouges that it might have been salvaged from the Roman Colosseum. Whenever I stepped on one of its pustulent brown blisters, the stuff let off a nasty hiss and I made a mental note to find out if color can cause nausea.

Against the far wall, in a chromium wheelchair, an

ancient man sat. gazing straight up into the air, mouth
agape, as if expecting an imminent miracle to take place
somewhere near the ceiling.

Off to one side a desk, bare except for a silver bell and
a smudged card marked *Ring Plse.*, hinted at some official,
yet unseen, presence.

I gave the striker four brisk strokes. At each *ting* of the
bell, the old man blinked violently, but did not take his
eyes from the air above his head.

Suddenly, as if she had slipped through a secret panel
in the woodwork, a wisp of a woman materialized. She
wore a white uniform and a blue cap, under which she was
busily poking limp strands of damp straw-colored hair with
one of her forefingers.

She looked as if she had been up to no good, and knew
perfectly well that I knew.

"Yes?" she said, in a thin but busy, standard-issue hospital voice.

"I've come to see Dr. Kissing," I said. "I'm his great-
granddaughter."

"Dr. *Isaac* Kissing?" she asked.

"Yes," I said, "Dr. Isaac Kissing. Do you keep more than
one?"

Without a word the White Phantom turned on her
heel and I followed, through an archway into a narrow so-
larium which ran the entire length of the building. Halfway along the gallery she stopped, pointed a thin finger
like the third ghost in *Scrooge*, and was gone.

At the far end of the tall-windowed room, in the single
ray of sunshine that penetrated the overhanging gloom of
the place, an old man sat in a wicker bath chair, a halo of
blue smoke rising slowly above his head. In disarray on a

small table beside him, a heap of newspapers threatened to slide off onto the floor.

He was wrapped in a mouse-colored dressing gown—like Sherlock Holmes's, except that it was spotted like a leopard with burn holes. Beneath this was visible a rusty black suit and a tall winged celluloid collar of ancient vintage. His long, curling yellow-gray hair was topped with a pillbox smoking cap of plum-colored velvet, and a lighted cigarette dangled from his lips, its gray ashes drooping like a mummified garden slug.

"Hello, Flavia," he said. "I've been expecting you."

AN HOUR HAD PASSED: an hour during which I had come to realize truly, for the first time, what we had lost in the war.

We had not got off to a particularly good start, Dr. Kissing and I.

"I must warn you at the outset that I'm not at my best conversing with little girls," he announced.

I bit my lip and kept my mouth shut.

"A boy is content to be made into a civil man by caning, or any one of a number of other stratagems, but a girl, being disqualified by Nature, as it were, from such physical brutality, must remain forever something of a *terra incognita*. Don't you think?"

I recognized it as one of those questions which doesn't require an answer. I raised the corners of my lips into what I hoped was a Mona Lisa smile—or at least one that signaled the required civility.

"So you're Jacko's daughter," he said. "You're not a bit like him, you know."

"I'm told I take after my mother, Harriet," I said.

"Ah, yes. Harriet. What a great tragedy that was. How terrible for all of you."

He reached out and touched a magnifying glass that perched precipitously atop the glacier of newspapers at his side. With the same movement he pried open a tin of Players that lay on the table and selected a fresh cigarette.

"I do my best to keep up with the world as seen through the eyes of these inky scribblers. My own eyes, I must confess, having been fixed on the passing parade for ninety-five years, are much wearied by what they have seen.

"Still, I somehow manage to keep informed about such births, deaths, marriages, and convictions as transpire in our shire. And I still subscribe to *Punch* and *Lilliput*, of course.

"You have two sisters, I believe, Ophelia and Daphne?"

I confessed that such was the case.

"Jacko always had a flair for the exotic, as I recall. I was hardly surprised to read that he had named his first two offspring after a Shakespearean hysteric and a Greek pincushion."

"Sorry?"

"Daphne, shot by Eros with a love-deadening arrow before being transformed by her father into a tree."

"I meant the madwoman," I said. "Ophelia."

"Bonkers," he said, pressing out his cigarette butt in an overflowing ashtray and lighting another. "Wouldn't you agree?"

The eyes that looked out at me from his heavily lined face were as bright and beady as those of any teacher who had ever stood watch at a blackboard, pointer in hand, and I knew that I had succeeded in my plan. I was no longer a "little girl." Whereas the mythical Daphne had been transformed into a mere laurel tree, I had become a boy in the lower Fourth.

"Not really, sir," I said. "I think Shakespeare meant Ophelia to be a symbol of something—like the herbs and flowers she gathers."

"Eh?" he said. "What's that?"

"Symbolic, sir. Ophelia is the innocent victim of a murderous family whose members are all totally self-absorbed. At least that's what I think."

"I see," he said. "Most interesting.

"Still," he added suddenly, "it was most gratifying to learn that your father retained enough of his Latin to name you Flavia. She of the golden hair."

"Mine is more of a mousy brown."

"Ah."

We seemed to have reached one of those impasses that litter so many conversations with the elderly. I was beginning to think he had fallen asleep with his eyes open.

"Well," he said at last, "you'd better let me have a look at her."

"Sir?" I said.

"My Ulster Avenger. You'd better let me have a look at her. You *have* brought her along, haven't you?"

"I—yes, sir, but how—?"

"Let us deduce," he said, as quietly as if he had said *let us pray*.

"Horace Bonepenny, onetime boy conjurer and long-time fraud artist, turns up dead in the garden of his old school chum, Jacko de Luce. Why? Blackmail is most likely. Therefore, let us suppose blackmail. Within hours, Jacko's daughter is ransacking newspaper archives at Bishop's Lacey, ferreting out reports of the demise of my dear old colleague, Mr. Twining, God rest his soul. How do I know this? I should think it obvious."

"Miss Mountjoy," I said.

"Very good, my dear. Tilda Mountjoy indeed—my eyes and ears upon the village and its environs for the past quarter century."

I should have known it! Miss Mountjoy was a spook!

"But let us continue. On the last day of his life, the thief Bonepenny has chosen to take up lodgings at the Thirteen Drakes. The young fool—well, no longer young, but still a fool, for all that—then manages to get himself done in. I remarked once to Mr. Twining that that boy would come to no good end. I hesitate to point out that I was correct in my prognostication. There always was a whiff of sulphur about the lad.

"But I digress. Shortly after his launch into eternity, Bonepenny's room at the inn is rifled by a maiden fair whose name I dare not utter aloud but who now sits demurely before me, fidgeting with something in her pocket which can hardly be anything other than a certain bit of paper the shade of Dundee marmalade, upon which is printed the likeness of Her Late Majesty Queen Victoria, and bearing the check letters, TL. *Quod erat demonstrandum.* Q.E.D."

"Q.E.D." I said, and without a word I pulled the glassine envelope from my pocket and held it out to him. With trembling hands—though whether they trembled from age or excitement I could not be certain—and using the tissue-thin paper as makeshift tweezers, he peeled back the flaps of the envelope with his nicotine-stained fingers. As the orange corners of the Ulster Avengers came into view,

I could not help noticing that his nicotine-stained finger-tips and the stamps were of a nearly identical hue.

"Great Scott!" he said, visibly shaken. "You've found AA. This stamp belongs to His Majesty, you know. It was stolen from an exhibition in London just weeks ago. It was in all the papers."

He shot me an accusing look over his spectacles, but his gaze was drawn away almost at once to the bright treasures that lay in his hands. He seemed to have forgotten I was in the room.

"Greetings, my old friends," he whispered, as if I weren't there. "It's been far too long a time." He took up the magnifying glass and examined them closely, one at a time. "And you, my cherished little TL: What a tale *you* could tell."

"Horace Bonepenny had both of them," I volunteered. "I found them in his luggage at the inn."

"You rifled his luggage?" Dr. Kissing asked, without looking away from the magnifying glass. "Phew! The Constabulary will hardly caper in delight upon the village green when they hear of that . . . nor will you, I'll wager."

"I didn't exactly rifle his luggage," I said. "He had hidden the stamps under a travel sticker on the outside of a trunk."

"With which, of course, you just happened to be idly fiddling when out they tumbled into your hands."

"Yes," I said. "That's precisely how it happened."

"Tell me," he said suddenly, swinging round to look me in the eye, "does your father know you're here?"

"No," I said. "Father's been charged with the murder. He's under arrest in Hinley."

"Good Lord! Did he do it?"

"No, but everyone seems to think he did. For a while, even I thought so myself."

"Ah," he said. "And what do you think now?"

"I don't know," I said. "Sometimes I think one thing and sometimes another. Everything's such a muddle."

"Everything is always a muddle just before it settles in. Tell me this, Flavia: What is it that interests you above all else in the universe? What is your one great passion?"

"Chemistry," I said in less than half a heartbeat.

"Well done!" said Dr. Kissing. "I've put that same question to an army of Hottentots in my time, and they always prattle on about this and that. Babble and gush, that's all it is. You, by contrast, have put it in a word."

The wicker creaked horribly as he half twisted round in his chair to face me. For an awful moment I thought his spine had crumbled.

"Sodium nitrite," he said. "Doubtless you are acquainted with sodium nitrite."

Acquainted with it? Sodium nitrite was the antidote for cyanide poisoning, and I knew it in all its various reactions as well as I know my own name. But how had he known to choose it as an example? Was he psychic?

"Close your eyes," Dr. Kissing said. "Imagine you are holding in your hand a test tube half-filled with a thirty percent solution of hydrochloric acid. To it, you add a small amount of sodium nitrite. What do you observe?"

"I don't need to close my eyes," I said. "It becomes orange...orange and turbid."

"Excellent! The color of these wayward postage stamps, is it not? And then?"

"Given time, twenty or thirty minutes perhaps, it clears."

"It clears. I rest my case."

As if a great weight had been lifted from my shoulders, I grinned a stupid grin.

"You must have been a wizard teacher, sir," I said.

"Yes, so I was . . . in my day."

"And now you've brought my little treasure home to me," he said, glancing at the stamps again.

This was something I hadn't counted upon; something I hadn't really thought through. I had meant only to discover if the owner of the Ulster Avenger was still alive. After that, I would hand it over to Father, who would surrender it to the police, who would, in due course, see that it was restored to its rightful owner. Dr. Kissing spotted my hesitation at once.

"Let me pose another question," he said. "What if you had come here today and found that I'd hopped the twig, as it were; flown off to my eternal reward?"

"You mean died, sir?"

"That's the word I was fishing for: died. Yes."

"I suppose I should have given your stamp to Father."

"To keep?"

"He'd know what to do with it."

"I should think that the best person to decide that is the stamp's owner, wouldn't you agree?"

I knew that the answer was "yes" but I couldn't say it. I knew that, more than anything, I wanted to present the stamp to Father, even though it wasn't mine to give. At the same time, I wanted to give both stamps to Inspector Hewitt. But why?

Dr. Kissing lighted another cigarette and gazed out the window. At length, he plucked one of the stamps from the folder and handed me the other.

"This is AA," he said. "*It is not mine; it don't belong to me,* as the old song says. Your father may do with it as he wishes. It is not my place to decide."

I took the Ulster Avenger from him and wrapped it carefully in my handkerchief.

"On the other hand, the exquisite little TL *is* mine. Mine own, without the shadow of a doubt."

"I expect you'll be happy to be sticking it back into your album, sir," I said with resignation, slipping its mate into my pocket.

"My album?" He gave a croaking laugh that ended in a cough. "My albums are, as dear, dead Dowson put it, gone with the wind."

His old eyes turned towards the window, gazing without seeing at the lawn outside where the two old ladies still fluttered and pirouetted like exotic butterflies beneath the sun-dappled beeches.

> " 'I have forgot much, Cynara! Gone with the wind,
> Flung roses, roses riotously with the throng,
> Dancing, to put thy pale, lost lilies out of mind;
> But I was desolate and sick of an old passion,
> Yea, all the time, because the dance was long:
> I have been faithful to thee, Cynara! In my fashion.'

"It's from his *Non Sum Qualis Eram Bonae Sub Regno Cynarae.* Perhaps you know it?"

I shook my head. "It's very beautiful," I said.

"To remain sequestered in such a place as this," Dr.

Kissing said with a broad sweep of his arm, "for all its dowdy decrepitude is, as you will appreciate, a most ruinous financial undertaking."

He looked at me as if he had made a joke. When I offered no response, he pointed to the table.

"Fetch out one of those albums. The uppermost, I think, will do."

I now noticed for the first time that there was a shelf wedged in below the tabletop, upon which were two thick bound albums. I blew off the dust and handed him the top one.

"No, no . . . open it yourself."

I opened the book to the first page, which contained two stamps: one black, the other red. By the slight marks of gummy residue and the ruled lines, I could see that the page had once been filled. I turned to the next page . . . and the next. All that remained of the album was a gutted hulk: a sparse, ravaged thing that even a schoolboy might have hidden away in shame.

"The cost, you see, of housing a beating heart. One disposes of one's life one little square at a time. Not much of it left, is there?"

"But the Ulster Avenger!" I said. "It must be worth a fortune!"

"Indeed," said Dr. Kissing, glancing once more through the magnifier at his treasure.

"One reads in novels," he said, "of the reprieve that comes when the trap's already sprung; of the horse whose heart stops an inch past the finish line." He chuckled dryly, and pulled out a handkerchief to wipe his eyes. "'Too late! Too late! the maiden cried'—and all that. 'Curfew shall not ring tonight!'

"How Fate loves a jest," he went on in a half whisper. "Who said that? Cyrano de Bergerac, was it not?"

For just a fraction of a second, I thought how much Daffy would enjoy talking to this old gentleman. But only for a fraction of a second. And then I shrugged.

With a slightly amused smile, Dr. Kissing removed his cigarette from his mouth, and touched its lighted tip to the corner of the Ulster Avenger.

I felt as if a ball of fire had been thrown into my face; as if my chest had been bound with barbed wire. I blinked, and then, frozen with horror, watched as the stamp began to smolder, then burst into a tiny flame which licked slowly, inexorably, across Queen Victoria's youthful face.

As the flame reached his fingertips, Dr. Kissing opened his hand and let the dark ashes float to the floor. From beneath the hem of his dressing gown, a polished black shoe ventured out and stepped daintily on the remains then, with a few quick twists, ground them beneath the toe.

In three thunderous heartbeats, the Ulster Avenger was no more than a black smudge on the linoleum of Rook's End.

"The stamp in your pocket has just doubled in value," said Dr. Kissing. "Guard it well, Flavia. It is now the only one of its kind in the world."

twenty-two

WHENEVER I'M OUT-OF-DOORS AND FIND MYSELF wanting to have a first-rate think, I fling myself down on my back, throw my arms and legs out so that I look like an asterisk, and gaze at the sky. For the first little while, I'm usually entertained by my "floaters," those wormy little strings of protein that swim to and fro across one's field of vision like dark little galaxies. When I'm not in a hurry, I stand on my head to stir them up, and then lie back to watch the show, as if it were an animated cinema film.

Today, though, I'd had too much on my mind to bother, so when I had bicycled no more than a mile from Rook's End, I threw myself down on the grassy bank and stared up into the summer sky.

I could not get out of my mind something that Father had told me, namely that the two of them, he and Horace Bonepenny, had killed Mr. Twining; that they were personally responsible for his death.

Had this been no more than one of Father's fantastic ideas I should have written it off at once, but there was more to it than that. Miss Mountjoy, too, believed they had killed her uncle, and had told me so.

It was easy enough to see that Father felt a real sense of guilt. After all, he had been part of the push to view Dr. Kissing's stamp collection, and his onetime friendship with Bonepenny, even though it had cooled, made him an accomplice in a roundabout sort of way. But still . . .

No, there had to be more to it than that, but what it might be, I could not think.

I lay on the grass, staring up at the blue vault of Heaven as earnestly as those old pillar-squatting fakirs in India used to stare directly into the sun before we civilized them, but I could think of nothing properly. Directly above me, the sun was a great white zero, blazing down upon my empty head.

I visualized myself pulling on my mental thinking cap, jamming it down around my ears as I had taught myself to do. It was a tall, conical wizard's model, covered with chemical equations and formulae: a cornucopia of ideas.

Still nothing.

But wait! Yes! That was it! Father had done nothing. Nothing! He had known—or at least suspected—from the instant it happened that Bonepenny had pinched the Head's prize stamp . . . and yet he had told no one.

It was a sin of omission: one of those offenses from the ecclesiastical catalogue of crime Feely was always going on about that seemed to apply to everyone but her.

But Father's guilt was a moral thing and, as such, hardly my cup of tea.

Still, there was no denying it: Father had kept silent,

and by his silence had perhaps made it seem necessary for the saintly old Mr. Twining to shoulder the blame and pay for the breach of honor with his life.

Surely there must have been some talk at the time. The natives in this part of England have never been known for their reticence; far from it. In the last century, the Hinley pond-poet Herbert Miles had referred to us as "that gaggle o' geese who gossip gaily 'pon the gladdening green," and there was a certain amount of truth in his words. People love to talk—especially when the talking involves answering the questions of others—because it makes them feel wanted. In spite of the gravy-stained copy of *Inquire Within Upon Everything* which Mrs. Mullet kept on a shelf in the pantry, I had long ago discovered that the best way to obtain answers about anything was to walk up to the closest person and ask. Inquire without.

I could not very well question Father about his silence in those schoolboy days. Even if I dared, which I did not, he was shut up in a police cell and likely to stay there. I could not ask Miss Mountjoy, who had slammed a door in my face because she viewed me as the warm flesh and blood of a cold-blooded killer. In short, I was on my own.

All day, something had been playing away in the back of my mind like a gramophone in a distant room. If only I could tune in to the melody.

The odd feeling had begun when I was browsing through the stacks of newspapers in the Pit Shed behind the library. It was something someone said . . . but what?

Sometimes, trying to catch a fleeting thought can be like trying to catch a bird in the house. You stalk it, tiptoe towards it, make a grab . . . and the bird is gone, always just beyond your fingertips, its wings . . .

Yes! Its wings!

"He looked just like a falling angel," one of the Greyminster boys had said. Toby Lonsdale—I remembered his name now. What a peculiar thing for a boy to say about a plummeting schoolmaster! And Father had compared Mr. Twining, just before he jumped, to a haloed saint in an illuminated manuscript.

The problem was that I hadn't searched far enough in the archives. *The Hinley Chronicle* had stated quite clearly that police investigations into Mr. Twining's death, and the theft of Dr. Kissing's stamp, were continuing. And what about his obituary? That would have come later, of course, but what did it say?

In two shakes of a dead lamb's tail I was aboard Gladys, pedaling furiously for Bishop's Lacey and Cow Lane.

I DIDN'T SEE THE "CLOSED" SIGN until I was ten feet from the front door of the library. Of course! Flavia, sometimes you have tapioca for brains; Feely was right about that. Today was Tuesday. The library would not open again until ten o'clock on Thursday morning.

As I walked Gladys slowly towards the river and the Pit Shed, I thought about those sappy stories they tell on *The Children's Hour*: those moral little tales of instruction such as the one about the Pony Engine ("I think I can . . . I think I can . . .") which was able to pull an entire freight train over the mountain just because it thought it could, it thought it could. And because it never gave up. Never giving up was the key.

The key? I had returned the Pit Shed's key to Miss Mountjoy: I remembered it perfectly. But was there by chance a duplicate? A spare key hidden under a windowsill to be used in the event some forgetful character wandered off on holiday to Blackpool with the original in her pocket? Since Bishop's Lacey was not (at least not until a few days ago) a notable hotbed of crime, a concealed key seemed a distinct possibility.

I ran my fingers along the lintel above the door, looked under the potted geraniums that lined the walkway, even lifted a couple of suspicious-looking stones.

Nothing.

I poked in the crevices of the stone wall that ran from the lane up to the door.

Still nothing. Not a sausage.

I cupped my hands to a window, and peered in at the stacks of crumbling newspapers sleeping in their cradles. So near and yet so far.

I was so exasperated I could spit, and I did.

What would Marie-Anne Paulze Lavoisier have done? I wondered. Would she have stood here fuming and foaming like one of those miniature volcanoes which results when a heap of ammonium dichromate is ignited? Somehow I doubted it. Marie-Anne would forget the chemistry and tackle the door.

I gave the doorknob a vicious twist and fell forward into the room. Some fool had been here and left the stupid thing unlocked! I hoped no one had been watching. Good thing I thought of that, though, since I realized at once that it would be wise to wheel Gladys inside where she wouldn't be spotted by passing busybodies.

Skirting the mouth of the boarded-over pit in the middle of the room, I eased my way gingerly round to the racks of yellowed newspapers.

I had no trouble finding the relevant issues of *The*

Hinley Chronicle. Yes, here it was. As I thought it might, Mr. Twining's obituary had appeared on the Friday after the account of his death:

> **Twining,** Grenville, M.A. (Oxon.) Passed away suddenly on Monday last at Greyminster School, near Hinley, at the age of seventy-two. He was predeceased by his parents, Marius and Dorothea Twining, of Winchester, Hants. He is survived by a niece, Matilda Mountjoy, of Bishop's Lacey. Mr. Twining was buried from the chapel at Greyminster, where Rev. Canon Blake-Soames, Rector of St. Tancred's, Bishop's Lacey, and Chaplain of Greyminster, led the prayers. Floral tributes were numerous.

BUT WHERE HAD THEY BURIED HIM? Had his body been returned to Winchester and laid to rest beside his parents? Had he been buried at Greyminster? Somehow I doubted it. It seemed much more likely that I would find his grave in the churchyard of St. Tancred's, no more than a two-minute walk from where I was standing.

I would leave Gladys behind in the Pit Shed; no point in attracting unnecessary attention. If I crouched down and kept behind the hedgerow that bordered the towpath, I could easily pass from here to the churchyard without being seen.

As I opened the door, a dog barked. Mrs. Fairweather, the Chairman of the Ladies' Altar Guild, was at the end of the lane with her corgi. I eased the door shut before she or the dog could spot me. I peeked out the corner of the window and watched the dog snuffling at the trunk of an oak as Mrs. Fairweather stared off into the distance, pretending she didn't know what was going on at the other end of the lead.

Blast! I'd have to wait until the dog had done its business. I looked round the room.

On either side of the door were makeshift bookcases whose rough-cut, sagging boards looked as if they'd been hammered together by a well-meaning but inept amateur carpenter.

On the right, generations of outdated reference books— year upon year of *Crockford's Clerical Directory*, *Hazell's Annual*, *Whitaker's Almanack*, *Kelly's Directories*, *Brassey's Naval Annual*—all jammed uncomfortably cheek-by-jowl on shelves of unpainted boards, their once regal bindings of red and blue and black now bleached brown by time and seeping daylight, and all of them smelling of mice.

The shelves on the left were filled with rows of identical gray volumes, each with the same gold-leaf title embossed on its spine in elaborate Gothic letters: *The Greyminsterian*; I remembered that these were the yearbooks from Father's old school. We even had a few of them at Buckshaw. I pulled one from the shelf before noticing that it was marked 1942.

I returned it to its place and ran my index finger to the left along the spines of the remaining volumes: 1930 . . . 1925 . . .

Here it was—1920! My hands shook as I took down the book and flipped quickly through it from back to front. Its pages overflowed with articles on cricket, rowing, athletics, scholarships, rugger, photography, and nature study. As far as I could see, there was not a word about the Magic Circle or the Stamp Society. Scattered throughout were photographs in which row upon row of boys grinned, and sometimes grimaced, at the eye of the camera.

Opposite the title page was a photographic portrait edged in black. In it, a distinguished-looking gentleman in cap and gown perched casually upon the end of a desk, Latin grammar in hand as he gazed at the photographer with a look of ever-so-slight amusement. Beneath the photo was a caption: "Grenville Twining 1848–1920."

That was all. No mention of the events surrounding his death, no eulogy, and no fond recollections of the man. Had there been a conspiracy of silence?

There was more to this than met the eye.

I began slowly turning pages, scanning the articles and reading the photo captions wherever one was provided.

Two thirds of the way through the book my eye caught the name "de Luce." The photograph showed three boys in shirtsleeves and school caps sitting on a lawn beside a wicker hamper which rested on a blanket littered with what appeared to be food for a picnic: a loaf of bread, a pot of jam, tarts, apples, and jars of ginger beer.

The caption read "Omar Khayyam Revisited— Greyminster's Tuck Shop Does Us Proud. Left to right: Haviland de Luce, Horace Bonepenny, and Robert Stanley pose for a tableau from the pages of the Persian Poet."

There was no doubt that the boy on the left, cross-legged on the blanket, was Father, looking more happy and jolly and carefree than I had ever known him to be. In the center, the long, gangling lad pretending he was about to bite into a sandwich was Horace Bonepenny. I'd have recognized him even without the caption. In the photograph, his flaming red curls had registered on the film as a ghostly pale aura round his head.

I couldn't suppress a shiver as I thought of how he had looked as a corpse.

Slightly apart from his comrades, the third boy, judging by the unnatural angle at which he held his head, seemed to be taking pains to show off his best profile. He was darkly handsome and older than the other two, with a hint of the smoldering good looks of a silent movie star.

It was odd, but I had the feeling that I had seen that face before.

Suddenly I felt as if someone had dropped a lizard down my neck. Of course I had seen this face—and recently too! The third boy in the photograph was the person who only two days ago had introduced himself to me as Frank Pemberton; Frank Pemberton, who had stood with me in Buckshaw Folly in the rain; Frank Pemberton, who this very morning had told me that he was off to view a shroud tomb in Nether Eaton.

One by one the facts assembled themselves, and like Saul I saw as clearly as if the scales had been ripped from my eyes.

Frank Pemberton was Bob Stanley and Bob Stanley was "The Third Man," so to speak. It was *he* who had murdered Horace Bonepenny in the cucumber patch at Buckshaw. I'd be willing to stake my life on it.

As everything fell into place my heart pounded as if it were about to burst.

There had been something fishy about Pemberton from the outset, and again this was something I had not thought about since Sunday at the Folly. It was something he had said . . . but what?

We had talked about the weather; we had exchanged names. He had admitted that he already knew who I was, that he had looked us up in *Who's Who*. Why would he need to do that when he had known Father for most of his life? Could that have been the lie that set my invisible antennae to twitching?

There had been his accent, I remembered. Slight, but still . . .

He had told me about his book: *Pemberton's Stately Homes: A Stroll Through Time*. Plausible, I suppose.

What else had he said? Nothing of any great importance, some load of twaddle about us being fellow castaways on a desert island. That we should be friends.

The bit of tinder that had been smoldering away in the back of my mind burst suddenly into flames!

"I trust we shall become fast friends."

His exact words! But where had I heard them before?

Like a ball on a rubber string my thoughts flew back to a winter's day. Although it had been still early, the trees outside the drawing-room window had gone from yellow to orange to gray; the sky from cobalt blue to black.

Mrs. Mullet had brought in a plate of crumpets and drawn the curtains. Feely was sitting on the couch looking at herself in the back of a teaspoon, and Daffy was stretched out across Father's old stuffed chair by the fire. She was reading aloud to us from *Penrod,* a book she had commandeered from the little shelf of childhood favorites which had been preserved in Harriet's dressing room.

Penrod Schofield was twelve, a year and some months older than I, but close enough to be of passing interest. To me, Penrod seemed to be Huckleberry Finn dragged forward in time to World War I and set down in some vaguely midwestern American city. Although the book was full of stables and alleys and high board fences and delivery vans which were, in those days, still drawn by horses, the whole thing seemed to me as alien as if it had taken place upon the planet Pluto. Feely and I had sat entranced through Daffy's readings of *Scaramouche*, *Treasure Island*, and *A Tale of Two Cities*, but there was something about Penrod which made his world seem as far removed from us in time as the last Ice Age. Feely, who thought of books in terms of musical signatures, said that it was written in the key of C major.

Still, as Daffy plodded through its pages, we had laughed once or twice, here and there, at Penrod's defiance of his parents and authority, but I had wondered at the time what there was about a troublesome boy that had captured the imagination, and possibly the love, of the young Harriet de Luce. Perhaps now I could begin to guess.

The most amusing scene, I remembered, had been the one in which Penrod was being introduced to the sanctimonious Reverend Mr. Kinosling, who had patted him on the head and said, "A trost we shall bick-home fawst frainds." This was a kind of condescension with which I lived my life, and I probably laughed too loud.

The point, though, was that *Penrod* was an American book, written by an American author. It was not likely as well known here in England as it would have been abroad.

Could Pemberton—or Bob Stanley, as I now knew him to be—have come across the book, or the phrase, in England? It was possible, of course, but it seemed unlikely. And hadn't Father told me that Bob Stanley—the same Bob Stanley who was Horace Bonepenny's confederate—had gone to America and set up a shady dealing in postage stamps?

Pemberton's slight accent was American! An old Greyminsterian with just a touch of the New World.

What an imbecile I had been!

Another peek out the window showed me that Mrs. Fairweather was gone and Cow Lane was now empty. I left the book lying open on the table, slipped out the door, and made my way round the back of the Pit Shed to the river.

A hundred years ago the river Efon had been part of a canal system, although there was now little left of it but the towpath. At the foot of Cow Lane were a few rotting remnants of the pilings which had once lined the embankment, but as it flowed towards the church, the river's waters had swollen from their decaying confines to widen in places into broad pools, one of which was at the center of the low marshy area behind the church of St. Tancred.

I scrambled over the rotted lych-gate into the churchyard, where the old tombstones leaned crazily like floating buoys in an ocean of grass so long I had to wade through it as if I were a bather waist-deep at the seaside.

The earliest graves, and those of the wealthiest former parishioners, were closest to the church, while back here along the fieldstone wall were those of more recent interments.

There was also a vertical stratum. Five hundred years of constant use had given the churchyard the appearance of a risen loaf: a fat loaf of freshly baked green bread, puffed up considerably above the level of the surrounding ground. I gave a delicious shiver at the thought of the yeasty remains that lay beneath my feet.

For a while I browsed aimlessly among the tombstones, reading off the family names that one often heard mentioned in Bishop's Lacey: Coombs, Nesbit, Barker, Hoare, and Carmichael. Here, with a lamb carved on his stone, was little William, the infant son of Tully Stoker, who, had he lived, would by now have been a man of thirty, and older brother to Mary. Little William had died aged five months and four days "of a croup," it said, in the spring of 1919, the year before Mr. Twining had leaped from the clock tower at Greyminster. There was a good chance, then, that the Doctor, too, was buried somewhere nearby.

For a moment I thought I had found him: a black stone with a pointed pyramidal top had the name *Twining* crudely cut upon it. But this Twining, on closer inspection, turned out to be an Adolphus who had been lost at sea in 1809. His stone was so remarkably preserved that I couldn't resist the urge to run my fingers over its cool polished surface.

"Sleep well, Adolphus," I said. "Wherever you are." .

Mr. Twining's tombstone, I knew—assuming he had one, and I found it difficult to believe otherwise—would not be one of the weathered sandstone specimens which leaned like jagged brown teeth, nor would it be one of those vast pillared monuments with drooping chains and funereal wrought-iron fences that marked the plots of Bishop Lacey's wealthiest and most aristocratic families (including any number of departed de Luces).

I put my hands on my hips and stood waist-deep in the weeds at the churchyard's perimeter. On the other side of the stone wall was the towpath, and beyond that, the river. It was somewhere back here that Miss Mountjoy had vanished after she had fled the church, immediately after the Vicar had asked us to pray for the repose of Horace Bonepenny's soul. But where had she been going?

Over the lych-gate I climbed once more, and onto the towpath.

Now I could clearly see the stepping-stones that lay

spotted among streamers of waterweed, just beneath the surface of the slow-flowing river. These wound across the widening pool to a low muddy bank on the far side, above and beyond which ran a bramble hedge bordering a field which belonged to Malplaquet Farm.

I took off my shoes and socks and stepped off onto the first stone. The water was colder than I had expected. My nose was still running slightly and my eyes watering, and the thought crossed my mind that I'd probably die of pneumonia in a day or two and, before you could say "knife," become a permanent resident of St. Tancred's churchyard.

Waving my arms like semaphore signals, I made my way carefully across the water and flat-footed it through the mud of the bank. By grasping a handful of long weeds I was able to pull myself up onto the embankment, a dike of packed earth that rose up between the river and the adjoining field.

I sat down to catch my breath and wipe the muck from my feet with a hank of the wild grass which grew in knots along the hedge. Somewhere close by a yellowhammer was singing "a little bit of bread and no cheese." It suddenly went silent. I listened, but all I could hear was the distant hum of the countryside: a bagpipe drone of far-off farm machinery.

With my shoes and socks back on, I dusted myself off and began walking along the hedgerow, which seemed at first to be an impenetrable tangle of thorns and brambles. Then, just as I was about to turn and retrace my steps, I found it—a narrow cutting in the thicket, no more than a thinning, really. I pushed myself through and came out on the other side of the hedge.

A few yards back, in the direction of the church, something stuck up out of the grass. I approached it cautiously, the hair at the nape of my neck prickling in Neanderthal alarm.

It was a tombstone, and crudely carved upon it was the name Grenville Twining.

On the tilted base of the stone was a single word: *Vale!*

Vale!—the word Mr. Twining had shouted from the top of the tower! The word Horace Bonepenny had breathed into my face as he expired.

Realization swept over me like a wave: Bonepenny's dying mind had wanted only to confess to Mr. Twining's murder, and fate had granted him only one word with which to do so. In hearing his confession, I had become the only living person who could link the two deaths. Except, perhaps, for Bob Stanley. My Mr. Pemberton.

At the thought, a cold shiver ran down my spine.

There were no dates given on Mr. Twining's tombstone, almost as if whoever had buried him here had wanted to obliterate his history. Daffy had read us tales in which suicides were buried outside the churchyard or at a crossroads, but I had scarcely believed these to be any more than ecclesiastical old wives' tales. Still, I couldn't help wondering if, like Dracula, Mr. Twining was lying beneath my feet wrapped tightly in his Master's cape?

But the gown I had found hidden on the tower roof at Anson House—which was now reposing with the police—had not belonged to Mr. Twining. Father had made it clear that Mr. Twining was wearing his gown when he fell. So, too, had Toby Lonsdale, as he told *The Hinley Chronicle*.

Could they both be wrong? Father had admitted, after

all, that the sun might have dazzled his eyes. What else had he told me?

I remembered his exact words as he described Mr. Twining standing on the parapet:

"His whole head seemed to be aglow," Father had said. "His hair like a disk of beaten copper in the rising sun; like a saint in an illuminated manuscript."

And then the rest of the truth rushed in upon me like a wave of nausea: It had been Horace Bonepenny up there on the ramparts. Horace Bonepenny of the flaming red hair; Horace Bonepenny the mimic; Horace Bonepenny the magician.

The whole thing had been a skillfully planned illusion!

Miss Mountjoy had been right. He *had* killed her uncle.

He and his confederate, Bob Stanley, must have lured Mr. Twining to the roof of the tower, most likely under the pretense of returning the stolen postage stamp which they had hidden there.

Father had told me of Bonepenny's extravagant mathematical calculations; his architectural prowlings would have made him as familiar with the tiles of the tower as he was with his own study.

When Mr. Twining had threatened to expose them, they had killed him, probably by bashing his head in with a brick. The fatal blow would have been impossible to detect after such a terrible fall. And then they had staged the suicide—every instant of the thing planned in cold blood. Perhaps they had even rehearsed.

It had been Mr. Twining who fell to the cobbles, but Bonepenny who trod the ramparts in the morning sun and Bonepenny, in a borrowed cap and gown, who had shouted "*Vale!*" to the boys in the Quad. "*Vale!*"—a word that could suggest only suicide.

Having done that, he had ducked down behind the parapet just as Stanley dropped the body through the drainage opening in the roof. To a sun-blinded observer on the ground, it would have appeared that the old man had fallen straight through. It was really nothing more than the Resurrection of Tchang Fu performed on a larger stage, dazzled eyes and all.

How utterly convincing it had been!

And for all these years Father had believed that it was his silence that had caused Mr. Twining to commit suicide, that it was he who was responsible for the old man's death! What a dreadful burden to bear, and how horrible!

Not for thirty years, not until I found the evidence among the tiles of Anson House, had anyone suspected it was murder. And they had almost got away with it.

I reached out and touched Mr. Twining's tombstone to steady myself.

"I see you've found him," said someone behind me, and at the sound of his voice my blood ran cold.

I spun round and found myself face-to-face with Frank Pemberton.

twenty-three

WHENEVER ONE COMES FACE-TO-FACE WITH A KILLER in a novel or in the cinema, his opening words are always dripping with menace, and often from Shakespeare.

"Well, well," he will generally hiss, "'Journeys end in lovers meeting,'" or "'So wise so young, they say, do never live long.'"

But Frank Pemberton said nothing of the sort; in fact, quite the contrary:

"Hullo, Flavia," he said with a lopsided grin. "Fancy meeting you here."

My arteries were throbbing like stink, and I could already feel the redness rising in my face, which, in spite of the chills, had instantly become as hot as a griddle.

A single thought went racing through my mind: I mustn't let on...I mustn't let on. Mustn't show that I know he's Bob Stanley.

"Hello," I said, hoping my voice wasn't shaking. "How was the shroud tomb?"

I knew instantly that I was fooling no one but myself. He was watching my face the way a cat watches the family canary when they're alone in the house.

"The shroud tomb? Ah! A confection in white marble," he said. "Remarkably like an almond marzipan, but larger, of course."

I decided to play along until I could formulate a plan.

"I expect your publisher was pleased."

"My publisher? Oh, yes. Old . . ."

"Quarrington," I said.

"Yes. Quite. Quarrington. He was ecstatic."

Pemberton—I still thought of him as Pemberton—put down his knapsack and began to unfasten the leather straps of his portfolio.

"Phew!" he said. "Rather warm, isn't it?"

He removed his jacket, threw it carelessly across his shoulder, and jerked a thumb at Mr. Twining's tombstone.

"What's the great interest?"

"He was my father's old schoolmaster," I said.

"Ah!" He sat down and lounged against the base of the stone as casually as if he were Lewis Carroll and I were Alice, picnicking upon the river Isis.

How much did he know? I wondered. I waited for him to make his opening move. I could use the time to think.

Already I was planning my escape. Could I outrun him if I took to my heels? It seemed unlikely. If I went for the river, he'd overtake me before I was halfway across. If I headed for the field towards Malplaquet Farm, I'd be less likely to find help than if I ran for the High Street.

"I understand your father is something of a philatelist," he said suddenly, looking unconcernedly off towards the farm.

"He collects stamps, yes. How did you know?"

"My publisher—old Quarrington—happened to mention it this morning over at Nether Eaton. He was thinking of asking your father to write a history of some obscure postage stamp, but couldn't think quite how best to approach him. Couldn't begin to understand it all . . . far beyond me . . . too technical . . . suggested that perhaps he should have a word with you."

It was a lie and I detected it at once. As an accomplished fibber myself, I spotted the telltale signs of an untruth before they were halfway out of his mouth: the excessive detail, the offhand delivery, and the wrapping-up of it all in casual chitchat.

"Could be worth a bundle, you know," he added. "Old Quarrington's pretty flush since he married into the Norwood millions, but don't let on I told you. I expect your father wouldn't say no to a bit of pocket change to buy a New Guinea ha'penny thingummy, would he? It must take a pretty penny to keep up a place like Buckshaw."

This was piling insult onto injury. The man must take me for a fool.

"Father's rather busy these days," I said. "But I'll mention it to him."

"Ah, yes, this—sudden death you spoke of . . . police and all that. Must be a damnable bore."

Was he going to make a move or were we going to sit here gossiping until dark? Perhaps it would be best if I took the initiative. That way, at least, I'd have the advantage of surprise. But how?

I remembered a piece of sisterly advice, which Feely once gave Daffy and me:

"If ever you're accosted by a man," she'd said, "kick him in the Casanovas and run like blue blazes!"

Although it had sounded at the time like a useful bit of intelligence, the only problem was that I didn't know where the Casanovas were located.

I'd have to think of something else.

I scraped the toe of my shoe in the sand; I would grab a handful and toss it in his eyes before he knew what had hit him. I saw him watching me.

He stood up and dusted the seat of his trousers.

"People sometimes do a thing in haste and later come to regret it," he said conversationally. Was he referring to Horace Bonepenny or to himself? Or was he warning me not to make a foolish move? "I saw you at the Thirteen Drakes, you know. You were inside the front door looking at the register when my taxi pulled up."

Curses! I had been spotted after all.

"I have friends who work there," I said. "Mary and Ned. I sometimes drop in to say hello."

"And do you always rifle the guests' rooms?"

I could feel my face going all scarlet even as he said it.

"As I suspected," he went on. "Look, Flavia, I'll be frank with you. A business associate had something in his possession that didn't belong to him. It was mine. Now, I know for a fact that, other than my associate, you and the landlord's daughter were the only two people who were in that room. I also know that Mary Stoker would have no reason to take this particular object. What am I to think?"

"Are you referring to that old stamp?" I asked.

This was going to be a tightrope act, and I was already putting on my tights. Pemberton relaxed at once.

"You admit it?" he said. "You're an even smarter girl than I gave you credit for."

"It was on the floor under the trunk," I said. "It must have fallen out. I was helping Mary clean up the room. She'd forgotten to do a few things, and her father, you see, can be—"

"I do see. So you stole my stamp and took it home."

I bit my lip, wrinkled my face a bit, and rubbed my eyes. "I didn't actually steal it. I thought someone had dropped it. No, that's not entirely true: I knew that Horace Bonepenny had dropped it, and since he was dead, he wouldn't have any further need for it. I thought I'd make a present of it to Father and he'd get over being angry with me about the Tiffany vase I smashed. There. Now you know."

Pemberton whistled. "A Tiffany vase?"

"It was an accident," I said. "I shouldn't have been playing tennis in the house."

"Well," he said, "that solves the problem, doesn't it? You hand over my stamp and it's case closed. Agreed?"

I nodded happily. "I'll run home and get it."

Pemberton burst into uncomplimentary laughter and slapped his leg. When he had recovered himself, he said, "You're very good, you know—for your age. You remind me of myself. Run home and get it indeed!"

"All right, then," I said. "I'll tell you where I hid it and you can go and get it yourself. I'll stay here. On my honor as a Girl Guide!"

I made the Girl Guide three-eared bunny salute with

my fingers. I did not tell him that I was technically no longer a member of that organization, and hadn't been since I was chucked out for manufacturing ferric hydroxide to earn my Domestic Service badge. No one had seemed to care that it was the antidote for arsenic poisoning.

Pemberton glanced at his wristwatch. "It's getting late," he said. "No more time for pleasantries."

Something about his face had changed, as if a curtain had been drawn across it. There was a sudden chill in the air.

He made a lunge for me and grabbed my wrist. I let out a yelp of pain. In a few more seconds, I knew, he'd be twisting my arm behind my back. I gave in at once.

"I hid it in Father's dressing room at Buckshaw," I blurted. "There are two clocks in the room: a large one on the chimneypiece and a smaller one on the table beside his bed. The stamp is stuck to the back of the pendulum of the chimneypiece clock."

And then something dreadful happened—dreadful and, as it would turn out, quite wonderful, rolled together into one: I sneezed.

My head cold had been lingering, nearly forgotten, for most of the day. I had noticed that, in the same way they recede when you're sleeping, head colds often let up when you're too preoccupied to pay them attention. Mine was suddenly back with a vengeance.

Forgetting for a moment that the Ulster Avenger was nestled inside it, I went for my handkerchief. Pemberton, startled, must have thought my sudden move was the prelude to my bolting—or perhaps an attack upon his person. Whatever the case, as I brought the handkerchief up towards my nose, before it was even opened he deflected my hand with a lightning-quick grab, crumpled the cotton into a ball, and rammed it, stamp and all, into my mouth.

"Right, then," he said. "We'll see what we shall see."

He pulled his jacket from his shoulder, spread it out like a matador's cape, and the last thing I saw as he threw the thing over my head was Mr. Twining's tombstone, the word "*Vale!*" carved on its base. *I bid you farewell.*

Something tightened round my temples and I guessed that Pemberton was using the straps of his portfolio to lash the jacket firmly in place.

He hoisted me up onto his shoulder and carried me back across the river as easily as a butcher does a side of beef. Before my head could stop spinning he had dumped me heavily back onto my feet.

Gripping the nape of my neck with one hand, he used the other to seize my upper arm in a vise-like grip, shoving me roughly ahead of him along the towpath.

"Just keep putting one foot in front of the other until I tell you to stop."

I tried to call out for help, but my mouth was jammed chock-full of wet handkerchief. I couldn't produce anything more than a swinish grunt. I couldn't even tell him how much he was hurting me.

I suddenly realized that I was more afraid than I had ever been in my life.

As I stumbled along, I prayed that someone would spot us; if they did, they would surely call out, and even with my head bound up in Pemberton's jacket, I would almost certainly hear them. If I did, I would wrench sharply away from him and make a dash towards the sound of their voice. But to do so prematurely, I knew, risked tumbling headlong into the river and being left there by Pemberton to drown.

"Stop here," he said suddenly, after I had been frog-marched what I judged to be a hundred yards. "Stand still."

I obeyed.

I heard him tinkering with something metallic and a moment later, what sounded like a door grating open. The Pit Shed!

"One step up," he said. "That's right . . . now three ahead. And stop."

Behind us, the door closed like a coffin lid, with a wooden groan.

"Empty your pockets," Pemberton said.

I had only one: the pocket in my sweater. There was nothing in it but the key to the kitchen door at Buckshaw. Father had always insisted that each of us carry a key at all times in case of some hypothetical emergency, and because he conducted the occasional spot check, I was never without it. As I turned my pocket inside out, I heard the key fall to the wooden floor, then bounce and skitter. A second later there was a faint clink as it landed on concrete.

"Damn," he said.

Good! The key had fallen into the service pit, I was sure of it. Now Pemberton would have to drag back the boards that covered it, and clamber down into the pit. My hands were still free: I would rip his jacket off my head, run out the door, pull the handkerchief out of my mouth, and scream like old gooseberries as I ran towards the High Street. It was less than a minute away.

I was right. Almost immediately, I heard the unmistakable sound of heavy planks being dragged across the floor.

Pemberton grunted as he pulled them away from the mouth of the pit. I'd have to be careful which way I ran: one wrong step and I'd fall into the open hole and break my neck.

I hadn't moved since we came in the door, which, if I was correct, must now be behind me with the pit in front. I'd have to estimate a hundred-and-eighty-degree turn blindfolded.

Either Pemberton had a finely tuned psychic ability or he detected some minute motion of my head. Before I could do anything, he was at my side, spinning me round half a dozen times as if we were beginning a game of blind-man's buff, and I was It. When he finally stopped, I was so dizzy I could barely stand up.

"Now then," he said, "we're going down. Watch your step."

I shook my head rapidly from side to side, thinking, even as I did so, how ridiculous it must look, swathed in his tweed jacket.

"Listen, Flavia, be a good girl. I'm not going to hurt you as long as you behave. As soon as I have the stamp from Buckshaw in my hands, I'll send someone to set you free. Otherwise..."

Otherwise?

"...I shall be forced to do something most unpleasant."

An image of Horace Bonepenny breathing his final breath into my face floated before my covered eyes, and I knew that Pemberton was more than capable of following through on his threat.

He dragged me by the elbow to a spot I assumed was the edge of the pit.

"Eight steps down," he said. "I'll count them. Don't worry, I'm holding on to you."

I stepped off into space.

"One," he said as my foot came down on something solid. I stood there teetering.

"Easy does it . . . two . . . three, you're almost halfway there."

I put out my right hand and felt the edge of the pit nearly level with my shoulder. As my bare knees detected the cold air in the pit, my arm began to tremble like a dead branch in the winter wind. I felt a tightness gripping at my throat.

"Good . . . four . . . five . . . just two more to go."

He was shuffling down the steps behind me, one at a time. I wondered if I could seize his arm and pull him sharply into the pit. With any luck he'd crack his head on the concrete and I'd scramble over his body to freedom.

Suddenly he froze, his fingers digging into the muscle of my upper arm. I let out a muted bellow and he relaxed his grip a little.

"Quiet!" he said in a snarl that wasn't to be trifled with.

Outside, in Cow Lane, a lorry was backing up, its gears whining in a rising and falling wail. Someone was coming!

Pemberton stood perfectly still, his quick breath rasping in the cold silence of the pit.

With my head muffled in his jacket, I could only faintly hear the voices outside, followed by the clanging of a steel tailgate.

Oddly enough, the thought that came to mind was of Feely. Why, she would demand, didn't I scream? Why didn't I rip the jacket from my head and sink my teeth into

Pemberton's arm? She would want to know all the details, and no matter what I said, she would rebut every argument as if she were the Lord Chief Justice himself.

The truth was that I was having difficulty just managing to breathe. My handkerchief—a sturdy no-nonsense piece of cotton—was stuffed so tightly into my mouth that my jaws were in agony. I had to breathe through my stuffed-up nose, and even by taking the deepest breaths I was only just able to draw in enough oxygen to keep afloat.

I knew that if I began coughing I was a goner; the slightest exertion made my head spin. Besides that, I realized, a couple of men standing out there beside an idling lorry would hear nothing but the noise of its motor. Unless I could contrive something earsplitting, I'd never make myself heard. Meanwhile, it was best to keep still and to keep quiet. I would save my energy.

Someone closed the lorry's tailgate with a clang of steel; two doors slammed shut, and the thing lumbered off in first gear. We were alone again.

"Now then," Pemberton said, "... down you go. Two steps more."

He gave my arm a sharp pinch and I slid my foot forward.

"Seven," he said.

I paused, reluctant to take the last step that would put me in the bottom of the pit.

"One more. Careful."

As if he were helping an old lady across a busy street.

I took another step and was instantly ankle-deep in rubbish. I could hear Pemberton stirring around in the stuff with his foot. He still had a fierce grip on my arm, which he relaxed only for an instant as he bent to pick something up. Obviously the key. If he could see it, I thought, there must be a certain amount of daylight at the bottom of the pit.

The daylight at the bottom of the pit. For some unfathomable reason, the thought brought back to me Inspector Hewitt's words as he drove me home from the County Constabulary in Hinley: *Unless some sweetness at the bottom lie, Who cares for all the crinkling of the pie?*

What did it all mean? My mind was awhirl.

"I'm sorry, Flavia," Pemberton said suddenly, breaking into my thoughts, "but I'm going to have to tie you up."

Before his words had time to register, he had whipped my right hand round behind me and tied my wrists together. What had he used, I wondered. His necktie?

As he tightened it, I remembered to press my fingertips together to form an arch, just as I had done when Feely and Daffy had locked me in the closet. When had that been? Last Wednesday? It seemed a thousand years ago.

But Pemberton was no fool. He saw at once what I was up to, and without a word, he pinched the backs of my hands between his thumb and forefinger and my little arch of safety collapsed in pain. He pulled the bonds tight until my wrists were squeezed together, then double- and triple-knotted the thing, giving it a hard, tight tug at each step.

I ran a thumb over the knot and felt the slick smoothness of it. Woven silk. Yes, he had used his necktie. Precious little chance of picking my way out of *these* bonds!

My wrists were already perspiring, and I knew that the moisture would soon cause the silk to shrink. Well, not precisely: Silk, like hair, is a protein, and does not itself shrink, but the way in which it is woven can cause it to tighten mercilessly when it is wetted. After a while, the circulation in my hands would be cut off, and then . . .

"Sit," Pemberton commanded, pushing down on my shoulders—and I sat.

I heard the click of his belt buckle as he removed it, whipped it round my ankles, and pulled it tight.

He didn't say another word. His shoes grated on concrete as he climbed the steps of the pit, and then I heard the sound of the heavy boards being dragged back across its mouth.

A few moments later, all was silence. He was gone.

I was alone in the pit, and no one but Pemberton knew where I was.

I would die down here, and when eventually they found my body, they would lift me into a gleaming black hearse and transport me to some dank old morgue where they would lay me out on a stainless-steel table.

The first thing they would do would be to open my mouth and extract the soggy ball of my handkerchief, and as they spread it out flat on the table beside my white remains, an orange stamp—a stamp belonging to the King— would flutter to the floor: It was like something right out of an Agatha Christie. Someone—perhaps even Miss Christie herself—would write a detective novel about it.

I would be dead, but I'd be splashed across the front page of the *News of the World*. If I hadn't been so frightened, so exhausted, so short of breath, and in such pain, it might even have seemed amusing.

twenty-four

BEING KIDNAPPED IS NEVER QUITE THE WAY YOU imagine it will be. In the first place, I had not bitten and scratched my abductor. Nor had I screamed: I had gone quietly along like a lamb to the September slaughter.

The only excuse I can think of is that all my powers were being diverted to feed my racing mind, and that nothing was left over to drive my muscles. When something like this actually happens to you, the kind of rubbish that comes leaping immediately into your head can be astonishing.

I remembered, for instance, Maximilian's claim that in the Channel Islands you could raise the hue and cry merely by shouting, "*Haroo! Haroo, mon Prince! On me fait tort!*"

Easy to say but hard to do when your mouth's stopped up with cotton and your head's wrapped in a stranger's tweed jacket that fairly reeks of sweat and pomade.

Besides, I thought, there is a notable shortage of princes in England nowadays. The only ones I could think of at the moment were Princess Elizabeth's husband, Prince Philip, and their infant son, Prince Charles.

This meant that, for all practical purposes, I was on my own.

What would Marie-Anne Paulze Lavoisier have done? I wondered. Or for that matter, her husband, Antoine?

My present predicament was far too vivid a reminder of Marie-Anne's brother, cocooned in oiled silk and left to breathe through a straw. And it was unlikely, I knew, that anyone would come bursting into the Pit Shed to haul me off to justice. There was no guillotine in Bishop's Lacey, but neither were there any miracles.

No, reflecting upon Marie-Anne and her doomed family was simply too depressing. I'd have to look to the other great chemists for inspiration.

What, then, would Robert Bunsen, for instance, or Henry Cavendish have done if they had found themselves bound and gagged at the bottom of a grease pit?

I was surprised by how quickly the answer came to mind: They would take stock.

Very well, I would take stock.

I was at the bottom of a six-foot pit, which was uncomfortably close to the dimensions of a grave. My hands and feet were tied and it would not be easy to feel my way around. With my head wrapped up in Pemberton's jacket—and doubtless tied tightly in position with its arms—I could see nothing. My hearing was muffled by the heavy cloth; my sense of taste disabled by the handkerchief stuffed in my mouth.

I was having difficulty breathing and, with my nose

partially covered, the slightest exertion used up what little oxygen was reaching my lungs. I would need to remain quiet.

The sense that seemed to be working overtime was my sense of smell, and in spite of my wrapped-up head, the stench of the pit came seeping at full strength into my nostrils. At bottom, it was the sour reek of soil that has lain for many years directly beneath a human dwelling: a bitter scent of things best not thought about. Superimposed upon that background was the sweet odor of old motor oil, the sharp undulating tang of ancient petrol, carbon monoxide, tire rubber, and perhaps a faint whiff of ozone from long-burnt-out spark plugs.

And there was that trace of ammonia I had noticed before. Miss Mountjoy had mentioned rats, and I wouldn't be surprised to discover that they flourished in these neglected buildings along the riverbank.

Most unsettling was the smell of sewer gas: an unsavory soup of methane, hydrogen sulphide, sulphur dioxide, and the nitrogen oxides—the smell of decomposition and decay; the smell of the open pipe from the riverbank to the pit in which I was trussed.

I shuddered to think of the things that might even now be making their way up such a conduit. Best to give my imagination a rest, I thought, and get on with my survey of the pit.

I had almost forgotten that I was seated. Pemberton's order to sit, and his pushing me down, had been so surprising I had not noticed what it was that I sat upon. I could feel it beneath me now: flat, solid, and stable. By wiggling my behind, I was able to detect the slightest give in the thing, along with a wooden creaking sound. A large tea chest, I thought, or something very like one. Had Pemberton put it here in anticipation, before he accosted me in the churchyard?

It was then that I realized I was famished. I had eaten nothing since my skimpy breakfast, which, come to think of it, had been interrupted by the sudden appearance of Pemberton at our window. As my stomach began to send out little pangs of complaint, I began to wish I'd been more attentive to my toast and cereal.

Moreover, I was tired. More than tired: I was totally exhausted. I had not slept well, and the lingering effects of my head cold were further choking off my oxygen intake.

Relax, Flave. Keep a cool head. Pemberton will soon be arriving at Buckshaw.

I had counted on the fact that when he entered the house to retrieve the Ulster Avenger, he would be accosted by Dogger, who would put paid to him in no uncertain terms.

Good old Dogger! How I missed him. Here was this Great Unknown living under the same roof and I had never thought to ask him, face-to-face, about his past. If ever I managed to find my way out of this infernal fix, I vowed that, at the earliest opportunity, I would take him on a private picnic. I would punt with him to the Folly, where I would ply him with Marmite on bread and pump him like billy-ho for all the gory details. He would be so relieved at my escape that he would hardly dare refuse to tell me all.

The dear man had pretended that it was he who had killed Horace Bonepenny, albeit by accident during one of his spells, and he had done so to protect Father. I was sure of it. Hadn't Dogger been there with me in the corridor outside Father's study? Hadn't he overheard, as I had, the row that preceded Bonepenny's death?

Yes, whatever happened, Dogger would look after it. Dogger was fiercely loyal to Father—and to me. Loyal even unto death.

Very well, then. Dogger would tackle Pemberton and that would be that.

Or would it?

What if Pemberton actually made his way into Buckshaw undetected and gained entry to Father's dressing room? What if he stopped the chimneypiece clock, reached behind the pendulum, and found nothing there but the mutilated Penny Black? What would he do then?

The answer was a simple one: He would come back to the Pit Shed and put me to the torture.

One thing was clear: I had to escape before he could return. There was no time to waste.

My knees popped like dry twigs as I struggled to my feet.

The first and most important thing was to make a survey of the pit: to map its features and discover anything that might aid in my escape. With my hands tied behind me at the wrists, I could only map out the concrete wall by going slowly round its perimeter, my back steadied against it, using my fingertips to feel every inch of the surface. With any luck, I might find a sharp projection to use as a tool in freeing my hands.

My feet were tied so tightly I could feel my anklebones grating together, and I had to invent a kind of hopping frog gait. My every move was accompanied by the rustling of old papers underfoot.

At what I judged to be the far end of the pit, I could

feel a current of cold air blowing on my ankles, as if there were an opening down near the floor. I turned and faced the wall, trying to hook a toe into something, but my bonds were too tight. Every move threatened to pitch me forward onto my face.

I could feel that my hands were quickly becoming covered with a rancid filth from the walls; the smell of the stuff alone was making me queasy.

What if, I thought, I could climb up onto the tea chest? That way, my head should be above the level of the pit, and there might be some kind of hook higher up the wall: something, perhaps, that had once been used to suspend a bag of tools, or a work light.

But first I had to find my way back to the chest.

Bound and tied as I was, this took far longer than I expected. But sooner or later, I knew, my legs would crash into the thing and, having completed my circumnavigation of the pit, I'd be back where I started.

Ten minutes later I was panting like an Ethiopian hound and still hadn't come up against the tea chest. Had I missed it? Should I carry on or go back the way I came?

Perhaps the thing was in the middle of the pit and I had been tiring myself by hopping in rectangles all round it. By what I could recall of the pit from my first visit—although it had been covered with boards and I had not actually looked down into it—I thought that it could be no more than eight feet long and six wide.

With my ankles trussed, I could hop no more than about six inches at a time in any direction: say, twelve hops by sixteen. It was easy enough to conclude that with my back to the wall, the center of the pit would be either six or eight hops away.

By now fatigue was overtaking me. I was jumping about like a grasshopper in a jam jar and getting nowhere. Then, just when I was about to give up, I barked my shin on the tea chest. I sat down on it at once to catch my breath.

After a time, I began moving my shoulders, back a bit and to the right. When I shifted to the left, my shoulder touched concrete. This was encouraging! The box was up against the wall—or close enough to it. If I could somehow manage to climb on top of the thing, there might be a chance I could throw myself up and over the rim of the pit like a sea lion at the aquarium. Once out of the pit, there would be far more likelihood I might find some hook or projection to help me rip Pemberton's jacket from my head. Then I would be able to see what I was doing. I would free my hands, and then my feet. It all seemed so simple in theory.

As carefully as possible I turned ninety degrees so that my back was to the wall. I shifted my behind to the rear edge of the tea chest and brought my knees up until they touched the part of the jacket that was under my chin.

There was a very slightly raised edge round the top of the chest, and I was able to hook my heels onto it. Then slowly . . . carefully . . . I began to extend my legs, sliding my back, inch by inch, up the wall.

We were a right-angled triangle. The wall and the top of the chest formed the adjacent and opposite sides and I was the shaky hypotenuse.

A sudden spasm shot through my calf muscles and I wanted to scream. If I let the pain overtake me, I would tumble off the box and likely break an arm or a leg. I steeled myself and waited for the pain to pass, biting the inside of my cheek with such ferocity that I tasted, almost instantly, my own warm, salty blood.

Steady on, Flave, I told myself: There are worse things. But for the life of me, I couldn't think of one.

I don't know how long I stood there trembling but it seemed like an eternity. I was soaked through with sweat, yet cool air was blowing in from somewhere; I could still feel its draughty breath on my bare legs.

After a long struggle, I found myself at last standing upright on the tea chest. I ran my fingers over as much of the wall as I could, but it was maddeningly smooth.

Awkwardly, like an elephant ballerina, I rotated one hundred and eighty degrees until I thought I was facing the wall. I leaned forward and felt—or thought I felt—the rim of the pit beneath my chin. But with my head swaddled in Pemberton's jacket, I could not be sure.

There was no way out; not, at least, in this direction. I was like a hamster that had climbed to the top of the ladder in its cage and found there was nowhere to go but down. But surely hamsters knew in their hamster hearts that escape was futile; it was only we humans who were incapable of accepting our own helplessness.

I dropped slowly to my knees on the tea chest. Climbing down, at least, was easier than climbing up, although the rough splintered wood, and what felt painfully like a tin rim running round the top of the box, made a hash of my bare knees. From there, I was able to twist sideways into a sitting position and swing my legs over the edge until I felt them touch the floor.

Unless I could find the opening through which the cold air was entering the pit, the only way out was up. If there *was* in fact a pipe or conduit leading to the river, would it be of sufficient diameter for me to crawl through? And even if it was, would it be free of blockage, or would I suddenly crawl face-first—like a mammoth blindworm—into some ghastly thing in total darkness and become jammed in the pipe, unable to go either forward or back?

Would my bones be found in some future England by a baffled archaeologist? Would I be put on display in a glass case at the British Museum, to be stared at by the masses? My mind raced through the pros and cons.

But wait! I'd forgotten about the stairs at the end of the pit! I would sit on the bottom step and go up backwards, one step at a time. When I reached the top, I would push up with my shoulders and lift the boards that covered the pit. Why hadn't I thought of this in the first place, before I'd worn myself down to this state of quivering exhaustion?

It was then that something came over me, smothering my consciousness like a pillow. Before I could recognize my total exhaustion for what it was, before I could muster a fight, I was vanquished. I felt myself sinking to the floor amid the rustling papers: papers which, in spite of the cold air from the conduit, now seemed surprisingly warm.

I shifted a little as if to burrow into their depths, and pulling my knees up towards my chin, I was instantly asleep.

I DREAMED THAT DAFFY WAS PUTTING on a Christmas pantomime. The great hallway at Buckshaw had been transformed into an exquisite jewel box of a Viennese theater, with a red velvet curtain and a vast crystal chandelier in which the flames of a hundred candles bobbed and flickered.

Dogger and Feely and Mrs. Mullet and I sat side by side on a single row of chairs, while nearby at a wood-carver's bench, Father puttered away at his stamps.

The play was *Romeo and Juliet,* and Daffy, in a remarkable display of quick-change artistry, was playing all the parts. One moment she was Juliet on the balcony (the landing at the top of the west staircase) and the next, having vanished for no more than a blink of a magpie's eye, she reappeared on the mezzanine as Romeo.

Up and down she flew, up and down, wringing our hearts with words of tender love.

From time to time, Dogger would put a forefinger to his lips and slip quietly out of the room, returning moments later with a painted wheelbarrow spilling over with postage stamps which he would dump at Father's feet. Father, who was busily snipping stamps in half with a pair of Harriet's nail scissors, would grunt without so much as looking up, and go on about his work.

Mrs. Mullet laughed and laughed at Juliet's old nurse, blushing and shooting glances at us one and all as if there were some message encoded in the words which only she could understand. She mopped her red face with a polka-dot handkerchief, twisting it round and round in her hands before rolling it into a ball and shoving it in her mouth to stop up her hysterical laughter.

Now Daffy (as Mercutio) was describing how Mab, the Fairy Queen, gallops:

> O'er ladies' lips, who straight on kisses dream,
> Which oft the angry Mab with blisters plagues
> Because their breaths with sweetmeats tainted are.

I took a surreptitious peek at Feely who, in spite of the fact that her lips looked like something you might see on a fishmonger's barrow, had attracted the attentions of Ned who was sitting behind her, leaning forward over her shoulder, his own lips pursed, begging a kiss. But each time Daffy flitted down from the balcony to the mezzanine below in the role of Romeo (looking, with his pencil-thin mustache, more like David Niven in *A Matter of Life and Death* than a noble Montague), Ned would leap to his feet with a volley of applause punctuated by fierce two-fingered whistles as Feely, unmoved, popped Mint Imperial after Mint Imperial into her open mouth, gasping suddenly as Romeo burst into Juliet's marbled tomb:

> For here lies Juliet, and her beauty makes
> This vault a feasting presence full of light.
> Death, lie thou there—

I woke up. Damnation! Something was running over my feet: something wet and furry.

"Dogger!" I tried to scream, but my mouth was full of a wet mess. My jaws were aching and my head felt as if I had just been dragged from the chopping block.

I kicked out with both feet and something scuttered through the loose papers with an angry chittering noise.

A water rat. The pit was likely swarming with the things. Had they been nibbling at me while I slept? The very thought of it made me cringe.

I pulled myself upright and leaned back against the wall, my knees beneath my chin. It was too much to expect that the rats would nibble at my bonds as they did in fairy tales. They'd more than likely gnaw my knuckles to the bone and I'd be powerless to stop them.

Stow it, Flave, I thought. Don't let your imagination run away with you.

There had been several times in the past, at work in my chemical laboratory or lying in bed at night, when I unexpectedly caught myself thinking, "You are all alone with Flavia de Luce," which sometimes was a frightening thought and sometimes not. This was one of the scarier occasions.

The scurrying noises were real enough; something was rummaging about in the papers in the corner of the pit. If I moved my legs or my head, the sounds would cease for a moment, and then begin again.

How long had I been asleep? Had it been hours or minutes? Was it still daylight outside, or was it now dark?

I remembered that the library would be closed until Thursday morning, and today was only Tuesday. I could be here for a good long while.

Someone would report me missing, of course, and it would probably be Dogger. Was it too much to hope that he would catch Pemberton in the act of burgling Buckshaw? But even if he was caught, would Pemberton tell them where he had hidden me away?

Now my hands and feet were growing numb and I thought of old Ernie Forbes, whose grandchildren were made to pull him along the High Street on a little wheeled float. Ernie had lost a hand and both feet to gangrene in the war, and Feely once told me that he had to be—

Stop it, Flave! Stop being such a monstrous crybaby!

Think of something else. Think of anything.

Think, for instance, of revenge.

twenty-five

THERE ARE TIMES—ESPECIALLY WHEN I'M CONFINED—
that my thoughts have a tendency, like the man in Stephen
Leacock's story, to ride madly off in all directions.

I'm almost ashamed to admit to the things that crossed
my mind at first. Most of them involved poisons, a few involved common household utensils, and all of them involved Frank Pemberton.

My mind flew back to our first encounter at the
Thirteen Drakes. Although I had seen his taxi pull up at
the front door, and had heard Tully Stover shout at Mary
that Mr. Pemberton had arrived early, I had not actually
laid eyes on the man himself. That did not take place until
Sunday, at the Folly.

Although there had been several odd things about
Pemberton's sudden appearance at Buckshaw, I really hadn't
had time to think about them.

In the first place, he hadn't arrived in Bishop's Lacey

until hours after Horace Bonepenny had expired in my face. Or had he?

When I looked up and saw Pemberton standing at the edge of the lake, I had been taken by surprise. But why? Buckshaw was my home: I had been born and lived there every minute of my life. What was so surprising about a man standing at the edge of an artificial lake?

I could feel an answer to that question nibbling at the hook I'd lowered into my subconscious. Don't look straight at it, I thought, think of something else—or at least pretend to.

It had been raining that day, or had just begun to rain. I had looked up from where I was sitting on the steps of the little ruined temple and there he was, across the water on the south side of the lake: the southeast side, to be precise. Why on earth had he made his appearance from that direction?

That was a question to which I had known the answer for quite some time.

Bishop's Lacey lay to the northeast of Buckshaw. From the Mulford Gates, at the entrance to our avenue of chestnut trees, the road ran in easy twists and turns, more or less directly into the village. And yet Pemberton had appeared from the southeast, from the direction of Doddingsley, which lay about four miles across the fields. Why then, in the name of Old Stink, I had wondered, would he choose to come that way? The choices had seemed limited, and I had quickly jotted them down in my mental notebook:

1.   If (as I suspected) Pemberton was the murderer of Horace Bonepenny, could he have been, as all mur-

derers are said to be, drawn back to the scene of the crime? Had he perhaps left something behind? Something like the murder weapon? Had he returned to Buckshaw to retrieve it?

2. Because he had already been to Buckshaw the night before, he knew the way across the fields and wanted to avoid being seen. (See 1 above)

What if on Friday, the night of the murder, Pemberton, believing that Bonepenny was carrying the Ulster Avengers, had followed him from Bishop's Lacey to Buckshaw and murdered him there?

But hold on, Flave, I thought. Hold your horses. Don't go galloping off like that.

Why wouldn't Pemberton simply waylay his victim in one of those quiet hedgerows that border nearly every lane in this part of England?

The answer had come to me as if it were sculpted in red neon tubing in Piccadilly Circus: because he wanted Father to be blamed for the crime!

Bonepenny had to be killed at Buckshaw!

Of course! With Father a virtual recluse, it was unlikely to expect that he would ever happen to be away from home. Murders—at least those in which the murderer expected to escape justice—had to be planned in advance, and often in very great detail. It was obvious that a philatelic crime needed to be pinned on a philatelist. If Father was unlikely to come to the scene of the crime, the scene of the crime would have to come to Father.

And so it had.

Although I had first formulated this chain of events—

or, at least, certain of its links—hours ago, it was only now, when I was at last forced to be alone with Flavia de Luce, that I was able to fit together all the pieces.

Flavia, I'm proud of you! Marie-Anne Paulze Lavoisier would be proud of you too.

Now then: Pemberton, of course, had followed Bonepenny as far as Doddingsley; perhaps even all the way from Stavanger. Father had seen them both at the London exhibition just weeks ago—proof positive that neither one was living abroad permanently.

They had probably planned this together, this blackmailing of Father. Just as they had planned the murder of Mr. Twining. But Pemberton had a plan of his own.

Once satisfied that Bonepenny was on his way to Bishop's Lacey (where else, indeed, would he be going?), Pemberton had got off the train at Doddingsley and registered himself at the Jolly Coachman. I knew that for a fact. Then, on the night of the murder, all he had to do was walk across the fields to Bishop's Lacey.

Here, he had waited until he saw Bonepenny leave the inn and set out on foot for Buckshaw. With Bonepenny out of the way and not suspecting that he was being followed, Pemberton had searched the room at the Thirteen Drakes, and its contents—including Bonepenny's luggage—and had found nothing. He had, of course, never thought, as I had, to slit open the shipping labels.

By now, he must have been furious.

Slipping away from the inn unseen (most likely by way of that steep back staircase), he had tracked his quarry on foot to Buckshaw, where they must have quarreled in our garden. How was it, I wondered, that I hadn't heard them?

Within half an hour, he had left Bonepenny for dead,

his pockets and wallet rifled. But the Ulster Avengers had not been there: Bonepenny had not had the stamps upon his person after all.

Pemberton had committed his crime and then simply walked off into the night, across the fields to the Jolly Coachman at Doddingsley. The next morning, he had rolled up with much ado in a taxicab at the front door of the Thirteen Drakes, pretending he had just come down by rail from London. He would have to search the room again. Risky, but necessary. Surely the stamps must still be hidden there.

Parts of this sequence of events I had suspected for some time, and even though I hadn't yet put together the remaining facts, I had already verified Pemberton's presence in Doddingsley by my telephone call to Mr. Cleaver, the innkeeper of the Jolly Coachman.

In retrospect, it all seemed fairly simple.

I stopped thinking for a moment to listen to my breathing. It was slow and regular as I sat there with my head resting on my knees, which were still pulled up in an inverted V.

At this moment I thought of something Father had once told us: that Napoleon had once called the English "a nation of shopkeepers." Wrong, Napoleon!

Having just come through a war in which tons of trinitrotoluene were dumped on our heads in the dark, we were a nation of survivors, and I, Flavia Sabina de Luce, could see it even in myself.

And then I muttered part of the Twenty-third Psalm for insurance purposes. One can never be too sure.

Now: the murder.

Again the dying face of Horace Bonepenny swam

before me in the dark, its mouth opening and closing like a landed fish gasping in the grass. His last word and his dying breath had come as one: "*Vale,*" he had said, and it had floated from his mouth directly to my nostrils. And it had come to me on a wave of carbon tetrachloride.

There was no doubt whatsoever that it was carbon tetrachloride, one of the most fascinating of chemical compounds.

To a chemist, its sweet smell, although very transient, is unmistakable. It is not far removed in the scheme of things from the chloroform used by anesthetists in surgery.

In carbon tetrachloride (one of its many aliases) four atoms of chlorine play ring-around-a-rosy with a single atom of carbon. It is a powerful insecticide, still used now and then in stubborn cases of hookworm, those tiny, silent parasites that gorge themselves on blood sucked in darkness from the intestines of man and beast alike.

But more importantly, philatelists use carbon tetrachloride to bring out a stamp's nearly invisible watermarks. And Father kept bottles of the stuff in his study.

I thought back to Bonepenny's room at the Thirteen Drakes. What a fool I had been to think of poisoned pie! This wasn't a Grimm's fairy tale; it was the story of Flavia de Luce.

The pie shell was nothing more than that: just a shell. Before leaving Norway, Bonepenny had removed the filling, and stuffed in the jack snipe with which he planned to terrorize Father. That was how he'd smuggled the dead bird into England.

It wasn't so much what I had found in his room as what I hadn't found. And that, of course, was the single item that was missing from the little leather kit in which Bonepenny carried his diabetic supplies: a syringe.

Pemberton had come across the syringe and pocketed it when he rifled Bonepenny's room just before the murder. I was sure of it.

They were partners in crime, and no one would have known better than Pemberton the medical supplies that were essential to Bonepenny's survival.

Even if Pemberton had planned a different way of dispatching his victim—a stone to the back of the head or strangulation with a green willow withy—the syringe in Bonepenny's luggage must have seemed like a godsend. The very thought of how it was done made me shudder.

I could imagine the two of them struggling there in the moonlight. Bonepenny was tall, but not muscular. Pemberton would have brought him down as a cougar does a deer.

Out comes the hypodermic and into the base of Bonepenny's brain it goes. Just like that. It wouldn't take more than a second, and its effect would be almost instantaneous. This, I was certain, was the way in which Horace Bonepenny had met his death.

Had he ingested the stuff—and it would have been a near impossibility to force him to swallow it—a much larger quantity of the poison would have been required: a quantity which he would have promptly vomited.

Whereas five cc's injected into the base of the brain would be sufficient to bring down an ox.

The unmistakable fumes of the carbon tetrachloride would have been quickly transmitted to his mouth and nasal cavities as I had detected. But by the time Inspector

Hewitt and his detective sergeants arrived, it had evaporated without a trace.

It was almost the perfect crime. In fact it would have been perfect if I had not gone down into the garden when I did.

I hadn't thought about this before. Was my continued existence all that stood between Frank Pemberton and freedom?

There was a grating noise.

I could not tell which direction it was coming from. I swiveled my head and the noise stopped instantly.

For a minute or more there was silence. I strained my ears but could hear only the sound of my own breathing, which I noticed had become more rapid—and more jagged.

There it was again! As if a piece of lumber were being dragged, with agonizing slowness, across a gritty surface.

I tried to call out "Who's there?" but the hard ball of the handkerchief in my mouth reduced my words to a muffled bleat. At the effort, my jaws felt as if someone had driven a railway spike into each side of my head.

Better to listen, I thought. Rats don't move lumber, and unless I was sadly mistaken, I was no longer alone in the Pit Shed.

Like a snake, I moved my head slowly from side to side, trying to take advantage of my superior hearing, but the heavy tweed binding my head muffled all but the loudest of sounds.

But the grating noises were not half as unnerving as the silences between them. Whatever it was in the pit was trying to keep its presence unknown. Or was it keeping quiet to unnerve me?

There was a squeak, then a faint *tick,* as if a pebble had fallen onto a large stone.

As slowly as a flower opening, I stretched my legs out in front of me, but when they met with no resistance, I pulled them back up beneath my chin. Better to be coiled up, I thought; better to present a smaller target.

For a moment, I focused my attention on my hands, which were still lashed behind me. Perhaps there had been a miracle; perhaps the silk had stretched and loosened, but no such luck. Even my numbed fingers could sense that my bonds were as tight as ever. I hadn't a hope of getting free. I really was going to die down here.

And who would miss me?

Nobody.

After a suitable period of mourning, Father would turn again to his stamps, Daphne would drag down another box of books from the Buckshaw library, and Ophelia would discover a new shade of lipstick. And soon—too painfully soon—it would be as if I had never existed.

Nobody loved me, and that was a fact. Harriet might have when I was a baby, but she was dead.

And then, to my horror, I found myself in tears.

I was appalled. Brimming eyes were something I had fought against as long as I could remember, yet in spite of my bound-up eyes I seemed to see floating before me a kindly face, one I had forgotten in my misery. It was, of course, Dogger's face.

Dogger would be desolate if I died!

Get a grip, Flave . . . it's just a pit. What was that story Daffy read us about a pit? That tale of Edgar Allan Poe's? The one about the pendulum?

No! I wouldn't think about it. I wouldn't!

Then there was the Black Hole of Calcutta in which the Nawab of Bengal had imprisoned a hundred and forty-six British soldiers in a cell made to hold no more than three.

How many had survived a single night in that stifling oven? Twenty-three, I remembered, and by morning, stark raving mad—every last one of them.

No! Not Flavia!

My mind was like a vortex, spinning...spinning. I took a deep breath to calm myself, and my nostrils were filled with the smell of methane. Of course!

The pipe to the riverbank was full of the stuff. All it needed was a source of ignition to set it off and the resulting explosion would be talked about for years.

I would find the end of the pipe and kick it. If luck were on my side, the nails in the soles of my shoe would create a spark, the methane would explode, and that would be that.

The only drawback to this plan was that I would be standing at the end of the pipe when the thing went off. It would be like being strapped across the mouth of a cannon.

Well, cannon be damned! I wasn't going to die down here in this stinking pit without a struggle.

Gathering every last ounce of my remaining strength, I dug in my heels and pushed myself against the wall until I was in a standing position. It took rather longer than I expected but at last, although teetering, I was upright.

No more time for thinking. I would find the source of the methane gas or die in the attempt.

As I made a tentative hop towards where I thought the conduit might be, a chill voice whispered into my ear:

"And now for Flavia."

twenty-six

IT WAS PEMBERTON, AND AT THE SOUND OF HIS voice, my heart turned inside out. What had he meant? "And now for Flavia"? Had he already done some terrible thing to Daffy, or to Feely...or to Dogger?

Before I could even begin to imagine, he had seized my upper arm in a paralyzing grip, jabbing his thumb into the muscle as he had done before. I tried to scream, but nothing came out. I thought I was going to vomit.

I shook my head violently from side to side, but only after what seemed like an eternity did he release me.

"But first, Frank and Flavia are going to have a little talk," he said, in as pleasant a conversational tone as if we were strolling in the park, and I realized at that instant I was alone with a madman in my own personal Calcutta.

"I'm going to take the covering off your head, do you understand?"

I stood perfectly still, petrified.

"Listen to me, Flavia, and listen carefully. If you don't do exactly as I say, I'll kill you. It's that simple. Do you understand?"

I nodded my head a little.

"Good. Now keep still."

I could feel him tugging roughly at the knots he had tied in his jacket, and almost at once its slick silk lining began to slide across my face, then dropped away entirely.

The beam of his torch hit me like a hammer blow, blinding me with light.

I recoiled in shock. Flashing stars and patches of black flew alternately across my field of vision. I had been so long in darkness that even the light of a single match would have been excruciating, but Pemberton was shining a powerful torch directly—and deliberately—into my eyes.

Unable to throw up my hands to shield myself, I could only wrench my head away to one side, squeeze my eyes shut, and wait for the nausea to subside.

"Painful, isn't it?" he said. "But not half so painful as what I'm going to do if you lie to me again."

I opened my stinging eyes and tried to focus them on a dark corner of the pit.

"Look at me!" he demanded.

I turned my head and squinted at him with what must have been a truly horrible grimace. I could see nothing of the man behind the round lens of his torch, whose fierce beam was still burning into my brain like a gigantic white desert sun.

Slowly, taking his time about it, he swung the glaring beam away and pointed it at the floor. Somewhere behind the light he was no more than a voice in the darkness.

"You lied to me."

I gave something like a shrug.

"You lied to me," Pemberton repeated more loudly, and this time I could hear the strain in his voice. "There was nothing hidden in that clock but the Penny Black."

So he *had* been to Buckshaw! My heart was fluttering like a caged bird.

"Mngg," I said.

Pemberton thought this over for a moment but could make nothing of it.

"I'm going to take the handkerchief out of your mouth, but first let me show you something."

He picked up his tweed jacket from the floor of the pit and reached into the pocket. When his hand came out, it was holding a shiny object of glass and metal. It was Bonepenny's syringe! He held it out for my inspection.

"You were looking for this, weren't you? At the inn *and* in your garden? And here it was all the while!"

He laughed through his nose like a pig and sat down on the steps. Holding the torch between his knees, he held the syringe upright as he rummaged once more in the jacket and pulled out a small brown bottle. I barely had time to read the label before he removed the stopper and swiftly filled the syringe.

"I expect you know what this stuff is, don't you, Miss Smart-Pants?"

I met his eye but gave no other sign I'd heard him.

"And don't think I don't know precisely how and where to inject it. I didn't spend all those hours in the dissecting room at the London Hospital for nothing. Once I'd knocked out old Bony, the actual injection was almost ridiculously simple: angle in a bit to the side, through the *splenius capitus* and *semispinalis capitis*, puncture the atlantoaxial ligament, and slide the needle over the arch of the axis. And whap! It's lights out. The carbon tet evaporates in no time, with hardly a trace. The perfect crime, if I may say so myself."

Just as I had deduced! But now I knew *precisely* how he'd done it! The man was stark, staring mad.

"Now listen," he said. "I'm going to take that handkerchief out of your mouth and you are going to tell me what you've done with the Ulster Avengers. One wrong word ... one wrong move and ..."

Holding the syringe upright, almost touching my nose, he squeezed the plunger slightly. A few drops of the carbon tetrachloride appeared for an instant, like dew, at the point of the needle, then dripped onto the floor. My nose caught the familiar reek of the stuff.

Pemberton put the torch on the steps and adjusted its position to illuminate my face. He placed the syringe beside it.

"Open," he said.

This is what rushed through my mind: He would stick a thumb and forefinger into my mouth to remove the handkerchief. I would bite down with all my might—bite them clean off!

But then what? I was still bound hand and foot, and even badly bitten, Pemberton could easily kill me.

I opened my aching jaws a little.

"Wider," he said, holding back. Then quick as a wink he darted in and fished the sodden handkerchief from my mouth. For a single instant the light of the torch was blocked by the shadow of his hand, so that he did not see, as I saw, the slightest flash of orange as the wet ball dropped in darkness to the floor.

"Thank you," I whispered hoarsely, making my first move in the second part of the game.

Pemberton seemed taken aback.

"Someone must have found them," I croaked. "The stamps, I mean. I put them in the clock—I swear it."

I knew instantly that I had gone too far. If I were telling the truth, Pemberton no longer had any reason to keep me alive. I was the only one who knew that he was a killer.

"Unless..." I added hastily.

"Unless? Unless what?"

He fell on my words like a jackal on a downed antelope.

"My feet," I whimpered. "The pain. I can't think. I can't...Please, at least loosen them—just a bit."

"All right," he said, with surprisingly little thought. "But I'm leaving your hands tied. That way you won't be going anywhere."

I nodded eagerly.

Pemberton knelt down and loosened the buckle of his belt. As the leather dropped from my ankles I gathered my strength and kicked him in the teeth.

As he reeled back, his head cracked against the concrete, and I heard the sound of a glass object hitting the floor and skipping away into the corner. Pemberton slid heavily down the wall to a sitting position as I limped towards the steps.

Up I went...one...two...my clumsy feet kicked the torch, which went tumbling end over end down onto the floor of the pit where it came to rest with its beam illuminating the sole of one of Pemberton's shoes.

Three...four...my feet felt like stumps hacked off at the ankles.

Five ...

Surely by now my head must be above the level of the pit, but if it was, the room was in darkness. There was no more than a faint bloodred glow from the windows in the folding door. It must be dark outside; I must have slept for hours.

As I tried to remember where the door was, there was a scrabbling in the pit. The beam of the torch arced madly across the ceiling and suddenly Pemberton was up the steps and upon me.

He threw his arms around me and squeezed until I couldn't breathe. I could hear the bones crackling in my shoulders and elbows.

I tried to kick him in the shins, but he was quickly overpowering me.

To and fro we went, across the room, like spinning tops.

"No!" he shouted, overbalancing, and fell backward into the pit, dragging me with him.

He hit the bottom with an awful thud and at the same instant I landed on top of him. I heard him gasp in the darkness. Had he broken his back? Or would he soon be on his feet again, shaking me like a rag doll?

With a sudden eruption of strength, Pemberton threw me off, and I went flying, facedown, into a corner of the pit. Like an inchworm, I wiggled my way up onto my knees, but it was too late: Pemberton had a fierce grip on my arm, and was dragging me towards the steps.

It was almost too easy: He squatted and grabbed the torch from where it had fallen, then reached out towards the stairs. I thought the syringe had been knocked to the floor, but it must have been the bottle I heard, for a moment later I caught a quick glimpse of the needle in his hand—then felt it pricking the back of my neck.

My only thought was to stall for time.

"You killed Professor Twining, didn't you?" I gasped. "You and Bonepenny."

This seemed to catch him unawares. I felt his grip relax ever so slightly.

"What makes you think that?" he breathed into my ear.

"It was Bonepenny on the roof," I said. "Bonepenny who shouted '*Vale!*' He mimicked Mr. Twining's voice. It was you who dumped his body down the hole."

Pemberton sucked air in through his nose. "Did Bonepenny tell you that?"

"I found the cap and gown," I said, "under the tiles. I figured it out myself."

"You're a very clever girl," he said, almost regretfully.

"And now you've killed Bonepenny the stamps are yours. At least, they would be if you knew where they were."

This seemed to infuriate him. He tightened his grip on my arm, again drilling the ball of his thumb into the muscle. I screamed in agony.

"Five words, Flavia," he hissed. "Where are the bloody stamps?"

In the long silence that followed, in the numbing pain, my mind took refuge in flight.

Was this the end of Flavia? I wondered.

If so, was Harriet watching over me? Was she sitting at this very moment on a cloud with her legs dangling over, saying, "Oh no, Flavia! Don't do this; don't say that! Danger, Flavia! Danger!"

If she was, I couldn't hear her; perhaps I was farther

removed from Harriet than Feely and Daffy. Perhaps she had loved me less.

It was a sad fact that of Harriet's three children I was the only one who retained no real memories of her. Feely, like a miser, had experienced and hoarded seven years of her mother's love. And Daffy insisted that, even though she was hardly three when Harriet disappeared, she had a perfectly clear recollection of a slim and laughing young woman who dressed her up in a starched dress and bonnet, set her down on a blanket on a sunlit lawn, and took her photograph with a folding camera before presenting her with a gherkin pickle.

Another jab brought me back to reality—the needle was at my brain stem.

"The Ulster Avengers. Where are they?"

I pointed a finger to the corner of the pit where the handkerchief lay balled up in the shadows. As the beam of Pemberton's torch danced towards it, I looked away, then looked up, as the old-time saints were said to do when seeking for salvation.

I heard it before I saw it. There was a muffled whirring noise, as if a giant mechanical pterodactyl were flapping about outside the Pit Shed. A moment later, there was the most frightful crash and a rain of falling glass.

The room above us, beyond the mouth of the pit, erupted into brilliant yellow light, and through it clouds of steam drifted like little puffing souls of the departed.

Still rooted to the spot, I stood staring straight up into the air at the oddly familiar apparition that sat shuddering above the pit.

I've snapped, I thought. I've gone insane.

Directly above my head, trembling like a living thing, was the undercarriage of Harriet's Rolls-Royce.

Before I could blink, I heard the sound of its doors opening and feet hitting the floor above me.

Pemberton made a leap for the stairs, scrabbling up them like a trapped rat. At the top he paused, trying wildly to claw his way between the lip of the pit and the front bumper of the Phantom.

A disembodied hand appeared and seized him by the collar, dragging him up out of the pit like a fish from a pond. His shoes vanished into the light above me, and I heard a voice—Dogger's voice!—saying, "Pardon my elbow."

There was a sickening crunch and something hit the floor above me like a sack of turnips.

I was still in a daze when the apparition appeared. All in white it was, slipping easily through the narrow gap between chrome and concrete before making its rapid, flapping descent down into the pit.

As it threw its arms around me and sobbed on my shoulder, I could feel the thin body shaking like a leaf.

"Silly little fool! Silly little fool!" it cried over and over, its raw red lips pressing into my neck.

"Feely!" I said, struck stupid with surprise, "you're getting oil all over your best dress!"

OUTSIDE THE PIT SHED, in Cow Lane, it was a fantasy: Feely was on her knees sobbing, her arms wrapped fiercely round my waist. As I stood there motionless, it was as if everything dissolved between us, and for a moment Feely and I were one creature bathing in the moonlight of the shadowed lane.

And then everyone in Bishop's Lacey seemed to materialize, coming slowly forward out of the darkness, clucking like aldermen at the torchlit scene, and at the gaping hole where the door of the Pit Shed had been; telling one another what they had been doing when the sound of the crash had echoed through the village. It was like a scene from that play *Brigadoon*, where the village comes slowly back to life for a single day every hundred years.

Harriet's Phantom, its beautiful radiator punctured by having been used as a battering ram, now stood steaming quietly in front of the Pit Shed and leaking water softly into the dust. Several of the more muscular villagers—one of them Tully Stoker, I noticed—had pushed the heavy vehicle backwards to allow Feely to lead me up out of the pit and into the fierce intensity and the glare of its great round headlamps.

Feely had got to her feet but was still clinging to me like a limpet to a battleship, babbling on excitedly.

"We followed him, you see. Dogger knew that you hadn't come home, and when he spotted someone prowling round the house..."

These were more consecutive words than she had ever spoken to me in my entire lifetime, and I stood there savoring them a bit.

"He called the police, of course; then he said that if we followed the man...if we kept the headlamps off and kept well back...Oh, God! You should have seen us flying through the lanes!"

Good old silent Roller, I thought. Father was going to be furious, though, when he saw the damage.

Miss Mountjoy stood off to one side, pulling a woolen

shawl tightly about her shoulders and glaring balefully at
the splintered cavern where the door of the Pit Shed had
been, as if such wholesale desecration of library property
were beyond the last straw. I tried to catch her eye, but she
looked nervously away in the direction of her cottage as if
she'd had too much excitement for one evening and ought
to be getting home.

Mrs. Mullet was there, too, with a short, roly-poly
dumpling of a man visibly restraining her. This must be
her husband, Alf, I thought: not at all the Jack Spratt I had
imagined. Had she been by herself, Mrs. M would have
dashed in and thrown her arms round me and cried, but
Alf seemed to be more aware that public displays of famil-
iarity were not quite right. When I gave her a vague smile,
she dabbed at one of her eyes with a fingertip.

At that moment, Dr. Darby arrived upon the scene as
casually as if he had been out for an evening stroll. In spite
of his relaxed manner, I couldn't help noticing that he had
brought his black medical bag. His surgery-cum-residence
was just round the corner in the High Street, and he must
have heard the crash of breaking wood and glass. He
looked me over keenly from head to toe.

"Keeping well, Flavia?" he asked as he leaned in for a
close look at my eyes.

"Perfectly well, thank you, Dr. Darby," I said pleasantly.
"And you?"

He reached for his crystal mints. Before the paper sack
was halfway out of his pocket, I was salivating like a dog;
hours of captivity and the gag had made the inside of my
mouth taste like a Victorian ball-float.

Dr. Darby rummaged for a moment among the mints,

carefully selected the one that seemed most desirable, and popped it into his mouth. A moment later he was on his way home.

The little crowd made way as a motorcar turned off into Cow Lane from the High Street. As it bumped to a stop beside the stone wall, its headlamps illuminated two figures standing together beneath an oak: Mary and Ned. They did not come forward, but stood grinning at me shyly from the shadows.

Had Feely seen them there together? I don't believe she had because she was still prattling on tearfully to me about the rescue. If she had spotted them, I might quickly have found myself referee at a rustic bare-knuckles contest: up to my knees in torn-out hair. Daffy once told me that when it comes to a good dustup, it's generally the squire's daughter who gets in the first punch, and no one knows better than I that Feely has it in her. Still, I'm proud to say that I had the presence of mind—and the guts—to give Ned a furtive congratulatory thumbs-up.

The rear door of the Vauxhall opened and Inspector Hewitt climbed out. At the same time, Detective Sergeants Graves and Woolmer unfolded themselves from the front seats and stepped with surprising delicacy out into Cow Lane.

Sergeant Woolmer strode quickly to where Dogger was holding Pemberton in some kind of contorted and painful-looking grip, which caused him to be bent over like a statue of Atlas with the world on his shoulders.

"I'll take him now, sir," Sergeant Woolmer said, and a moment later I thought I heard the *snick* of nickel-plated handcuffs.

Dogger watched as Pemberton slouched off towards

the police car, then turned and came slowly towards me. As he approached, Feely whispered excitedly into my ear, "It was Dogger who thought of using the tractor battery to get the Royce started up. Be sure to compliment him."

And she dropped my hand and stepped away.

Dogger stood in front of me, his hands hanging down at his sides. If he'd had a hat, he would have been twisting it. We stood there looking at one another.

I wasn't about to begin my thanks by chatting about batteries. I wanted rather to say just the right thing: brave words that would be talked about in Bishop's Lacey for years to come.

A dark shape moving in front of the Vauxhall's head-lamps caught my attention as, for a moment, it cast Dogger and me into the shadows. A familiar figure, silhouetted in black and white, stood out like a paper cutout against the glare: Father.

He began shambling slowly, almost shyly, towards me. But when he noticed Dogger at my side, he stopped and, as if he had just thought of something vitally important, turned aside to have a few quiet words with Inspector Hewitt.

Miss Cool, the postmistress, gave me a pleasant nod but kept herself well back, as if I were somehow a different Flavia than the one who—had it been only two days ago?—had bought one-and-six worth of sweets from her shop.

"Feely," I said, turning to her, "do me a favor: Pop back into the pit and fetch me my handkerchief—and be sure to bring me what's wrapped up inside it. Your dress is already filthy, so it won't make much difference. There's a good girl."

Feely's jaw dropped about a yard, and I thought for a moment she was going to punch me in the teeth. Her whole face grew as red as her lips. And then suddenly she spun on her heel and vanished into the shadows of the Pit Shed.

I turned to Dogger to deliver my soon-to-be-classic remark, but he beat me to it.

"My, Miss Flavia," he said quietly. "It's turning out to be a lovely evening, isn't it?"

twenty-seven

INSPECTOR HEWITT WAS STANDING IN THE CENTER of my laboratory, turning slowly round, his gaze sweeping across the scientific equipment and the chemical cabinets like the beam from a lighthouse. When he had made a complete circle, he stopped, then made another in the opposite direction.

"Extraordinary!" he said, drawing the word out. "Simply extraordinary!"

A ray of deliciously warm sunlight shone in through the tall casement windows, illuminating from within a beaker of red liquid that was just coming to a boil. I decanted half of the stuff into a china cup and handed it to the Inspector. He stared at it dubiously.

"It's tea," I said. "Assam from Fortnum and Mason. I hope you don't mind it being warmed-over."

"Warmed-over is all we drink at the station," he said. "I settle for no other."

As he sipped, he wandered slowly round the room, examining the chemical apparatus with professional interest. He took down a jar or two from the shelves and held each one up to the light, then bent down to peer through the eyepiece of my Leitz. I could see that he was having some difficulty in getting to the point.

"Beautiful bit of bone china," he said at last, raising the cup above his head to read the maker's name on the bottom.

"Quite early Spode," I said. "Albert Einstein and George Bernard Shaw drank tea from that very cup when they visited Great-Uncle Tarquin—not both at the same time, of course."

"One wonders what they might have made of one another?" Inspector Hewitt said, glancing at me.

"One wonders," I said, glancing back.

The Inspector took another sip of his tea. Somehow, he seemed restless, as if there was something he would like to say, but couldn't find a way to begin.

"It's been a difficult case," he said. "Bizarre, really. The man whose body you found in the garden was a total stranger—or seemed to be. All we knew was that he came from Norway."

"The snipe," I said.

"I beg your pardon?"

"The dead jack snipe on our kitchen doorstep. Jack snipe are never found in England until autumn. It had to have been brought from Norway—in a pie. That's how you knew, isn't it?"

The Inspector looked puzzled.

"No," he said. "Bonepenny was wearing a new pair

of shoes stamped with the name of a shoemaker in Stavanger."

"Oh," I said.

"From that, we were able to follow his trail quite easily." As he spoke, Inspector Hewitt's hands drew a map in the air. "Our inquiries here and abroad told us that he'd taken the boat from Stavanger to Newcastle-upon-Tyne, and traveled from there by rail to York, then on to Doddingsley. From Doddingsley he took a taxi to Bishop's Lacey."

Aha! Precisely as I had surmised.

"Exactly," I said. "And Pemberton—or should I say, Bob Stanley?—followed him, but stopped short at Doddingsley. He stayed at the Jolly Coachman."

One of Inspector Hewitt's eyebrows rose up like a cobra. "Oh?" he said, too casually. "How do you know that?"

"I rang up the Jolly Coachman and spoke with Mr. Cleaver."

"Is that all?"

"They were in it together, just as they were in the murder of Mr. Twining."

"Stanley denies that," he said. "Claims he had nothing to do with it. Pure as the driven snow, and all that."

"But he told me in the Pit Shed that he had killed Bonepenny! Besides that, he more or less admitted that my theory was correct: The suicide of Mr. Twining was a staged illusion."

"Well, that remains to be seen. We're looking into it, but it's going to take some time, although I must say your father has been most helpful. He's now told us the whole story of what led up to poor Twining's death. I only wish he had decided earlier to be so accommodating. We might have saved . . .

"I'm sorry," he said. "I was speculating."

"My abduction," I said.

I had to admire how quickly the Inspector changed the subject.

"Getting back to the present," he said. "Let me see if I've got this right: You think Bonepenny and Stanley were confederates?"

"They were always confederates," I said. "Bonepenny stole stamps and Stanley sold them abroad to unscrupulous collectors. But somehow they had never managed to dispose of the two Ulster Avengers; those were simply too well known. And with one of them having been stolen from the King, it would have been far too risky for any collector to be caught with them in his collection."

"Interesting," the Inspector said. "And?"

"They were planning to blackmail Father, but somewhere along the line, they must have had a falling-out. Bonepenny was coming over from Stavanger to do the deed, and at some point Stanley realized that he could follow him, kill him at Buckshaw, take the stamps, and leave the country. As simple as that. And it would all be blamed on Father. And so it was," I added, with a reproachful look.

There was an awkward silence.

"Look, Flavia," he said at last. "I didn't really have much choice, you know. There were no other viable suspects."

"What about me," I said. "I was at the scene of the crime." I waved my hand at the bottles of chemicals that lined the walls. "After all, I know a lot about poisons. I might be considered a very dangerous person."

"Hmm," the Inspector said. "An interesting point. And you *were* on the spot at the time of death. If things hadn't gone exactly as they did, it might well be your neck in the noose."

I hadn't thought of that. A goose walked over my grave and I shivered.

The Inspector went on. "Arguing against it, however, are your physical size, your lack of any real motive, and the fact that you haven't exactly made yourself scarce. Your average murderer generally gives the police as wide a berth as possible, whereas you . . . well, *ubiquitous* is the word that springs to mind. Now then, you were saying?"

"Stanley ambushed Bonepenny in our garden. Bonepenny was a diabetic, and—"

"Ah," the Inspector said, almost to himself. "Insulin! We didn't think to test for that."

"No," I said. "Not insulin: carbon tetrachloride. Bonepenny died from having carbon tetrachloride injected into his brain stem. Stanley bought a bottle of the stuff from Johns, the chemists, in Doddingsley. I saw their label on the bottle when he filled the syringe in the Pit Shed. You've probably already found it under all the rubbish."

I could tell by his face that they hadn't.

"Then it must have rolled down the pipe," I said. "There's an old drain that runs down to the river. Someone will have to fish it out."

Poor Sergeant Graves! I thought.

"Stanley stole the syringe from the kit in Bonepenny's

room at the Thirteen Drakes," I added, without thinking. Damn!

The Inspector pounced. "How do you know what was in Bonepenny's room?" he asked sharply.

"Uh...I'm coming to that," I said. "In a few minutes."

"Stanley believed you'd never detect any possible traces of carbon tetrachloride in Bonepenny's brain. Jolly good thing you didn't. You might have assumed it came from one of Father's bottles. There are gallons of the stuff in the study."

Inspector Hewitt pulled out his notebook and scrawled a couple of words, which I assumed were *carbon tetrachloride*.

"I know it was carbon tet because Bonepenny blew the last whiff of the stuff into my face with his dying breath," I said, wrinkling my nose and making an appropriate face.

If an Inspector's complexion can be said to go white, Inspector Hewitt's complexion went white.

"You're certain about that?"

"I'm quite competent with the chlorinated hydrocarbons, thank you."

"Are you telling me that Bonepenny was still alive when you found him?"

"Only just," I said. "He...uh...passed away almost immediately."

There was another one of those long, crypt-like silences.

"Here," I said, "I'll show you how it was done."

I picked up a yellow lead pencil, gave it a couple of turns in the sharpener, and went to the corner where the articulated skeleton dangled at the end of its wire.

"This was given to my great-uncle, Tarquin, by the naturalist Frank Buckland," I said, giving the skull an affectionate rub. "I call him Yorick."

I did not tell the Inspector that Buckland, in his old age, had given his gift in recognition of young Tar's great promise. "To the Bright Future of Science," Buckland had written on his card.

I brought the sharpened point of the pencil round to the top of the spinal column, shoving it slowly in under the skull as I repeated Pemberton's words in the Pit Shed:

"'Angle in a bit to the side . . . in through the *splenius capitus* and *semispinalis capitis*, puncture the atlantoaxial ligament, and slide the needle over the—'"

"Thank you, Flavia," the Inspector said abruptly. "That's quite enough. You're quite sure that's what he said?"

"His precise words," I said. "I had to look them up in *Gray's Anatomy*. *The Children's Encyclopaedia* has several plates, but not nearly enough detail."

Inspector Hewitt rubbed his chin.

"I'm sure Dr. Darby could find the needle mark on the back of Bonepenny's neck," I added helpfully, "if he knew where to look. He might inspect the sinuses, as well. Carbon tetrachloride is stable in air, and might still be trapped there, since the man was no longer breathing.

"And," I added, "you might remind him that Bonepenny had a drink at the Thirteen Drakes just before he set out to walk to Buckshaw."

The Inspector still looked puzzled.

"The effects of carbon tetrachloride are intensified by alcohol," I explained.

"And," he asked with a casual smile, "do you have any

particular theory about why the stuff might still be in his sinuses? I'm no chemist, but I believe carbon tetrachloride evaporates very rapidly."

I did have a reason, but it was not one I was willing to share with just anyone, particularly not the police. Bonepenny had been suffering from an extremely nasty head cold: a head cold which, when he breathed the word "*Vale*" into my face, he had transmitted to me. Thanks buckets, Horace! I thought.

I also suspected that Bonepenny's plugged nasal passages might well have preserved the injected carbon tetrachloride, which is insoluble in water—or in snot, for that matter—which would also have helped inhibit the intake of outside air.

"No," I said. "But you might suggest that the lab in London carry out the test suggested by the British Pharmacopoeia."

"Can't say I recall it, offhand," Inspector Hewitt said.

"It's a very pretty procedure," I said. "One that checks the limit of free chlorine when iodine is liberated from cadmium iodide. I'm sure they're familiar with it. I'd offer to do it myself, but I don't expect Scotland Yard would be comfortable handing over bits of Bonepenny's brain to an eleven-year-old."

Inspector Hewitt stared at me for what seemed several aeons.

"All right," he said at last, "let's have a dekko."

"At what?" I said, putting on my mask of injured innocence.

"Whatever you've done. Let's have a look at it."

"But I haven't done anything," I said. "I—"

"Don't play me for a fool, Flavia. No one who has had

the pleasure of your acquaintance would ever believe for an instant that you haven't done your homework."

I grinned sheepishly. "It's over here," I said, moving towards a corner table upon which stood a glass tank shrouded with a damp tea towel.

I whisked the cloth away.

"Good Lord!" the Inspector said. "What in the name of—?"

He fairly gaped at the pinkish gray object that floated serenely in the tank.

"It's a nice bit of brain," I said. "I pinched it from the larder. Mrs. Mullet bought it at Carnforth's yesterday for supper tonight. She's going to be furious."

"And you've . . . ?" he said, flapping his hand.

"Yes, that's right. I've injected it with two and a half cubic centimeters of carbon tetrachloride. That's how much Bonepenny's syringe held.

"The average human brain weighs three pounds," I went on, "and that of the male perhaps a little more. I've cut an extra five ounces to allow for it."

"How did you find *that* out?" the Inspector asked.

"It's in one of the volumes of Arthur Mee's books. *The Children's Encyclopaedia* again, I think."

"And you've tested this . . . brain, for the presence of carbon tetrachloride?"

"Yes," I said, "but not until fifteen hours after I injected it. I judged that's how much time elapsed between the stuff being shot into Bonepenny's brain and the autopsy."

"And?"

"Still easily detectable," I said. "Child's play. Of course I used *p-Aminodimethylaniline*. That's rather a new test, but an elegant one. It was written up in *The Analyst* about five years ago. Pull up a stool and I'll show you."

"This isn't going to work, you know." Inspector Hewitt chuckled.

"Not work?" I said. "Of course it will work. I've already done it once."

"I mean you're not going to dazzle me with lab work and skate conveniently round the stamp. After all, that's what this whole thing is about, isn't it?"

He had me cornered. I had planned on saying nothing about the Ulster Avenger and then quietly handing it over to Father. Who would ever be the wiser?

"Look, I know you have it," he said. "We paid a visit to Dr. Kissing at Rook's End."

I tried to look unconvinced.

"And Bob Stanley, your Mr. Pemberton, has told us that you stole it from him."

Stole it from him? The idea! What cheek!

"It belongs to the King," I protested. "Bonepenny nicked it from an exhibition in London."

"Well, whomever it belongs to, it's stolen property, and my duty is to see that it's returned. All I need to know is how it came into your possession."

Drat the man! I could dodge it no longer. I was going to have to confess my trespasses at the Thirteen Drakes.

"Let's make a deal," I said.

Inspector Hewitt burst out laughing. "There are times, Miss de Luce," he said, "when you deserve a brass medal. And there are other times you deserve to be sent to your room with bread and water."

"And which one of those times is this?" I asked.

Hooo! Better watch your step, Flave.

He waggled his fingers at me. "I'm listening," he said.

"Well, I've been thinking," I told him. "Father's life hasn't been exactly pleasant lately. In the first place, you arrive at Buckshaw and before we know it you've charged him with murder."

"Hang on . . . hang on," the Inspector said. "We've already been through this. He was charged with murder because he confessed to it."

He did? This was something new.

"And no sooner had he done so, than along came Flavia. I had more confessions walking in the door than Our Lady of Lourdes on a Saturday night."

"I was just trying to protect him," I said. "At that point, I thought he might have done it."

"And whom was *he* trying to protect?" Inspector Hewitt asked, watching me carefully.

The answer, of course, was Dogger. That was what Father meant when he said "I feared as much" after I told him that Dogger, too, had overheard the scene in his study with Horace Bonepenny.

Father thought Dogger had killed the man; that much was clear. But why? Would Dogger have done it out of loyalty—or during one of his peculiar turns?

No—best to leave Dogger out of this. It was the least I could do.

"Probably me," I lied. "Father thought I had killed Bonepenny. After all, wasn't I the one who was found, so to speak, at the scene of the crime? He was trying to protect *me*."

"Do you really believe that?" the Inspector asked.

"It would be lovely to think so," I said.

"I'm sure he was," the Inspector said. "I'm quite sure he

was. Now then, back to the stamp. I haven't forgotten about it, you know."

"Well, as I was saying, I'd like to do something for Father; something that will make him happy, even for a few hours. I'd like to give him the Ulster Avenger, even if it's only for a day or two. Let me do that, and I'll tell you everything I know. I promise."

The Inspector strolled over to the bookcase, fetched down a bound volume of the *Proceedings of the Chemical Society* for 1907, and blew a cloud of dust from the top of the spine. He leafed idly through its pages, as if looking for what to say next.

"You know," he said, "there is nothing my wife, Antigone, detests more than shopping. She told me once that she'd rather have a tooth filled than spend half an hour shopping for a leg of mutton. But shop she must, like it or not. It's her fate, she says. To dull the experience, she sometimes buys a little yellow booklet called *You and Your Stars*.

"I have to admit that up until now I've scoffed at some of the things she's read out to me at breakfast, but this morning my horoscope said, and I quote, 'Your patience will be tried to the utmost.' Do you suppose I could have been misjudging these things, Flavia?"

"Please!" I said, giving the word a gimlet twist.

"Twenty-four hours," he said, "and not a minute more."

And suddenly it all came gushing out, and I found my-self babbling on about the dead jack snipe, Mrs. Mullet's really quite innocent (although inedible) custard pie, my rifling of Bonepenny's room at the inn, my finding of the stamps, my visits to Miss Mountjoy and Dr. Kissing, my encounters with Pemberton at the Folly and in the churchyard, and my captivity in the Pit Shed.

The only part I left out was the bit about my poisoning Feely's lipstick with an extract of poison ivy. Why confuse the Inspector with unnecessary details?

As I spoke, he made an occasional scribble in a little black notebook, whose pages, I noticed, were filled with arrows and cryptic signs that might have been inspired by an alchemical formulary of the Middle Ages.

"Am I in that?" I asked, pointing.

"You are," he said.

"May I have a look? Just a peek?"

Inspector Hewitt flipped the notebook shut. "No," he said. "It's a confidential police document."

"Do you actually spell out my name, or am I represented by one of those symbols?"

"You have your very own symbol," he said, shoving the book into his pocket. "Well, it's time I was getting along."

He stuck out a hand and gave me a firm handshake. "Good-bye, Flavia," he said. "It's been . . . something of an experience."

He went to the door and opened it.

"Inspector . . ."

He stopped and turned.

"What is it? My symbol, I mean."

"It's a *P*," he said. "Capital *P*."

"A *P*?" I asked, surprised. "What does *P* stand for?"

"Ah," he said, "that's best left to the imagination."

DAFFY WAS IN THE DRAWING ROOM, sprawled full-length on the carpet, reading *The Prisoner of Zenda*.

"Are you aware that you move your lips when you read?" I asked.

She ignored me. I decided to risk my life.

"Speaking of lips," I said, "where's Feely?"

"At the doctor's," she said. "She had some kind of allergic outbreak. Something she came in contact with."

Aha! My experiment had succeeded brilliantly! No one would ever know. As soon as I had a moment to myself, I'd record it in my notebook:

Tuesday, 6th of June 1950, 1:20 p.m. Success! Outcome as postulated. Justice is served.

I let out a quiet snort. Daffy must have heard it, for she rolled over and crossed her legs.

"Don't think for a moment you've got away with it," she said quietly.

"Huh?" I said. Innocent puzzlement was my specialty.

"What witch's brew did you put in her lipstick?"

"I haven't the faintest what you're talking about," I said.

"Have a peek at yourself in the looking-glass," Daffy said. "Watch you don't break it."

I turned and went slowly to the chimneypiece where a cloudy leftover from the Regency period hung sullenly reflecting the room.

I bent closer, peering at my image. At first I saw nothing other than my usual brilliant self, my violet eyes, my pale complexion: but as I stared, I began to notice more details in the ravaged mercury reflection.

There was a splotch on my neck. An angry red splotch! Where Feely had kissed me!

I let out a shriek of anguish.

"Feely said that before she'd been in the pit five seconds she'd paid you back in full."

Even before Daffy rolled over and went back to her stupid sword story, I had come up with a plan.

ONCE, WHEN I WAS ABOUT NINE, I had kept a diary about what it was like to be a de Luce, or at least what it was like to be this particular de Luce. I thought a great deal about how I felt and finally came to the conclusion that being Flavia de Luce was like being a sublimate: like the black crystal residue that is left on the cold glass of a test tube by the violet fumes of iodine. At the time, I thought it the perfect description, and nothing has happened over the past two years to change my mind.

As I have said, there is something lacking in the de Luces: some chemical bond, or lack of it, that ties their tongues whenever they are threatened by affection. It is as unlikely that one de Luce would ever tell another that she loved her as it is that one peak in the Himalayas would bend over and whisper sweet nothings to an adjacent crag.

This point was proven when Feely stole my diary, pried open the brass lock with a can opener from the kitchen, and read aloud from it while standing at the top of the great staircase dressed in clothing she had stolen from a neighbor's scarecrow.

These thoughts were in my mind as I approached the door of Father's study. I paused, unsure of myself. Did I really want to do this?

I knocked uncertainly on the door. There was a long silence before Father's voice said, "Come."

I twisted the knob and stepped into the room. At a table by the window, Father looked up for a moment from his magnifying lens, and then went on with his examination of a magenta stamp.

"May I speak?" I asked, aware, even as I said it, that it was an odd thing to be saying, and yet it seemed precisely the right choice of words.

Father put down the glass, removed his spectacles, and rubbed his eyes. He looked tired.

I reached into my pocket and pulled out the piece of blue writing paper into which I had folded the Ulster Avenger. I stepped forward like a supplicant, put the paper on his desk, and stepped back again.

Father opened it.

"Good Lord!" he said. "It's AA."

He put his spectacles back on and picked up his jeweler's loupe to peer at the stamp.

Now, I thought, comes my reward. I found myself focused on his lips, waiting for them to move.

"Where did you get this?" he said at last, in that soft voice of his that fixes its hearer like a butterfly on a pin.

"I found it," I said.

Father's gaze was military—unrelenting.

"Bonepenny must have dropped it," I said. "It's for you."

Father studied my face the way an astronomer studies a supernova.

"This is very decent of you, Flavia," he said at last, with some great effort.

And he handed me the Ulster Avenger.

"You must return it at once to its rightful owner."

"King George?"

Father nodded, somewhat sadly, I thought. "I don't know how you came to have this in your possession and I don't want to know. You've come this far on your own and now you must see it through."

"Inspector Hewitt wants me to hand it over to him."

Father shook his head. "Most kind of him," he said, "but also most official. No, Flavia, old AA here has been through many hands in its day, a few of them high and many low. You must see to it that your hands are the most worthy of them all."

"But how does one go about writing to the King?"

"I'm sure you'll find a way," Father said. "Please close the door on your way out."

AS IF TO COVER UP THE PAST, Dogger was shoveling muck from a wheelbarrow into the cucumber bed.

"Miss Flavia," he said, removing his hat and wiping his brow on his shirtsleeve.

"How should one address a letter to the King?" I asked.

Dogger leaned his shovel carefully against the greenhouse.

"Theoretically, or in actual practice?"

"In actual practice."

"Hmm," he said. "I think I should look it up somewhere."

"Hold on," I said. "Mrs. Mullet's *Inquire Within Upon Everything*. She keeps it in the pantry."

"She's shopping in the village," Dogger said. "If we're quick about it, we may well escape with our lives."

A minute later we were huddled in the pantry.

"Here it is," I said excitedly, as the book fell open in

my hands. "But wait—this was published sixty years ago. Would it still be correct?"

"Sure to be," Dogger said. "Things don't change as quickly in royal circles as they do in yours and mine, nor should they."

The drawing room was empty. Daffy and Feely were off somewhere, most likely planning their next attack.

I found a decent sheet of writing paper in a drawer, and then, dipping the pen in the inkwell, I copied out the salutation from Mrs. Mullet's greasy book, trying to make my handwriting as neat as possible:

> Most Gracious Sovereign:
>   May it please Your Majesty,
>   Please find enclosed an item of considerable value belonging to Your Majesty which was stolen earlier this year. How it fell into my hands (a nice touch, I thought) is unimportant, but I can assure Your Majesty that the criminal has been caught.

"Apprehended," Dogger said, reading over my shoulder.

I changed it.

"What else?"

"Nothing," Dogger said. "Just sign it. Kings prefer brevity."

Being careful not to blot the page, I copied the closing from the book:

> I remain, with the profoundest veneration, Your Majesty's most faithful subject and dutiful servant.
>   Flavia de Luce (Miss)

"Perfect!" Dogger said.

I folded the letter neatly, making an extra-sharp crease with my thumb. I slipped it into one of Father's best envelopes and wrote the address:

> His Royal Highness King George the Sixth
> Buckingham Palace, London, SW1
> England

"Shall I mark it Personal?"

"Good idea," Dogger said.

A WEEK LATER, I was cooling my bare feet in the waters of the artificial lake, revising my notes on coniine, the chief alkaloid in poison hemlock, when Dogger appeared suddenly, waving something in his hand.

"Miss Flavia!" he called, and then he waded across to the island, boots and all.

His trouser legs were soaking wet, and although he stood there dripping like Poseidon, his grin was as bright as the summer afternoon.

He handed me an envelope that was as soft and white as goose down.

"Shall I open it?" I asked.

"I believe it's addressed to you."

Dogger winced as I tore open the flap and pulled out the single sheet of creamy paper which lay folded inside:

> *My Dear Miss de Luce,*
> *I am most grateful to you for your recent communication and for the restoration of the*

splendid item contained therein, which has, as you must know, played a remarkable part, not only in the history of my own family, but in the history of England. Please accept my heartfelt thanks.

And it was signed simply "George."

ACKNOWLEDGMENTS

Whenever I pick up a new book, I always turn to the acknowledgments first because they provide me with a sort of aerial photograph of the work: a large-scale map that shows something of the wider environment in which the book was written, where it has been, and how it came to be.

No work-in-progress was ever more kindly nurtured than *The Sweetness at the Bottom of the Pie*, and it gives me tremendous pleasure to express my gratitude to the Crime Writers' Association and the panel of judges who chose the book for the Debut Dagger Award: Philip Gooden, chair of the CWA; Margaret Murphy; Emma Hargrave; Bill Massey; Sara Menguc; Keshini Naidoo; and Sarah Turner.

Additional and special thanks are due to Margaret Murphy, who not only chaired the Debut Dagger Awards

Committee, but also stole time from her own hectic schedule on awards day to personally welcome a wandering alien to London.

To Meg Gardiner, Chris High, and Ann Cleeves for making me feel as if I'd known them all my life.

To Louise Penny, a Dagger winner herself, whose warm generosity and encouragement is exemplified in the beacon her website has become for aspiring writers. Louise truly knows how to "give back" for the things she has received. Besides that, her Chief Inspector Armand Gamache novels are simply terrific!

To my agent, Denise Bukowski, for flying the Atlantic to be there and, in spite of my jet lag, for getting me to the church on time.

Again, to Bill Massey, of Orion Books, who had faith enough to buy the novel—and the series—on the strength of that first handful of pages, and for treating me to a memorable lunch at the onetime Bucket of Blood, in Covent Garden, the very spot where the poet and critic John Dryden was set upon by ruffians in a passageway. No one has ever been blessed with a better editor than Bill. He is truly a kindred spirit!

To Kate Miciak and Molly Boyle, of Bantam Dell in New York, and Kristin Cochrane of Doubleday Canada, for their early faith and encouragement.

Special thanks to Janet Cooke, vice president, director of sales, the Bantam Dell Publishing Group, whose enthusiasm has contributed so much to the world of Flavia de Luce.

To Robyn Karney and Connie Munro, copy editors at Orion Books and at Bantam Dell, respectively, for their excellent and perceptive suggestions. And to Emma

Wallace and Genevieve Pegg, also at Orion Books, for their enthusiastic and friendly welcome.

To the helpful and friendly staff of the British Postal Museum and Archive, at Freeling House, Phoenix Place, London, for so cheerfully answering my questions and allowing me access to materials in their care relating to the history of the Penny Black.

To my longtime Saskatoon friends and connoisseurs of crime, Mary Gilliland and Allan and Janice Cushon for putting into my hands the Edwardian equivalent of the Internet: a complete set of the eleventh edition (1911) of the *Encyclopaedia Britannica,* which must surely be every detective novelist's dream.

To David Whiteside, of the Bukowski Agency, for his yeoman work in bringing order to the necessary mountains of paperwork and red tape.

To my dear friends Dr. John and Janet Harland, who were there at every step along the way with many useful and often brilliant suggestions. Without their enthusiasm, *The Sweetness at the Bottom of the Pie* would have been a lesser book and much less fun to write.

All of these kind people have given me their best advice; if any mistakes have crept in, they are mine alone.

And finally, with love and eternal thanks to my wife, Shirley, who urged me—no, insisted that I allow Flavia and the de Luce family to emerge from the bundle of notes in which they had been languishing for far too long.

ABOUT THE AUTHOR

ALAN BRADLEY was born in Toronto and grew up in Cobourg, Ontario. Prior to taking early retirement to write in 1994, he was director of television engineering at the University of Saskatchewan media center for twenty-five years. His versatility has earned him awards for his children's books, radio broadcasts of his short stories, and national print for his journalism. He also co-authored *Ms. Holmes of Baker Street*, to great acclaim and much controversy, followed by a poignant memoir, *The Shoebox Bible*. In 2007, Bradley won the Debut Dagger Award of the Crimewriter's Association for *The Sweetness at the Bottom of the Pie*, the first book in a new series featuring the brilliant young British sleuth Flavia de Luce. Alan Bradley lives in Kelowna, British Columbia, with his wife and two calculating cats. He is at work on the second Flavia de Luce novel.